Praise for Leah Cutter's debut novel _Paper Mage_

"I don't believe that there are enough superlatives to describe this book. Splendid comes to mind, as do magnificent, wonderful, excellent, and superb. Leah's writing is at one and the same time both powerful and delicate. Setting her story in the era of the Tang Dynasty, Leah captures the culture just perfectly, with a heroine who is torn between tradition and following her own heart. This is an exceptional tale by an exceptional writer; this is writing at its finest. It doesn't get any better than this."
—Dennis L. McKiernan, author of _Once Upon a Winter's Night_

"Leah Cutter has written an enchanting novel, skillfully rooted in Chinese history and myth. The 'paper magic' at its core is a wonderful creation: mystical, unusual, and thoroughly convincing. I wholeheartedly recommend _Paper Mage_ to all lovers of fine fantasy. It's a strong debut, and I look forward to reading more of Cutter's work in the years ahead."
—Terri Windling, editor of _The Year's Best Fantasy and Horror_

"Magic, myth, and adventure unfold in this intriguing tale by Leah Cutter of a young mage who must prove herself in a time and place where traditional roles are the rule. _Paper Mage_ is a terrific first novel."
—Kristen Britain, author of _Green Rider_

"Leah Cutter has created a magical world as solid and believable as our own, meticulously researched and drawn with loving attention to detail."
—Cecilia Dart-Thornton, author of _The Ill-Made Mute_ and _The Lady of the Sorrows_

PAPER MAGE

Leah R. Cutter

PUBLISHER'S NOTE

This is a work of fiction. Names, characters, places, and incidents either are the product of the author's imagination or are used fictitiously, and any resemblance to actual persons, living or dead, business establishments, events, or locales is entirely coincidental.

A ROC BOOK

ROC
Published by New American Library, a division of
Penguin Putnam Inc., 375 Hudson Street,
New York, New York 10014, U.S.A.
Penguin Books Ltd, 80 Strand,
London WC2R 0RL, England
Penguin Books Australia Ltd, 250 Camberwell Road,
Camberwell, Victoria 3124, Australia
Penguin Books Canada Ltd, 10 Alcorn Avenue,
Toronto, Ontario, Canada M4V 3B2
Penguin Books (N.Z.) Ltd, Cnr Rosedale and Airborne Roads,
Albany, Auckland 1310, New Zealand

Penguin Books Ltd, Registered Offices:
Harmondsworth, Middlesex, England

First published by Roc, an imprint of New American Library,
a division of Penguin Putnam Inc.

First Printing, March 2003
10 9 8 7 6 5 4 3 2 1

Cover art by Mark Harrison

REGISTERED TRADEMARK—MARCA REGISTRADA

Printed in the United States of America

...rt of

...ectronic,
...or written
...f this

...either

To Amy, Charlotte, and Rachel—
the original inspirations for Xiao Yen

NAMES

Nickname	Meaning	Relationship to Xiao Yen/Description
Wang Tie-Tie/Mei-Mei	Auntie Wang, Plum Blossom	Aunt from father's side
Xiao Yen	Little Sparrow; *Xiao* also means filial piety	
Fu Be Be	Mama Fu (Fu as in Teacher)	Mother
Gan Ou	Lotus Blossom	Older sister
Han Wanju	Lovely Toy	Cousin
Ling-Ling	Dragonfly	Cousin
Master Wei		Teacher
Fat Fang	Fang as in square, same Fang as in Bao Fang	Classmate, Fifth son of governor of Bao Fang
Long Yen	Dragon Eye	Classmate, Youngest son of head of Weavers' Guild
Bing Yu	Ice Jade	Friend, Sister of Fat Fang
Bei Xi	White Petal	Friend, Sister of Nügua
Jhr Bei		Sister to Bei Xi
Udo		Foreigner
Ehran		Udo's half-brother
Frauke		Udo's love
Vakhtang		Northern barbarian warlord
Young Lu		Wang Tie-Tie's younger sister
Tuo Nu		Northern magician
Zhang Gua Lao		Fisherman, Immortal

Hours

Midnight	Rat
2 A.M.	Ox
4 A.M.	Tiger
6 A.M.	Hare
8 A.M.	Dragon
10 A.M.	Snake
Noon	Horse
2 P.M.	Sheep
4 P.M.	Monkey
6 P.M.	Rooster
8 P.M.	Dog
10 P.M.	Pig

Prologue

Mei-Mei paused at the gate of the abandoned kiln and called out, "Is anyone there?"

No one answered.

She looked up and down the dirt road again. It was empty. Not many merchants traveled the trade routes since the Tibetans sacked Xian, the capital of the Middle Kingdom. Farmers only came to her city, Bao Fang, on market days. But bandits, soldiers—or worse, foreign soldiers—could appear at any time. Cold *shouzhi* walked down Mei-Mei's spine in spite of the summer sun beating on her head.

Maybe she should just leave the basket of cakes for her sister and run back home. Mei-Mei had always been accompanied by someone when outside Bao Fang's walls, either her mother, her siblings, or her nurse. This was the first time she'd gone beyond any of the city gates by herself.

But the cakes would spoil in the heat, and she wouldn't see Young Lu. Mei-Mei made herself call again, her voice barely rising above the chorus of cicadas hidden in the grass.

No response.

Was she at the right building? She thought so. It was the first kiln outside Bao Fang. Abandoned kilns made fine houses for those who weren't allowed to live inside the city walls. This one was in much better shape than its neighbors: the yard had been raked; a small altar, dedicated to Kuan Yin, goddess of mercy, stood next to the door; and a geomancer's mirror decorated with red and green *ba gua* hung over the entrance, protecting those inside from evil spirits. At the same time, the white building had been patched with plain mud, and garbage lay piled as high as the garden wall.

A soft clank came from inside the kiln, the sound of a lid being placed on a teapot. Mei-Mei crossed the yard, then hesitated and peered into the semidarkness.

Young Lu stood on the far side of the room, her back to the door. Mei-Mei would recognize the slender figure anywhere, her long thin neck, the coltish way she tilted her head.

"*Nin hau,*" Mei-Mei called, using the formal greeting.

Young Lu turned around. She raised her cane above her head, holding it like a soldier's staff. She drew in a deep breath, as if to scream, then let it out with a huff.

"Mei-Mei?" she asked.

"*Nin hau,*" Mei-Mei repeated.

Young Lu dropped her cane and rushed, limping, to where Mei-Mei stood. Wordlessly she hugged her older sister.

Mei-Mei returned the hug just as fiercely. Though her father had disowned his youngest daughter, and Uncle Li now called her evil, Mei-Mei still missed her.

After a moment Young Lu pulled back and scolded Mei-Mei as if Mei-Mei were the younger one. "What are you doing? You know you shouldn't be here." Young Lu clutched Mei-Mei's arms while she spoke. "It isn't safe outside the city walls. Come inside." She pulled Mei-Mei across the threshold. "Does Mother know you're here?" she asked.

Mei-Mei didn't meet Young Lu's eye. "I told her I was visiting my sister."

"But not that you were visiting your youngest sister,

eh?" Young Lu shook her head. "What would happen if Father found out?"

Now Mei-Mei looked up. "I'm not his favorite," she said, then covered her mouth as if hiding the source of her thoughtless words.

Bitterness tinged the edge of Young Lu's smile. "True. He'd probably only beat you. But your reputation could be ruined if someone saw you here. Prostitutes live in the kiln next door. Why did you come?"

Mei-Mei stuttered, trying to put unaccustomed emotions into words. "It—it, it was so hot, waiting in Grandma's room, the—the air wasn't good. I felt . . . stifled." She paused again.

Just after lunch, while Mei-Mei had tucked her grandmother in for her nap, her grandmother had told a story of when she'd been a little girl, taking care of a sick aunt. She'd commented on how someday, one of Mei-Mei's descendants would take care of her.

Normally, Mei-Mei felt comforted by such stories. The cycle of death, rebirth, and life swirled by, but her place was as fixed as the stars in the king of Heaven's crown.

Today was different. Maybe it was because she'd accompanied her mother to the White Temple that morning, to light incense for her cousins who had been killed defending the mountain passes against the Tibetans. She still remembered them leaving for battle, eager and optimistic, their naïve enthusiasm louder than their mother's tears. They'd laughed at the change in their fortune.

While Mei-Mei had listened to her grandmother's tale in the afternoon, she'd realized her life would never change. She'd marry, move into the woman's compound of her husband's house, and rarely leave. She'd have children, grow old, be revered, and die. When she thought hard about her future, the air grew thick, like a winter quilt, and threatened to smother her. So she'd had to leave.

"My *xiao*—filial duty—is important." Mei-Mei held up her hand so Young Lu would let her finish. "But so is my entire family. Please," she said, extending her basket. "It would be my honor if you would accept this inadequate token of my high esteem and regard for you." Mei-Mei pressed the basket into her sister's hands.

"Thank you so much," Young Lu replied. "You don't know how much this means to me," she said, her voice cracking. She turned away so Mei-Mei couldn't see her tears and indicated with her free hand that Mei-Mei should sit.

"Thank you for being my relation," Mei-Mei said formally, kneeling on the cracked and dusty bamboo mats covering the dirt floor.

"Please, let me get you something to eat," Young Lu said, turning back to Mei-Mei.

"No, I'm not hungry. I couldn't eat anything," Mei-Mei replied.

"It won't be any trouble."

"I just had lunch. I wouldn't touch a bite. Really." Mei-Mei let some iron creep into her voice. Young Lu had always been as slender as spring bamboo. Now she was even skinnier. Her cheeks were hollow, which made her cheekbones stand out, and her lips were drawn and pale. She looked more delicate than one of Master Kung's statues, made of clay so soft it could be carved with flower petals. Mei-Mei wouldn't put any strain on her sister's household by eating even a little of what they had.

Young Lu nodded, her face saved, but still shamed. "Let this unworthy person at least offer you some tea," she insisted.

Mei-Mei accepted. She had to give Young Lu some way to show her hospitality.

Young Lu limped across the floor to the back of the kiln, where a small hearth held an iron pot with a cracked lid. Mei-Mei pretended not to notice her sister's infirmity by looking down at her lap and smoothing her silver robe, running both hands over the embroidered white cranes.

"That's one good thing about living here in the kiln,"

Young Lu said over her shoulder. "Pieces of coal are scattered all over the ground."

Mei-Mei couldn't help but smile. Only Young Lu could find any good in being cast out of their family, shunned by their father and mother, and forced to live outside the city walls. The kiln was tiny and filthy: it had only two rooms, the back one just large enough to hold a bed; the walls were covered with soot from a fire a former tenant had let burn out of control; and the incense Young Lu burned couldn't hide the smell of the garbage next door. The light from the single eastern-facing window didn't shine all the way through the front room, and didn't bring any fresh air in with it.

On the right side of the hearth, Young Lu, or her husband, Old Lu, had installed a small wooden altar. Pasted between the flimsy split-bamboo uprights was a brightly colored picture of Zhao Wang, the kitchen god. Under the picture sat a tiny white-and-blue porcelain bowl filled with rice. It had three sticks of incense poking out of it.

Mei-Mei shook her head. How could Young Lu afford even a small sacrifice? She looked at her sister. Young Lu swayed in time to her own silent music, like ivy in a breeze. From that angle, Mei-Mei saw the bulge in Young Lu's abdomen.

Young Lu's gaze followed Mei-Mei's. She brushed her fingertips across her stomach, looking more serene than the Buddha meditating under the *bodhi* tree.

Mei-Mei pressed her lips together in a polite smile, hiding her surprise. She wanted to know, but couldn't ask.

Young Lu told her anyway. "Five and a half moons," she said. She hobbled from the stove—tiny, awkward steps—and knelt next to her sister. "Isn't it exciting? I never expected to be blessed so soon."

Mei-Mei hugged Young Lu. "That's wonderful! Ten thousand blessings," she said, feeling Young Lu's shoulder blades through her robe. She was too thin to be that far along.

Young Lu pulled back and said with a mischievous smile, "Old Lu was so happy when I told him. It made him feel more like a tiger again."

Mei-Mei looked down at her hands, embarrassed at the shared intimacy. Young Lu struggled to get to her feet. Mei-Mei said, "Let me help you."

Young Lu admonished her. "The guest shouldn't serve the tea. It isn't a problem."

Mei-Mei gave her a skeptical look.

Young Lu continued. "I barely feel it anymore. See?" She got to her feet and walked to the stove, limping.

Mei-Mei turned away. When their father had heard Old Lu's marriage proposal, he'd forbidden it. Young Lu had pleaded with Father. She told him Old Lu and she were meant to be with each other. The moon god had tied their ankles together with a red ribbon at birth, even if she was only fourteen and they were second cousins. Father and daughter fought for weeks. Girls weren't supposed to pick their own husbands. It wasn't proper.

Young Lu tried to run away. Father caught her and treated her like a slave, not like a daughter. He put her right ankle in a press and squeezed the two boards together until the bones shattered.

As soon as she could walk, Young Lu ran away again, this time successfully, and the marriage was consummated. Both families renounced Young Lu and Old Lu. All of Bao Fang had gossiped about the scandal for weeks. Old Lu worked hard to earn a few coins in the market, fetching and carrying from place to place, but it wasn't enough. Many merchants wouldn't serve them.

As Young Lu poured the tea, Mei-Mei asked, "Have you heard from Old Lu's friend in the north?"

Young Lu sighed and sipped her tea. "It's so hard. I don't want to leave. Our family's here. All our ancestors are buried here." She paused. "Can you imagine leaving?"

Mei-Mei didn't respond. To go to live with strangers

for the rest of her life? To never again tell stories with her aunts all afternoon, read one of her mother's poems, listen to her father construct a faultless argument, or talk with her sisters, her brothers, her cousins? It was the most horrible fate she'd ever contemplated. Yet when she got married . . .

Young Lu continued. "Bao Fang is the only city I've ever known. But Old Lu wants to leave. And I'll follow him. Even to the Hell of Iron and Acid, if necessary."

"You're so brave," Mei-Mei said, marveling.

Young Lu giggled. "I'm not brave," she said, sounding like a carefree girl for the first time that afternoon. "I'm just stubborn, like an old ox."

Mei-Mei also giggled at her petite sister comparing herself to such a huge beast.

Young Lu took a sip of tea and said, "Tell me about your engagement to Wang Po Kao. Everyone in Bao Fang speaks well of him. They say he'll make a lot of money in trading."

Mei-Mei tried to make herself smile at the thought of her husband-to-be, but failed. She drank her tea instead. The hot liquid failed to warm her belly, and left a bitter, metallic taste on the back of her tongue. She looked at her cup instead of meeting her sister's eye. It had splashes of orange, green, and yellow under a thick glaze, not fine, but artistically done. The parts of her life mingled like the colors—her family, her sister, her husband-to-be. Would the last color wash over all the others, until her life was a muddy brown, like the bottom of the river Quang?

"When Old Lu looks at you, he sees a treasure, and thinks himself the luckiest man in the world," she started.

"Stop!" Young Lu interrupted, hiding her smile behind her hand.

"The one time I met Wang Po Kao, at Mother's birthday party, he also looked at me like I was a treasure. But one he'd never share, like . . ."

Mei-Mei bit down on her lip, but her unspoken

comment, "like Father," still echoed through the room.

Young Lu didn't say anything.

Mei-Mei continued. "It's a good match, good for the family. The Wangs have a cousin who has a son who is friends with the horsemen up north. If Father has horses he can sell through the winter, our family will thrive. The price for horses has tripled since the war."

" 'Our family will thrive,' " Young Lu repeated. "And you'll do what Father wants, won't you?"

Mei-Mei replied without thinking, "Of course. He's my father. I'm his daughter. It's my duty to obey him."

"Of course," Young Lu said.

Mei-Mei's blush spread from her cheeks all the way to her ears. Young Lu had defied Father. She'd changed her life, wrenched it out of the fixed shape laid out for her by all the generations of women who'd come before her. Like their dead cousins, she'd paid a horrible price. Mei-Mei couldn't imagine doing anything like that. She'd end her days at home, surrounded by her family, secure, safe, and stifled.

"Let's be cheerful," Mei-Mei said. "Marrying Wang Po Kao means I'll soon have my own babies. And that *is* something I look forward to. As well as to the birth of your little one. I'm sure you'll have a fine son."

When the bells tolled the change from the hour of the Sheep to the hour of the Monkey, Young Lu got up and escorted her sister to the door. She made Mei-Mei wait inside the kiln while she went out to the road to check that it was empty. Then she beckoned for Mei-Mei.

Mei-Mei approached with her hands out, saying the traditional words of parting, "Until we meet again, may . . ."

Young Lu held up her hand, indicating Mei-Mei should stop. Without another word, Young Lu limped back into the kiln. Mei-Mei blinked hard to keep the tears out of her eyes. She might never see her sister again. Then her chin stiffened. She *would* see her, at least one more time. Plus, she wouldn't just bring a few cakes from the market. She'd bring the biggest basket of food she could carry.

The next afternoon, after Mei-Mei had sung her grandmother to sleep, she decided to go light incense for Young Lu and her unborn child. Though Mei-Mei and her family considered themselves Buddhist, they were also practical, and prayed at a number of different temples, depending on the occasion. Today, Mei-Mei decided to go to the Fire Mountain Temple and pray to Fu Xi and Nü-gua. Though they'd been brother and sister, the other gods had decreed that they should be together, and so had invented marriage just for them. Mei-Mei loved the representation of the two that hung on the wall above the altar—the top, human-halves of their bodies faced away from each other, while their snake tails intertwined together, inseparable, as white as crane feathers.

The Fire Mountain Temple was just up the street from the southern gate. Before she could approach the altar in the main building, a priest in a tan robe stopped her.

"Can I help you?" he asked. He was a skinny man, tall like a foreigner, and looked down his nose at Mei-Mei.

"No, thank you, sir," Mei-Mei responded. It was always better to be polite to priests. Her grandmother believed priests talked directly with the gods. Mei-Mei thought priests were more like scholars, whose knowledge came from study, not divine intervention.

"Are you certain? Tell me who you pray for. I can help." The man licked his thin lips, like a cat smelling a treat.

Mei-Mei couldn't tell him that she prayed for Young Lu. He might have heard of the scandal, and forbidden it. Plus, she didn't have any coins to pay him for his services, as he was obviously anticipating.

"Please, sir, just let me—"

"Are you here alone?" the priest interrupted. He peered past her shoulder. "Where's your mother? Or your nurse? Nice girls like you shouldn't be going to temples by themselves," he admonished.

The priest was right. Mei-Mei shouldn't be there alone. It wasn't proper. More than one market tale of illicit romance took place in a temple. Her anger flared. She remained silent.

"You need to go home now," he said. "You don't want another disgrace to mar your family's name." The priest turned away and walked back into the main temple.

Alternate courses of shame and rage washed through Mei-Mei. The priest *had* recognized her. But she wasn't doing anything wrong. Someone needed to pray for Young Lu.

The anger won. Mei-Mei turned on her heel and stormed out of the Fire Mountain Temple compound. Instead of turning to her right and going back into the city, she turned to her left, and marched out the southern gate. Then she continued along the path, straight to a small pavilion that sat next to the river Quang. The previous summer, her family had picnicked there. An unattended altar to the river dragon sat in one corner of the pavilion.

Without another thought, Mei-Mei lit her incense, knelt, pressed the incense to her forehead, and bowed the customary three times, praying for a son for Young Lu. Then she bowed three more times, praying for Young Lu herself.

"There," thought Mei-Mei as she reached above her head to place the incense in the brazier. That would show that meddlesome priest. She sat back on her heels and watched with satisfaction as the thin curls of smoke rose above the red lacquered altar table.

How dare that priest question why she prayed alone? Someone needed to burn incense and ask for kindness for Young Lu's unborn child. Just because Mei-Mei wasn't escorted by her mother didn't mean she was willful, like Young Lu. . . .

Mei-Mei looked back the way she'd come. She couldn't see the city walls. On her left, the river Quang ran slick and gray in the morning sunshine, full of melted snow from the northern mountains. Crickets chirped in the low grass, and small fluffy clouds played tag with each other across a perfect blue sky.

It looked so peaceful, but soldiers could be hiding in the stand of oaks on the far side of the river. Mei-Mei jumped to her feet, suddenly regretting her rash behavior. She needed to hurry back before anyone discovered she was gone.

A rattling sound came from behind her, rhythmic and hollow, like metal against a dry reed. She turned toward the noise.

An old fisherman stood on the far side of the pavilion. He held one hand out over the river, shaking a long bamboo pole. Something inside the pole made the clanking noise. His face held only a light map of wrinkles, yet Mei-Mei had the impression he was extremely old. He smiled with childlike joy. His jacket had faded to a muddy beige from too many washings. Muscular calves bulged beneath his rolled-up pant legs. Mysterious bags hung from his wide leather belt.

The old man's rhythm grew faster, sharper. He called out to Mei-Mei, excited and happy, "Come here, miss."

Mei-Mei hesitated. He was obviously poor. It wasn't safe here beyond Bao Fang's wall. She should go home.

"Come see!" the old man called out again.

Duty to all elders compelled Mei-Mei to walk toward him.

The old man gestured with his free hand at the river. Mei-Mei caught her breath in surprise. A school of fish had gathered under the clear water. They moved forward and back, turned a quarter turn together, then moved from side to side. The fish danced in time to the old man's rhythm.

Was he a sorcerer? Mei-Mei took two steps backward.

He turned to smile at her. His teeth were faultlessly placed—no gaps or irregularities—white with fine shading, like bright jade. How could such an old man have perfect teeth? The wrinkles around his eyes reflected many summers of looking into the sun. His laughter, though, was carefree. "Oh, gentle miss," he said, still smiling, "might I have the honor of knowing your name?"

Mei-Mei bowed her head low at his quaint request. "My surname is Li, my formal name is Kong-Jing."

"And what do you call yourself?" the old man asked.

It wasn't proper for him to ask. Only family and close friends used a person's milk name. On the other hand, his smile warmed her heart more than the sun warmed her back. "My friends call me Mei-Mei."

"Ah, Mei-Mei, you're as fair as the plum blossoms for which you're named. You may call me Old Zhang." He bowed deeply. Without straightening up, he twisted his head and grinned at her.

Mei-Mei couldn't help herself. He looked so comical, stooped over with his head at such an odd angle. She put her hand in front of her mouth and giggled.

Old Zhang laughed with her as he stood up. "Good," he said. "You can tell more about a person when they laugh. You—" he paused, then nodded "—are young, not quite conventional, and as precise as a dagger in the hands of an assassin. I like that."

Mei-Mei didn't like his mention of assassins, but she was too polite to let it show.

"I'm a stranger here. Tell me about this city," he said, leading her back to the pavilion.

They sat on one of the benches next to the altar and talked. Mei-Mei told him which merchants had the best goods, which ones would try to cheat him, and a little about her family. Of course, she never mentioned Young Lu. Then their conversation wandered. They tried to define the exact color of the setting sun, the different sounds water makes, which flowers bloom first in the spring and why. From flowers, they moved to peaches.

"Would you accept a peach from the garden of Xi Mong Yu? If one were offered to you?" Old Zhang asked.

"A peach that would make me immortal?"

The old man frowned for the first time that afternoon. "Peaches from Xi Mong Yu's garden allow you to leave the eternal wheel of death, rebirth, and suffering. But you don't become one of the eight immortals that wander the earth. Instead, you live on Peng Lai, the Isle of the Blessed, forever at peace."

The crickets in the grass stopped their calls, and the river hushed, as if holding its breath. The stillness went straight to Mei-Mei's heart. She tried to shake off the feeling with a laugh. "Of course, I'd accept," she said. "Wouldn't everyone? It'd be such an honor for my family to have a daughter who was immortal, who'd pray for them and look over them forever. It might make up for . . ." Mei-Mei paused, not wanting to discuss family matters. Her mother had always told her, "Wear your broken arm *inside* your sleeve."

"Even if you had to say good-bye to your family? Once you reach the Isle of the Blessed, you can never return to this sweet Middle Kingdom," the old man said, leaning forward.

Mei-Mei didn't know what to say. To leave her family forever seemed a great price, even for the honor of immortality. Yet, to change the set pattern of her life, to be immortal, reverenced forever, her name a legend . . .

In the distance, the evening bells rang in deep, somber tones. It was the hour of the Rooster. She was late for dinner. "I must go home," she said. She'd never had such a fascinating conversation, or talked so easily with someone, not even Young Lu.

"Please meet me again. I wish to talk with you more," Old Zhang said.

"I don't know," Mei-Mei said, hesitating. "I shouldn't be here. What if someone saw?"

"Doesn't your grandmother nap every afternoon? You can slip away then," he said in a reassuring voice.

"But I have someone else I must visit. . . ." Mei-Mei said. She must go see Young Lu at least one more time.

"I predict your mother will send you on errands tomorrow morning so you'll be able to see your friend. Then, your grandmother will sleep so well after lunch you'll be able to come straight here," Old Zhang said.

Mei-Mei pulled back from him a little. *Was* he a sorcerer? She liked him so much, but if he hurt her family . . .

Her concern must have shown on her face because Old Zhang laughed and said, "Don't worry. I'm lonely, and in your company my soul feels complete."

Mei-Mei smiled and her cheeks burned. Now she knew how Young Lu felt about Old Lu.

"Until tomorrow, then," he said as she turned to go.

Mei-Mei said, "Only if I can. If Father finds out . . ." She couldn't finish. She didn't know what her father would do if he thought he had two wild daughters. She'd come to the altar of the river dragon that afternoon because she hadn't been thinking. To come back deliberately was something different. She couldn't risk making Father angry. Not even for a soul mate. Or an immortal peach.

She turned and ran back toward the safety of Bao Fang.

The next morning, as Mei-Mei approached the kiln, she heard shouting. She paused. Should she go back? What if Young Lu was in trouble? Mei-Mei made herself hurry forward.

A pale white water buffalo stood in front of the kiln. A small wagon piled with goods rested behind the animal. Old Lu and another man argued with each other on the far side of the buffalo. Old Lu wanted the man to tie the bed down tighter, while the man thought it was tight enough. They didn't see Mei-Mei, so she walked around the wagon into the kiln.

The cracked, yellowing bamboo mats still lay on the

floor, but everything else had been removed. Young Lu stood in the center of the room waving a piece of paper, as if it were a magic wand that had made everything disappear.

"Young Lu?" Mei-Mei called, holding her basket with both hands in front of her.

Young Lu whipped around, the spell broken. "Mei-Mei! Why did you come here again? I told you it was dangerous," she said, folding her arms over her chest.

Mei-Mei looked down at the heavy basket in her hands, surprised by Young Lu's welcome, unsure of what to say.

"I *am* glad you came," Young Lu said, relenting. "Old Lu's friend in Khan Hua sent word. He has work. One of the traders here is taking a caravan north, and hired Old Lu as a guard. We're meeting the rest of the caravan within the hour." Young Lu paused and took a deep breath. "I wrote you a farewell note, so you'd know what happened to us." She held the forlorn piece of paper out to her sister.

Mei-Mei made herself smile and handed her basket to Young Lu. "A fair exchange. You need some food for the road," she said. She glanced at the letter, the characters flowing in firm lines, telling of Young Lu's good fortune. "Is there anyone else . . . ?" Mei-Mei asked, pausing.

"No," Young Lu replied. "Father still wants me dead." She hesitated, then continued. "I wish I could talk with him, at least one more time, before I go. I may never see him again." She turned away from Mei-Mei, her voice full of unshed tears. "I know I should hate Father, hate all this," she said, gesturing at the blackened walls of the kiln. "I should be happy I have a new chance in a new place, that won't have heard of the scandal. But I'm not. I can't be. He's my father. And I'm leaving." Young Lu turned back toward Mei-Mei.

Mei-Mei took a step toward her. She wanted to hug her little sister, to hold her apart from the world and protect her, just for a moment.

Young Lu held up her hand. "Don't," she said. "Or I might squeeze you to death like a snake demon. We have to say good-bye too."

The silence in the room lengthened. The voices outside faded. The two sisters stood at arm's length from each other, trying to say with their eyes all the things they'd never speak aloud.

"It's time to go," Mei-Mei heard from behind her. Young Lu looked away from Mei-Mei, switching her gaze to Old Lu. Though their gaze held fire, Mei-Mei felt cold. She was alone with these two people, on the outside. Young Lu limped to where Old Lu stood.

"Can't I walk with you? At least to the river?" Mei-Mei asked.

"You're a good sister," Old Lu said, taking the basket from Young Lu. He weighed it in his hands. "A very good sister. But I won't have others blacken your name."

"I don't care," Mei-Mei replied.

"I do," Young Lu said. "It was dangerous for you to come see me."

"But I met this fisherman—he reflects my soul—I want to talk with you. . . ."

"You can always talk with me in your heart," Young Lu said, ending the conversation.

Old Lu led Young Lu to the wagon. He gave the basket to the other man and lifted his wife onto the seat as if she were a fragile present from the Emperor. He nodded once to Mei-Mei, then walked beside the wagon as it trundled along. Young Lu never looked back.

Mei-Mei had a wild impulse to run after the wagon, to ask Young Lu to take her with them. But no, that was just a dream. Her mother always told her that a person who followed their dreams spent their life asleep. Mei-Mei waited awhile more, then plodded back to Bao Fang, alone.

Old Zhang had been right. Mei-Mei had been able to visit Young Lu in the morning while doing the er-

rands her mother had sent her on, and her grandmother had gone right to sleep after lunch.

Mei-Mei hurried toward the pavilion covering the
river dragon altar. She didn't have much time. Today
was the twenty-fifth day of the seventh moon. That
evening was the family dedication ceremony. Every
year just before ghost month, her entire family—all
her cousins and aunts and uncles—knelt before the
family poem and swore to uphold its tenets: be loyal
to the Emperor, show obedience to family elders, uphold the family honor, and bring prosperity to all.

The pavilion was empty. Mei-Mei circled the eight-
sided structure, trying not to step on the profuse blue-
bells. She didn't see Old Zhang anywhere. Her heart
thudded heavily in her ears, louder than the river.
Maybe he was a sorcerer, and yesterday had been a
dream. Or maybe the soldiers . . .

Notes from a sad, solitary flute floated from the
trees beyond the pavilion. Mei-Mei followed the sor-
rowful melody along a trail, away from the river. Old
Zhang sat on a bench enclosed by bushes and trees,
playing a black lacquered flute. The river sounded
louder here, though she could no longer see it. It was
the perfect place for a tryst. A warm glow started in
her belly, but she didn't sit down.

Old Zhang finished playing with a pensive trill that
placed a question mark between them. "You're wary.
Good. But you have nothing to fear from me. I'm just
lonely, like a wind whispering bad news. I didn't want
to see anyone except you, so I hid back here. Please
join me, won't you?" He smiled at her with his perfect teeth.

Mei-Mei still didn't sit, but she did take a step forward. "I shouldn't be here. What if someone saw us?
I'm worried. . . ."

Old Zhang laughed. "I'd be disappointed if you
weren't. You're a pretty young girl, with eyebrows
curved as softly as a butterfly's wing. I'm not asking
for solace, just for the company of a dear friend on
this sad, fleeting day."

Mei-Mei cautiously sat on the bench. A quick breeze through the curtain of green in front of her entangled the leaves and branches until she couldn't see the trail. Before she could say anything, a brilliant sapphire-colored bird landed near her feet. It sang a song, pecked at the ground, then looked up at her, first with one eye, then the other. Mei-Mei giggled and forgot about being nervous.

Old Zhang told her about the begging birds in the west. Monks trained them to fetch food from the people in the nearby village and bring it back to the monastery. Then their talk wandered all over the world, from the barbarians and dwarves north of the Tian mountains, to the kindhearted people south of the Yellow River, and the terrible dragons in the eastern sea. Eventually they arrived again at Peng Lai, the Isle of the Blessed.

"Are you certain you'd choose to be an immortal?" Old Zhang asked.

Mei-Mei began the speech she'd prepared the night before. "Of course, if someone favored such an unworthy person as myself with that choice, I'd have to consider it for a long while. But in the end, the honor would be too great to turn down."

"And your family?" he asked.

Mei-Mei bit her lip. She didn't want to hurt her family. They'd lost so many relatives during the war, and now they'd lost Young Lu. Who would take her place in the ceremony that night? But a chance to be free of her marriage to Wang Po Kao, away from Father's wicked temper . . .

"Watching a child pass beyond the Great River is the hardest thing in the world," Old Zhang said, rubbing his hands. "Even if they've lived a long full life."

Mei-Mei examined the fisherman, noting again the discrepancy between his old eyes and his young face. "You're an immortal, aren't you? One of the eight who wander the Middle Kingdom?" she asked.

The breeze rattled the bushes again and the sound

of the river died. The silence was muted, expectant.
"Yes. I am." Old Zhang hesitated, then continued. "I
love wandering the Middle Kingdom, helping people
in small ways. Now, though, it isn't enough. The barbarian horseman, Vakhtang, just killed the last of my
family. Nothing holds me to the earth anymore. I'm
afraid when I sleep at night, if I don't tie myself to
the ground, I'll turn into a wind and blow away."

Mei-Mei knew there weren't enough tears in the
world to ease his heart. "What about the other seven
immortals?" she began.

"They can't help. Immortality just means being
alone, without your family, forever."

Mei-Mei nodded. She knew a little of his sorrow,
and of being alone. She suspected she'd learn more.

She took the old man's face in her hands and
rubbed his cold nose with hers. She didn't know what
made her do it: whether it was his bleak words; because she wanted to touch his magic; or because she
wanted to hold, just for a moment, the kind of feelings
Young Lu had.

Old Zhang placed his warm hands on hers and
pulled her into his arms.

Then the dragon played with the pearl, the hen
showed her teeth, and they entered the land of thunder and rain.

Mei-Mei's knees ached even though she knelt on a
silk cushion her grandmother had embroidered for
her. She'd been kneeling with the rest of the family
for the entire hour of the Dog while her father and
uncles performed the family dedication ceremony. Another trickle of sweat squeezed out from where her
thighs met her calves.

The family poem hung above a skinny black-lacquer
altar, its characters dark and solid on the yellowing
silk. Many narrow, crimson tablets stood on top of the
altar, each about the length of an arm from fingertips
to elbow. Every lacquered tablet had the name of one

of Mei-Mei's ancestors written on it in raised gold characters. Tendrils of sweet smoke rose from the ball-shaped silver filigree censer that also sat on the altar.

The empty spot next to Mei-Mei nagged at her worse than her younger cousins begging for sweets. This was the first time Young Lu hadn't been there to read her stanza. Who would take her place?

When the men finished, one by one the women rose, prostrated themselves before the altar, and read a stanza from the family poem. Mei-Mei trembled inside. Her mother stood up, read her part of the poem; then her two older sisters did the same. She would be next. How could she swear to uphold the family honor when she'd stained it that afternoon with Old Zhang?

Her knees unbent slowly, like leather stiff with age. How could she be part of her family anymore? She should accept the immortal peach from Old Zhang, and become another tablet in her family's Hall of Ancestors. She walked toward the altar, unable to feel her feet. Yet she didn't trip or stumble. At least her association with Old Zhang hadn't brought her bad luck.

Mei-Mei knelt back on the ground, then prostrated herself. She stayed flat on the floor for a moment, not wanting to continue. What if her throat suddenly closed and she couldn't speak? She forced herself up to a kneeling position. She had to continue. It was the only path she knew.

She began reading. The words flowed out of her mouth like rain from the heavens, cleansing her conscience, bathing her soul. She could dedicate herself, from this moment on, to her family. She took a deep breath when she finished her part. She wanted the relief she felt to continue, so she read the next stanza as well, the one that Young Lu usually read. She wasn't trying to take Young Lu's place. She would never be called the youngest daughter.

Mei-Mei bowed and touched her forehead to the ground three times before she got up and joined the rest of her family standing in a line near the door. She trembled again. What if she'd overstepped her bounds? She watched the ground as she walked, not wanting to meet her father's eye. After her two younger brothers finished their parts, the family stood silently for a while, letting the echoes of their reading float up to the Heavenly Court.

The back of Mei-Mei's neck pricked and chicken skin moved across her shoulders, though the room was warm. She felt compelled to look up. Her father stared at her. Mei-Mei shrank inside at the fierceness of his gaze. Then it softened, and he nodded, moving his head just a fraction. Mei-Mei risked a small smile. Her father didn't smile back with his mouth, but his eyes looked tender. He wasn't angry with her. She'd done the right thing. For the second time that night relief flooded through her.

Mei-Mei's smile drained away as the weight of her choice settled into her bones. She couldn't leave. She'd just established the pattern of her life. She was her father's daughter. For better and for worse, she was part of her family, here, in the Middle Kingdom.

Old Zhang was fishing in the river when Mei-Mei walked up to him. He looked at her, his eyes sucking at her, pulling her toward him. He didn't say anything, so she tried. "I—ah—I've decided to—ah—to not accept . . ." she stuttered.

"You've decided to stay in this world, and not travel to the next. Very wise of you," Old Zhang said. He pulled his bare hook out of the water and wrapped the line around the long bamboo pole.

Mei-Mei didn't know what to say. She looked down at her hands. Such small hands, so pale. She knew now that strong bones grew underneath that soft skin.

Old Zhang said, "Imagine the great black sky that is the life of an immortal. There are so few bright points. You, my dear, are one of those stars."

Mei-Mei's cheeks burned. How could she live with the memory of their afternoon together?

Old Zhang answered her unspoken question. "If

jade isn't polished, it can't become a thing of use. You'll remember what you need to remember, and use it, like a tailor with a silver needle, to sew your happiness together."

Mei-Mei looked up and made herself smile at him. She bit her tongue hard, to hurt to prevent herself from crying.

Old Zhang returned her sad smile. He laid his pole on the ground next to him and took a brilliant piece of white paper from one of the bags hanging from his belt. He scooped up some water from the river and sprinkled a few drops on the paper. Then he blew on it.

The paper unfolded itself rapidly, fold upon fold, like a giant lotus blossom. Mei-Mei stepped back, her heart beating fast, not with fear, but with wonder. A deep tone came from the waist-high paper, like echoes from a bronze bell. Two more times the paper unfolded, then a full-sized donkey stood where the paper had been, motionless as a white statue.

The old man blew on the paper a second time. The white faded to gray. The donkey's mane stirred, and the beast shuddered and shook itself. It looked at Old Zhang, then lowered its head to pull up some grass. The old man laughed, grabbed a handful of the donkey's mane, and swung himself up on its back. He turned back to Mei-Mei and said, "I respect your decision." He paused, then continued. "Maybe one of your descendants will make a different choice."

He clucked once and the donkey started trotting. Old Zhang didn't say another word or turn around again.

As Mei-Mei watched him disappear behind the river bend, she vowed that when one of her descendants showed merit, she'd move heaven and earth to let her have that choice.

Chapter I

❧

Bao Fang and on the Trail

Xiao Yen marveled at how the peaceful morning air grew charged with anticipation the moment Wang Tie-Tie woke up.

"Good morning, Aunt," Xiao Yen said from where she was kneeling. She bowed from her waist, put her hands on the floor, and touched her forehead to the ground to show respect for the eldest member of her family. Wang Tie-Tie's dark eyes stared out at Xiao Yen from a collection of wrinkles. Her forehead held deep lines, and her long hair was all white, with only a few strands of black. The front of her neck was hollow, like an old rooster's, but her gaze was steady, and her hands didn't shake as she pushed herself up into a seated position.

Xiao Yen kept her own eyes averted, observing instead the scarlet, orange, and green quilt that covered her aunt. She traced the tiny stitches attaching the seemingly random-colored pieces together. Only when Xiao Yen let herself look beyond the minute could she see that the colors made exotic flowers.

"You leave today," Wang Tie-Tie said, breaking the silence. "Good. You will be worthy, perform your duty, and do great deeds while you're traveling. You will make Old Zhang proud of you," she said, gesturing toward the altar set up in the corner of her room.

An ink drawing of the immortal hung above a black lacquered table. He stood between his donkey and a river, holding his long bamboo fish drum in his hand. A peach tree grew just behind him. His cheeks and brow were broad and wide, youthful and without flaws. The artist had drawn the immortal's eyes extra large and bulging, with many wrinkles around them. Old Zhang seemed to be staring at Xiao Yen, judging her worth.

"And when I come back?" Xiao Yen asked without thinking. She put her hand in front of her mouth. She'd never questioned her aunt before. Wang Tie-Tie didn't seem to notice her impoliteness.

"When you come back, I shall arrange other employment for you."

Employment. Not marriage, though she'd just turned seventeen, and should be married. Gan Ou, her older sister, had been engaged by the time she was fifteen. Xiao Yen wondered again if the reason her aunt never talked about Xiao Yen getting married was because her own husband had been so unpleasant before he'd been killed in the same river accident that had taken Xiao Yen's father and elder brothers. Wang Tie-Tie's husband was honored. Her aunt performed the proper rituals to appease his ghost every month. On the other hand, no one talked about him, or told stories about the funny or clever or even brave things he'd done. Xiao Yen's mother lamented about how improper the household was now that Wang Tie-Tie was the head of the family, how in the old days the servants did all the shopping and the women were strictly confined to the women's quarters. Yet Xiao Yen suspected her mother secretly enjoyed being able to go to the market and to the White Temple without having to beg permission.

"Now go. It is time for my morning tea," Wang Tie-Tie said.

Xiao Yen swallowed hard, sadness dimming the morning sunlight. Though she knew better than to expect warm words at their parting, she'd still hoped.

Xiao Yen didn't want to go, didn't know when she'd be returning, and if she ran into bandits, or worse . . . She unbent her knees slowly, as if they held Wang Tie-Tie's age, bowed again to her aunt, and started for the door.

"Xiao Yen," Wang Tie-Tie called out.

Did her tone hold some softness? Xiao Yen stopped, but didn't turn around.

"I have every faith in you. You will do well, and Old Zhang will come to reward you. He promised me."

Xiao Yen turned around. Had the immortal really visited her aunt when she was Xiao Yen's age? She'd heard the story almost every day since she'd been a little girl. And about his promise.

It had always been easy for Xiao Yen to agree to her aunt's plan: learn paper magic, perform some great deed, and be rewarded with an immortal peach from Zhang Gua Lao. Now the plan had to be put into action. She was about to start her first appointment as a paper mage, protecting horses. How could she prove herself worthy of such important, rare charges, let alone an immortal's attention? Especially with foreigners, going to a foreign place? The impossibility of her task threatened to crush her.

"And when he does reward you . . ." Wang Tie-Tie started.

"I'll bring the immortal peach to you," Xiao Yen finished the litany. Every time Xiao Yen saw Wang Tie-Tie, they repeated this phrase. It was their pact, their bond. It was how Xiao Yen would repay Wang Tie-Tie for letting her study with Master Wei. It was her duty. No matter what else happened, Xiao Yen would do her duty.

Wang Tie-Tie smiled, her eyes kind. "You are my hope. My dream." The soft voice hardened. "I don't understand why you have such a sad face. You're lucky. You've always been lucky."

Xiao Yen forced her hands to stay at her sides, to not reach up to grasp the empty place around her neck. The amulet that held her luck was gone. A ragged hole ripped through the morning and darkness poured through, threatening to suffocate Xiao Yen. She kept her face calm, placid, so Wang Tie-Tie wouldn't know anything was wrong.

"You will do well. I'm sure of it." Her aunt paused, then said, "I will see you again when you return."

Xiao Yen bowed at the dismissal, turned, and walked out the door.

She couldn't tell her aunt. She couldn't tell anyone.

Bright spring sunlight peeped over the front wall of the family compound. Pale sky filled the area above the walls—the sky well. Xiao Yen only saw darkness. She held herself rigid, not blinking until she was sure she could move again without screaming her loss aloud. She'd lost her luck. Jing Long, the dragon living at the bottom of the city well, had caused her amulet, the source of her luck, to fall into the well at the center of the city. Now she had to leave her family, go on an impossible journey with foreigners, and protect their horses, each one worth more than her life.

She took a deep breath, trying to capture the stillness of the morning air. She failed. She couldn't stop trembling inside. She closed her eyes and tried to find her center, her quiet place, but all she saw were the gray backs of her eyelids.

A moment later, she felt a tug on her sleeve, and opened her eyes. Her old nurse, Ama, stood beside her. She held out a dark blue bundle. Xiao Yen recognized her mother's favorite jacket. Without a word, Ama folded it again and put it into Xiao Yen's pack. Fu Be Be hadn't understood why Xiao Yen had wanted to take her old jacket. It was worn, the cuffs were covered with plaques to hide their raveling, and the embroidered threads were breaking. But Xiao Yen had wanted something of her mother's with her, to remind her of her family, to comfort her while she traveled. It was Xiao Yen's favorite jacket too.

Ama bowed deeply to Xiao Yen, almost bending in half. Then she scuttled away, heading toward the servants' quarters at the far end of the compound. They'd already said their good-byes. Xiao Yen knew Ama didn't want to be seen crying again.

Fu Be Be came up before Xiao Yen could take another deep breath. Her skin glowed like a white peony in the sunlight. She'd added only the slightest pink to her cheeks and lips. Her eyebrows arched across her forehead like gull wings, showing her great intelligence. She wore her rich black hair piled loosely on top of her head, held in place with three black-and-red lacquered hairpins. Glittering sunlight reflected off her best silver jacket, and fired the golden pine boughs embroidered on it.

Xiao Yen's throat tightened. Although her mother didn't approve of her employment, Fu Be Be was going to see her daughter off with all due ceremony.

Fu Be Be sniffed with disapproval when Xiao Yen picked up her own bag. To forestall another argument about hiring porters, Xiao Yen turned and walked toward the gate that separated the family courtyard from the front, formal courtyard. Though her mother stood a good head shorter than Xiao Yen, and was thinner than a river willow, Xiao Yen would rather face Hu Xien, the demon-slayer strong enough to jump and touch the moon, than have another fight with her mother.

Old Gardener had sprinkled water mixed with oil over the stones that morning, so the formal courtyard, also known as the Yard of Greeting, sparkled in the sunlight. The Hall of Politeness, the only building in the Yard of Greeting, sat like a shadow in the sunlight. Small brass bells hung under the eaves and rang when the wind touched them. Xiao Yen hurried past, with only the slightest nod to show her respect. Fu Be Be hadn't paused, and already stood waiting at the front gate, beyond the bright red spirit wall.

Evil spirits could only travel in straight lines, so families built spirit walls behind their front gates, preventing direct access into the courtyards beyond. A circling gold-and-white dragon was painted on the side of the wall facing the gate of Xiao Yen's family compound. Xiao Yen wanted to stroke the dragon's long, drooping whiskers, to say good-bye, as she had when she'd been younger. But she couldn't. Not in front of her mother.

Old Gardener opened the gate silently, eyes downcast. As Xiao Yen passed through, he reached out and patted the dragon's snout for her. Xiao Yen bit her lip, refusing to cry. Instead, she hurried after her mother.

"*Hú-ah,*" cried an old woman sitting on the street corner next to a covered iron pot. "Porridge for sale!" High-pitched tings rang from the coppersmith shop. Heated bargaining spilled out onto the street from the tailor's next door. Steam clouds billowed across the sidewalk. They smelled like almonds and obscured the bun stand.

Xiao Yen slowed as she passed the line of customers. She would like to buy a sweet bun for breakfast, but her mother wouldn't stop. Fu Be Be walked without hesitation, like the ghost Wu Quang Yin on her way to collect more souls. Dutifully, Xiao Yen hurried on.

The rain from the night before had left large puddles in the center of the road, squeezing traffic into two tight lines. Xiao Yen paused at the first line to let a man with a wheelbarrow full of baskets pass in front of her. She found a narrow path between two puddles in the center, then paused again to wait for an ox pulling a cart laden with spring grain. Fu Be Be was already on the other side of the street. Xiao Yen hurried to catch up.

Just as Xiao Yen reached her mother, she stepped in a small puddle. Her shoe stuck in the mud at the bottom of the hole and Xiao Yen fell onto her knees and hands. Her head snapped forward and she bit her tongue. "Ow!" she cried.

Fu Be Be rushed to her daughter's side, gripped Xiao Yen's elbow, and pulled her up.

Xiao Yen looked down in dismay. Mud covered her new gray travel pants. The palms of her hands burned and the mud on her knees grew chill in the cool morning air. Xiao Yen grasped her mother's arm to steady herself. The warm silk slid under her hand. Xiao Yen let go, but it was too late. An ugly stain, like a black arrow, circled the silver sleeve.

Xiao Yen stared, horrified. She'd just ruined her new travel clothes and her mother's best jacket. A roaring like wet thunder filled Xiao Yen's ears. How could she have done this? She'd rarely tripped before, and had never fallen like this. Not when she'd had her luck. She rubbed the faint scar on the back of her left hand, remembering when she once thought of herself as the luckiest girl in the world.

Fu Be Be leaned over and brushed at the mud on Xiao Yen's pants, but only dirtied her own hands. She straightened up and looked at Xiao Yen, her dark eyes cutting through Xiao Yen's cloud of silence.

"This is a bad omen. Wang Tie-Tie should never have signed that contract. It's shameful. Sending you away from your family, to work with those dirty foreigners. You must keep yourself apart and pure." Fu Be Be pulled Xiao Yen's arm down, jerking her forward, and hurrying along again.

Xiao Yen stopped. "Mother, I'm sure it'll be fine. It'll be good experience for me." Xiao Yen regretted the words as soon as they left her mouth.

Fu Be Be turned and came back to where Xiao Yen was standing. Xiao Yen flinched under her mother's angry gaze.

"Good experience? The only experience you should be getting is listening to matchmakers and swaddling babies. Who's going to make an offer for you after you spend three months away from your home, traveling with foreigners?"

"Shhh, Mother," Xiao Yen said, conscious of the stares from the people passing them.

Fu Be Be wouldn't be shushed. "Wang Tie-Tie, your own aunt, has robbed you. I don't care how much money we're getting from this contract. A girl without family is poor."

A water carrier, his empty buckets dangling on a pole carried over his broad shoulders, leaned against the wall next to the sidewalk to watch. Xiao Yen gestured at him and told her mother, "Remember what they say: wear your broken arm *inside* your sleeve."

Fu Be Be glared at the young man, then dismissed him with a wave of her hand. Holding her nose high, she turned and walked down the sidewalk again, as proud as royalty. Xiao Yen suppressed a giggle and followed.

A small crowd had gathered in the courtyard of the merchant inn. The two foreign brothers stood next to their horses, packed and ready to go. A group of people gathered in a circle around them, staring, pointing, and whispering to each other. The brothers towered over everyone by a head at least. Xiao Yen gasped as she and Fu Be Be approached. She'd never been this close to a foreigner before. They really were as ugly as her cousins said. Wang Tie-Tie's partner, Fu Ling, detached himself from the crowd to greet them.

Fu Ling bowed low with his hands pressed together across his chest. He wore makeup around his eyes to make them seem small and squinting, as if he spent his nights studying. His broad red nose told the truth—the only thing he studied was a wine pot. He wore a black cap with a high-standing brim and long ear flaps, like an official's cap, but without the sign of Heaven embroidered on it. His russet silk robe had a pattern of golden blossoms embroidered across his skinny chest and long sleeves.

"Greetings, Lady Fu," he said in a voice like silk caressing silk. "I welcome you and your"—he paused, glancing at Xiao Yen—"daughter."

Everyone always said how much Xiao Yen looked like her mother, the same long fine fingers, well-formed nose, and oval face. Xiao Yen's training had left her bulkier though. Her sister had teased her once, that with Xiao Yen's shoulders, if she cut her hair, she could pass for a man. The remark still burned.

Fu Ling paused again. Fu Be Be bowed to him, a

very short, curt bow, as one would give to an inferior. Xiao Yen did the same. The crowd in the courtyard now stared at her. She wished she could disappear. It was bad enough that her family knew of her position. Now all of Bao Fang would know. Gossip ran faster through the city than the goddess Chang-e could fly from the Tien Moutains in the west to the sea in the east.

Fu Be Be started to walk past Fu Ling, but he touched her sleeve and said, "Oh, gracious lady, perhaps you can untie the knot the foreigners have presented me."

"Continue," Fu Be Be commanded.

Xiao Yen caught her breath. If there was some way out of the current contract, her mother would find it. Xiao Yen didn't know whether to feel sadness or joy. On the one hand, she didn't want to go. Who would want to be separated from their family, their home, for weeks, traveling with foreigners? On the other hand, she had to go. She must do her duty. She had to fulfill her obligation to Wang Tie-Tie.

"It seems the foreigners have, ah, met someone. She calls herself Bei Xi. She also travels the merchant trail, and wants to join the brothers and their horses."

"Does this person, this Bei Xi, expect my daughter to protect her as well?" Fu Be Be asked.

"She has her own guard, but, if they're all traveling together, how could Xiao Yen protect one and not the other?" Wang Tie-Tie's partner ended with an elegant shrug.

One of the two foreigners walked up to them. Xiao Yen couldn't take her eyes off his blond hair. It was like someone had taken a piece of the sun and placed it on his head. Maybe it had happened because he was so tall. Fu Ling introduced him as Udo, then bowed and said something in a foreign language, his voice like oil running off water, though he struggled with the words.

The tall foreigner pointed to Xiao Yen and said a single word, incredulously. Xiao Yen's cheeks burned.

She could guess what had happened. Wang Tie-Tie's partner had never told the foreigners, or had lied, about her being so young. Or about her being a girl. No one thought girls could provide good protection.

Udo's eyes, the color of summer thunderstorms, flashed with anger. He drew himself up straight, his face turning more red, about to argue more, when a sweet voice called out. The voice spoke fluently in the foreigner language. The man turned and answered roughly.

The most beautiful woman Xiao Yen had ever seen appeared from behind the foreigner, gliding like silk on the wind. She was petite as the blossoms on a *wutong* tree, with skin finer than imperial jade. Though the pink of her cheeks had been only slightly enhanced, her lips were as red as poppies. She wore a lovely off-white silk jacket decorated with cicadas, tied loosely with sleeves that didn't cover her wrists, giving improper glimpses of her under jacket when she moved.

Xiao Yen looked down at her feet, conscious again of her stained pants. *This* was the person who wanted to travel with the foreigners? From the way Bei Xi wore her clothes and the amount of makeup covering her face, she was obviously a courtesan. Equally obvious, from the quality of the jacket she wore, her cultured tones, and the number of jewels adorning her, she was from some lord's court, possibly even a lord who knew the Emperor.

Fu Be Be made a disapproving noise. Xiao Yen knew Fu Be Be didn't approve of second wives, let alone other women in a household. Would her mother let her travel with such a woman? Xiao Yen was certain that Wang Tie-Tie would approve of Xiao Yen associating with Bei Xi. Her aunt always sought to better their family's social position. Besides, Xiao Yen knew that Wang Tie-Tie thought second wives, courtesans, even prostitutes, could help keep discord from a marriage.

Patiently, Bei Xi listened to the story told by the

foreigner. She spoke in a reassuring tone, and eventually mollified the tall blond man. He walked away, still shaking his head. The woman watched him, her head tilted to one side, as if she listened to the wind. She raised her arms, clapped her hands, then turned to Fu Be Be.

A servant came running into the courtyard, breathless, carrying a large sack.

"Of course, because your talented daughter is now protecting twice as many people, you should receive twice the fee," Bei Xi said, indicating that the servant should hand the money to Fu Be Be.

Xiao Yen felt the anger radiating from her mother. The courtesan had done the right thing, the proper thing. Her mother couldn't back out now. "The contract . . ." she started to say.

"Is still valid," Wang Tie-Tie's partner smoothly inserted as he reached for the bag.

Xiao Yen looked at her feet. Of course it was. She still had to go, to do her duty, to make Wang Tie-Tie proud.

The foreign brothers had traveled the entire length of the Great Merchant road, from the fabled city of Constantinople, over the Mountains of Heaven, through the Bone Desert, and down to Xian, the capital of the Middle Kingdom. Their home was a town called Reric, on the other side of the world, just east of the kingdom of Jutland. They'd hired Xiao Yen to protect their merchandise, their horses, as they made their way through the Middle Kingdom to the seaport Khuangho. They'd make much more money selling the horses on the coast than selling them inland. Xiao Yen didn't know how they'd gotten permission to do it. Almost all horses were the property of the Emperor or his men.

The brothers had traveled to Xian with a different mage, one who enchanted cloth. He'd conjured blankets that changed the appearance of the horses. Xiao Yen wished she could have met him, though she'd been warned by her master many times that all other mages would be a threat to her. The brothers dismissed the cloth mage when he tried to steal their horses while at the capital.

The brothers wanted to go back home by sea. A sea route back to the foreign lands of the west had been open for ten years or so. It wasn't a safe journey, but the land route was less safe than it had been. When Emperor Dezong had forged the peace treaty with the Tibetans to the west and the kingdom of Turic—the land of the horsemen—to the north, and the Great Merchant road to the west had reopened, all three kingdoms had dedicated soldiers to keeping merchants safe from robbers. Now, the horsemen ignored the treaty, raiding both merchants and the villages on the border between their lands and the Middle Kingdom. In addition, on the other side of the trade route, the great foreign king, Charlemagne, had died, and his son was old and weak. His lands, too, were under attack.

Everything happened quickly in the courtyard. One of Bei Xi's servants led Xiao Yen to her horse. It had a ragged, dark brown coat with matching mane, and the character for "ox" branded on its right shoulder. The characters branded on the left side of its tail indicated that the horse was foreign. The brands on the right showed that it could be used privately. It smelled of hay and dust.

Xiao Yen remembered another brand she'd seen, only once. She shivered, and wished she could ask the horse if it still hurt.

Xiao Yen's head didn't crest the horse's back, while the foreigners' heads stood almost as high as their horses! Xiao Yen had never been on a horse before. Her fear hollowed out the pit of her stomach as she looked up at it. What if she injured it? If she took all the money from her contract, maybe she could pay for one horse.

Bei Xi's servant tied Xiao Yen's bags across the back of the horse, and showed her how to step on the mounting block, and how to swing one leg up and over the horse. Xiao Yen forced herself to follow his instructions precisely, trying to make the foreign movements seem natural. She couldn't let anyone guess how full of fear she was. She was their defense against mercenaries and bandits on the road. She couldn't be afraid of what she was protecting.

From her high perch, Xiao Yen could see over the heads of everyone in the courtyard. Maybe this wouldn't be too bad. She wasn't afraid of falling off. Her training with Master Wei had given her an excellent sense of balance.

Then the horse took a step.

Xiao Yen stopped looking around and concentrated on her horse. She'd never sat in a cart or ridden in a palanquin. Moving without taking a step was an odd sensation. It reminded her of her dreams of flying.

A sharp whistle cut through the air. Xiao Yen's horse turned around and started walking toward the gate, following the rest of the horses. Xiao Yen clutched at the reins and looked around for her mother. This was it. She was leaving. Leaving Bao Fang. Leaving her family.

Xiao Yen bent her head as she passed through the arch of the merchant's inn, though she didn't need to, unlike the foreigners. Her mother came hurrying up, pushing her way through the crowd. Xiao Yen wasn't sure how to stop her horse. She couldn't dismount. She'd never be able to get back on it again without help.

Fu Be Be handed Xiao Yen a small willow branch, saying, "I look forward to your return."

Xiao Yen squeezed her lips together, biting them. The willow branch was a traditional parting gift. It cried all the tears that the parties saying good-bye could never shed. Xiao Yen didn't know what to say. She'd never thought her mother would shed any tears, real or metaphorical, at her departure.

"Be well," her mother said, falling away.

"I'll try," Xiao Yen called over her shoulder. She couldn't look backward for more than a moment. Though she had good balance, it was still unsettling.

Besides, she didn't want to see her mother actually cry.

Xiao Yen held the reins to her horse in one cold hand and clutched the willow branch in the other. Her thighs trembled and her buttocks ached. She'd never ridden a horse before that day. Now she'd been on one all day, and wasn't sure she could dismount. Everyone in camp seemed too busy to help her. The long-haired guard, a barbarian horseman from the north, Gi Tang, was setting up a tent for Bei Xi on the eastern edge of camp. The trail guide looked after the horses, lifting up hooves one at a time, checking for rocks.

The foreign brothers, Udo and Ehran, worked together; Ehran built a fire and Udo unpacked large cast-iron cooking pots. They yelled at each other with big, hearty voices, as if they stood many *li* apart. Their voices dominated the other sounds in the camp: the grunts from the barbarian guard as he raised the center pole of a tent, the chorus of frogs from the river, the horses nickering as the trail guide led them to the edge of camp. Xiao Yen longed to be outside of all the noise, in the woods with only the wind speaking to her. Though the oaks still held their leaves, the other trees were only budding, so the blazing orange sunset shone through the clearing. From her high perch, Xiao Yen smelled the damp ground. Her horse was warm against her thighs, but her shoulders were cold. At least her legs had finally dried.

She suppressed a shudder remembering the river crossing that morning. Only her horse had stumbled, dropping to its knees. Only Xiao Yen had soaked her legs. The foreigners had laughed, saying she was now "baptized," whatever that meant. Xiao Yen knew it was the river dragon trying to drag her under, angry with her because the city dragon was angry with her.

She was glad they didn't have to cross the river again, though they would ride beside it for weeks as they traveled north along the merchant trail. It would provide their water the entire trip.

Udo approached her. He was the uglier of the two foreigners, with a large nose and the grin of a carnivore. His best feature was his hair, golden as summer wheat. It rested in waves across the top of his head, and he tied it in a ponytail in the back. He wore the cuffs of his gray pants loose, like a woman, instead of bound tightly around his ankles, like a man. Over his reddish cotton shirt he wore a short black vest, lined with brown fur.

Udo said something to her in his harsh, guttural foreign tongue, and held out his hands. She assumed he wanted to help her down so she said, "Yes, down please," in his tongue. He looked surprised and rattled off more words at her.

Xiao Yen didn't know what he'd said. She smiled as if she agreed, hoping that was the right answer. He yelled at his brother—something about a flower? Then he turned back and smiled at her, showing all his teeth like an angry dog. Xiao Yen suppressed a shudder and didn't flinch when he touched her elbow and helped her slide off her horse. His warm fingers held her upper arm, steadying her. When Xiao Yen found she could stand, she pulled away from him.

Udo untied her bags, hanging on either side of her horse. He grunted as he lifted them over the horse, then dropped them to the ground. Xiao Yen let go of her willow branch and picked her bags up. Why hadn't he just handed them to her? He said something more that she didn't understand.

"He's asking how you can carry such heavy bags," came a soft voice over her right shoulder. Xiao Yen spun around, clutching her bags to her chest like a shield. Bei Xi the courtesan stood there, more beautiful than the painting Wang Tie-Tie had of Kuan Yin, the goddess of mercy. A sweet scent flowed from Bei Xi to Xiao Yen. In the dimming light her skin glowed like a new moon. Her teeth looked like little pearls, expertly strung.

Xiao Yen realized that both Bei Xi and Udo stared at her, waiting for an answer. One word popped out from her terror of addressing such a perfect being. "Practice."

Udo roared with laughter when Bei Xi repeated the word to him in his language. The courtesan smiled politely, though her eyes laughed as well. Xiao Yen turned away, taking small steps with her shaky legs. Udo came up beside her before she was halfway across the camp clearing and took her bags from her. He grunted again at their weight.

He led her to a small tent set up next to Bei Xi's. Xiao Yen glanced at Bei Xi's tent, then looked away. Why had they put her tent next to Bei Xi's? The courtesan's tent was made from off-white cloth, like the muslin used for mourning clothes. Xiao Yen had often heard the northern barbarians referred to as "the ones who sleep in death tents."

Xiao Yen's tent, provided for her by her foreign patrons, was made of black oiled leather. It was long enough for Xiao Yen to lie down and be covered. A padded comforter covered the floor of the tent. The apex of the tent was high enough for her to sit upright. After Udo placed her bags inside, Xiao Yen sank down, glad to sit on ground that didn't move.

Udo yelled again at his brother. Why couldn't they address each other in normal tones? Ehran came over to where Udo stood. Xiao Yen decided that, in dim light, he might pass for a wealthy merchant from her land, the Middle Kingdom. He wasn't as tall as Udo. Ehran also weighed more. He carried his extra weight around his belly. His beard grew out of his chin, thin and black. He let his black hair hang loose around his shoulders. His skin was darker than Udo's, and his features were much wider. His nose spread across his face like it had melted. Only his round eyes ruined the illusion.

Ehran spoke rapidly to Udo, gesturing at Xiao Yen.

She caught the word "protection." She stifled a groan and wished the earth would open up and swallow her whole. All she wanted to do was to sleep. How could riding a horse all day make her so tired? Her legs ached at the thought of getting up, but she knew she must. She needed to set up the defenses for the camp that night.

She reached up to touch her luck. When her fingers closed upon the empty space around her neck she nearly growled. She had no luck. She rubbed the back of her left hand. The faint scar there held no magic. As she flexed her fingers she remembered the willow branch her mother had given her. Where was it?

She looked under her bags. The branch wasn't there. She remembered holding the branch when she'd been on her horse, letting it cry the tears she couldn't. Then she'd dropped it when Udo had put her bags on the ground. Xiao Yen got out of her tent and stood up. The edges of her vision dimmed. Xiao Yen closed her eyes and took three deep breaths to steady herself.

She opened her eyes in time to see the trail guide throw her willow branch on the cooking fire.

Xiao Yen wanted to turn around and crawl back into her tent, pull her comforter over her head, and never get up again. The green willow wood sizzled and crackled on the fire. Any hope that things would be better after she left Bao Fang also went up in smoke.

Udo said something from behind her. Xiao Yen acquiesced without fully understanding what he asked. It was time for her to do her duty, in front of these strangers, luck or no. Master Wei had said she had skill as well as luck. She hoped he was right.

She followed Udo around the edges of the camp, memorizing landmarks. Then she went to her tent. Her special bag was there, made of stiff oiled leather, the sides supported with straight pieces of wood, so that the paper she carried wouldn't get wet or be crushed. She sent another quick prayer of thanks to Master Wei for such a thoughtful parting gift. She reverently pulled out a sheet of paper and put her bag over her shoulder. Then she walked to the southern edge of the camp, the one closest to her home.

Xiao Yen sat on the cold ground with the paper in her lap. She breathed deeply, pulling her breath down past her fast-beating heart into her center where she imagined a pebble tumbling over and over. She concentrated on the revolving rock. She filled herself with the sound of the night wind pulling at the winter leaves and the scent of the spring hidden in the thawing ground. The image of a silver river came to Xiao Yen, the place where she felt most comfortable, her still place, the home of her quiet.

Calmer now, Xiao Yen bowed three times to the west, the direction of Xian and the Emperor, touching her forehead on the cold earth each time. Then she lifted her hands and prayed to Zhang Gua Lao, the immortal. When she finished, she raised her arms, glad to see they were as steady and as motionless as the arms of a carved Buddha.

She picked up the piece of paper and made her first two folds, mountain-folds, bringing the lower corners to the back of the paper, close to the middle. Then she valley-folded the top layer only, creasing the paper from the lower edge to just past the center. She made a valley-fold of the small remaining square, pulling the fold between her nails so it was sharp. Then she unfolded the paper and looked at the resulting lines. They were crisp, well defined, like the trimmed edges of a wooden fan. Pleased, she folded more.

When she finished, her creation wasn't much bigger than her outstretched hand, but its legs were solid, its ears large, and its tail supple. Even the two fangs looked sharp. Xiao Yen was happy with her tiger. She was also relieved her first try had worked, that she didn't have to make a second attempt in front of her new employers. She put her beast on the ground where she had previously touched her forehead. Still feeling the folds in her fingers, she closed her eyes and let the tiger grow larger and larger in her mind.

She imagined its soft fur rippling as it paced, its whiskers bobbing, its paws as big as her thigh, ready to rend any strangers to pieces.

The collective gasp behind her told her she'd succeeded. She opened her eyes to a golden tiger glow. A surety and wildness filled its eyes. Xiao Yen didn't know she possessed or could have imparted such emotion.

Holding her tiger's gaze, Xiao Yen let the path around their camp, a series of landmarks she had memorized earlier, saturate her vision. The first landmark was just north of the tents: a little bush, buds only, no leaves; next was a thin sapling with more white than gray in its trunk; and then a small rock with brown veins on the right and a hollow in a tree on the left. She thought about every spot she'd chosen around the border of their camp in sequence, visualizing the unique aspects of each. When she thought of the last marker, finishing the circle around their camp, the tiger, with a sudden jump, sprang to its duty. It would patrol from one place to the next, protecting their camp with its presence as it prowled the perimeter for the entire night.

Xiao Yen pulled five candles out of her bag. She placed them at the five compass points around the paper figure still on the ground: north, south, east, west, and center. Then she stood to fetch a small branch from the fire with which to light the candles.

Udo, Ehran, Bei Xi, and her guard stood in a line behind her. Udo asked something in a choked tone. Bei Xi translated.

"How long . . . ?"

"Until the sun comes up," Xiao Yen replied, indicating with her hand, palm raised.

Ehran asked something, his voice a little more normal than his brother's. Ehran didn't look up as he asked the question. His gaze stayed focused on his fingers, fiddling with the knife hilt sticking out from his belt.

Bei Xi translated. "Will it stay outside the camp?"

"Outside, yes. It will follow the path I made."

"Is it dangerous?" Udo asked, his voice now under his control again.

Finally a question that Xiao Yen could answer without translation. "To others, if they see it. It can kill," Xiao Yen lied. Xiao Yen's teacher, Master Wei, could create a deadly tiger, but Xiao Yen didn't have the wisdom or understanding yet.

Bei Xi smiled. "Ay! We're lucky to have you with us."

Lucky? Was she lucky to be here, so far away from her family and everything she'd ever known? She'd lost her luck, maybe forever. With her luck gone, how could she gain enough merit to win Wang Tie-Tie an immortal peach? Xiao Yen was certain she was the unluckiest girl in the world.

Chapter 2

❦

Bao Fang

Xiao Yen yawned loudly, knowing it was disrespectful, hoping Mama would notice her boredom just the same. Instead, Gan Ou, her sister, hissed at her. Gan Ou was older, almost ten. She was supposed to take care of Xiao Yen, baby-sit her seven-year-old sister, but all she did was tease Xiao Yen and pull her hair when they were alone. In front of Mama, Gan Ou pretended to be the best daughter.

Xiao Yen raised her hands again and tried to pray. She was so tired of praying. She was sorry Papa and her three older brothers had gone to the Heavenly Pavilion, but hadn't they always been gone anyway? Working or traveling or trading? And how would praying to Jing Long, the dragon at the bottom of the well in the center of the city, help them at the bottom of the river Quang? Xiao Yen had hoped they'd go to the altar next to the river to pray that day, but Mama had taken them to the White Temple instead.

The priest that morning had talked to Mama about the dragon being the symbol of change. He'd told the story of how the dragon rose out of the water in the spring to bring the summer rains. Mama had only thanked him and told her daughters to continue to pray for the change to stop, or reverse itself.

The candles on either side of the altar flickered.

Xiao Yen followed the smoke rising to the ceiling. The aqua and scarlet scales of the dragon painted on the wall shimmered, and its white belly looked hard. It played with a pearl as it rose through the clouds. Xiao Yen imagined riding the dragon, floating through the sky, her hair blown back like the dragon's golden whiskers. Its back would feel solid and warm under her legs, like a sunny rock near the river. They would spiral up and up, above the clouds, into the sky where the blue was so pure and thick it would be like swimming.

Mama put her hands on the ground and touched her forehead to the earth. Xiao Yen watched out of the corner of her eye, hopeful. Was Mama finished? Xiao Yen sighed again when Mama sat back, still absorbed in prayer. It gave her an idea though.

Xiao Yen put her hands on the ground and lowered her head, like her mother had. Then she pushed with her hands, scooting backward. She did this three times, until she was behind her mother and her sister.

She stood up, holding her breath in case Mama or her sister noticed. Her legs wobbled. Mama still prayed. Gan Ou still pretended to pray. The candlelit dragon flew above them, out of the shadows, toward the light. A bubble of excitement filled Xiao Yen's chest. The strain of being quiet for so long expanded inside her, racing down her arms and legs to her fingers and toes, tingling. The tension stretched tighter and tighter until it snapped. She spun and ran into the sunlit courtyard.

It felt so good to run, to move freely. The warm sunlight on Xiao Yen's head and back soothed her. She watched the ground as she ran. Chalk was mixed in with the stone in the courtyard, and if she stamped hard enough, sometimes tiny clouds of white powder rose from her feet. She slowed as she approached the spirit wall in front of the gate on the far side of the temple complex, tapped a hinge on the gate, then took off again. She decided to run the full length of the courtyard five times, once for each of the five compass points.

To the right of the courtyard stood a large Buddhist temple. Round pillars held up the blue-tiled sloped roof. The Buddha sat cross-legged with one hand on his knee, three fingers pointing toward the ground, summoning the earth goddess Ma Tou to witness his enlightenment. The wooden shutters along the sides of the temple had been taken down so the monks could sit in their alcoves and fill the courtyard with their chanted prayers.

Xiao Yen had reached Jing Long's temple and was going back toward the gate when a pair of feet and a brilliant flash of saffron appeared before her. Xiao Yen squealed and lurched to the side, landing on her shoulder.

When she looked up, kind brown eyes smiled at her over a silver tray. Xiao Yen stammered and used the most formal phrases she knew to address the monk.

"Excuse me, honorable sir."

"Are you hurt?"

"No," Xiao Yen replied as she stood up. She tried to stand very tall, but she still couldn't see what the monk carried on his tray.

"You were lucky you didn't run into me and spoil all my hard work."

Xiao Yen felt comforted by his words. Everyone told her she was lucky. She reached up and touched the gold amulet hanging around her neck. Wang Tie-Tie had given it to her forty days after she'd been born, as part of her naming ceremony. It brought her luck. It had a stylized dragon claw on one side, representing the year of her birth, and the character for luck, *Fù*, on the other. *Fu* was also her family name, but it had a different character, and meant "teacher."

"Would you like to see?" the monk asked.

"Please," Xiao Yen replied.

The monk bent at the waist and lowered the silver tray to Xiao Yen's eye level. A delicate tree grew out of the center, strung out of tiny white jasmine blossoms. Eight yellow-gold peaches rested on the tray, circling the tree, attached to the branches with intricate knots. The sweet scent made Xiao Yen smile.

"Do you know who this is for?" the monk asked.

Xiao Yen replied more casually, "Yes, it's for Old Zhang and the other immortals."

The monk raised his eyebrows. "I'm glad you're so familiar with them."

Xiao Yen thought the monk was making fun of her, but she wasn't sure, so she spoke more formally again. "My aunt, Wang Kong-Jing, admires the immortal Zhang Gua Lao. She often tells me stories about him and his paper mule."

"Does your auntie tell good stories?" the monk asked as he straightened up.

"They're very good stories," Xiao Yen replied.

"It's good you listen to your Tie-Tie," the monk said. "You might want to go see her now, and not run around the courtyard."

Xiao Yen's cheeks grew hot as she blushed. The monk walked toward the main temple, where the big Buddha sat. Xiao Yen didn't want to go back inside. She sighed and looked around the courtyard. Emerald green ivy covered the northern wall with leaves as large as her hand. Xiao Yen walked along the wall, dragging her fingers through them. They bounced when she tapped them. It made her laugh. She sat down to watch them.

On the ground, in the warm sunshine, she couldn't feel any wind. There must have been some though, because the ivy leaves sometimes moved in circles or bounced up and down. The wall behind the ivy was made of mud bricks painted over with white plaster. Something shiny had gotten mixed in with the plaster. When the leaves bounced out of the way and the sun touched the wall, it glittered. Xiao Yen laughed again.

"What are you laughing at?" asked someone from behind her. She didn't like the voice. It sounded like a grown-up version of her sister. Gan Ou sometimes pretended to be interested in what Xiao Yen was doing just so she could ridicule Xiao Yen.

Xiao Yen turned to see where the voice came from. A man stood behind her. He was old, maybe as old as Wang Tie-Tie, the oldest person Xiao Yen knew. Though his skin was smooth and few wrinkles gathered around his mouth, his eyes told her he'd seen ten thousand sunsets. His lips were thin and his nose hooked on the end like a hawk's beak. His eyebrows, still thick and black, flew across his forehead like raven's wings. His neck was as long and skinny as a crane's. He wore black shoes, black pants bound around his ankles with black and silver wrappings, and a long black jacket that had a pattern of dancing cranes on it.

"You laugh? Why?" he asked again.

The simple language astonished Xiao Yen. Did he think she was like Chu Long Yi's baby, who'd been three years old before he'd learned to crawl? She'd show him. She turned and pointed to the wall, addressing him directly, like an equal, instead of as an elder.

"I'm watching the glass-colored salamanders. See? There goes one!" she said, her finger following the path of the wind. "It's racing another one under the ivy leaves. That's what sparkles in the sun. And see there?" She pointed to a leaf bobbing up and down. "There's one sitting under that leaf. It has its three tails spread across the wall. It's tickling the stem, telling the leaf to grow. Its fingers are long and jointed, like bamboo. See?" Xiao Yen laughed again at the picture in her head.

The old man stared at Xiao Yen as if she had glass salamanders climbing all over her, and he was a bird that ate such things. "Might I have the honor of knowing your name?" he asked, very formally.

"My family name is Fu, my formal name is Xi Wén, but everyone calls me Xiao Yen."

" '*Xiao*' as in little?" the man asked.

"Yes," Xiao Yen said. "And '*Yen*' is the bird, the

little brown one, that Wang Tie-Tie tells me stories about, that would die before it stole food."

"A sparrow," the man said.

"Correct," Xiao Yen replied.

The man bowed his head to her. "My surname is Wei. I am opening a school here, the Dancing Crane Defense school."

Xiao Yen bowed in return, not sure what he meant.

"I hope my improper daughter hasn't been disturbing you."

Xiao Yen hadn't heard any footsteps, but her mother now stood behind her. Hastily Xiao Yen stood up. What had she been thinking, talking with such familiarity to a stranger? An older person at that? Wang Tie-Tie would speak strictly to her for an hour or more when she found out.

"No, she's been politeness itself," the old man replied.

Gan Ou shot Xiao Yen a look that implied the improbability of that.

"I'm here to ask the priests for blessings for my new school. Might I have the honor of calling upon your household after we're finished, gracious Lady Fu?"

Fu Be Be replied, "You may. Now please excuse us, honorable sir. We must be going."

The old man bowed low as they passed. When Xiao Yen looked back, he was still watching her with that hungry look, even though a monk had come up to him and was trying to lead him toward the main temple.

"My turn!" Xiao Yen called. She turned her back to her two cousins and threw the ball over her head. It landed in the dirt with a solid *thunk,* the grain inside the sewn-leather bag giving it extra weight. It bounced once, then rolled a little.

Xiao Yen turned around and urged the ball to roll more with her hands. However, the ball was a plain ball, not magic like the one in the story of Princess Lu: it wouldn't go wherever its owner wished. It stopped moving five paces away from the line drawn in the dirt.

"Drat," Xiao Yen said. The ball had to be within one pace for her to win.

Ling-Ling, her older cousin, laughed and said, "Now it's my turn to tell you what to do." She walked to where Xiao Yen stood.

Xiao Yen met her eye and refused to show any fear. Ling-Ling could be mean. It showed in her sharp teeth and thin lips. For her first turn, she'd demanded Xiao Yen eat four spicy peppers. The trick had turned against Ling-Ling. Xiao Yen's mother had grown up in the south, and Xiao Yen was used to spicy food.

Sudden laughter came from the corner of the family courtyard. Ama, Xiao Yen's nurse, sat on the steps telling a story to half a dozen of Xiao Yen's younger cousins. Xiao Yen looked at them with longing. Not too long ago she'd always sat with the storytelling group. Now she only got to hear stories at night. Ama had all the children waving their arms. Xiao Yen guessed the story: "The Mandarin and the Hundred Butterflies." She wished Ling-Ling would have listened harder to that story, which taught that cruelty was always "rewarded" with more cruelty.

"Hurry up," called Han Wanju, another of Xiao Yen's cousins, as Ling-Ling circled Xiao Yen again. "Or it'll be time for lunch before you decide." Han Wanju was always concerned about food, as evidenced by her fat cheeks and pudgy fingers.

The sun shone down in the square family compound. The outer walls of the "sky well" were solid stone, light yellow-red in color. One-story wooden rooms sitting on squat stilts lined the walls. If the courtyard flooded in the spring rains, the rooms didn't. Also, during the winter, fires on either side of the rooms were set up, and warm air traveled through a collection of pipes under the floors.

"I've decided," Ling-Ling announced after she'd circled Xiao Yen a third time. "I want you to spin—"

"Wang Tie-Tie has a visitor!" Gan Ou interrupted

as she rushed through the full-moon-shaped gate that separated the front courtyard from the family courtyard. Two servants hurried behind her. One went straight ahead, heading toward the far back courtyard where the kitchen was. The other cut diagonally across the family courtyard to the gate shaped like a vase. Beyond that gate lay the Garden of Sweet Scents, where Fu Be Be, Wang Tie-Tie, and the other aunts sat drinking tea.

"Girls! Come here, out of the way," Ama called.

Xiao Yen turned and started walking toward the far corner where Ama and the other children sat.

Ling-Ling scooped up the ball and called, "Hey! It's still my turn to tell you what to do!"

"That's right, Xiao Yen. You need to get used to other people telling you what to do," Gan Ou added.

Xiao Yen stopped short of the safety of the other children. "What?" she asked as she turned around. "Who's the visitor? Isn't it Chu Tie-Tie?" Aunty Chu was a *cha-ping* of Wang Tie-Tie. When she came over, she and Wang Tie-Tie sat and drank tea together for hours, telling stories from their childhood. Wang Tie-Tie was always jovial after a visit from one of her "tea-friends," not upset like she'd been that morning. The incense the servants had bought at the market was poor quality and wouldn't stay lit. Wang Tie-Tie had yelled at them, calling them things Xiao Yen hadn't understood. Then her mother had started yelling at Wang Tie-Tie. Xiao Yen had been glad when her cousins had arrived and everyone had to be nice to each other again.

"No, it isn't her," Gan Ou said with a smile so sharp its ends glistened. At seven years old, Xiao Yen didn't know all of her sister's smiles, but she suspected this one wasn't a good one. Fu Be Be always said Gan Ou was prettier than Xiao Yen. Xiao Yen doubted her mother looked beyond Gan Ou's smiles.

"Who is it?" Xiao Yen asked.

Gan Ou didn't respond.

Wang Tie-Tie appeared in the gateway and walked

across the courtyard, not deigning to look at anyone there. Her gray hair was piled high on her head and held in place by three long hairpins with pearls stretched between them. Two strands of hair hung loose from the arrangement and curled next to her ears. Her mouth was the color of spring cherries, a startling contrast to her powdered face. She wore a coat of plum-colored silk with an elegant pattern of peonies woven into it. The sleeves were longer and tighter than was fashionable. They always covered her arms to the wrist. She never drew them back.

Xiao Yen took a deep breath and felt her chest fill with pride. Wang Tie-Tie was so beautiful. Her skin was as white and fine as the statue at the Fire Mountain Temple of Nü-gua, the half-human, half-snake goddess who'd brought civilization to the Middle Kingdom.

Servants followed, carrying the best tea service, the one with fine thin cups the color of old jade. The visitor must be important.

Xiao Yen sneaked a quick look at her sister. Gan Ou wore her good red jacket, so pale it was almost pink. Xiao Yen wondered if it was good enough to greet the visitor in, or if Gan Ou would have to change into her festival clothes. At ten years old, Gan Ou was old enough to be presented. She'd put on her best smile and charm everyone with her good manners. Being younger, Xiao Yen would probably stay behind with the rest of the children.

Before Xiao Yen could look down, Gan Ou had turned around. The color of her jacket reflected in her cheeks, a very pretty pink. Her smile was sharper than before.

"I bet they're going to send for you next," Gan Ou said. Ling-Ling and Han Wanju stood shoulder to shoulder next to Gan Ou, facing Xiao Yen.

Xiao Yen asked, "Why?" She folded her arms in front of her chest. The three girls looked like vultures waiting for her, the tiny bird, to make one wrong move.

"Because that man you were talking with at the temple this morning is our visitor," Gan Ou said.

"What man?" Ling-Ling demanded.

"Really?" Xiao Yen asked, almost whispering. Why was he here? She remembered the hungry look in his eyes. A small tremor of fear ran through the center of her chest. She swallowed hard.

Gan Ou told the story, then turned back to Xiao Yen. "You're right to be afraid." She dropped her voice and came closer to Xiao Yen. "Do you know why he's here? Do you know what Wang Tie-Tie's going to do?"

Xiao Yen said no. Had he talked about a school of cranes? She didn't remember.

Gan Ou reached out and touched Xiao Yen's shoulder. "He buys children, trains them at this school of his, then sells them as servants to rich houses. You know, everyone knows, we need money. Ever since Papa died, we've been at the mercy of Wang Tie-Tie. Now, Wang Tie-Tie is going to sell you, so Mama and I can stay here. That was her bargain with Mama, you know."

Xiao Yen scowled. "Mama wouldn't sell me."

"I bet she would," Ling-Ling said. "Your mother told my mother how she despaired of you. She had to bring you to Wang Tie-Tie to be scolded three times last week, didn't she? Selling you would solve her problems, and Wang Tie-Tie's. I feel sorry for you."

Xiao Yen bit her lip. True, Mama did scold her often, more often than she scolded Gan Ou. Plus, Mama didn't have to bring Gan Ou in front of Wang Tie-Tie for a lecture as often as she had to take Xiao Yen. Would she sell her youngest daughter? Ama told many stories of children being sold as servants.

Gan Ou put her hands together in front of her chest as if in prayer and said, "I'll never forget you, Xiao Yen. I swear by the Buddha himself. If I ever have enough money to buy your contract back, I will. I swear it."

Xiao Yen trusted Gan Ou's words. She'd do the

same for Gan Ou. She'd walk across the sea or battle a thousand demons to help her family, or do her duty. She peered into her sister's face. Gan Ou stared back, eyes wide and sincere. Yet, that smile still lurked. Xiao Yen didn't believe that smile. She repeated, "Mama wouldn't sell me."

Gan Ou said, "It isn't Mama who's selling you. It's Wang Tie-Tie. Why do you think she was so angry this morning? It wasn't because of the incense. It was because she and Mama had been fighting about you."

Xiao Yen heard some truth in her sister's words. "I don't believe you," Xiao Yen said, though not as fiercely.

Another servant rushed into the family courtyard, going straight to Ama sitting in the corner, then whispering in her ear. Ama looked up and stared at Xiao Yen.

"I'll never forget you, Xiao Yen," Gan Ou said as Ama got up and came toward where the girls stood.

"Me neither," said Ling-Ling. "I'll always remember how pretty your hands were before they got ruined by working." Ling-Ling smiled politely at Xiao Yen, her sharp teeth showing.

Ama reached out to Xiao Yen and said, "Let me look at you." She spun Xiao Yen around, brushing her hand over Xiao Yen's pants. "I suppose your jacket is fine enough," she said.

Xiao Yen glanced at her jacket. It was made from light blue cotton, with a pattern of white waves embroidered around the hem. Her pants were a darker blue, plain, but well made.

"Why do I have to go?" Xiao Yen asked as Ama took her hand and led her toward the gate. "Why doesn't Gan Ou have to go?" Xiao Yen looked over her shoulder at Gan Ou, who mouthed the words "never forget you" with exaggerated motions.

"Because Wang Tie-Tie didn't send for Gan Ou. She sent for you. Quit dawdling," Ama said. "Master Wei is an important man. And your aunt doesn't like to be kept waiting."

The formal courtyard, also called the Yard of Greeting, was covered with large whitish, quarried stones, like tile. The Hall of Politeness was the only building in the Yard of Greeting. Knobby ridges went from the high point of the roof to the four lifted corners. Small brass bells hung under the eaves and rang when the wind touched them. All the tall sliding doors on the long southern side of the hall were open. The doors on the short side of the hall, facing east, were closed, but the shutters were open so light could pass through the finely carved latticework. Incense floated from the hall, filling the courtyard with a heavy, solemn scent.

Xiao Yen walked in front of Ama up the three broad steps to the hall, then paused at the threshold. After the brilliant sunshine she couldn't see inside the dark hall. Ama came up behind her and nudged her forward.

Slowly the room resolved itself. Wang Tie-Tie sat at the long low table, facing Xiao Yen. The man Xiao Yen had met at the temple sat around the corner from Wang Tie-Tie, with his back to an altar dedicated to Kuan Yin, the goddess of mercy. He sat on the best pillow, the one reserved for the most important guests. He wore the same all-black jacket. The embroidered cranes caught the light every now and again as he moved his arms. His gray beard formed a neat point just past his chin. He looked proper, worthy of being treated like an important guest. But his words made no sense.

"The immortality of the crane is reflected in the dance. Learning it helps one manifest *qi,* which feeds the *shan.* It also increases the *jing.* One grows in harmony with the nobility of the crane. The *qi* rises with the wings of the crane, sinks with each landing. *Jing* swells with movement and understanding."

A scowl tugged down the edges of Wang Tie-Tie's fine mouth. She sipped her tea, watching her hands as she brought the cup up to her lips and returned it to the table, instead of politely regarding her visitor. The room was too dark for Xiao Yen to see the expression in her aunt's eyes, but she suspected they held anger.

Wang Tie-Tie sat in front of the altar dedicated to Xiao Yen's ancestors. The family poem hung above her aunt, drawn with beautiful firm strokes in black ink on yellowing silk. Once a year the head of the household swore to uphold the values listed there. The second name of sons often came from the family poem. An altar table stood under the poem, holding a sand-filled brazier. Three sticks of incense burned in it, sending long curving streamers toward the high ceiling. A small bowl of rice, three gold cups filled with wine, and two sprigs of jasmine also lay below the poem.

Xiao Yen held her head up higher, less afraid. Wang Tie-Tie was so beautiful, framed by her family poem and the altar, almost like a goddess herself. She wouldn't sell Xiao Yen.

"One is taught to appreciate and understand nature, the light and dark sides of the day, both the mountain and the valley. Only by fully understanding the nature of a creature and the nature of your materials can one infuse an image with its own *jing,* or life force. It isn't a matter of compelling an artifact. You must mold yourself to it and it to you."

Suddenly Master Wei stopped babbling and said, "May I show you?" Without waiting for a response, he reached inside his sleeve and drew out a snowy white piece of paper.

Wang Tie-Tie's attention froze on his hands. The room grew still.

Xiao Yen only drew shallow breaths as she watched. Master Wei's fingers were stiff and precise, a counterpoint to his arms, which moved in a graceful dance, folding one over the other as he folded the paper. The last two folds he did with his hands above the paper, hiding it. When he finished, he revealed a beautiful paper dove.

Master Wei stared at the dove. His smooth brow

didn't wrinkle, but Xiao Yen could tell he concentrated hard. Xiao Yen thought his cheeks glowed with the effort until she realized the light came from his creation. A small white cloud covered where the paper dove had stood. The cloud swelled until it was almost the same size as Master Wei's head. Then the edges sharpened and solidified. A real dove, gray and white, now stood on the table.

The bird pecked at its feet a few times, before spreading its wings and hopping into the air. It flew around the room three times before flying over Xiao Yen's head and out the door. She gasped with delight as it winged its way toward the bright blue sky. In a moment, it was a speck on the horizon. A moment after that, it was gone.

Xiao Yen felt her smile spread from her face all the way to her toes. She was so lucky to have seen that! Who would have thought Master Wei was a magician? Just wait until she told Gan Ou and Ling-Ling. No one she knew had ever seen a mage before, though their work was rumored to be everywhere. Her eldest cousin said he had a friend who knew someone whose sister had married a man who had a magic trident that caught eels every time he stuck it in the water. Plus, Xiao Yen had never heard of magic being done with paper. All the stories Ama told used magic mirrors or hairpins.

An ashlike dove still stood on the table. Master Wei picked it up. It disintegrated into dust in his hands. He poured the remains of his creation into a bag at his waist.

When Master Wei looked up, Wang Tie-Tie asked in a strangled voice, "How much?"

An icicle plunged through Xiao Yen's chest. Was her aunt going to sell her after all?

"We can discuss terms later," Master Wei said. "I'm sure we can come up with something agreeable."

"And you're sure Xiao Yen is the one you want? Not one of my sons?" Wang Tie-Tie asked, sipping her tea with shaking hands.

Xiao Yen felt even colder. Was Wang Tie-Tie afraid of this man? Was that why she was selling Xiao Yen?

"No, your sons are too old. The training must start when they're Xiao Yen's age."

"And she'll be able to do . . . to cast . . . to make paper come alive?" Wang Tie-Tie asked, looking hard at Master Wei.

Master Wei rubbed his hands across the table as if smoothing out a wrinkle. "She must work hard. She must study the nature of things, through paintings, through poems, through observation. She must be able to control the flow of essential energies, both through herself and to her creations. If she can imagine enough, and understand enough, after many years, then she'll be able to do paper magic."

Paper magic? Master Wei wanted to teach her paper magic? Gan Ou and Ling-Ling were going to be so jealous. Xiao Yen couldn't wait to tell them.

Wang Tie-Tie motioned for Xiao Yen to come farther into the hall.

Xiao Yen felt shy in front of the great magician, so she moved forward slowly.

Master Wei stood and looked down at her. His dark eyes glittered under his bushy eyebrows, like a fierce demon hunter.

Xiao Yen backed up, afraid.

"Ah, hmmm," he said.

"Is something wrong?" Wang Tie-Tie asked.

"Ah, well, when I saw her at the temple, she was, not so shy. She needs to be, um, well, less restrained, I guess, if she's going to succeed."

Wang Tie-Tie said, "I'll make sure of it."

Xiao Yen didn't like the cold sound of her aunt's words.

"You understand that I've only agreed to test her for the school, to see if she'll work out. If she fails the first exam in six months, well . . ."

Wang Tie-Tie said with a little impatience, "I do understand."

Master Wei replied in a tired voice, "I'm sure you do." They bowed many times saying their good-byes.

After Master Wei had gone, Wang Tie-Tie called Xiao Yen to her side, then pulled her niece closer so Xiao Yen's face was next to hers. "You're a wonder, child. My hope. My true descendant. Do you understand why he asked for you? What he wants to do for you?"

Xiao Yen said she understood, wishing she could melt into the floor. Wang Tie-Tie had never looked so pretty, or so fierce. Her perfume mingled with her breath, sweet flowers and bitter tea. This was worse than being scolded, because for all her kind words, Xiao Yen had the feeling Wang Tie-Tie was angry at her. She didn't know why.

"He wants to teach you paper magic. You will learn it. I was promised once . . . Never mind. I'll tell you later."

Wang Tie-Tie turned and looked out the door, across the courtyard and into the sky, as if she followed the path the dove had taken.

"More independent, hmm? Old fool thought I didn't know what he meant. But I do. And you'll learn, all your lessons, very well. No matter how poor it may make you."

Xiao Yen didn't reply. Wang Tie-Tie's words sounded threatening. Yet, if Xiao Yen could learn to make doves out of paper like that, she was certain she would be the luckiest girl in all of Bao Fang.

Chapter 3

❧

On the Trail

Even Xiao Yen recognized the shouted foreign word. "Dinner!" She crawled out of her tent and struggled to her feet, her legs still sore from her first day's ride. The night was quiet. It was too early in the year for crickets or cicadas. An occasional wind stirred the winter leaves. Sounds of the river—gurgling water, quietly croaking toads—came from the wrong direction. Bao Fang, where Xiao Yen had grown up, sat west of the river Quang. For the first time, Xiao Yen was east of it.

Gi Tang, the courtesan's guard, sat on the ground between Xiao Yen's tent and the fire. He had a nose as sharp as a dagger, hooded eyes, and a face unused to smiling. His cloak hung below his waist, made out of a thick red material, with a stylized horse embroidered in black on the back, marking him as one of the horsemen soldiers. Under his cloak he wore a light blue shirt and bands of leather across his chest. He bound his heavy wool pants around his ankles with leather straps. He had small knives strapped to his waist. During the day, Xiao Yen had seen him carrying a long bow and two quivers of arrows.

He stared at Xiao Yen as she passed him, one hand reaching across his chest to touch the hilt of a knife. His face tightened with the intensity of his stare. Was he afraid of her? He glanced away from her as the circling tiger passed. He obviously didn't like her magic. Xiao Yen bowed her head to Gi Tang, to be polite. He wrinkled his nose in a sneer, as if he'd smelled something bad, then turned back to his dinner.

Xiao Yen walked away quickly. She'd seen his fear. She didn't want him to see hers. She hoped he wouldn't test the strength of her tiger. Xiao Yen could only affect the mundane world a little. Maybe her tiger could bend a leaf or break a twig. She didn't have the experience to animate a tiger that could kill a man. She'd have to study many years before she would. Her employers didn't know that though. No one did. And no one would. She had to keep a strong face. She had to keep them all from knowing she had any weaknesses.

Udo, Ehran, and Bei Xi stood near the cooking pot. Bei Xi's perfect skin reflected the fire with a rosy glow. The firelight picked up the red highlights in Udo's hair. Pieces of it that had escaped from his ponytail fanned out around his face like a fiery mane. Xiao Yen smiled, thinking maybe Udo could pass for a fox fairy. Though fox fairies were usually female, they brought luck if they were good. Ehran's face was in shadows, his eyes hidden.

Xiao Yen smelled cooking vegetables over the earthy scent of the thawed ground near the fire. Her stomach clenched and she realized how hungry she was. Udo handed Xiao Yen a cold tin bowl, a small spoon, and a ladle, then gestured toward the two pots sitting in the ashes next to the fire. The bigger pot held a thick gruel. The wonderful smell came from the smaller pot, which was filled with stew.

Xiao Yen filled her bowl and returned to the group. Ehran handed her a small pouch. The leather was well oiled, waterproof. Inside was something red that had been dried and crushed. The smell went all the way down the back of her throat, dark and slightly bitter.

Udo pointed at the bag, then at his mouth, and said,

"Ow, Ow!" Then he said something in a condescending tone, lecturing her.

Bei Xi translated. "Don't laden your food with too much pepper. It's spicy. You might burn your mouth."

Xiao Yen bristled at the suggestion. "Please tell my respected client that I appreciate his warning. However, my mother grew up in the south, where they eat much hotter foods than in Bao Fang. I'm used to eating spicy food."

Bei Xi smiled, shrugged, and stepped back. Xiao Yen tried to read her face in the flickering light. She couldn't see beyond Bei Xi's lovely smile. Udo had a smirk on his face. Ehran kept his face without emotion, unreadable, like someone born in the Middle Kingdom.

Xiao Yen used her spoon to put the peppers in her bowl. She knew better than to use her fingers. She took only half as many as she would have if the peppers had been from Fu Be Be's village. She could always get more later. She almost put on more when Udo's smirk grew larger and Ehran's face took on a serene smile, like the Buddha's. She'd show them who could eat hot food. It had always been a pleasure to hear the amazement of her classmates when they saw her heap peppers on her food. In that way, she'd excelled beyond them.

After the first bite Xiao Yen knew her mistake. The bitterness she'd smelled didn't manifest, but the darkness did, burning the back of her throat like the black heart of a piece of coal. Her eyes smarted and her nose started running. The peppers she was used to were more subtle, increasing their power throughout the meal. What would these peppers be like after a few more bites? She ate a spoonful of the gruel, knowing water would set her whole mouth on fire.

The grain cooled her tongue enough that she could take another nibble. The spiciness stayed intense. Xiao Yen couldn't taste the vegetables beyond the pain. Her eyes watered. She sucked in the night air to cool her throat.

Someone tried to suppress a snort.

Xiao Yen looked up, suddenly aware of her audience. The wind against her cheeks told her she had tears streaming down her face. She couldn't imagine how red her nose must be.

Udo howled with laughter, while Ehran merely chuckled. Even Bei Xi's smile widened to show her flawless teeth. They'd known how hot the peppers were. Why had they tricked her? Why had they warned her in such a manner as to make sure she'd take too many, and make a fool of herself?

Xiao Yen handed her bowl to the still-grinning Udo, saying, "I'm not hungry anymore." Then she walked away. First she headed toward her tent, but she swerved to avoid Gi Tang. She didn't want any more witnesses to her humiliation. She walked east instead, toward the river.

Another small clearing stood beyond the tethered horses. The moon broke through the patchy clouds as she crossed it, coating the winter grass with silver. Xiao Yen stopped short of the circle the tiger followed around the camp. Maybe tomorrow night she would start the camp defense after dinner, in case she needed to get away.

Xiao Yen stared out through the night and the trees. She could still hear Udo and Ehran laughing. Why had they been so mean to her? Her stomach growled with hunger. She'd always been proud of her ability to eat spicy foods. Now she'd made a fool of herself, disgracing both herself and her mother's cooking. Wang Tie-Tie always told her to not show any weaknesses to strangers, and not to family either, if she could help it. Xiao Yen had not only been overpowered by the peppers, she'd shown she was vulnerable to her employer's tricks. Maybe she should have stayed and laughed with them at her mistake. Maybe she'd laugh at herself in a while, but not now.

A horse behind her neighed, high pitched, almost a squeal. Xiao Yen turned around. The horses had backed up and were pulling on their lines, trying to get away from something in front of them. Their large backs blocked Xiao Yen's view. Her mouth went dry with fear. She had no paper with her. How could she protect the horses? She tried to shout but she couldn't force any words past her burning throat.

Abruptly, the night grew still. The wind died and the quiet trickling of the river stopped. The horses strained against their leads for another moment, then relaxed and shuffled forward, acting normal again. The sounds of the night resumed.

What had frightened the horses? Why were they no longer scared? The guide had told her the horses were mostly good tempered, staid, only scared of loud noises and snakes.

Bei Xi came into view, walking around the horses in a wide arc. Had she scared the horses? Or was she afraid of them? Xiao Yen dismissed the thought. Bei Xi wasn't afraid of anything. If Zhu Tse Guo, the demon of nightmares, appeared, rattling the skulls around its neck and flicking its forked tongue at her, Bei Xi would have it kneeling at her feet and cooing in a matter of moments.

Xiao Yen felt a pang of jealousy. She would never be as cultured nor as beautiful as Bei Xi. Xiao Yen was just a merchant's daughter. Though her family had better social connections now than they'd had when she was a child, they weren't lords, or part of the court. Xiao Yen didn't think even Wang Tie-Tie could change that.

Bei Xi glowed like a second moon as she crossed the clearing. She held a small bowl in her hands, carrying it with her arms extended, as if it were an offering. Bei Xi walked straight to Xiao Yen, handed the bowl to her, and said, "I thought you might still be hungry."

Xiao Yen caught a whiff of dark spice from the bowl. She raised her eyebrows at Bei Xi, who responded, "Yes, there are peppers in it. Only a sprinkling, to flavor the dish, not enough to burn your mouth."

Xiao Yen nibbled at the stew. It was wonderful, spicy, yet not too hot. She attacked her food, but found herself watching Bei Xi over the edge of her bowl. Xiao Yen tried to drown her uneasiness with the warm food sliding down her throat. Bei Xi was lovely, more beautiful than a painting. She'd been thoughtful as well, bringing Xiao Yen some food. Where did Xiao Yen's feeling of uneasiness come from?

In her mind's eye, Xiao Yen tried to see beyond Bei Xi's form. There was something special about Bei Xi, the way her image shimmered. Xiao Yen couldn't see beyond Bei Xi's shining face.

"It's because they're scared," Bei Xi said.

Xiao Yen took another bite of her stew and said nothing. Wang Tie-Tie and Master Wei both had encouraged Xiao Yen to ask more questions, to overcome her innate shyness. Her sister, however, had taught Xiao Yen that she sometimes learned far more by being quiet.

"Udo and Ehran are far from their home, in foreign lands," Bei Xi explained, her hands pressed together, palm to palm, as if in prayer. "They watched you perform your magic, and it scared them. In their eyes you grew fierce and large, like your tiger. They needed to force you into human form again. So they gave you the peppers."

Xiao Yen replied, "But I'm the one in foreign lands now. I'm the one far from my family."

"Udo and Ehran don't see the world through your eyes. They think of this ground as *your* land."

Xiao Yen wondered at her strange emphasis on "your." Why didn't Bei Xi say "our"?

Bei Xi continued. "You think you're far from your family? Udo and Ehran haven't seen theirs for more than four years. Ehran's worried about their father. That's why they're traveling, the real reason. Not because they're merchants or they want gold. The brothers were banished for protecting their father's land."

Xiao Yen nodded. She hadn't known the brothers'

status, but she wasn't surprised that they were land-owners, from either an equal or higher class than her family. Wang Tie-Tie wouldn't have let her work for them otherwise.

"What happened?" she asked, when Bei Xi didn't go on.

"It's a story older than the Tien Mountains. A wealthy lord coveted their father's land. He tricked Ehran into signing a lien against it. Though the contract wasn't legal, the man could buy a judgment in his favor."

Though an official's corruption was a familiar story in the Middle Kingdom, Xiao Yen was astonished. Maybe foreigners were more similar to her people than she'd thought.

Bei Xi went on. "Ehran went to talk with him one night. They argued. When the man attacked him, Ehran defended himself too well with his knife. He was banished for it. Udo came with his brother."

"Why wasn't the whole family banished? How did they protect their father?" Xiao Yen asked.

"Foreigners think an individual is responsible for his actions. They rarely punish the whole family for the crimes of one."

Xiao Yen shook her head. Entire villages were sometimes burned to the ground for the crimes of a few. She'd always assumed that foreigners acted irresponsibly because they were so far from their families and possible repercussions. Now she wondered if they always acted that way.

"At first the brothers stayed in a neighboring country. Then they started traveling, buying, selling, trading as they went. I think Udo wanted to leave. The adventure of the Great Merchant trail caught them and wouldn't let them go, not until they'd traveled the length of it. But now, they want to go home."

Xiao Yen sighed. The story sounded so romantic in the telling, without the sweat of living through it. "Will they make enough money selling the horses on the coast?" she asked.

Bei Xi's smile barely lifted the corners of her mouth. "I . . . I don't know."

Xiao Yen's heart sank. They wouldn't make enough. From the falseness of Bei Xi's smile, Xiao Yen knew they might not make enough for their passage back to their lands, which would be a shame. The brothers were so foreign. They didn't belong in the Middle Kingdom.

"What about your tale? Why are you going north?" Xiao Yen said, trying to brighten Bei Xi's smile.

"I will tell you about myself. But only if you tell me about yourself. Agreed?"

"Agreed," Xiao Yen said.

"You first," Bei Xi replied. "You're younger."

Xiao Yen opened her mouth and closed it again. How could she have allowed herself to be tricked so easily again? Grudgingly, Xiao Yen began. "I'm the youngest in my family. I have an older sister, Gan Ou. My father, my uncles, and my three older brothers were all killed in an accident, taken by the river dragon." This was ancient history, that Bei Xi could find out about from anyone in Bao Fang. It wasn't that important.

"The river dragon!" Bei Xi said. "That was why it was difficult for you to cross the river this morning, wasn't it?"

"It was," Xiao Yen replied. She hadn't meant to share anything private with Bei Xi, but maybe Xiao Yen's past was too connected to her present to let her hide anything.

"My aunt, Wang Tie-Tie, put me into Master Wei's school when I was very young. And that has been my life, school and home. Now I am here." Xiao Yen looked up, defying Bei Xi to find out her secrets.

"That must have been hard, living between school and home, divided, all the time," Bei Xi remarked.

Xiao Yen shook her head. She couldn't say anything without Bei Xi seeing through to the essence of the matter. "Every person must face difficulties in their life, to learn and grow." At least that's what Wang Tie-Tie and Master Wei had always told her.

"Your trials have given you great strength," Bei Xi said.

Xiao Yen didn't know what to say. She felt as though she'd failed her trials. She'd lost herself, lost her luck.

"You'll see," Bei Xi said. "I've had some . . . difficulties in my life as well."

"Please continue," Xiao Yen said. "I'm eager to hear your tale, which must be more interesting than mine." She hoped Bei Xi would take her statements as politeness. Xiao Yen didn't want Bei Xi to peer at her own life anymore.

Bei Xi tilted her head to the side, as she had in the courtyard of the merchant's inn that morning, then lifted her eyes skyward, as though talking with the moon. The moon must have said something funny, because Bei Xi's laughter rang out, high and tinkling over the quiet river sounds.

When she turned to look at Xiao Yen, her face carried the moon's glow. A gust of wind tugged at her clothes, raising her coat a little.

"Do you know the story of Princess Zhao Jun?" Bei Xi said, running her hands down her sides, pushing her jacket back into place with a wiggle, like a sensual snake adjusting its skin.

"Wasn't Emperor Han Zo tricked into giving the princess to a northern lord as part of a peace treaty? He thought she was ugly, but she wasn't, right?"

"Exactly. Our stories are similar. The court painter did an inappropriate painting of me. My lord accused the painter and me of being lovers."

"Were you?" Xiao Yen blurted out. Bei Xi had seen through to the center of Xiao Yen's life, so Xiao Yen asked the first question that came to her, even though it was rude. Bei Xi owed her a truth. "Were you lovers?"

Bei Xi answered quietly, barely speaking above the

sounds of the night. "No. He loved another. He put my face on her body, as his love for her was even more inappropriate."

Xiao Yen sighed. Life at court must be as interesting as all the storytellers in the marketplace made it.

Bei Xi continued. "Instead of taking my head, as was my lord's right, he gave me to the barbarian horseman Vakhtang, as part of a bribe for continued peace. There has been no war for so many years now, between the kingdom of Tibet to the west, and the kingdom of the Turic, to the north. But now these horsemen, the Uighiers, attack the border towns, threatening our peace."

Xiao Yen knew about the raids. Wang Tie-Tie had already started moving the family's business interests farther south. Her aunt believed all the treaties would be broken soon, and war would come again, like it had in her childhood. Xiao Yen had seen refugees in the markets of Bao Fang, driven from their own lands by the horsemen.

Bei Xi peered into the darkness. She looked remote, like a statue coalesced out of fairy dust, silver and white. Even more than Wang Tie-Tie, she resembled the statue of the goddess Nü-gua in the Fire Mountain Temple. Her skin was as white as the goddess' snake tail, joined with her brother's as they peered out in different directions.

Almost to herself, Bei Xi said, "There must be peace between our lands. I'll sacrifice whatever I have to." She paused for a moment, then turned to look at Xiao Yen. Her face was as smooth and unreadable as a porcelain mask, but her eyes held darkness. "I speak some of the language of the kingdom of Turic—the horsemen's language. My sister lived at Vakhtang's court for a while. I also know the language Udo and Ehran speak. Please, let me teach you. Let me help you."

"Why?" Xiao Yen wondered. She put her hand in front of her mouth when she realized she'd spoken her impolite question aloud.

Bei Xi laughed her tinkling, high-pitched laugh, but only until she saw Xiao Yen's expression. Then she gazed soberly at Xiao Yen.

"I was going to tell you a fantastic tale. Family matters should be private. You've shared some of your tale with me, though, so I will tell you the truth. I was supposed to look after my sister. Teach her the ways of the world. She was my responsibility."

Xiao Yen understood. She'd been Gan Ou's responsibility for many years.

"But I didn't do my duty as well as I should have. I played games, instead of guiding her. She left . . . our home. Now, she sings beyond the Yellow River. I don't want that to happen to you as well."

Xiao Yen found herself agreeing to Bei Xi's tutelage. The story of Bei Xi's sister sounded true, even if there was still something about Bei Xi that made Xiao Yen uneasy.

"Let me see," Bei Xi said, pausing for a moment. "I'd like something that would tie us together, your family and mine. I know! I can show you something I learned at my lord's court. It's a silly thing, not real magic, but you might like it. I'm sure you won't have any problem learning it."

She drew a long piece of red cord from her sleeve. The moon bled away most of the color, but Xiao Yen could still see it was very rich. It slid like silk through Bei Xi's fingers.

Bei Xi made three loops, then drew the ends of cord through them, twisting this way and that. She finished with a three-looped knot, the cord wrapped around itself across the bottom and with the ends coming out of the center loop.

"Very pretty, don't you think?" Bei Xi asked, holding it out to Xiao Yen. The knot took up Bei Xi's entire palm.

Xiao Yen agreed, not sure what she was supposed to say.

Bei Xi said, "Now watch." The knot seemed to draw in on itself, as if unseen hands pulled on the ends, tightening it. The color grew darker as well. The knot shrank until it resembled a small, wooden bead with the pattern of a knot carved on it. Now it took up less than a quarter of Bei Xi's palm.

Xiao Yen looked up from the knot into Bei Xi's smile. Her eyes looked younger, as if the knot had pulled away some of her years. Her pure white teeth glowed like small pearls.

Bei Xi said, "You tie two of the loops through something you want to keep closed, like the two ends of a chest. Then you shrink the knot, and even though it's just tied, everyone believes it's sealed. Privacy, as well as trustworthy locks, can be difficult to find when there are many ladies in a court. Here, you try it." Bei Xi urged the cord onto Xiao Yen. As it left her hand, the magic faded, and Xiao Yen held a knot.

"Untie that and tie your own knot," Bei Xi instructed.

"What kind of knot?" Xiao Yen asked as she slid the ends through the loops and unraveled the knot.

"A knot you're familiar with, that won't confuse you as you think about which end goes over which," Bei Xi replied.

Xiao Yen tied a simple bowline. She started with an overhand loop, threaded one end through the loop, around and over the hanging bit of cord, then back through the loop. When she tightened the knot, pulling on the hanging bit of cord while holding the rest of the knot with her other hand, she was left with a large loop, closed tightly with her knot.

When Xiao Yen finished, Bei Xi said, "That's a very practical knot. Now feel the knot in your fingers, the looping cord, how it's tied together."

Xiao Yen took two deep breaths and felt for the knot, the same way she felt the folds in one of her paper creations. The image came quickly, of the looping and gathering, the tension of the cord, the ends straining against each other.

From a distance she heard Bei Xi say, "Good. Now pull the ends tighter, shrink the distances between the loops in your mind. Imagine it isn't cord anymore, but thread. See the gaping holes between the loops? Make them smaller, make the knot tighter. Imagine the loops as one solid entity. Wonderful!"

Xiao Yen opened her eyes. The cord was as it had been, a large loop on one side, the two ends dangling between her fingers. A small, flat wooden bead now connected the parts, not a knot.

"Now, I want to show you something else. It was one of the first things I taught my sister, Jhr Bei." Bei Xi lifted the knot up and held it above Xiao Yen's palm. "Do you see the shadow the knot casts? Look carefully, not with your eyes, but with your mind's eye."

Xiao Yen thought hard as she stared. The knifelike edges of the shadow blurred, and became tinged with blue.

"Is that a trick of the moonlight?" Xiao Yen asked. Master Wei had said there were ways to "see" magic, but that they were unreliable.

Bei Xi said, "Almost anything that's magic, that has been enchanted, casts a shadow with a blue hue. It isn't an absolute test. Some things completely magical cast solid black shadows, and some things with only a hint of magic are all blue. It's always worth checking."

"Oh," Xiao Yen replied. She glanced down at her own shadow. Blue ran around the edges of it, and around Bei Xi's. She pointed to it and said, "But I'm not magic. Why is my shadow blue?"

Bei Xi laughed and said, "I told you it isn't always reliable."

Xiao Yen looked again at her palm. Though she'd shrunk the knot the first time she'd tried, she knew that was from her practice as a paper mage. The magic was more complicated than Bei Xi realized. Understanding the knot and how it looped, seeing what you wanted it to become, took a clear mind and good imaging. Though it followed the nature of all magic Xiao Yen knew about—it only changed an artifact, not an element—it still wasn't a simple court lady trick.

Xiao Yen was going to ask Bei Xi about it when she heard a horse whinny. Xiao Yen and Bei Xi both turned toward the sound. Ehran appeared, walking close to the horses, stroking them, talking to them in a low voice. He held up his hand in greeting when he saw Bei Xi and Xiao Yen. Then he walked across the clearing to where they stood, moving like a dark cloud. He held himself with dignity, like Master Wei when he was thinking about a problem.

When he joined them on the far side of the clearing, Xiao Yen half expected him to greet them in her tongue, but he spoke in his language instead. Xiao Yen recognized that he asked them how they were and what they were doing. Then she was lost.

After more conversation Xiao Yen couldn't follow, Bei Xi said to Xiao Yen, "Why don't you go back to camp. I'm sure you must be weary to the bone after today's travels."

Xiao Yen took two steps, then looked back, expectantly. She hid a yawn behind her hand.

Bei Xi noticed Xiao Yen's hesitance. "Please don't be concerned about us. We will follow you on the shortest wind."

Xiao Yen didn't move. It wasn't right for Bei Xi to be alone with one of the foreigners, far from camp and from her guard. Bei Xi laughed. Xiao Yen felt wrapped from head to toe by the warm, comforting sound.

"I am responsible for my actions. We don't need a chaperone," Bei Xi said, still trying to reassure Xiao Yen.

Ehran asked a question, and whatever Bei Xi said made him turn and smile patronizingly at Xiao Yen. He rested his right hand on the haft of a knife hanging from his belt. Was that the knife he'd used to kill that man?

Xiao Yen said, "I wish you both a good night." Then she turned and walked back toward the camp. She stopped again next to the horses to look back. Ehran and Bei Xi seemed deep in conversation.

Xiao Yen's anger flared through her. The two stood too close together. It wasn't proper. No wonder Bei Xi's lord had accused her of being unfaithful, if this was how she acted.

As quickly as Xiao Yen's anger sprang into life, it drained out of her. What could she do about it? Gi Tang, the barbarian guard, wouldn't understand her if she tried to tell him about it. Udo didn't like her, so he wouldn't believe her. Besides, maybe nothing improper was going on.

Xiao Yen looked at the knot in her hand, then at the two in the clearing. Ehran's shadow flowed out behind him like a black river on a moonless night.

Bei Xi's shadow held hints and sparkles of blue.

Xiao Yen resolutely turned back toward the camp. She couldn't trust her luck to keep her from jumping to the wrong conclusion just then. It was just the moonlight and Xiao Yen's exhaustion that had turned the concubine's shadow blue. Bei Xi couldn't be magical. Xiao Yen didn't want to be any more embarrassed than she already had been that night by believing anything else.

Chapter 4

❧

Bao Fang

Xiao Yen checked the incense clock again, then sighed. The coin resting on top of the burning stick had only slipped down the width of her finger since the last time she'd looked. It would be a long time before the incense finished burning and the coin fell to the bottom of the brass bowl, signaling with a *ting* the end of the hour of the Monkey. Even that wouldn't be the end of Xiao Yen's torment. She'd have to wait until the end of the following hour, the hour of the Rooster, before she'd be allowed to leave the Garden of Sweet Scents.

Xiao Yen heard her cousins and her sister playing in the family courtyard, yelling as they chased a rolling hoop, trying to get it between one of two goals. Wang Tie-Tie forbade Xiao Yen to play with her cousins, to listen with the other children to stories told by Ama, or even to go to the White Temple. Instead, she banished Xiao Yen to the garden, away from everyone. Xiao Yen only saw her sister and mother in the morning and at night. She took all her midday meals alone.

The only person Xiao Yen saw during the day was Wang Tie-Tie, who visited Xiao Yen two or three times a day. Seeing her aunt was almost as bad as being alone. Wang Tie-Tie made Xiao Yen tell stories. Not the traditional ones Ama told, but ones Xiao Yen made up. Wang Tie-Tie never seemed satisfied with Xiao Yen's stories, either.

Xiao Yen sat on a raised platform at the end of the garden. A large oiled umbrella with bamboo leaves painted on it protected her from the sun. The garden was full of summer flowers: shaggy pink and red petunias, black-spotted tiger lilies, purple dragon-nose flowers with petals as long as Xiao Yen's hand.

On the west side of the platform was the fox altar. It stood about as high as Xiao Yen's knee, made of white stone, with pillars supporting a domed roof. The stone on the top and sides was pitted and flaking from age. Wang Tie-Tie said fox fairies helped people in trouble and brought them luck. Fu Be Be said they acted mischievously and added to a person's problems. Gan Ou said they stole life from men during sex. Xiao Yen didn't know who was right, but she sometimes burned incense at the altar anyway.

Xiao Yen studied the altar, tracing the spiderwebs that ran from its back to the plants behind it. She sighed again. She had a story ready for Wang Tie-Tie, but she was sure her aunt wouldn't like it.

"To spend your life dreaming is the same as spending your life asleep," said a voice from behind her. Xiao Yen jumped and turned around, her heart racing. Maybe a fox fairy *had* come to rescue her. But no, it was Wang Tie-Tie, standing as still as if she'd been planted.

Xiao Yen jumped to her feet, bowed, and said, "Please, dear aunt, take this unworthy cushion and come out of the sun."

Wang Tie-Tie inclined her head slightly, then sat. She indicated with her hand that Xiao Yen should sit next to her. Wang Tie-Tie surveyed the garden, like a matriarch overlooking undeserving descendants. Xiao Yen couldn't help but be impressed. Wang Tie-Tie looked beautiful and regal, like an empress. She wore a coat made of creamy ivory, close in color to the yellow of royalty, with a pattern of tiny, pale green maple leaves woven into it.

Xiao Yen tugged at the hem of her own jacket. Wang Tie-Tie had had it made for her after Master Wei had come to visit. It was as finely made as Wang Tie-Tie's, of silk dyed a green so dark it was almost black, with only the simplest pattern of white willow leaves edging the hems and sleeves. Ling-Ling, her cousin, had made fun of it, calling it servant's clothing because of the dark color and lack of design. Xiao Yen tugged on it again, wishing for her old clothes, ones she could play and fall on the ground in without making someone angry.

When Xiao Yen looked up, she started at Wang Tie-Tie's stare. For all the soft paint on her face, Wang Tie-Tie's eyes burned. Xiao Yen grew still, like a rabbit sitting before a snake, afraid to twitch her nose.

Abruptly, Wang Tie-Tie broke the gaze and looked out over the garden again. "Tell me a story," she commanded. She picked up her fan and began to fan herself with a steady, slow beat. The fan had been a gift from Wang Tie-Tie's youngest son. An elegant butterfly was painted on the face of the fan, floating up near the top edge of it.

Xiao Yen had a story about a butterfly prepared. She didn't know if it was a good omen or not that her aunt had decided to use the butterfly fan, so she hesitated until Wang Tie-Tie turned and stared at her.

"Once, in the country north of here, there lived a lonely butterfly. He had a beautiful garden to play in, with many colorful flowers, but no friends. So one day he flew over the garden walls—"

Wang Tie-Tie interrupted her. "What did the butterfly look like? What color was it?" She laid her fan on the platform and pointed to the one painted there. "See? A butterfly's wings are separated into two parts. Was the top part colored the same as the bottom part? Were the two parts the same size? Was the edge of the wing scalloped? How big was the butterfly?"

Wang Tie-Tie reached across the empty space between them. "Was it as big as your hand?" Wang Tie-

Tie held Xiao Yen's hand in front of her face. "As long as your arm?" she said, pulling Xiao Yen's arm toward her, then dropping it. "You have to *see* these things, every detail. Use your imagination. Master Wei told me you had a good one. Use it." With that, Wang Tie-Tie looked out over the garden again, as still as a stone.

Xiao Yen took a deep breath. She thought a moment, then started again. "Once, in the country north of here, there lived a butterfly. Every morning as he dried his wings in the new sun, he felt lonely. The garden he lived in had many beautiful flowers—yellow mums, white foxglove, blue morning glories—but there weren't any other butterflies.

"The butterfly's wings were black and white, striped like a tiger, with sharp edges. He had two black tails, shaped like teardrops, hanging off the ends of his wings. He was about the size of Old Gardener's palm. The two tails were about the size of the top of your little finger." Xiao Yen held up her hand to demonstrate.

Wang Tie-Tie gestured for her to continue.

"One day he flew above the garden walls." Xiao Yen paused for a moment.

"What did he see?" Wang Tie-Tie asked.

"There were fields all around, stretching to the horizon, long and flat, filled with bright green summer wheat. When the wind blew, the grass rippled, like water on a pond. The butterfly flew over the sea of grass. It took him three days to cross."

Wang Tie-Tie raised her eyebrows at Xiao Yen.

Hastily, she explained, "It's because butterflies fly slowly. It would have taken you or me only a day walking. The butterfly had to stop often. When he came out of the thick blue sky, he'd rest on a stem. It would bend under his weight."

"What did the butterfly eat?" prompted Wang Tie-Tie, more gently this time.

Xiao Yen thought a moment. "There wasn't anything for the butterfly to eat as he crossed the plain of grass. But maybe, he could suck dew out of the folds of grass stems in the early morning."

Wang Tie-Tie didn't say anything, so Xiao Yen continued. "Beyond the grasslands lay a river. It was"—she paused—"a dark river. Darker than the wood in the Hall of Greeting. And wide. The butterfly couldn't see the far side of it. It flowed deep and fast, but silent, so he couldn't hear how dangerous it was. The butterfly walked up and down on the shore, looking at the river, wondering if he could fly, without stopping, to the far side, wondering what was on the far side, wondering if there would be someone there for him to play with." Xiao Yen paused as she'd planned when she'd rehearsed the story. She waited until Wang Tie-Tie looked at her before she continued.

"Suddenly," she said, holding her hands out like something big was coming at her, "there was a rumbling in the water, and the river dragon poked its head out. The head was . . . was . . . about as big as this garden," she said, indicating the space before them.

Wang Tie-Tie smiled and said, "Continue."

Xiao Yen said, "The dragon was beautiful and terrifying. Her, I mean, its"—Xiao Yen looked at Wang Tie-Tie, but she didn't seem to have noticed the slip—"its eyes were like two small plates. The outer part was light yellow, almost white. The inner part was so dark and black it looked like a hole, like you could fall into those eyes and drown." Xiao Yen didn't add what she was thinking: like your eyes, Wang Tie-Tie.

"The eyebrows above the terrible eyes were soft and graceful, like willow leaves. The nose was long and black with red streaks, like lightning bolts, running along either side. Its nostrils blew water and smoke. Right behind its nostrils hung golden whiskers. They dripped water, and glittered in the sunlight. Everything else on the dragon shone with darkness.

"The dragon asked the butterfly, 'Why have you come so far from your garden?' Its voice sounded deep and low, like the stone bell at the White Temple," she added at Wang Tie-Tie's look.

"The butterfly said, 'I'm lonely in my garden. Will you play with me?'

"The dragon laughed a terrible laugh. It laughed so loudly it hurt the butterfly's ears. The dragon dropped back into the water and laughed more. Huge waves splashed on the shore. The butterfly had to jump up in the air so he wouldn't drown. Finally the dragon stopped laughing and came back to talk to the butterfly.

" 'Dragons don't play with butterflies,' he said, in a mean voice, like how Ling-Ling talks to Han sometimes. 'Go back to your garden, where you belong. Or you may be sorry.' Then the dragon lifted itself out of the river, toward the sky. Its whole body was as black as temple shadows, with red streaks running down its sides. Its belly looked like hard river crystal, white and cold.

"The butterfly turned around and flew as fast as he could back to his garden. He knew that if he didn't get away quickly, he'd be caught by the thunderstorm the dragon was making. There was no safe place for him, no blade of grass in all those fields big enough for him to hide under when the rain started.

"So he flew and he flew, not pausing at all. It took him only one day to fly back to his garden. When he got there, he was very tired. His wings shook. It felt like heavy rocks rested on them. He landed on the fox fairy altar.

"That altar looked very much like our altar," Xiao Yen said, pointing to the altar standing at the foot of the platform. "It, too, was made of white stone. But it was newer, and was painted red on the inside.

"The butterfly looked around his garden. Maybe another butterfly had come while he'd been gone. But he was still alone. And if he left the garden again, the dragon would get him. Dragons can be mean like that," Xiao Yen added, almost under her breath. She hastily continued before Wang Tie-Tie could say anything.

"Two tears fell from the butterfly's eyes and landed

on the stage of the altar, where you put incense and flowers. Suddenly, a lovely fox fairy sprung up out of the ground. She said, 'Why are you—' "

"What did she look like?" Wang Tie-Tie said, interrupting again.

Xiao Yen jerked her head up. She'd gotten too involved in her story. "The fox fairy had a broad forehead, like a melon. She painted her eyebrows far above her eyes, with thin, graceful strokes, like gull wings. Her nose was tiny, almost like she'd forgotten to put one on her face. But if you looked closely, you could see it was as sharp as a broken rock. Her golden eyes reminded the butterfly of warm summer afternoons. Her lips were the color of ripe plums. She wore ivory silk that had circles of bamboo embroidered in light green, and—"

Wang Tie-Tie interrupted Xiao Yen again. "What did her teeth look like?"

Xiao Yen paused, then asked, "Are a fox fairy's teeth like an immortal's teeth?"

Wang Tie-Tie replied, "It is so."

Xiao Yen continued. "Her teeth were like fine white jade, strung together like impossibly perfect jewels." She paused for a moment, forgetting where she'd stopped. She bit her lip. Was that enough description to satisfy Wang Tie-Tie? She hoped so. "The fox fairy asked the butterfly what was wrong. The butterfly told his tale of flying for days to see the dragon, only to have the dragon laugh at him and send him home. The fairy wrinkled her brow, thinking for a while, then she said, 'I can help you.'

"The butterfly was very excited. 'Can you make me a friend to play with?' he asked, dancing along the top of the altar.

"The fairy smiled at him, a warm, real smile, the kind you feel in your belly. 'No,' she said, 'but I can make you not miss them so much.'

"The butterfly was puzzled. How could she do that? He would always miss having friends, wouldn't he? But fox fairies sometimes do things their own way."

Xiao Yen paused again. Wang Tie-Tie sat fanning herself, not looking at Xiao Yen, so she went on.

"The butterfly agreed, and the fox fairy changed him into a beautiful white-and-black-striped flower. His petals were as soft as swan feathers. Black stripes ran from the outside of the flower toward the center in harsh, straight lines. The edges of the petals were fluffy. In the center of the flower hung two black stems, shaped like teardrops. That was what was left of the butterfly's tail.

"He was still different. There wasn't another flower like him in the entire garden. But he was a flower, like all the other flowers, and so he wasn't alone anymore.

"And that's the tale I heard." Xiao Yen ended her story with the traditional ending and stared down at her hands, afraid to face Wang Tie-Tie.

The silence dragged on. Xiao Yen sneaked a look at Wang Tie-Tie. A half-smile crept slowly across her aunt's lips, though the rest of her was as unmoving as a stone. Abruptly, Wang Tie-Tie snorted, then started laughing. Though her laugh was quiet, it sounded like the dragon laugh Xiao Yen had imagined. She shivered.

Wang Tie-Tie stopped laughing and turned to Xiao Yen, her eyes terrible and beautiful. "Yes, I am a horrible dragon, aren't I?" Wang Tie-Tie laughed again and shook her head. "Maybe someday you'll understand that I'm doing this because you must learn to stand by yourself. You, alone, must be taller than if you stood on the shoulders of all your family."

How could she grow that tall? Why did she have to? Xiao Yen didn't understand.

"Family isn't always a blessing," Wang Tie-Tie said, her gentle words carrying sorrow as they spoke themselves in Xiao Yen's ear. "And when you do your famous deeds, you may have to be far from here, far from your mother and sister." Wang Tie-Tie's voice grew stern. "And why must you do famous deeds?"

"So Zhang Gua Lao will notice me."

Wang Tie-Tie prompted. "And when he notices you . . . ?"

Xiao Yen dutifully finished Wang Tie-Tie's sentence. "Zhang Gua Lao will give me an immortal peach so I can give it to you."

Wang Tie-Tie always responded in one of two ways at the end of this litany: either she laughed, clapped her hands, and called Xiao Yen a good girl, or she tested Xiao Yen's resolve. This time, she did the latter.

"You don't have to bring the peach to me," she said in a wheedling voice that reminded Xiao Yen of Ling-Ling.

"Oh, no, Aunt, I want to give it to you," Xiao Yen replied. It was her duty to do whatever the head of her household told her to do, even giving up her family, if she must.

Wang Tie-Tie fanned herself a couple of times, then put the fan on the table, stretching her left arm out toward Xiao Yen. She rubbed her forearm as if it itched.

"I'm so tired of this life. I want to get off the wheel of death, rebirth, and sorrow, to have some peace, and more time to pray for forgiveness," she said in a melancholy tone. She folded her sleeve back toward her elbow, and rubbed the wrinkled, startlingly white flesh.

Xiao Yen had never seen her aunt's naked arm before. She didn't recognize what she saw at first.

Some of Wang Tie-Tie's wrinkles formed straight lines. No, not wrinkles—scars, scarred lines, whiter than her flesh. Lines that crossed each other. Lines that resolved into the character for "possession," often branded on horses, to indicate they were owned by a lord or the Emperor.

"My father and my husband were well matched in their temperaments," Wang Tie-Tie said, speaking under her breath, so quietly Xiao Yen could barely hear her. "They treated me like merchandise, not like a daughter or a wife. Now, I am old. I need another lifetime at least to let go of the hate I've held. I still pray, every morning, that I will be able to forgive them. And myself."

Wang Tie-Tie looked at Xiao Yen and spoke to her as if to an equal. "You don't have to give me the peach. Not if you're in a situation like mine and you need it for yourself. Not if your life has turned to bitter ash and you cannot survive the regret and hate."

Xiao Yen responded fervently, addressing Wang Tie-Tie's scarred flesh, no longer using her duty-bound voice. "I will do famous deeds so you can leave this world of tears. I will bring you an immortal peach."

Wang Tie-Tie pushed down her sleeve, her melancholy banished. "Good." She looked at Xiao Yen, her fierce eyes dissecting Xiao Yen like a butterfly under a knife. "You'll learn Zhang Gua Lao's type of magic. You'll be the best at it. You'll be the one offered the choice. And when the offer comes, if you don't want the peach yourself, you'll remember Wang Tie-Tie."

Every word bored into Xiao Yen's skull. She knew she'd never forget the still afternoon, the fan lying on the platform, the smell of the blossoms opening in the heat, the silent scars, and Wang Tie-Tie's eyes drilling holes into her and hooking ropes there, ropes that only Wang Tie-Tie knew how to pull.

"I'll remember," Xiao Yen replied, shifting in her seat.

Wang Tie-Tie stared for a moment longer, then laughed. The sound sent a chill down Xiao Yen's back. "Yes, you'll remember," her aunt said. "And you'll learn to stand on your own, away from the center of your family, as poor as that will make you. It's the only way you'll be a good paper mage. You're lucky to have me for an aunt. No one else would teach you this. No one else has been as alone as you must be, locked away for only one person's private pleasure."

Wang Tie-Tie rose and announced, "At the end of the hour of the Rooster, you may come back into the household and be with your mother and sister. Not before." She walked out of the garden without looking back.

Xiao Yen watched her aunt leave, the empty pit in her stomach growing wider. Alone again, and for so long. Xiao Yen steeled herself to wait some more, refusing to cry for herself. She would do her duty, as she'd been taught. She'd help Wang Tie-Tie end her pain. And hope that she'd never be taught to hate as her aunt had been.

Chapter 5

❧

On the Trail

Xiao Yen had already passed the two arrows, thinking they were skinny, broken branches, before she realized what she was seeing.

"Stop!" she called. She made her horse turn around and go back. The arrows protruded from the back of a man wearing a gray merchant's coat. She surmised he was recently dead as not many flies rose from the body as she approached.

Before she could get off her horse, Udo came up and asked, "Why?" He said other things she didn't understand, but she guessed the gist of it: it was dangerous to stop, unhealthy for the horses, and they didn't have time. The same things Udo always said whenever she asked him to stop.

"I study defense," Xiao Yen said, gesturing in the direction where she thought the dead man's camp lay. After three weeks on the trail under Bei Xi's tutelage, she could communicate much better in his language.

Bei Xi and her guard, Gi Tang, rode up. Before Bei Xi spoke, Udo made another long speech. Xiao Yen didn't try to follow it. Instead, she dismounted, draped her reins in a nearby bush so her horse wouldn't wander off, and approached the body.

This wasn't the first time she'd seen a dead body. Criminals were hung on Bao Fang's walls as a warning to others, and beggars were allowed to decompose outside the city's gates. But this was the first occasion she'd had to study one.

Xiao Yen didn't know what she was looking for, so she tried to memorize all the details: the stillness of the corpse, never mistaken for sleep; his head twisted to one side, covered by his bleeding hand; and his bare feet, impossibly pale against the dark ground. A belt lay next to him, like a disemboweled snake, the money and trinkets gutted.

Gi Tang also dismounted. He ignored Xiao Yen while he walked around the body. Then he sniffed the air in the direction Xiao Yen thought the camp would be. She sniffed as well: the air smelled of mud, the dry lichen growing on the tree trunks, and a faint undercurrent of blood. Without a word, he walked in that direction. Xiao Yen followed him.

"Xiao Yen!" Bei Xi called.

Her tone held enough worry that Xiao Yen stopped, took two steps back toward Bei Xi, and said, "I have to do this. It's my duty."

Bei Xi didn't reply. She stayed on her horse and looked down at Xiao Yen, her concern apparent in her eyes. Xiao Yen crossed her arms over her chest and stared back. She wasn't three years old. Bei Xi broke their gaze and looked away. Xiao Yen turned and started walking again.

Bei Xi called after her, "Be careful! Don't be long."

Xiao Yen didn't turn around a second time. She now understood why Jhr Bei, Bei Xi's younger sister, hadn't stayed with her older sister. Bei Xi vacillated between overprotecting and ignoring her charge. Xiao Yen didn't know which she disliked more, when Bei Xi smothered her, or when she spent all her time laughing, talking—and, Xiao Yen presumed, flirting—with Ehran. Maybe Fu Be Be was right about courtesans. Bei Xi's behavior was so improper, especially for someone from the court.

A cracking sound alerted Xiao Yen to where Gi Tang was. She hesitated about going any closer to him.

When they camped at night, she avoided the barbarian guard. He spat every time she walked past, and more than once had pulled his knife halfway out of its holder and scowled at her. Yet, she had to see this camp, see what defenses they'd had, and if possible, why they hadn't worked. It was her duty.

As Xiao Yen entered a clearing holding three torn and slashed tents, Gi Tang kicked a corpse in the face. Teeth flew, light catching them as they scattered. Xiao Yen gasped, horrified. Though the Buddhists believed the body was like an old shell, discarded and unimportant once the soul left, most merchants believed if a body wasn't whole when it was burned or buried, the spirit wouldn't rest. They persecuted the Taoists who used human bones, generally dug up from graveyards, in their magic and elixirs. Xiao Yen tried to reassure herself that Gi Tang was a barbarian and didn't know what he was doing, but the grin on his face told her he'd desecrated the body on purpose. Xiao Yen shuddered and forced herself to look away.

The earth around the camp was packed and baked, and didn't hold many footprints. The rest of the bodies lay in their tents. She speculated that they'd had a single guard circling the camp, the man near the trail. Or maybe not. Maybe he'd been asleep and had woken and run, leaving his boots in his tent. The fire pit held no embers. If they'd banked a fire to last all night, it would have still been warm.

The tents were like hers, dark oiled leather, low to the ground. They weren't cheap, and would have fetched a good price if they hadn't been purposefully ruined. Xiao Yen bent down and peered in the doorways to look at the bodies. In both the first and the second tent there hadn't been any struggle. The men had had their throats slit in their sleep. Whoever had done this had been professional, and quiet. The last tent was empty. Any goods the men carried were gone.

Xiao Yen heard Gi Tang leave. She walked in the opposite direction, into a small clearing beyond the first. The remains of a second camp were there, but she couldn't tell if it was from the night before or not. No fire.

She went around the perimeter of the second clearing, thinking. The attackers must have been well provisioned, otherwise they would have stolen the merchants' tents and clothes. Fresh horse droppings spotted the second clearing, so the attackers had been on horseback. Why hadn't the merchants posted a guard? Arrogance? Stupidity? Or had they felt themselves safe? Had there been a second camp, and had it attacked the first?

Xiao Yen had more questions than answers. She walked back to the first camp, then paused. She wished she could do something for the bodies, but she wasn't strong enough to bury them herself. Gathering enough wood for a pyre would take too long. Udo would never allow it.

An idea came to her. She kicked out the sticks holding the tents up so they collapsed over the bodies, like earth-colored shrouds. The third tent she dragged over the body desecrated by Gi Tang. Then she took out a single sheet of paper, divided it into three pieces, and folded simple long boats from each portion, one for each tent. She used one of her precious matches to burn them. The match, also known as a "lady finger," was slim and tapered, longer than Xiao Yen's fingers. While the boats burned, Xiao Yen prayed for the ghosts of the murdered men to cross the Yellow River and go to the next kingdom, and not stay and haunt this one. She wished she was like Udo and Ehran's first magician, the one who could enchant cloth, so the bodies wouldn't be discovered by some Taoist on his quest for eternal youth.

Udo didn't ask any questions when she came back. Someone had covered the body near the trail with an old, torn blanket. Gi Tang was already mounted, looking satisfied. Xiao Yen tried to dismiss the thought that came to her: that barbarian soldiers, like Gi Tang, had camped next to the merchants, and had killed them. Not for money and goods, but for spite. She shivered, and resolved to make a stronger defense that night, maybe a tiger again.

Bei Xi's and Ehran's horses stood close together, and they leaned toward each other, flirting. As Xiao Yen mounted her horse, Bei Xi's laughter rang out. When Xiao Yen turned to look, both Ehran and Bei Xi looked in her direction, then looked away. Xiao Yen assumed they'd been laughing at her. Bei Xi laughed too much with Ehran, and some nights Xiao Yen saw them leave together. It wasn't proper behavior for a woman, even a courtesan.

Xiao Yen was too worried about Ehran to blame him for Bei Xi's behavior. Though he was still heavier than most men his height, he'd lost weight. He no longer looked fat and healthy. His eyes had sunk into his cheeks. Black circles ran under them. He always rode at the back, always tired. He refused to listen to Xiao Yen's suggestion that he might be sick. He wouldn't pay attention to her, or take her concerns about his health seriously. He only teased her, or laughed at her, as Fat Fang, her classmate, had.

Bei Xi laughed again at something Ehran said. Xiao Yen wondered if Bei Xi was trying to teach him the language of the Middle Kingdom again. Xiao Yen hoped not. Bei Xi used archaic language, words so old and formal not even Wang Tie-Tie used them. If Ehran learned their language from Bei Xi, no one would understand him.

Xiao Yen turned forward, then glanced down. The sunlight coming through the trees was too dappled to cast strong shadows. Since the night three weeks ago in the clearing, Xiao Yen had never seen Bei Xi in a strong light, so she'd never been able to check Bei Xi's shadow again.

Xiao Yen had checked her own shadow, often. The blue tinge she saw sometimes disturbed her. She wasn't magic, was she? Her creatures cast blue shadows as well, but their shadows were also tinged with black. Her creatures were strictly magical, only able to affect the magic realm. Why weren't their shadows solid blue?

Bei Xi and Ehran laughed some more. Pangs of

loneliness assailed Xiao Yen. Bei Xi could talk with Ehran. The only person Xiao Yen could talk with easily was Bei Xi, and more often than not, Bei Xi just wanted to teach her something. At least the first thing Bei Xi had taught Xiao Yen, the knot magic, was a comfort. Xiao Yen often pulled her practice string out of her sleeve and tied knot after knot, growing them together then shrinking them down. Knot magic took less effort than paper magic, though Xiao Yen did sometimes review the steps necessary to fold creatures while she rode. She'd found that she couldn't stay in her quiet space while riding. She'd nearly fallen off the first time she'd tried. Instead, every time they set up camp, she practiced some aspect of her magic, and escaped to her quiet space whenever she could.

As the trail opened up at a clearing, Bei Xi called out, "Let's race!"

Without looking back, Xiao Yen kicked her horse and cantered across the clearing. When she reached the far end, she made her horse wheel around. Though Xiao Yen sometimes still felt nervous about the beast she rode, at least she could make it do her bidding. She no longer worried about hurting it inadvertently. She called her horse "Sunset Flying Roan," after one of the famous ten chargers Emperor Tai Zhung had owned.

Xiao Yen had expected Bei Xi to be on her heels, but she and Ehran were still on the far side of the clearing. Bei Xi encouraged Ehran to run with her, but he just smiled and shook his head, looking down at his reins.

Why wouldn't he race? Bei Xi gave up on him. Xiao Yen grinned. The clearing was in full sunlight. At last she'd be able to see Bei Xi's shadow. To her disappointment, Bei Xi unstrapped her umbrella from her saddle and rode shaded across the clearing. The tan color of her umbrella set off her dark hair and made her skin luminous. Her robe was made of off-white silk, with large beige patterns of flying swallows. Xiao Yen looked down at her own unembroidered blue jacket. It was a good jacket, well made and functional, but dull in Xiao Yen's eyes.

Bei Xi reined in her horse and stopped next to Xiao Yen, in the shade, of course. When they turned back, they saw Udo on the far side of the clearing with Ehran. Udo gestured sharply. Ehran didn't respond. Udo jerked the reins of his horse and came trotting across the clearing to where Xiao Yen and Bei Xi waited. Ehran followed at a slow walk.

Udo asked how they were, if they were hungry. When Ehran joined them, Udo told them that lunch would be soon.

"Good," Ehran replied with exaggerated relief. "I need to rest."

"My brother," Udo said to Xiao Yen with a laugh, "he sleeps, all the time."

Xiao Yen didn't respond. Udo didn't take her worries about Ehran seriously either.

Udo continued up the trail first. Xiao Yen followed him. Bei Xi and Ehran stayed side by side. Xiao Yen flinched at their laughter. She could catch up to Udo, but what would she say? Though Xiao Yen could speak a little of the brothers' language now, she didn't know enough to say anything meaningful. Plus, even if she could talk with Udo fluently, she still wouldn't want to. Udo seemed harsh compared with his brother. He always said cutting things, both to her and Bei Xi. The only person he was ever nice to was Ehran. And the horses. He spoke to them like a mother talked to her children.

It had been better when Xiao Yen had been at home, when Wang Tie-Tie had tried to teach her how to be alone. At least, at the end of the day, she'd been able to be with her family. Now there was no one.

Xiao Yen bit her tongue and concentrated on the pain. She would not cry. Not where anyone could see her.

Xiao Yen looked up from her bowl of noodles when the tone of Udo and Ehran's conversation changed. They were always louder than two excited five-year-olds chasing a ball, but now they were really yelling at each other.

Xiao Yen couldn't follow the rapid flow of their words. From the way Ehran held his hands open she could tell he was asking for something. Udo stood stiffly over him, his arms tightly folded across his chest. Udo didn't want to give it to him. Udo kept shaking his head, and Xiao Yen made out the word, "Late."

As quickly as it had started, it was over. Ehran closed his eyes and lay back, one arm under his head for a pillow. From his smug smile Xiao Yen surmised he'd won. Udo watched him for a moment, tight lipped, shoulders hunched, upset.

Xiao Yen bent her head over her bowl when Udo looked her way, not wanting him to see that she'd been watching. She watched his boots walk past her. She sighed and put more noodles in her mouth. The sauce on them had cooled and the noodles stuck together, salty and thick.

From over her left shoulder she heard Udo call, "Sanchen." The brothers always used the wrong tones when they tried to say her name, so they found a name for her in their language that sounded similar to her name. Bei Xi had assured her it was a good name, full of luck.

Xiao Yen looked up, her mouth full of noodles. Still looking at Ehran, Udo asked, "How short is your protection?"

Xiao Yen chewed and tried to swallow. She didn't understand his question. Though she'd spent many hours on the trail every day, either learning Udo and Ehran's language or the language of the horsemen, she was far from fluent.

She swallowed and asked, "Excuse me?" It was the phrase she knew the best.

Udo brought his hands together, indicating something small. "How short can you make your protection? Does it have to go all night? Or can you do it just for one hour?"

Xiao Yen didn't understand all Udo's words, but she could guess the meaning of them. The larger the creature, the longer it should stay animated, according to Master Wei. Otherwise it was a waste of the essential spirit. "Hour of Horse and hour of Sheep best. Just hour of Horse, possible, but not as good."

Udo looked around the camp, then stared at Ehran again. "We won't be here that long." He bit his upper lip and stood with his hands clenched together behind his back. "Stay close to camp. Those bandits may be nearby. If we're lucky, they won't be looking for horses. We're close to the next city, to Tan Yuan. We won't get there today, but maybe by tomorrow . . ." He bowed his head, then walked away.

Ehran lay as still as a large river stone. Xiao Yen worried about him. She felt responsible for Ehran. She'd been hired to protect the whole party, not just the horses. She didn't know what was wrong with Ehran. He just seemed drained of life. He didn't complain of fever or chills or loose stools. Xiao Yen hoped to talk with an alchemist in Tan Yuan. Maybe she could get some tea that would revive him.

Udo stopped at Bei Xi's tent, called out to her, speaking too fast for Xiao Yen to follow. Next, he walked to where the trail guide squatted, eating his lunch. Then he walked toward the horses. He talked to them as well, as if telling them the news. One of the horses leaned its head over and brushed it against Udo, like a shy child rubbing against its mother's skirt. After Udo patted the horses a few more moments, he walked into the woods.

Xiao Yen finished her noodles, rinsed her bowl out with water the trail guide had fetched from the river, then walked to her horse. She opened the bag containing her clothing. If they were going to be in Tan Yuan soon, maybe she could get more thread to sew the hole in her other set of pants. She reached in to bring the pants to the top, when her hand brushed against smooth silk.

Xiao Yen's heart came alive in her chest, pumping

hard, full of loneliness. Xiao Yen drew out a portion of the silk and held it to her cheek. It was her mother's jacket, Xiao Yen's favorite, the dark blue one with a pattern of cranes in lighter blue.

Xiao Yen looked back at the camp. Ehran's eyes were open. He raised his head and glanced around, searching for someone. Xiao Yen guessed he was looking for Udo. With a self-satisfied smirk, Ehran got up and walked over to Bei Xi's tent. As he approached, Gi Tang turned his head and looked away, purposefully not seeing him.

Xiao Yen, too, didn't want to see. It was just another reminder of how alone she was. She wrapped her arms around the jacket, hiding it from the others, hugging the sweet-smelling silk to her chest. She ran into the woods, tears streaming down her face.

When Xiao Yen couldn't see the camp anymore, or hear the horses, she stopped. She wiped her tears on her own sleeve. She took three deep breaths, placed the jacket under a nearby tree, then stood in the first pose, with her feet together, her arms by her side. Every morning, Master Wei had made his students go through a series of poses, a kind of slow dance. The poses were first straight or stretched, then contracted together, as if imitating the different types of paper folds. They also helped build *qi,* which in turn awakened the *jing,* or essential life force.

Xiao Yen went through the first series, paying attention to her breathing, trying to flow the "white crane" pose to "play flute" to "stroking the phoenix tail," but she felt awkward, out of balance. Besides, going through the poses just made her more homesick. She couldn't reach her calm place, a glassy river, shining like quicksilver between verdant banks. All she saw were the dark trees of the forest before her.

Xiao Yen stopped and walked over to where her mother's jacket lay. With steady hands, she undid the white frogs buttoning her jacket, both on the outer cotton layer and the inner soft layer. She folded both her jackets in half and laid them on a bush. Then she put on her mother's jacket. The silk slid up her arms and across her back like a soft breeze. It smelled of the incense from her bag and her mother's sweet perfume.

Xiao Yen hadn't ever worn her mother's jacket before. But she'd carried it with her, sneaking it into her bed, holding on to it like a three-year-old with a blanket. She felt ashamed of how much she needed it, how much comfort it gave her, how she longed for her home.

Xiao Yen held her hands out in front of her. The dark blue of the jacket made her skin look whiter, though not as fine as Bei Xi's. The scar on the back of Xiao Yen's left hand blazed. She ran a finger across one of the embroidered cranes. Some of the threads had broken, poking out of the cloth and curling like Udo's hair. The plackets that covered the raveling cuffs were coming undone as well. The gold threads looked brown in places, and some of the joining red boxes were missing.

Xiao Yen wrapped her arms around herself, hugging her aching chest. The silk slid under her hands, both cool and warm at the same time. She let her shoulders move and her chest convulse, heaving sobs without tears. She wouldn't damage this jacket any more than it already was.

Xiao Yen took deep breaths when she finished, pulling the sweet forest air into her center. Her chest still hurt; her stomach, though full of noodles, felt hollow; and her eyes burned with unshed tears. She was so alone. She tried to cheer herself up, reminding herself that she did have a family to go back to.

At least until Wang Tie-Tie found her another job, and she'd be alone again.

With steady fingers, Xiao Yen undid the elegant frogs at her neck, across her chest and down the front. She slid her right arm out from the jacket sleeve, then froze at the sound of snapped branches behind her. Startled, she turned around.

Ehran stood a few feet away.

Xiao Yen pulled the front of the jacket across her chest, trying to cover herself. A breeze blew across her bare back, raising chicken flesh across her shoulders and in the crevice between her breasts.

Ehran stared at her intently, the dark hollows under his eyes making his gaze more animallike. He was finally looking at her seriously, but this look scared her. She'd wanted him to pay attention to her warnings, not to her.

Ehran gestured with one hand and said something, slurring his words so she didn't understand. He fingered the haft of his knife with his other hand. Then he took a step forward and grinned at her, showing all his teeth. He looked like a fierce *ye ren*—the mythical wild men who were part human, part beast—that had found his lunch.

Xiao Yen took a step back and said the first word that came to her mind, "Friends?"

Ehran nodded and said, "Yes. Friends." But he kept looking at her strangely, and took another step forward.

Xiao Yen trembled inside, but she willed her arms to be as still as the tree trunks around her. His eyes held hers. She felt hypnotized, like a rabbit before a snake.

Xiao Yen took another step back and repeated, "Friends?"

Ehran said, "Oh, yes, friends."

Out of the corner of her eye, Xiao Yen could see his hands drop to his waist. She kept her eyes on his face, willing herself to not see that he was undoing his trousers. Xiao Yen had no paper defense, no knot to hold him back. They were far enough away from camp that no one would hear if she screamed.

She tried one last time, the whispered word barely making it across her dry and swollen lips. "Friends . . ."

Ehran took another step forward, but before he reached for her, Udo appeared next to him, his yellow hair like a ball of sun in the dark woods. Udo looked at Ehran, then at Xiao Yen. He spoke to Ehran in a low, angry tone.

Ehran looked away from Xiao Yen, down at the ground, and did up his pants. He looked back at Udo, laughed, then spoke, loudly and slowly so Xiao Yen could understand. "It was just for fun." He laughed again, shrugged his shoulders, and walked away, though Udo still asked questions like "what" and "why."

After Ehran was out of sight, Udo turned to Xiao Yen and said, "What are you doing? Didn't I tell you to stay at camp? There could be bandits out here. You could have been hurt."

Xiao Yen said, "I wanted to . . . It's my mother's . . ." She couldn't think of the words to say.

Udo didn't look in her face. Instead, he eyed the jacket she held across her chest. "For this?" he asked. He opened his mouth to say something more, then spat in disgust, and said, "Get back to camp." He turned and walked away.

Xiao Yen wanted to protest. *I know it's old, but it's my mother's! I was lonely! It isn't as elegant as any of Bei Xi's clothing, but it's still lovely!*

Then Xiao Yen realized what she'd been saying in her head. She was shocked by it. She sounded like a three-year-old defending a favorite toy. She looked down at the poor jacket, its raveling cuffs and broken embroidery. Maybe Udo was right to be disgusted. The jacket was too old. She shouldn't be carrying it anymore. She was too beholden to it. It was time to give up her childish need for it.

Xiao Yen put on her own jackets and did up the frogs. They smelled of her sweat and the horses and the campfire. She folded her mother's jacket. She pressed it one last time to her cheek and laid it at the foot of a pine tree. Then she walked away, crying inside. She felt as bad as the first day of her trip, when she'd left her family and Bao Fang.

When Xiao Yen reached the camp, everything was already packed up. Gi Tang and the trail guide had already started. Udo and Ehran sat on their horses, waiting for her. Xiao Yen pulled herself up on her horse. She sat until they went up the trail before she urged her horse forward.

The bright sun dappled the trail, making it seem like a tunnel of light through the dark surrounding trees. Xiao Yen followed the light blindly, trusting her horse to follow the others. She didn't try to see beyond the patterns on the ground, letting herself be hypnotized by the shapes of light and shadow. Her head bobbed with the gait of her horse. She'd left her family, all her childhood, behind. Again. This time it'd been her choice, not Wang Tie-Tie's. That didn't seem to make it any easier. Every time Xiao Yen swallowed, she felt a hard dry lump. The back of her throat ached, as if she were coming down with a cold. Her shoulders throbbed with tension. The spot in the middle of her shoulder blades burned as if pinpointed with the flame of a candle.

"Xiao Yen?"

Bei Xi was suddenly in front of her. Xiao Yen looked up at Bei Xi, but she didn't say anything.

Bei Xi now wore a dark red robe over her ivory silk jacket. Golden thread, woven around the edges, flashed, even in the dappled light, dancing before Xiao Yen's eyes.

"Xiao Yen?" Bei Xi hesitated. "I'm—I'm, sorry, about Ehran."

Xiao Yen's eyes snapped to Bei Xi's. Had she also followed Xiao Yen? Had she seen what had happened with Ehran? And not stopped it?

Or had Ehran told her, bragging of his dominance over Xiao Yen?

Xiao Yen's cheeks grew hot. She bit her tongue again, willing her tears to not surface. She urged her horse forward and pulled ahead of Bei Xi, afraid that if she opened her mouth, she'd wail with grief. The lump in her throat grew more solid, harder to swallow past. She had to blink hard at the sudden burst of light as her horse plodded into a clearing.

"Xiao Yen," Bei Xi called, riding up next to her.

Xiao Yen kept her eyes on the ground.

"Please, little one . . ."

What Xiao Yen saw registered slowly. There was no mistaking it. Bei Xi's shadow was solid blue.

Xiao Yen kicked her horse. Startled, it stumbled, then began to trot. Xiao Yen needed to get away from Bei Xi, away from everyone. She needed to think. Too many things bothered her about Bei Xi: the courtesan's archaic language, her ability to do knot magic, her facility with languages, her beautiful perfect teeth. And now, her blue shadow.

Another piece of the puzzle clicked into place.

Ehran was having the life sucked out of him.

Slowly, the answer came to Xiao Yen, resolving like a portrait held under the water and slowly raised to the surface.

Bei Xi wasn't human. She must be a fox fairy. And not a good fairy, bringing luck. She was sucking Ehran's *qi* from him every time they were together as man and wife. The thought of Ehran being drained of his male essence made Xiao Yen smile a little.

Once Xiao Yen was on the far side of the clearing, she slowed again. Udo rode just ahead. His golden hair flashed as spots of light struck it. He turned when he heard her coming and smiled at her, a wan smile. He didn't meet her eye. Then he looked forward again, his shoulders hunched. Xiao Yen looked past him to the cause of his concern. Ehran. Even though Udo wouldn't listen to Xiao Yen when she brought up her worries about Ehran's health, Udo still fretted about his brother.

Xiao Yen shook her head angrily. In her original contract she'd been hired to protect the brothers and their horses. This was her duty, and she must do her duty. Bei Xi was no longer her obligation, as she was hurting someone in their party. Xiao Yen would save Ehran from Bei Xi, though he deserved what he got. And maybe if she saved him, Udo would be less disgusted with her.

Chapter 6

❧

Bao Fang

Xiao Yen didn't dare wipe the sweat beading on her brow. Instead, she kept folding. She willed the sweat to stay where it was and not fall into her eyes. Then she forgot about it and concentrated on her little crane.

The paper between her fingers felt stiff, as if it were still made of bamboo. Though her biceps burned with the effort of holding her arms in front of her, her forearms, wrists, and hands moved with fluid grace. She did an inside reverse-fold to bring the legs down from the body of the bird and took a deep breath, sucking hot air from the Hall of Receiving deep into her gut. She was nearly finished.

Outside the hall, the unseasonably warm spring sun shone down on the front courtyard of the Dance of the Defending Crane paper mage school. It chased the snow away from the center of the courtyard, revealing black and white tiles. The snow clung bravely to the shadows at the bottom of the walls of the courtyard. When Xiao Yen had marched with the twelve other children from the student rooms to the front hall for their six-month exam, she'd thought the courtyard looked as pretty as one of the painted scrolls Master Wei made them study. Now, all she wanted was to melt the snow in her sweating hands.

At the far end of the hall, a boy shifted his weight and sighed. It was the only sound in the room. Xiao Yen felt, rather than saw, Master Wei's disapproval. She heard him rise and walk the length of the hall, moving stiffly, like a heron who'd just spotted a fish for lunch.

With his intense stare gone, Xiao Yen's shoulders relaxed a little. She did another inside reverse-fold through half the hidden back flap on the first leg, then did the same fold twice more, bending the leg up, then twisting it down, so the crane's leg bent backward. With her sharp nails, she split the bottom of the leg into three pieces, rolled each piece between her thumb and forefinger, then splayed them like a three-toed foot.

She did the same for the other leg, willing herself to see the webbing between the toes. She bent the ankles forward a little, then moved her fingers up the legs. She re-pressed the leg joints to make the folds more firm, then glanced up. Luckily, Master Wei was still at the other end of the hall and not looking in her direction. She took another deep breath. Master Wei didn't like to see wasted motion when folding, or for students to press a fold. He wanted the fold to be right the first time.

Xiao Yen brought her fingers up to the bird's body. Twisting her hands to echo a flying motion, she made the final fold and extended the wings. She brought her arms down and set the bird on the table, praying it would stand. It did. She opened her arms as she moved them back, completing the presentation. Then she brought them into her lap and relaxed.

"It's perfect." The whispered words, barely audible, floated to Xiao Yen's ears. Bing Yu, the only other female student in the paper mage school, took Xiao Yen's hot hand in her cool one. Xiao Yen smiled at her friend, who smiled back, wanly.

Under normal circumstances, Xiao Yen and Bing Yu would never have met, or been allowed to associate with each other. Bing Yu was the daughter of the governor, and Xiao Yen's family didn't have a high-enough social standing to associate with the ruling family in Bao Fang. As she was the only other girl in the school, the girls had ignored their different statuses, and had enjoyed each other's company.

The toad Bing Yu had folded had been far from perfect. Its front legs were stunted, and its hind legs were uneven, as if the toad were crawling. Master Wei wanted a strong, vital toad, one capable of leaping to the moon like the mythical three-legged toad.

Xiao Yen patted her friend's hand and looked again at her own creation. Its neck smoothly joined its head to its body, and the wings held a preflight energy, as if it were about to fly. At the same time, the folds in its legs were harsh. She'd been tired. Her crane wasn't worthy of being given *jing*, or life force, of its own. Only a perfectly crafted artifact was worthy of receiving magic, whether it was a cloak or a ring or a paper bird.

She hadn't yet learned how to give life to a creature. Master Wei would teach that skill only to the students who passed the six-month exam, and only if they studied hard and developed their understanding of the essence of the creatures they folded and the material they used. He'd send the rest of the students back to their families. They'd be able to retake the test after another year.

Xiao Yen looked up. Master Wei had bent over the table and put his face close to her crane. He blew gently on her bird. Its left leg was a fraction shorter than its right leg, so it rocked from one leg to the other in the slight wind. Xiao Yen was lucky as always though, and the crane stayed standing.

Master Wei straightened up. Not looking up from the table covered with paper animals, he said, "Please stand."

The students rose as one. Though Xiao Yen had only used her arms folding, her thighs ached. Her abdomen hurt as much as it had the first week of school, when she'd spent hours keeping it tucked in so she could sit straight without leaning on anything. Small tremors shook her forearms. She willed them to be still. Her apprehension intensified now that the strain of folding was gone. Despair hollowed the pit of her stomach. She was certain she hadn't passed, that she'd be sent back to Wang Tie-Tie in disgrace. Her cousin hadn't passed his civil exams the first time he'd taken them, and though that was normal, he'd had to live like a hermit, studying day and night, until he'd passed.

"Please stand over there." Master Wei pointed a long, skinny finger at the far end of the hall.

Xiao Yen stayed standing where she was, puzzled. Two of the boys exchanged looks.

"Now."

Master Wei's impatience and sharp tone made Xiao Yen wonder if any of the students had passed the exam. As one, the students turned and walked, single file toward the far wall. They bunched up in the corner. Bing Yu touched Xiao Yen's back. Xiao Yen reached behind her so Bing Yu could take her hand. Even if she were sent away from the paper mage school, at least she'd had a friend, for a while. Wang Tie-Tie's lessons about being alone had all gone to waste.

Master Wei picked up a tall screen lying against the wall and set it up. It had a village with golden buildings painted on it. A matching screen leaned against the opposite wall. Master Wei pointed to the two tallest boys in the class, then to the screen. Hastily, they picked it up and unfolded it across the space between that wall and the table.

Master Wei picked up a smaller screen and set it up on the table. Now the far end of the hall was completely blocked by the three screens. The students could no longer see their creations.

Master Wei peered around the first screen and said, "When I call your name, come into the other part of the hall."

He paused, then looked at each student. Xiao Yen

tried unsuccessfully to read his gaze. Was he trying to tell her she'd failed? She didn't know. She kept her own face still, willing herself to be as calm as a mountain waiting for a storm, though at the same time she squeezed Bing Yu's hand.

Master Wei finally said, "An Jon."

The boy moved a screen to one side so he could pass, then put it back into place.

Bing Yu and Xiao Yen exchanged glances, but neither of them spoke. Though Xiao Yen listened hard and the students were quiet, she couldn't hear what Master Wei said to An Jon. She didn't think he'd passed. He'd torn a leg off the dove he'd been folding as he'd been pressing it straight.

Master Wei asked for Xiao Li next. He'd folded a hummingbird. Its neck had been extended, as if reaching for a flower, full of energy and life. Xiao Yen had been certain he'd passed. She shot a puzzled look at Bing Yu, who shrugged her shoulders.

The small space where the students stood grew hotter. This end of the hall didn't have any open windows or doors. Bing Yu and Xiao Yen let go of each other's hands. Xiao Yen swayed on her feet. She wished she could sit, but none of the other students did, so she wouldn't either. She jumped every time Master Wei called another name.

There were seven students left when Master Wei called Bing Yu's name. She looked over her shoulder at Xiao Yen, biting her lower lip as she put the screen back into place. Xiao Yen touched her lucky amulet, wishing its luck for Bing Yu, knowing it wouldn't help. Master Wei hadn't asked for Bing Yu like he'd asked for Xiao Yen. He'd been forced to take her as a student because she was the youngest daughter of the governor.

At first, Xiao Yen had thought Master Wei picked on Bing Yu unfairly, but toward the end of the six months of study, Xiao Yen had learned to see the differences between Master Wei's creations and Bing

Yu's. Bing Yu moved her arms gracefully when she folded, but she couldn't concentrate. Her creatures never had any life. Still, Xiao Yen stuck by her friend, and helped her when she could.

Finally, only Xiao Yen, Fat Fang, and Long Yen were left.

Fat Fang was one of the governor's sons: a minor son, from his third wife, but still a son. He loved sweets, and his round arms and belly showed it. His lips were thick and heavy, like those of the Buddha at the White Temple, and often held a similar smile. Xiao Yen didn't like him. His dark eyes sucked at everything they saw, like greedy whirlpools. He also made fun of her, and his sister, for trying to learn "man's work." Fat Fang had bragged often about how he would defend Bao Fang from bandits, foreigners, or barbarians, even though the Middle Kingdom was at peace. He'd taken his studies seriously. The snake he'd folded for the exam had curves in its back that made it seem more like cloth than like paper.

Long Yen was the youngest son of the head of the Weavers' Guild. He'd always been nice to Xiao Yen. He was a medium-sized boy, with creamy skin and long curling eyelashes. Bing Yu had lamented that a boy had been born with such skin and eyes, and not a girl. He had a lazy smile and napped whenever he could. When he concentrated, his fingers flew like a shuttlecock. The bear he'd folded had a stocky body, like a late-summer bear. Xiao Yen could see the solid muscles running under its fur, but its front paws were weak. Like Xiao Yen, Long Yen had grown tired.

Master Wei didn't call any of their names. Maybe he'd forgotten about them. Xiao Yen tried to relax, but she kept leaning forward, a knotted rope tying itself tighter in her chest.

Xiao Yen didn't see Master Wei take down the screen standing on the table. The breeze on her cheek as the space opened up alerted her. Fat Fang and Long Yen folded up the other screens. Master Wei indicated for the children to resume their places behind the long table. Just their paper animals stood there. All the others were gone.

Xiao Yen sat, keeping her back straight. How embarrassing to be told her future in front of two other students! She knew she'd done badly. She hadn't thought she'd done that poorly. She held herself rigid, determined not to cry. She didn't want to imagine what Wang Tie-Tie would say to her. A cold knot formed in her throat, making it hard to swallow.

Master Wei paced on his side of the table for a while more, as if deciding what to say. Xiao Yen didn't think telling them they'd failed would take that much effort.

Finally, Master Wei stopped and stood in front of them. "For the next year you two"—Master Wei pointed at the boys—"will stay in the large rooms, next to the storage rooms, on the east side of the back courtyard." Master Wei paused again. "Xiao Yen, you will move into the room next to the library, on the west side. All of you have my permission to go home for the next two days to collect your things."

Xiao Yen kept herself rigid. Had she really heard what she'd thought she'd heard? She glanced to her left. The boys sat slack mouthed, staring. She was the first to find her voice. "Excuse me, honorable teacher, does that mean we passed?"

Master Wei looked surprised. "Of course, you did."

Xiao Yen smiled, a warm happiness melting the lump in her throat. The boys grinned and bobbed their heads. Wang Tie-Tie would be so pleased! Maybe she'd order fireworks, like she had for Xiao Yen's going-away party, when she'd started school. Gan Ou and Xiao Yen would stay up all night talking, snuggling together in their big bed. It would be so lovely to see her family again.

Then she thought of Fu Be Be, and ice water drowned her happiness. Her mother wouldn't like Xiao Yen living at the school. It wouldn't matter to her that Xiao Yen had passed her exam the first time, unlike her cousin. She'd sniff and not speak to Xiao Yen, as if she were one of the servant's children.

Master Wei spoke again. "You didn't pass because the creatures you folded were perfect. You're lucky, Xiao Yen, that bird of yours doesn't fall over. Fang, the belly on your snake isn't smooth. If you gave that poor creature life, it couldn't glide. Its stomach would always be catching on something. And the bear you did," Master Wei continued, turning to Long Yen, "the front paws are uneven. And the snout isn't turned down enough. It wouldn't be able to get food down its throat without spilling all over its chest."

The boys still grinned. Xiao Yen bit her lip. They weren't paper mages yet. Much more hard work was involved, including many hours of working with paper, studying paintings, and trying to capture the essence of a creature. All she and her fellow classmates knew how to do was to fold a few animals, and not very well.

Again she was the one who found her voice first. "Excuse me, sir, I know the piece I folded was a poor example of your lessons; not because you're a bad teacher, but because I'm such a slow student. But why did I pass? Why are you allowing me to continue to study with you?"

Master Wei said, "That's a good question, but not easy to answer, as are all good questions." He paused for a moment, stroking his long skinny beard. "Before this test, you all demonstrated excellent imagination, which is an essential part of paper magic. Those who folded well, but without heart or vision, were dismissed."

Ah, thought Xiao Yen. That explained Xiao Li. He could fold beautifully, but he'd had less imagination than Bing Yu's paper toad.

Master Wei continued. "Then, while you folded, each of you showed true concentration. A mage's mind must be focused. You all show glimmers of that. Also, you paid attention, not just to the folds, but to movements you made while folding. You must have grace, even under pressure, or your creation will be ungraceful, unnatural, and a danger to all." He paused for another moment.

"Look at Xiao Yen's crane. The head and neck flow smoothly into the body, the wings and legs flow out, making it all one creature. It echoes the grace you showed while folding. Toward the end, your arms grew tired, didn't they?"

Xiao Yen, her face burning with the unexpected attention, agreed.

"I thought so. That's why it barely stands."

Xiao Yen didn't respond.

"So I have a task for you, that you will perform every evening. After a while, you'll be able to fold at the end of your piece with as much grace as when you started." Master Wei looked at the boys and said, "I have tasks for you two as well."

Xiao Yen tried to pay attention to Master Wei's instructions for the boys. She knew she could learn much from everything he said. A voice in her head kept interrupting, singing over and over again, "I've passed! I'm going to be a real paper mage."

Two months later, Xiao Yen stood outside doing her nightly task. She tightened her sweating fingers around the rocks she held in her hands. She checked her elbows, making sure they bent like a gull's wings, then lifted her arms. Her shoulders ached. Sweat ran down her sides. She kept her arms at shoulder height and held them motionless in the air while she took a deep breath. Out, pause, in. She counted two more breaths, then she lowered her arms again.

The rocks in her hands felt cool against her thighs. Her forearms trembled. She'd be sore in the morning, but her arms would be stronger. She needed to have strong arms to fold difficult creatures, or so Master Wei had said. Wang Tie-Tie told her to do what Master Wei said.

At the thought of Wang Tie-Tie, Xiao Yen felt a pang in her stomach, as if it were empty, though she'd eaten a big bowl of seasoned grain for dinner. During the first six months of school, before the exam, the students had been allowed to go home every ten days or so. Now, going home was a privilege she had to earn. Suddenly the rocks in her hands felt as heavy as the stone the servants used to grind the grain. She sat on the steps leading to her room. When she put the rocks down, they made a solid thunk on the wood. She grinned. These rocks were a little heavier than the ones she'd started with. She was getting stronger.

From her seat, Xiao Yen looked across the courtyard. No lights burned through the window of the boys' room. She wondered if they were still awake. She remembered lying in the dark, talking with Gan Ou for hours, when she'd lived at home. She sighed. She'd loved those times, even though she and Gan Ou had often fought. At least she hadn't been alone. No one even lived in the building Xiao Yen lived in now. Next to her room was the Hall of Study, full of scholars' scrolls and painted silks. To her left, along the outer courtyard wall, were the servants' quarters and the kitchen. Just beyond them, in the corner, was the well.

Master Wei stayed in the front courtyard. The Hall of Reception was actually split in two, lengthwise. Master Wei lived in the long skinny room at the back of the hall. He said he needed the quiet. Xiao Yen didn't understand. Wasn't the whole compound quiet enough? She missed the sounds of her younger cousins yelling as they chased after a ball, or listening to Wang Tie-Tie and her tea friends tell stories and laugh in the Garden of Sweet Scents, and the noises of the crowded streets, the vendors hawking their wares. Xiao Yen felt as if she were the white snake Bei Si, imprisoned in her seven-story pagoda, only able to watch the life going on below.

The moon broke through the clouds, like a friendly beacon. It wasn't strong enough to fill the courtyard with light. The back corner where the well stood had thick shadows. Xiao Yen wondered if a dragon lived at the bottom of that well, too, like Jing Long, the one who lived at the bottom of the city well.

And if a dragon did live there, what did it bring? The dragon in the river Quang brought floods and fresh water every spring to the farmers. Jing Long brought the autumn rains. Maybe a dragon in the well of a paper mage school would bring luck? To the student who studied hardest?

Xiao Yen imagined the dragon rising out of the well, like the painting of Jing Long above the altar at the White Temple. The dragon she imagined was black, built out of shadows, not colors. It curled like smoke as it rose, undulating across the courtyard, outlined in silver by the moon. It held a special piece of dragon gold in its claws, in the shape of a pearl. It circled the courtyard, twisting and turning, playing with its ball.

A sudden gust of wind shook the trees, and a piece of fruit from the cork tree fell at Xiao Yen's feet. She blinked, startled. The dragon she'd imagined disappeared. Xiao Yen sighed, more sad than impatient with herself for letting her concentration be disrupted. It was too late in the day for her to imagine a fully grown dragon for long. She should go to bed. She sighed again. She felt too tired to move.

Maybe she could pick up the gold ball the well dragon had left behind. She held it in her mind's eye. It weighed less than one of the cork fruits, and was crunched together, like a wadded-up piece of paper. She had to hold it tightly or the wind would blow it away.

As she turned it, feeling the ridges under her fingers, she found a loose end. She tugged at it. The ball unraveled. Bit by bit, she unfolded it, tugging at it like dough. It grew in her hands to the size of a small blanket. She smoothed it and pressed it flat until it flowed like silk. Then Xiao Yen wrapped the gold around herself, letting it smother her in luck and fortune and all good things as she picked herself up and drifted to her room to sleep.

Chapter 7

On the Trail

Xiao Yen walked around the medicinal stele, marveling. Cures for at least a hundred ailments were carved on its sides. It was made of pale gray river rock, tall as a foreigner, and wide enough that she'd have to stretch to put her arms around it. The governor of Tan Yuan had placed seven medicinal pillars around the city's marketplace so that all people could get the same reliable treatment and live healthy lives.

Xiao Yen didn't see a cure for her problem written on the stele, but she knew what to do. All the tales she'd heard from Ama had taught her. The way to force Bei Xi back into her original fox-fairy form was to sprinkle sulfur in a circle around her.

Xiao Yen left the marketplace and headed toward the apothecary. She felt sad. Bei Xi had been so nice to Xiao Yen, teaching her the foreigners' language, and some of the northern barbarians' language as well. Plus, Bei Xi had paid for Xiao Yen's services, so contractually, Bei Xi was Xiao Yen's responsibility. However, Xiao Yen had originally only been hired to protect the foreign brothers, and Bei Xi was draining the life out of Ehran. Xiao Yen couldn't let her continue. Even if she thought Ehran deserved it.

Xiao Yen recognized the apothecary shop by the sign of the toad squatting on the compass. She also could have found the shop by the smell: the bitter herbs, sweet flowers, and incense all mingled with something that caught at the top of Xiao Yen's throat and dried it out.

Xiao Yen entered the shop and made her way to the counter at the back. A stout glass jar filled with thick red liquid and three floating geckos sat to one side. Strings of dried crab shells and squids hung above the counter. To the right of the counter hung a snakeskin. The body of the snake curled upon itself, forming a small nest, while the head stretched out, almost as if the snake had woken from a nap and was in search of food. The skin hung on thin wires and moved with the slightest breeze, as if it were alive.

"May I help you?" A skeletal man with dark, sunken eyes and pale skin came from behind the curtain separating the back from the front. His long neck and bony frame gave the impression of great height.

"I need some sulfur," Xiao Yen said, not giving the man her entire attention, staring instead at a thin bamboo cage containing hundreds of dried crickets.

The apothecary quoted a price. Xiao Yen continued to look around the shop. Her distracted pose was a bargaining ploy. If the merchant didn't think she was that interested, he'd drop the price more readily. Eventually, she responded with a price less than a third of the one the merchant had started with. They bargained. Xiao Yen threatened to leave the shop. Finally, they settled on a price, a little less than half the one originally stated.

Wang Tie-Tie had taught Xiao Yen how to bargain. Even Fu Be Be said Wang Tie-Tie was the best bargainer in the family. Xiao Yen had asked her aunt about it one afternoon, after watching her negotiate three pairs of shoes for the price of one. Wang Tie-Tie had said something about how if she didn't bargain hard, her husband would take every wasted penny out of her skin. After seeing the brand on her arm that day in the Garden of Sweet Scents, Xiao Yen wondered if Wang Tie-Tie had meant it literally.

The apothecary stepped into a back room to get Xiao Yen's purchase, and came back carrying a small bag. The sulfur was so strong, she could smell it when he got close to the counter.

"Here's your yellow fluid," the apothecary said. While Xiao Yen dug coins out of her bag, he asked, "Do you have a cold?" Sulfur was often used in an infusion to treat colds around the waist and kidneys.

Xiao Yen grinned at him and lied. "No. A mother-in-law."

He laughed. Mother-in-laws were notorious for finding fault with new brides. In more than one market tale, particularly evil mother-in-laws were discovered to be foxes in disguise.

"Maybe you should go to Ba Long's, the dragon temple, then. There's an altar there dedicated to Fu Xi and his wife Nü-gua."

Fu Xi was well known as the architect of all society. He'd invented fishing, farming, as well as writing. Nü-gua was known to come to the aid of hard-pressed heroes. Fu Xi and his wife Nü-gua were generally shown as human from the waist up, their bodies facing away from each other, while their lower snake halves intertwined.

Xiao Yen thanked him and asked directions to the temple. It was only three streets away. Xiao Yen bought incense from one of the sellers just outside the temple gate. Inside the complex, the main building across from the gate was dedicated to Ba Long, the city's dragon.

A smaller building stood to the right. Painted knots covered the façade. Before Fu Xi had brought writing to Xiao Yen's people, they'd communicated using knots. Considering the steles in the marketplace, Xiao Yen wasn't surprised that the scholarly aspects of the god and goddess were worshiped here in Tan Yuan.

Inside, the temple was dark, lit by only a few candles. Three different aspects of the pair hung above the altar. The center scroll had the traditional representation of the pair painted on it. To the left hung a scroll with Nü-gua standing in front of a group of beings who all looked like her, with snake bottom halves and human tops. Each held a different item, representing the things the goddess had given to humanity: different instruments, like the flute and mouth organ, to represent music; rocks and swords, to represent smelting; compasses and maps, to represent navigation. To the right hung a similar scroll, showing Fu Xi and his contributions: a square measure, fishing rods, plows, pens, paper and ink.

Xiao Yen lit her incense and placed five sticks, representing the compass points, in the brazier under the painting for Fu Xi. She placed the traditional three sticks in the center brazier, under the traditional painting. Then she placed the rest, a lucky eight, in the remaining brazier for Nü-gua. Xiao Yen knelt and prayed for a long while. Since she had no luck, she needed all the help she could get.

Xiao Yen examined her crane in the flickering candlelight. Its beak looked sharp enough to pluck out the eyes of a fox. Its wings flowed from its body, its neck and legs followed classic lines. Its splayed feet held the ground solidly. Master Wei would be proud of her. It was an artifact worthy of its own life, if only for a short while.

Would it be good enough to affect a fox fairy? She hoped so. As fairies were magic, not mundane, her magic was probably strong enough to affect them, but she wasn't certain.

She tucked the crane into the sleeve of her jacket, blew out her candle, and took a deep breath, breathing in the stillness of the night air. An owl hooted above her head. The moon hadn't risen yet, so there was little light. Trees whispered to each other in the evening breeze. A few crickets chirped in the high grass. The rich taste of the campfire came to her, carried on the wind.

Xiao Yen sighed and made herself get up. She had to do this. She had to save Ehran from Bei Xi, even though every time he smiled at her, she shivered. It was her duty. Besides, he looked so pale and ill, she doubted he could hurt her. Though Udo joked about tying Ehran to his saddle so he wouldn't fall off, Xiao Yen heard the worry in Udo's voice. Maybe Udo was a foreigner, but he felt responsible for his little brother, just like siblings from her people did. Realizing this had made Xiao Yen like Udo a little more.

She heard the three of them laughing, like a cheerful chorus of bells in the night.

Waist-high bushes grew between the dark tree trunks. Xiao Yen blundered into more than one as she walked back to the camp. When she drew close enough to see by the fire's light, she stopped and studied the area. Bei Xi stood between Ehran and Udo on the far side of the fire. Gi Tang sat about a quarter of the way around, involved in a game of dice with the trail guide.

As quietly as she could, Xiao Yen circled around the fire until she was behind Bei Xi. Her heart beat hard in her chest, as if she'd just walked up a steep hill in midsummer heat. Sweat trickled down her side, and instantly cooled in the evening air. She reached into her sleeve, pulled out the bag of sulfur, and untied the knot. Her hands were steady. She smiled grimly. No matter what, her hands rarely shook. Master Wei had seen to that. At least the wind was blowing in her direction, so her scent wasn't carried to the group.

Xiao Yen crept closer behind Bei Xi. When the wind stopped for a moment, she threw some of the powder on the back of Bei Xi's legs.

"Wha—?" was all Bei Xi said before she froze.

Xiao Yen yelled, "Ehran. Udo. Move back!" Xiao Yen walked counter-sunwise around Bei Xi, sprinkling the sulfur on the ground as she walked, making a circle of powder around the courtesan. When she finished, she still had a little powder in the bottom of her bag, so she flung the remains on the fronts of Bei Xi's legs.

Bei Xi stood frozen, like a statue carved from white jade. Her mouth formed a perfect "O." Her eyes stared unblinking, like two dark almonds. She held her arms in front of her, as if to catch herself from a fall. She still looked impossibly beautiful.

Xiao Yen had been right. A real human wouldn't have reacted to the sulfur at all.

Ehran and Udo stood on either side of Bei Xi, amazement in their faces, and fear. She heard Gi Tang come up from behind, but he didn't try to stop her. Xiao Yen told the brothers again, "Move back." Then she took her crane out of her sleeve, placed it on the ground, and concentrated on animating it.

The fire cast a rosy glow on her paper bird, like light from the setting sun. Xiao Yen imagined the shadows under its wings growing longer, wider. The fire crackled. Xiao Yen imagined a happy bird picking up its feet and dancing to the sound. The sweat on her forehead cooled with a sudden breeze. Xiao Yen saw the same breeze ruffling the snow white feathers of a large crane.

When it turned its golden eyes to her, Xiao Yen filled them with one image, the face of Bei Xi. Her lovely curved cheeks, her small sharp nose, her perfect teeth. The crane dipped its head several times, then turned, its wings outspread.

Bei Xi was still frozen when Xiao Yen first looked up. The crane walked stiff legged in a circle around her. Abruptly, Bei Xi blinked, lowered her arms to her sides, and finished the "O" with the barest whisper. Her legs glowed and shimmered, as if being viewed through a heavy rain. A deep bell-like tone sounded once. Udo and Ehran stepped back, aware that something magical was going on.

Xiao Yen waited, expecting Bei Xi's fox tail to appear between her legs. Maybe her luck was changing. She rubbed at the scar on the back of her left hand. Her crane flexed its wings a couple of times, like a wrestler warming up before a match.

A tail never appeared. Instead, Bei Xi's legs fused together into a single white snake's tail.

Then she started growing. Her head shot up toward the trees. The snake tail ended at Bei Xi's waist, while her human half grew more beautiful than before. Her tail glittered like wet fish scales. A pearly white glow emanated from her human half, illuminating the shock and horror on Ehran and Udo's faces.

Bei Xi's eyes grew large and liquid, like a horse's eyes. She loomed above their heads like a living statue.

The pose was familiar to Xiao Yen. She placed her hands over her mouth. That afternoon. In the temple. Why hadn't she seen the likeness before? Bei Xi resembled Nü-gua, the goddess who had brought so many advances to the Middle Kingdom. Xiao Yen's stomach lurched.

Before Xiao Yen could stop her crane, it pecked at Bei Xi's tail. Bei Xi gave Xiao Yen a look of anger that shot straight into her heart. Then Bei Xi broke through the sulfur circle and hurried into the woods, the crane leaping from one foot to the other as it followed her, pecking at her tail as it disappeared into the brush.

Xiao Yen was the first to break out of her frozen stance. She ran in the same direction Bei Xi had gone. Udo grabbed her arm and stopped her. Even in the fire glow, Ehran's face looked deathly white. Udo's, on the other hand, was red, as if he were blushing.

"Why are you following her?" he asked.

The tone of his voice told Xiao Yen his cheeks were red in anger. Her stomach fell further. He had every right to be angry with her. She'd failed, ruined everything.

"It isn't safe," he continued, no longer glaring at her, but at Ehran. Maybe he wasn't angry with her. Maybe he was angry with his brother.

"I have to help, see if Bei Xi needs help," she said, knowing how ineffective her words sounded. Bei Xi didn't need her help.

"Why would you help that—that—monster?" Udo was shouting at her now.

How could he call Bei Xi a monster? Like some horrible animal that lived on human blood, as Bei Xi had translated the term for her? Abruptly, she understood. Udo was a foreigner. His land had never been civilized by Fu Xi and Nü-gua. He didn't know Bei Xi's heritage.

"Bei Xi is goddess, sister to goddess Nü-gua," Xiao Yen explained patiently. "She is good. Not evil. I must go, I must"—Xiao Yen searched for the foreign words—"say I'm sorry."

She yanked her arm out of Udo's grasp, turned, and ran into the woods. She heard Udo coming after her.

At first, Xiao Yen ran blindly. Once her eyes adjusted to the dark, she followed the white glow of Bei Xi. The goddess didn't make the trail easy. Xiao Yen stumbled on unseen tree roots. Bushes snagged her clothes. Low branches pulled her hair. The still air of the woods didn't cool her sweat. The unearthly point of light always seemed on the verge of disappearing. It was like a nightmare. Bei Xi played with Xiao Yen, just as she'd played with Ehran. Xiao Yen followed determinedly.

Xiao Yen tried not to think of the consequences of her actions as she ran. She'd exposed a goddess, forced her to take non-human shape. There was probably a special hell reserved for people like her. Xiao Yen fell again. Her palms burned as they slid across the earth. Her knees hurt from the rocks they landed on. Xiao Yen rested for a moment, her head hanging down, trying to catch her breath. She smelled dry leaves. She wanted to lie down in a soft pile of them, forget her shame, her duty. But she couldn't.

She forced herself to stand and follow the wavering light.

The point of light grew to a slim column. Bei Xi had stopped. Xiao Yen rubbed her stinging palms together, wiping off some of the dirt. She tugged on her braids, smoothing them as best as she could, then tried

to flatten the hair on top of her head. It was hopeless.
Ends stuck up in every direction. There was no time
to rebraid her hair now. The goddess was waiting.

Xiao Yen stepped out of the woods and into the
clearing. Bei Xi waited at the far edge. She glowed
like a small moon that had come to earth, turning the
meadow grass into a silvery lake. Xiao Yen hurried
across the clearing, keeping her arms at her sides, her
palms out, so Bei Xi could see she didn't carry any
weapons or paper defense.

Though Bei Xi's tail curled under her, her face was
far above Xiao Yen's. Her body had grown larger.
Just from the waist up she was taller than Udo. Her
curves had grown more pronounced, more feminine.
Though her arms were as thick as Xiao Yen's waist,
they floated gracefully at her sides. Her eyebrows
soared above her eyes, more lovely than a crane's
wings. Her nose was still sharp, like a point of beauty.
Her eyes held ancient suffering, passed down from the
earth itself. They filled Xiao Yen's heart with sorrow.
At the same time, they were beautiful, like black
pearls.

"Oh, Great One," Xiao Yen said. She knelt on the
ground and placed her forehead on the cool earth.
"Please forgive me. Please accept my most humble
apology. I—"

"Xiao Yen," Bei Xi interrupted, "stand up."

Xiao Yen stood. She couldn't control the trembling
in her knees.

"Please gaze upon my face," Bei Xi said.

Xiao Yen raised her head, then looked up, and
looked up some more. Her head tilted almost all the
way back before she could see Bei Xi's face.

Bei Xi's lovely tinkling laugh settled like rain on
Xiao Yen's shoulders. "You can take two steps back."

Xiao Yen obediently took two steps back.

"Little Sister—may I call you Little Sister?"

Xiao Yen gulped, not trusting her voice at being
given such an honor. She hoped Bei Xi understood
her silence for assent.

"You were fulfilling your duty. This is right. You were protecting your clients. Maybe I shouldn't have, ah, played with them. I was protecting you, as well. I thought if Ehran were distracted . . . But now, how am I supposed to stop Vakhtang?" Bei Xi added, almost to herself.

"I'm so sorry," Xiao Yen said, breaking in. "It's all my fault. I should have kept my suspicions to myself. I—"

"No, Xiao Yen. You did the right thing. How could you know that there were plans within plans? I should have taken you into my confidence. It was easy to fool the foreigners—what do they know of our land, of our people? They wouldn't suspect anything. But you would. I sincerely apologize, Little Sister, for not speaking directly to you," Bei Xi said, bowing slightly to Xiao Yen.

"No, it is I who must apologize," Xiao Yen said, bowing deeply in return.

"Now that we are both equally sorry," Bei Xi said seriously, though there was still laughter shining in her eyes, "I need to tell you my plans, and beg for your assistance."

"Anything." Xiao Yen breathed the word out, as if pledging her whole self to the unheard proposal. "I would consider it an honor if I can help you in even the smallest way."

"But what of your duty, the brothers . . . ?" Bei Xi asked.

"They're foreigners," Xiao Yen replied. "My duty lies with helping"—Xiao Yen paused, then continued—"you and your kind." She didn't want to call Bei Xi a goddess to her face. It seemed impolite, somehow.

Bei Xi thought for a moment, then acquiesced.

Xiao Yen drew her first comfortable breath. At last, she'd done something right.

"Vakhtang," Bei Xi started, "is evil. He doesn't want peace. He wants to use our blood for his wine, our souls for his meat, our children for his slaves. He must be stopped." She paused. In the distance, Udo called Xiao Yen's name. Bei Xi raised her eyebrows and asked, "Do you wish for me to let him find us?"

"Not Ehran," Xiao Yen blurted out.

Bei Xi's eyes took on a distant look. "He's still at the camp." She smiled a tight smile at Xiao Yen. "You must be careful of him. He doesn't have the heart of a snake, but he can be as treacherous as one."

Xiao Yen remembered the time he found her in the woods. She felt the blush starting in her cheeks and spreading to her ears, but she looked straight back at Bei Xi.

"My baby sister, Jhr Bei, had taken a special interest in the people from the north. She had many followers, temples dedicated to her alone, not just to our more famous brethren, Fu Xi and Nü-gua. She wanted to protect her people from the raids of the barbarian horsemen. She thought she could befriend Vakhtang, then use him and his soldiers as a barrier between the Middle Kingdom and the rest of the horsemen. We, her sisters, advised against it, but she wouldn't listen to us. She thought Vakhtang was good. Vakhtang feared death—the price for his help was invulnerability. Jhr Bei created a bubble around his heart that protected him from all wounds.

"What Jhr Bei didn't realize was how great Vakhtang's own magical ability had grown. He used his powers to corrupt her magic. The bubble was supposed to be powered by his own life force, but instead, he feeds it the essence of others. This makes the bubble too strong. It prevents him from having proper feelings. After he became invulnerable, he killed my sister, and used, still uses, her soul. There's no hope of rebirth for her, for any of his victims, until he dies." Bei Xi fell silent for a moment.

Xiao Yen felt awe. How could Vakhtang kill a goddess? And use her soul? He must be very powerful.

"Only something of the one who created the bubble

can be used to dissolve it. Vakhtang destroyed everything of Jhr Bei's, all her clothing, her jewelry, her combs, her shoes. But he missed one thing.

"Centuries before, a rat stole one of Jhr Bei's hairpins, and gave it in homage to the king of the rats, the rat dragon. This dragon still has the hairpin. It's the only thing that can harm Vakhtang. It just needs to break his skin, a single little scratch."

Xiao Yen was surprised that such a small act could do so much damage.

Bei Xi continued. "The first task is to get the hairpin from the dragon. This beast," she warned, "can only be killed by words not spoken or written."

Before Xiao Yen could ask Bei Xi to explain herself, Udo joined them. His upturned face shone with wonder and fear. Bei Xi addressed him for a minute, speaking faster than Xiao Yen could understand. He asked many questions. Finally he turned to Xiao Yen and asked, "She's good?"

Xiao Yen said, "She's a goddess. We, respect—*bài*—her."

"Worship," Bei Xi said, still smiling.

"Her people gave my people writing, houses, music, marriage, poetry, all that makes my people my people." Xiao Yen paused. "Is she good? She does good, but she also plays, like all people," Xiao Yen said, trying hard to make the distinction that Bei Xi was herself, not goodness incarnate like Kuan Yin, the goddess of mercy.

Udo seemed satisfied, so Bei Xi explained to him about Vakhtang, the hairpin, and the rat dragon.

"This dragon," Udo said. "Does it have much silver?"

Bei Xi replied, "Yes. Heaping piles of it. Its lair is full of tunnels and it guards them jealously. Many men have died for only a few handfuls of coins."

Udo bobbed his head and looked pleased.

Bei Xi went on. "Vakhtang doesn't know of the hairpin. He believes he is safe. So now, he is growing bold. He plans to invade the Middle Kingdom. This is why the King of Heaven let me return, to stop Vakhtang. Now I must petition the King of Heaven again, for him to change me into human form again, and let me return. I don't know how long that will take. Whether I will be allowed to return in a day or a year. Time moves differently in the Heavenly Pavilion."

Bei Xi unwound her tail a little and grew taller. "Little Sister, you pledged yourself to my aid."

"Vakhtang must be stopped," Xiao Yen said, forcing each word out. It was her duty, both to her people, and to Bei Xi, to stop him. It was her only chance for redemption after ruining Bei Xi's plans. And all it would take was one small scratch.

"I'll help too," Udo said.

Xiao Yen looked at him, surprised. He stood like a soldier, his chest out, hands behind his back, legs solidly under him.

More shouts came through the woods. Bei Xi said, "My guard. Gi Tang. He's one of Vakhtang's soldiers. He did not know of my deception. He cannot report to Vakhtang before you get there."

Udo nodded. "Ehran will take care of him."

Xiao Yen wondered at Udo. He said it with such finality. Xiao Yen remembered that Ehran had killed a man before. She was struck again by the image of Ehran fondling the hilt of the knife on his belt. She shivered and blamed the cool night air for her chicken skin.

"Vakhtang now makes Khan Hua, the next city, his capital. It's only two days north of here."

Xiao Yen blinked. Wang Tie-Tie's youngest sister lived in Khan Hua. Maybe her aunt would be able to help them in their task.

"And the dragon?" Udo asked, leaning forward on the balls of his feet.

Bei Xi smiled broadly. "Many people in the city can direct you to it." She glanced skyward for a moment, as if she'd heard a distant call. "The time I was allowed here is gone. I must go." She bowed to them, bending at her human waist, lowering herself with her tail. Then she rose like a pillar of white smoke and ascended to the sky. Like a comet she went across the night, blazing east, where the King of Heaven sat, with all his court.

Xiao Yen watched until Bei Xi's trail disappeared. It was a beautiful flight, like an ageless white bird flying free across the sky. When the glow trickled away, she felt her heart return to her body with a thud. Her burden felt like piles of stones on her shoulders. Why was she so unlucky?

Udo said, "Come. We have work to do." He almost smiled at her, but not quite.

Xiao Yen followed him blindly back to the camp.

Chapter 8

✣

Bao Fang

"My father pays a string of coins every week for my studies," Fat Fang confided in Long Yen. They walked ahead of Xiao Yen on the wide dirt road. Master Wei was taking his students on a field trip to study animals in nature. Predawn clouds stretched sketchy orange fingers across the sky as they walked toward the altar of the river dragon. The river Quang ran gray and quiet.

Xiao Yen didn't care for Fat Fang's tone of voice. He was up to something. His smile was always the same serene Buddha-like smirk, but he wasn't as good as Gan Ou at faking a sincere tone.

Fat Fang continued. "And I know your father pays about the same," he told Long Yen. "And how much does your father pay, Xiao Yen?" he asked over his shoulder.

Xiao Yen didn't know how much Wang Tie-Tie paid, but she was certain it wasn't as much as anyone else. Not because of any generosity from Master Wei, but because Wang Tie-Tie was the best bargainer Xiao Yen had ever seen.

After a moment, Xiao Yen replied to Fat Fang, "My *family* supports my schooling." She hoped to imply that many people supporting her were better than a single parent.

Fat Fang spoke reassuringly. "I'm sure they do. Isn't Master Wei a charitable person?" he asked of no one in particular.

Xiao Yen knew she shouldn't take offense, but he was disparaging Wang Tie-Tie, and she couldn't stand that.

"At least I'm here because of my skill, not because some official bribed my way."

Fat Fang shot her a mean look, his mouth cross, his chin pointing and hard. "I have just as much skill as you do."

Xiao Yen replied, "Maybe, but did Master Wei *ask* your family to send you to his school? Like he *asked* for me?"

Fat Fang stopped and stared at Xiao Yen.

Xiao Yen glared back.

"You were just lucky, a *girl* doing men's work," Fat Fang said. He paused. "Maybe you're always lucky." His serene Buddha smile reappeared. "At least I'm continuing in school because of my skill, not through sheer luck."

Xiao Yen's cheeks grew warm in the cool morning air. How dare he accuse her of being in school only because of her luck? Yet a tiny voice deep inside her questioned if he might be right.

Before she could think of a reply, Long Yen stepped between them, laughing.

"Stop bickering like old hens," he said. He pushed Fat Fang in the direction they'd been walking. "You know Master Wei will be angry if he has to wait for us."

"You're right," Fat Fang said. "Though we *are* with lucky Xiao Yen. If we walk too slowly, Master Wei will have gotten a pebble in his shoe, and will also be going slowly," he said, linking his arm through Long Yen's and walking forward.

Long Yen glanced back at Xiao Yen. He raised his eyebrows in a helpless look, then winked at her.

Xiao Yen gave him a small smile in return. Her smile fell when he turned away.

Was Fat Fang right? Things like that did happen to her. She'd be late for dinner on the one day dinner was delayed, or she'd accidentally tear the creature she was folding at the same time Master Wei discovered the paper was inferior. These incidents were as natural to her as breathing. She'd always been lucky.

Did that mean she had no skill? No, of course not. She was building skill in folding. Her aching shoulders attested to that. Plus, an important part of paper magic was being able to imagine things, and everyone always told her she had a good imagination. She reassured herself she'd passed her first exam, and the others since then, with more than just luck.

A kernel of doubt remained.

Xiao Yen unbent her left knee, lifting her foot from the earth until it was halfway between the ground and her waist. Then she bent her knee again, while at the same time she folded her right hip joint and brought her left arm across her chest. Xiao Yen tried to keep her mind empty as she moved, folding and unfolding her limbs like Master Wei had taught them. This morning the master and his students flowed through the poses, one melting into another. Sometimes Master Wei had them stop and hold a pose while paying attention to their breath and their *qi*. Xiao Yen felt more comfortable in the folded poses, with her *qi* surrounding her like a soft blue cocoon. Fat Fang and Long Yen both did better in the unfolded poses, with their *qi* stretched out, vibrant and red.

Master Wei continually stressed how important the *qi* was, and the interaction between it and the life force. Xiao Yen paid attention when Master Wei talked, but he used complex philosophical terms she didn't understand. It took her months to fully grasp some concepts. She hoped that someday she'd understand all the nuances Master Wei took for granted.

Only by transferring energies could she animate a paper creation. That was the fundamental nature of all magic—imbuing artifacts with just the right amount of life force. Anyone could fold a pretty crane. But to make it fly . . .

For the first three years of their schooling, Master Wei had only let his students fold creatures. They'd also spent much of their time poring over paintings of animals, insects, and landscapes by famous artists, or reading poems about them, trying to discover the essence of each animal or insect. At the start of their fourth year, he'd taught them how to animate small creatures, like ants or centipedes. Xiao Yen excelled at all her studies. It was easier for her than the boys. She didn't have any friends, no one to talk with, nothing to do but study all the time. The younger students wouldn't socialize with her. Xiao Yen couldn't say she was used to being alone because she still always felt lonely. Even with all of Wang Tie-Tie's training, she wasn't sure she'd ever get used to the loneliness.

Xiao Yen brought her hands together, palm to palm, in the final gesture. She bent her head in thanks for the morning, the clear air, the connections she felt with river, the rocks, the birds singing in the trees behind her, the trees themselves.

Master Wei led them to the eight-sided pavilion that held the altar of the river dragon. The pavilion's gray-tiled roof curved gracefully at the corners, supported by round, red-lacquered poles. Green planks ran at waist level between the pillars, perfect for leaning against and watching the river. The altar of the river dragon was a long and skinny table, covered with a red silk, embroidered cloth. A silver brazier stood in the center of the altar, holding sand and the remains of hundreds of sticks of incense.

Master Wei knelt and bowed to the altar. His students did the same behind him. After praying for a while, he reached into his sleeves and pulled out five perfectly folded doves made out of dazzling white paper. He arranged them on either side of the altar, then concentrated, head bowed. Little balls of fog covered the five paper birds.

After a moment, the fog melted away and live doves

appeared. The birds stood at attention, like soldiers, looking to Master Wei for instructions. As one, they bobbed their heads, wheeled, and took off. They flew in an arrow formation, sunwise, around the pavilion three times, then headed for the river. Again they spiraled, the sun reflecting off their brilliant white feathers. One by one they dove into the river, passing into the water as swiftly and silently as knives.

Master Wei produced another stiff piece of paper and gathered up the ashes of the paper birds still standing on the altar. He held it up above his head as he left the pavilion and walked to the river. With a graceful bow, he poured the ashes into the river, saying, "Please accept my most humble offering. I hope the birds find their way to your court and delight you with their flying."

Without turning around, Master Wei addressed his students. "Tell me about the birds."

Xiao Yen hid her grin. Master Wei was always a teacher, even when he was paying respect to a dragon. Master Wei wanted his students to be acute observers, not just when they studied, but all the time. They never knew when he'd turn to them and say, "Describe what you've just seen." It was like a game he played with them.

Xiao Yen blessed Wang Tie-Tie again for all the long hours of storytelling she'd made Xiao Yen do in the Garden of Sweet Scents. How could Wang Tie-Tie have known that keen observation was such an important part of being a paper mage?

Fat Fang started, describing the scales on the birds' feet, a detail Xiao Yen hadn't noticed. Long Yen described how their wings didn't start close to the birds' necks, but farther down, like shoulders, and how the wing feathers overlaid the tail.

Xiao Yen's heart sank down to her ankles. She didn't know what to add. The boys had described the birds completely. She couldn't dredge another detail about them from her memory. She wished she had more time to remember. Before the silence dragged on too long, she described the birds' flight, commenting on how they'd entered the water silently, without a ripple.

Master Wei turned around at her description. Xiao Yen didn't meet his eye, afraid of a reprimand. She hadn't described the physical birds at all.

"Exactly!" he said, startling her, making her look up. "Why is that detail so important?"

Xiao Yen looked at him blankly. She glanced at Long Yen. His face held the same look. Fat Fang turned to look at her. Silently he mouthed the word, "Luck."

Xiao Yen tried to concentrate on Master Wei's explanation of mundane and magic—how a magical creature couldn't affect the world around it, while a mundane creature couldn't affect magic. As the dragon was a magical creature, it was proper to send him magical doves, rather than earthly ones.

When Master Wei finished his lecture, he turned and walked up the river path. Fat Fang and Long Yen followed him closely. Xiao Yen also stayed close for a time, then she fell back, thinking.

It wasn't fair of Fat Fang to accuse her of being lucky. It was like accusing her of having black hair, or dark eyes. It wasn't something she consciously used. It was a part of who she was.

Yes, Master Wei had met her by chance, and she'd shown him her imagination through luck. But she hadn't stayed in school because of her luck. She also worked hard. It was just so unfair.

What would happen to her if she lost her luck? Xiao Yen swallowed hard. She reached up with her right hand to touch her amulet, to reassure herself it was still there.

Master Wei and the boys walked out of sight, beyond the next curve in the river path. Xiao Yen decided to find out how lucky she was. She wasn't going to follow them. She was going to stop here, and see if Master Wei became furious with her or if something would happen. She sat down on the river side, plucking long brown stems of grass and throwing them like spears into the river.

Nothing happened.

Xiao Yen couldn't see anything moving, not fish nor birds, not even ants. It was worse than sitting in the Garden of Sweet Scents, waiting for Wang Tie-Tie. Then she remembered Wang Tie-Tie saying, "If you grasp opportunity as it passes, you don't need lucky dreams." Maybe she wasn't as lucky as Fat Fang had said.

What would happen when Master Wei came back and found her sitting looking at nothing? Xiao Yen didn't want her teacher to be angry at her. He was a good man. He rarely yelled at his students and he never beat them. Maybe she shouldn't test her luck. It didn't seem to be holding, anyway.

She stood up, brushed off the seat of her pants, and started walking again. Maybe her luck couldn't come on demand. It was good to know. She was lucky, but it wasn't something she could use for cheating. She was in school because of her skill, not because of her luck, no matter what Fat Fang said.

A trumpeting sound split the air.

Xiao Yen stopped. Only one bird made a call like that. She looked up and caught her breath. Seven cranes came out of the sunrise, heading straight for the marsh in front of her. The cranes rarely came this far inland, preferring to stick to the coast, where they were assured of water. She stayed as still as when holding a pose for Master Wei, hoping the birds wouldn't see her.

The birds landed in the marsh and the waters next to it. From the light brown spots on their backs, Xiao Yen could tell they were juveniles, less than a year old. They'd lose their baby feathers over the winter, becoming white like the adults by the spring mating season.

Xiao Yen took a few cautious steps forward. The birds acted boisterous, trumpeting, picking up floating grass and throwing it at each other, hopping in the air, challenging. Two birds on the side approached each other like marching soldiers, lifting their feet high out of the water with each step. Xiao Yen watched, entranced. They were so graceful, head flowing into neck, chest becoming wings, legs supporting the whole. She tried to pay attention to every detail, to how the spots broke up the straight lines of their backs, their vermilion crests, the gold in their eyes.

The two on the side began to dance, wings spread, leaping high into the air, throwing their heads back and trumpeting to the sky. Xiao Yen forced herself to stay still. She wanted to join them, to celebrate the morning and the river and the sunshine.

"Xiao Yen!" she heard behind her. The flock took off without glancing back. Xiao Yen's heart rose to her throat as she followed their flight. The cranes sliced through the air, heads and legs stretched out, like the living arrows of the hero Hou Yi, who'd shot down the ten suns when they'd threatened to burn up the earth, leaving behind just the two, the sun and the moon.

Xiao Yen turned around. Master Wei stood alone, his face also turned toward the sky. Without looking at her, he spoke.

"Legends say that for the first hundred years of a crane's life, it eats fish, small frogs, and other creatures of the water. For the next hundred years, it eats less and less. After the first five hundred years of its life, it stops eating earthly food altogether, and instead lives entirely on sunshine. A few hundred years after that, it joins the phoenix in its search for a just Emperor. Or"—he paused to look at Xiao Yen—"a man with a true heart."

Xiao Yen didn't know how to respond. Was Master Wei saying she had a true heart?

Master and student stood silently for a moment, the cranes no longer in sight.

"You were lucky to see them," Master Wei said. He turned and started walking up the river path again.

Xiao Yen followed. She *had* been lucky, but only

after she'd given up trying to be lucky. So was she in school just because of her luck? She couldn't ask Master Wei. It was too silly a question to contemplate. Yet . . .

Chapter 9

On the Trail

"Of course, you're welcome to spend the night with us. But, surely, you don't want to stay for longer than that. Your aunt is very sick," Young Lu repeated, as if that were the end of the conversation.

Xiao Yen replied again, "I must finish my duty before I can go home." She didn't know how long she'd need to find the rat dragon, and the hairpin, and Vakhtang; however, she was sure it'd take more than one day. She also didn't know what to say to convince her aunt, Young Lu, Wang Tie-Tie's youngest sister, to let her stay. Should she say something about Bei Xi? Would her aunt believe her?

In addition, Young Lu had made it clear that though Xiao Yen might be welcome, Udo was another matter. While Young Lu fed Xiao Yen tea and delicate fan-shaped cookies, Udo had to sit outside the hall like a servant. At least her aunt had agreed to have pillows and an umbrella fetched for him. Xiao Yen had told Udo her aunt was afraid of foreigners and had counseled patience. Udo hadn't seemed surprised. He'd obviously run into other people from the Middle Kingdom who disliked foreigners.

Young Lu poured another cup of tea for her guest. Young Lu entertained Xiao Yen in the formal, front building of their compound. It wasn't as fine as the

Hall of Politeness from Xiao Yen's home. It was smaller, older, and the windows had no lattice covers. Only a tiny altar sat in the corner, dedicated to Kuan Yin, the goddess of mercy. The low table Xiao Yen and Young Lu sat at was made of a dark heavy wood, uncarved but highly polished. A musty smell filled the room, mingling with the smell of flower incense. The teacups they drank from had splashes of orange, green, and yellow under a thick glaze, not fine, but artistically done.

"Tell me about Gan Ou's wedding," Young Lu said, changing subjects again.

Xiao Yen told her how Gan Ou had looked. She'd worn a headpiece of pearls and diamonds, at least as tall as Xiao Yen's hand, and her hair had spilled from it like a black curtain. Her skin had glowed like a peach in morning sunlight. The red silk of her dress was so delicate it floated in the slightest breeze. Wang Tie-Tie gave Gan Ou the finest gold torc Xiao Yen had ever seen, covered with endless knots, the ends fashioned into dragon heads. The firecrackers set off when Gan Ou left home would have scared even Xing Mou, king of the demons.

Xiao Yen had felt the same at Gan Ou's wedding as she did now. Her family had been happy to see her, but she'd still been an outsider, an embarrassment. Then, she'd been the sister who wasn't married, not even engaged. Now, she was the niece on a strange quest, traveling with a foreigner, not unwelcome, but not wanted either.

After they'd talked about the wedding, Xiao Yen told Young Lu stories of the rest of the family, of her mother and cousins and nieces and nephews. Young Lu seemed starved for news, and served her guest two pots of tea during their conversation.

When Xiao Yen brought up staying again, Young Lu had a servant fetch the latest letter from Wang Tie-Tie and made Xiao Yen read it. The letter said her aunt was very ill, bedridden, waiting for Xiao Yen's return.

Xiao Yen sighed. She couldn't return to her family right away. She had to fulfill her duty to Bei Xi. And to do that, she needed to stay in Khan Hua. She wanted to stay with her aunt. She didn't want to spend a night camped outside of the city. Too many of Vakhtang's soldiers—horsemen wearing the same stylized black horse that Gi Tang had—were around. Udo provoked attention, just because he was a foreigner. Xiao Yen wanted to hide him in Young Lu's house, out of sight of any officials or soldiers. It was better to avoid trouble than to invite it. She should have traveled with Ehran, who would have blended in better, but he was guarding Gi Tang, keeping the horseman tied up and out of the way until Udo and Xiao Yen returned. Ehran hadn't understood why he had to do this, why he and Udo couldn't just continue on their way to the seaport Khuangho. The brothers had fought, and in the end Ehran had agreed to their plan.

Xiao Yen also needed information about the city, about Vakhtang, about everything. Bei Xi said they would find him here. But where?

As they finished their fourth pot of tea, Xiao Yen realized Young Lu was content to sit, share stories, and not move for the rest of the afternoon. Young Lu hadn't invited Xiao Yen to see the rest of the compound, even though she was family.

Desperate, Xiao Yen decided to risk a question. Bei Xi had said that her little sister had had her own temples in the north, so she asked, "Have you ever heard of Jhr Bei?"

Young Lu looked startled. A servant entered, bringing fresh tea. Young Lu waved the servant away. "You want to go there, pray?" She slurred her words together, so that "there, pray" sounded like Jhr Bei.

"Yes," Xiao Yen answered, not sure what her aunt was up to. "There. Pray." She, too, ran the words together so they sounded like Jhr Bei.

Young Lu gazed across the table, not seeing anything for a moment. When she turned to Xiao Yen, her voice was normal, but she pressed her lips together tightly, as if holding back what she really wanted to say.

"My old bones won't make it to the dragon temple this afternoon, though I pray for release every day. But we have a small altar here. Come, niece. Let's pray together here, first."

Xiao Yen didn't know if there was any hidden meaning in her aunt's words, so she waited without saying anything while her aunt rose. Something was wrong with Young Lu's ankle. She depended on a plain wooden cane to walk. She'd been lame a long time—the head of her cane was polished smooth from handling—although Xiao Yen would bet that her aunt hadn't been born that way. Young Lu held her head high, as if she were still a coltish girl. Xiao Yen wondered what had happened to her aunt, if her deformity had something to do with the scandal surrounding her life, why she lived up north, so far away from the rest of the family. Fu Be Be wouldn't talk about it. Neither would Wang Tie-Tie.

Udo lay with his head touching the top stair and his feet almost stretched out to the bottom stair. He opened his eyes as Xiao Yen and Young Lu passed.

"Soon," Xiao Yen said, not wanting to pause.

Udo grunted and closed his eyes again.

Young Lu took Xiao Yen through the gate separating the formal front courtyard from the back. The family courtyard was much like the one Xiao Yen had grown up in, with low wooden houses built on stilts, leaning against the walls. Young Lu led her niece straight to her own bedroom. An altar holding a single ancestor tablet stood in the corner opposite the door. Xiao Yen guessed it was for Young Lu's husband, who had died only a year ago or so. Fresh flowers lay on the altar, still holding morning dewdrops—or were they tears?

A bed stood against the far wall of the room, heaped high with colorful quilts and furs. At the foot of the bed stood an elegant black-and-gold lacquered wardrobe with several village scenes painted on it.

Young Lu made Xiao Yen wait by the dressing table next to the door. Xiao Yen couldn't see beyond her aunt's skinny shoulders as she fiddled with something in the opposite corner. She heard a quiet click. Her aunt backed away carrying something. It took a moment for Xiao Yen to realize that her aunt didn't hold a part of the wall, but a painting that looked like the wall. Xiao Yen stepped closer, to see what her aunt had revealed.

A tiny shrine stood recessed into the wall. It was as well kept as the ancestor altar, with fresh flowers and a thimble of wine. An ancient wooden plaque stood at the back of the shrine. The paint on it had been worn away. Xiao Yen had to lean closer to see the faint outline that remained. It looked like a half-snake, half-human picture of Nü-gua, except the face had more definition in it, and the hair, instead of being bound up, was long and flowing.

Xiao Yen said aloud, "Jhr Bei."

Young Lu's eyes filled with tears. "You know." After another moment, she continued in a conversational tone. "It's forbidden to worship Our Lady. Or even to grieve for her, after that monster Vakhtang ate her soul. If anyone found out about this shrine, the soldiers would throw me into the pits beneath the governor's house. I'd never see daylight again."

Young Lu spoke without emotion, as if she were describing the market in the city. She genuflected in front of the altar again, then straightened up.

"I keep the shrine anyway. I offer respect, and beg for vengeance." Young Lu was a small bird of a woman, with thin bones and fine skin. Yet Xiao Yen still saw the strength that held her aunt together.

"Aunt," Xiao Yen said. "I'm here to—"

Young Lu interrupted. "I don't want to know your plans. If Vakhtang's soldiers capture me, I don't want to be able to give you away."

Xiao Yen doubted that a barbed whip could tear a whisper from Young Lu if she decided not to talk. However, she saw the wisdom in her aunt's decision.

"Udo and I need supplies. We're going to the rat dragon's cave first, then Vakhtang's."

"The foreigner? He's going with you?" Young Lu asked. She looked surprised.

Xiao Yen said, "He is. Jhr Bei's sister said he should."

Young Lu's eyes grew large, but her voice remained calm. "What I have is yours. I can tell you of the rat dragon's cave, of Vakhtang, his soldiers, anything."

"Thank you," Xiao Yen said. She bowed to her aunt.

"I should be the one thanking you," Young Lu replied, bowing even deeper.

That evening, Xiao Yen and Udo ate dinner privately in his room, separate from the rest of the household. Though Young Lu had told her servants that they'd be whipped and thrown out if they gossiped about their guests, she didn't know for certain if they'd hold their tongues. It was best to keep both Xiao Yen and Udo out of sight. Young Lu trusted her in-laws and the other members of the household a bit more, but there were many children, and who knew what they'd say without thinking, and to whom?

Just as Xiao Yen and Udo finished their dinner of rabbit and celery stew, Young Lu joined them. She brought a small bowl of dried apple pieces with her, to help her guests clear their palates.

"Apples!" Udo cried out when he saw them. He took the bowl from Young Lu without asking, then picked out one of the pieces and examined it.

Xiao Yen blushed at his rudeness. Though she'd wanted to eat dinner with the rest of the household, to be with family, she'd agreed to Young Lu's plan to stay out of sight. Now, she was glad she'd agreed. She'd traveled with Udo and the others for long enough that she'd forgotten how little the foreigners knew about manners. At least the room was dark, and the candlelight hid her blush a little.

Young Lu knelt down next to Xiao Yen at the low

table holding the remnants of their dinner, then reached over and patted her niece's hand. "I see that even with foreigners, men are still boys."

Xiao Yen nearly giggled. At least, Young Lu hadn't taken offense. And she was right. Udo did look younger, his eyes even rounder with delight as he tasted an apple piece.

"My family owns an orchard. We grow apples, and other fruits," Udo said. "I haven't seen many apples since I left. This one seems different from the ones we grow. The flesh is more firm, even when it's dried. The fruit is smaller too. Can you tell me anything about how apples are grown here?"

"What's he saying?" Young Lu asked.

"If I understand him right, his family grew apples on their land. I think he's comparing the apples, and wants to know more about these."

Young Lu was happy to explain. "These apples grow wild in the hills, just south and west of the city. We get the best of the crop. My youngest son-in-law has a friend whose cousin oversees the crop as it comes in. He always directs our cooks to the best sellers in the market."

Xiao Yen translated as best she could, though family connections were always difficult to describe.

"You don't grow them? You gather them?" Udo asked, incredulous. "Why would you do that?" The criticism was obvious in his voice.

Young Lu sat up primly when she heard Udo's reaction, the flickering candlelight casting stern shadows across her face. "Wild apples have more natural essences in them. They're better for you than those grown in an orchard. Though you shouldn't ever eat apples if you're sick. You might keep the sickness with you, because the word for 'sick' is so similar to the word for 'apple.' "

Xiao Yen struggled with the translation, trying to explain "essence" and "natural" with her limited vocabulary.

Udo shook his head when he understood, as if he

didn't quite believe it. "Apples are healthy for you. If you don't eat dried apples during the winter, your teeth grow loose."

Young Lu made a quiet comment to Xiao Yen about "uncivilized foreigner."

Udo replied with a quiet comment about "superstitious barbarians."

Xiao Yen didn't translate either.

After a moment's strained silence, Xiao Yen said, "Tell us about your home, Udo."

Udo glared at her for a moment, as if he resented her trying to end the argument. Xiao Yen suspected he was still upset with Young Lu for making him wait outside the Hall of Politeness that afternoon.

He picked up another apple piece. His expression softened. "The orchard was a magical place. I always thought so, at least. My gran told me stories of the special creatures that lived in the orchard, the *Elfe* and *Heinzelmaennchen* and such." At Xiao Yen's puzzled look, he said, "Creatures that aren't real, that exist only in stories. Like, well, like Bei Xi. Stories you hear about, but know aren't true."

"Bei Xi is true," Xiao Yen said. How could he not believe in the goddess, especially after he'd seen her? Xiao Yen herself was a mage. Did he not believe in her magic either?

"Until I started traveling, I didn't believe those stories. But now, who knows?" Udo paused, his eyes growing bright and childlike again. "The first magician we traveled with never let us watch him enchant that cloth. Sometimes I wondered if he actually did it, or if he'd just bought a bunch of magic rugs. But now I've traveled with a mage who lives and breathes magic." Udo paused and smiled softly at Xiao Yen.

The admiration and wonder in Udo's voice made Xiao Yen blush again. She thought of herself as a girl who sometimes performed magic, not as someone magical.

"I'll never think of magic in the same way," Udo continued. "I've even met someone you call a goddess.

We're going to go fight a dragon. Maybe the stories my gran told were true too."

Xiao Yen shrugged. She didn't know. Yet, how could magic not exist in the foreign world? That would be very strange indeed. It must exist, just not in the way it existed in the Middle Kingdom.

"Tell me about the dragon. How are we going to fight it? I'm going to need a sword and shield," he said, addressing Young Lu.

Xiao Yen had already grilled her aunt that afternoon for information about the dragon, so she summarized her knowledge for Udo.

"The dragon isn't really a proper dragon. It's a mindless beast, created by a foreign magician out of a rat."

Young Lu, not understanding Xiao Yen's words, started piling dishes up onto a carrying tray. Xiao Yen helped herd dishes across the table toward her aunt.

"Vakhtang suffers the beast's existence because it's a good guard of the western mountain passes for him. It knows enough to not hunt the people from Khan Hua, but, instead, harries the caravans and other people from the east. It also feeds on prisoners Vakhtang sends it sometimes. There's a huge pile of garbage outside the main entrance, so it's easy to find the place where it lives."

"If it's so easy to find, why hasn't someone killed it?" Udo asked, chewing another apple piece with relish.

"The mountain is easy to find. The dragon itself is harder. As a rat chews through wood, the rat dragon gnaws through rock. Men get lost in its tunnels and die of starvation before they reach the creature. Here, Aunt, let me help you."

Xiao Yen sprang to her feet as Young Lu started to rise. Xiao Yen took the tray with the dishes and put it on the front stair outside the door. Then she came back in and sat down again. She continued, saying, "The men who do find the beast say they can't harm it. Mages, too, have failed to kill it. No one in the city knows what will harm it. Bei Xi started to tell me what would, but she was distracted before she could finish. I'm sure she didn't mean to keep it a secret. She said, though, that the dragon could only be killed by words not written or spoken."

Udo snorted. "I can kill the dragon. That thing has never seen a man from my country before. You just need to get me a sword and shield. I'll do the rest."

Xiao Yen was speechless in the face of his arrogance. Did he really think that little of Bei Xi's warning? Of Young Lu's information? Of the people in Khan Hua who had died trying to kill the beast?

Young Lu sniffed with disdain. She didn't understand Udo's words, but his tone of voice conveyed his meaning clearly enough. She leaned over and said to Xiao Yen, "Are you sure you want to take him with you?"

"Even a foreigner's help is better than none," Xiao Yen replied, hoping that it would be true.

Young Lu pressed her lips together and said, "If you don't want him to go with you, we can lie about where you've gone when you go."

"Thank you, Aunt," Xiao Yen said, meaning it.

"Do we go after the dragon tomorrow morning?" Udo asked.

Xiao Yen translated, then replied, "I need to meditate on the puzzle Bei Xi gave me about the dragon before we go attack it. I don't want to go in without some kind of plan."

"I'm all the plan you need," Udo said, leaning away from the table.

Xiao Yen ignored him. She turned to her aunt and asked, "What more can you tell me about Vakhtang?" Xiao Yen hadn't asked many questions about Vakhtang. Though it was more important to stop him than to get to the rat dragon's cave, she felt that she didn't have to worry about him yet. She would be able to ask Young Lu more questions and make plans after she and Udo had the hairpin. Besides, Xiao Yen felt uneasy about what Bei Xi expected her to do to Vakhtang. Just one little scratch with the hairpin would dissolve the bubble around his heart. But would it kill him? Killing went against all Xiao Yen's Buddhist teachings. She wasn't sure she could kill a man, even with a small wound.

"He lives in the governor's compound. No one has seen the governor for months. It is said—"

"What's she saying?" Udo interrupted.

Xiao Yen kept ignoring him.

Young Lu continued. "He keeps a harem in the inner courtyard, some of Our Lady's temple attendants—"

"You're plotting against me. You're planning on attacking the dragon without me," Udo said. "All of you are alike. You think you're so superior. You don't think a foreigner can do anything. You think we're not human, not as good as you are. I'm tired of it. I'm tired of you!"

How dare Udo say such things aloud? A civilized person showed their manners to others, not their emotions. Xiao Yen's shame about Udo was matched by her shame about herself, because she had been thinking about leaving him behind.

Young Lu stood stiffly, not waiting for Xiao Yen to translate Udo's words. "Come, niece. Let's leave the important *lord* to his plans." She walked out the door, head held high.

Xiao Yen rose as well. She walked to the door, then turned back.

"My aunt and I talk about Vakhtang. Not the dragon."

Udo sneered at her. "But you had talked about leaving me behind."

Xiao Yen didn't deny it. "The dragon is not only problem. Vakhtang—"

"Is your problem. Not mine. I'm going to kill the dragon, and get its gold. Nothing more. Killing a lord in your country, well, as you've told me, I *am* a foreigner. I'd never make it back to my own land alive."

Xiao Yen opened her mouth, then closed it again.

How could Udo be so selfish? The dragon wasn't the important part of their duty. Vakhtang was. Without another word, she walked out the door.

A cool night breeze ruffled through her hair. Above the walls of the compound she could see the stars. Master Wei had told her that identical points of light shone on the other side of the world, above the foreigners. In spite of similarities like that, Xiao Yen was certain Udo had come from someplace quite unknowable.

The next morning, Xiao Yen rose early and went to the local dragon temple. It squatted on the southern edge of a lake, just to the west of Khan Hua. Thick red and blue clay tiles covered the curved roof, making it look twice as big as the rest of the building.

The altar inside the temple was a simple thin table against one wall, with a clawed silver cup filled with pure water that the dragon could use, should it decide to manifest itself.

Xiao Yen made her offering of incense and candles, then went outside to sit next to the lake. On the side nearest the city a group of screaming children played a game of ball. The object seemed to be to get as close to the water as possible without going in, and to make as much noise as possible while doing it. Xiao Yen went to the far side of the lake, away from the city and the children.

She thought about the different ways one could say words—singing, shouting, whispering—but she knew Bei Xi had meant something else. Another idea, something linked to Bei Xi, tugged at Xiao Yen, but she couldn't grasp it. If only Udo hadn't interrupted. Bei Xi would have told her. She hadn't meant it to be a mystery, Xiao Yen was certain. She rubbed the scar on her left hand and sighed.

Finally, she pushed all her thoughts away, closed her eyes, and transported herself to her quiet place, a place that existed in her mind alone, beside a fast-running river, the moss on the banks softer than any pillows. Gentle winds caressed her cheeks, and the silence covered her with silky feathers.

When Xiao Yen came back to the present, she opened her eyes and looked at the lake. While she'd had her eyes closed, an old man and a young boy had started fishing. The top of the old man's head was bald—only a few wisps of white hair clung valiantly to the edges. His head was the color of old wood, lovingly polished. He wore a simple black jacket with loose-fitting gray pants.

The young boy played by himself near the shore. He moved with a surety that told Xiao Yen he'd been walking for a couple of years, so maybe he was four or five. He built himself a pile of rocks next to the water's edge and talked to it in an authoritative tone. Every once in a while, he'd pick up a stone and carry it over for the old man to see. The old man would pat the boy's head, but he never said anything.

The old man was lucky that day. Every other time he put his line in the water, a fish jumped on it. Xiao Yen was impressed. Several fish hung on his line by the time Xiao Yen decided to leave. She was about to stand up when the old man made a cawing noise, like a crow. The boy looked up. The old man gestured for him to come over.

The old man held out his hand to the boy, silently asking for something. The boy undid a rope wrapped around his waist. The man tied a large, complicated knot at one end, followed by several simple knots. Then he tied a different knot, counted his fish, and tied that number of smaller knots.

Xiao Yen grew very still. She watched the old man repeat the process for a different variety of fish he'd caught. Chicken flesh covered her back and went down her arms.

It was so simple.

The god Fu Xi, Bei Xi's uncle, had given Xiao Yen's people writing many centuries ago. Before they'd received this gift, her people had still had writing.

They'd used knots. "Words neither spoken or written." Xiao Yen remembered the knots adorning Fu Xi's temple in Tan Yuan.

That was why Bei Xi had been so insistent that Xiao Yen learn the knot magic.

Xiao Yen wanted to shout with joy, to hear her voice echo over the water, to shake the dragon temple and wrap the old man and the young boy in warmth. Instead, she stood, bowed deeply to them, and started walking around the lake. She had to tell Udo.

First she stopped at the dragon temple and lit three more sticks of incense. Maybe her luck was returning. Then she raced through the crowded city.

The Lu family courtyard was quieter than the streets. The door to Udo's room stood open. Xiao Yen went in. A fat old serving woman was opening the shutters over the window.

"Where's Udo?" Xiao Yen asked. The servant looked blank, so Xiao Yen added, "The tall foreigner with hair the color of wheat?"

"Oh, miss," the servant said, bowing several times. "He's gone."

"Where did he go?" Xiao Yen asked, fearing that he'd offended Young Lu one too many times and had been asked to leave.

The servant waddled over to Xiao Yen and dropped her voice to a conspiratorial whisper. "He's gone to kill the rat dragon! Foreigners get into such strange moods, ah? No one can kill that dragon." She bowed her head again to Xiao Yen and walked out the door.

Xiao Yen's elation drained out of her. She should have realized that Udo didn't trust her, wouldn't wait for her, and that he'd do something stupid like this. Now she had to find him, as well as face the rat dragon alone.

Her luck hadn't changed. It was still bad.

Chapter 10

Bao Fang

Xiao Yen watched enviously as Fat Fang's cranes danced together in an intricate pattern on the table-top. If only she'd thought of that! He was certain to win the privilege of going into Bao Fang to see his family for five days. After being at school for four years, all trips into the city were a treat. At least, if he did win, he couldn't accuse her of having all the luck. Xiao Yen almost smiled at the thought.

Xiao Yen's single crane stood tall in the corner, watching the dancing birds with disdain, preening its feathers now and again. Its thin head seemed to float at the end of its graceful neck, its chest curved like an inviting cushion, and the edges of its wings trailed behind it, like phoenix's wings.

Neither of Fat Fang's cranes were as graceful as her crane. Their legs were as thin as a spider's; both had chest feathers that protruded instead of lying flat; and their wings were shaped like sharp knives instead of graceful plumes. Plus, they were the size of roosters, not full sized, like Xiao Yen's. On the other hand, there were two of them, and they interacted. Xiao Yen marveled at how well they danced together, weaving their necks faster and faster, wings spread out. They barely missed stepping on each other. It wasn't the kind of crane dance she'd seen out in the wild, but it was just as beautiful.

Fat Fang's eyebrows almost touched each other as he scowled in concentration. Once a creature was animated, and had received its instructions, it had a will of its own. Only on rare occasions could a mage influence it after that. Fat Fang continued to stare at his cranes, as if the force of his will kept them dancing.

Long Yen's crane was no longer in the hall. He'd gone first in the contest. He'd never had control of his creature. It had flown in frightened circles over the courtyard before it had escaped. Determination now filled his usually happy face. He concentrated on Fat Fang, as if trying to wrest the secret of the two interacting birds from him by thought alone.

Xiao Yen's crane flapped its wings once, as if trying to get her attention. She looked over at it and sighed. She'd poured as much of her understanding of cranes as she could into her bird, filling its head with her observations of the birds. She'd let everything flow from herself into her crane, hoping to transfer enough essence that it would have its own life. It wouldn't have a soul, as it was only a created creature. It could only have a soul if Xiao Yen placed her own soul in it—and she had neither the ability nor the will to do that.

Her crane turned its head. Its dusky eyes bored into hers. Xiao Yen remembered watching the cranes dance by the river Quang in the golden morning sun. First one approached and bowed, then the other, like two officials meeting for the first time, each unsure of the other's rank. Then they'd thrown their heads back, proclaiming their delight to the flock. They'd leapt together, in celebration of the light and the water and the joy of being alive.

Now her crane tossed its head, as if beckoning her to join it. It moved its wings in a circular motion, fluffing its feathers, like a dancer stretching. It took two steps toward the table. Xiao Yen stood up, afraid that it might interfere with the other birds. She glanced over her shoulder at Master Wei. His whole attention was drawn to the birds dancing on the table. Xiao Yen walked to the corner.

The crane's eyes were at the same level as Xiao Yen's and held greater wisdom than Wang Tie-Tie's. Xiao Yen bowed to it, low. It bowed back, then leapt into the air. Xiao Yen's heart leapt with it. The crane snaked its head down and pecked at her feet, forcing her to lift one foot, then the other. The crane met her gaze again and raised its wings.

Xiao Yen hesitated. Master Wei wouldn't approve. Fat Fang was sure to tease her about it. The yearning in her crane's eyes tugged at Xiao Yen's heart. She bowed her head, lifted her arms in response, and joined her creation, dancing.

She didn't dance like the crane did. She didn't feel the beat it used. She moved her feet in time to her own sense of rhythm, swaying from side to side like the pine trees she'd observed, seeking grace. She wove her arms together, forming a ball, folding it and unfolding it into long strips of paper, echoing the poses Master Wei made them do every morning. The crane nodded its head in approval. For a moment, elation mingled with her sense of shame. She wasn't doing the right thing, but at least her creature approved.

The crane jumped and landed, then brought its wings close to its body and shuffled to its left. Xiao Yen moved as well, circling around so she stayed facing the crane.

As if it were part of the dance, the crane bent its head down to the table, snapped up one of Fat Fang's cranes, and tossed it out the open hall doors with a graceful flick of its head. It did the same to his other crane.

Xiao Yen froze. She held both her hands over her mouth, horrified. What would Master Wei think? She didn't dare meet his eyes. Where was her luck now? Her crane stepped forward, into their dance again. It snaked its head to either side of hers. Xiao Yen felt a slight sting on the back of her left hand, followed by the soft brush of feathers on her right.

Xiao Yen's cheeks flamed red with embarrassment. She flung her arms out, like a peasant woman shooing chickens. Her crane took a step backward, its gaze still locked on her eyes. Xiao Yen wished she could fly away and sport with clouds as white as her crane's wings. Maybe her crane understood her. It threw its head back, exalting, then with three hopping steps, leapt for the door and headed for the sky.

Xiao Yen turned around. Fat Fang had a surprised look on his face. Long Yen was smiling, and his eyes sparkled. Master Wei's face held no emotion that Xiao Yen could read. He indicated with his hands that she should proceed with the end of the ritual.

Xiao Yen walked to the table where her paper crane still stood. She picked it up with both hands, lifting the ashlike paper above her head, afraid her breath would disintegrate it. She carried it to the altar against the far wall.

Hanging above the altar was an ink drawing of the immortal Zhang Gua Lao, the patron of all paper mages. He sat backward on his white paper donkey, holding a peach in his hand. Tied to his back was his long bamboo fish drum. Under the painting stood a silver brazier, filled with sand and ashes and the remains of several dozen sticks of incense. Xiao Yen placed the paper figure in the center of the brazier, then took a lit candle standing on the altar and set the mundane remains of her creation on fire. This freed the crane essence, sending it heavenward, with the smoke.

She turned away, about to go sit down, then stopped. She reached back, put a finger in the ashes, then painted a dot in the center of her forehead, where her third eye was supposed to be, to show respect for her creation. Maybe she'd failed the test. Maybe her luck had failed her. Her crane hadn't failed her. She sat down, keeping her gaze on her hands in her lap, the wonder of her crane's dance vying with her shame.

Master Wei walked from the far corner where he'd been observing the contest to the opposite side of the table. "A unique performance," he said.

Xiao Yen's throat tightened and her stomach clenched. That was what Fu Be Be always said just before she punished Xiao Yen. "Unique" was a bad word, a brand of difference Xiao Yen had learned to hate. Her sister, Gan Ou, used it all the time to tease her.

"I think we can all agree that Xiao Yen deserves the prize," Master Wei continued.

"What . . . ?" Fat Fang stopped himself. It was acceptable to question the master; however, the questions had to be phrased properly.

"Excuse me, sir, but I don't understand why you say I won," Xiao Yen said, asking the question so Fat Fang wouldn't lose more face.

"There are three reasons why Xiao Yen should get the prize. Can any of you give me one of those reasons?" Master Wei said, his voice taking on its lesson tone.

Long Yen laughed and said, "I can. She tossed Fat Fang's birds out the door."

Xiao Yen kept her eyes on the table, still ashamed. How could that be a good thing? Fat Fang was her classmate.

Master Wei said, "That's right. She defeated the enemy, though I don't believe it was intentional. Xiao Yen passed more wild spirit to her creature than she contains herself." He paused for a moment, then said, "Xiao Yen."

She looked up.

"You must remember that outside this school, mages are enemies, people you will have to fight, or at least defend against. I've only encountered a handful of mages in all my life, but I've had to battle every one of them."

Xiao Yen bit her lip, but didn't respond. In the next phase of the school the students had to set their creatures against each other, to fight one another. Master Wei had already talked with Wang Tie-Tie about it. She'd approved. Fu Be Be had told Xiao Yen that fighting was bad. It wasn't a thing girls did.

"Fat Fang?" Master Wei asked.

The sullen boy didn't reply.

"No idea?" Master Wei continued. "The second reason is because the crane interacted with Xiao Yen. She's mundane, it is magic. Your cranes interacted with each other, which is good, but there's a tremendous difference between magic interacting with magic, versus magic interacting with the mundane."

"It doesn't count!" Fat Fang said.

Master Wei looked puzzled.

Fat Fang rushed to explain. "*She* created the creature. Maybe she had planned it, planned the dance, so *it* wasn't reacting to her, *she* was reacting to it!"

Master Wei pursed his lips. "That's possible, except for one thing. Xiao Yen's crane also reached the third, highest level. It affected the mundane world. Only the strongest mages can animate creatures like that. Xiao Yen transferred enough essence to give her creature its own, individual life force."

Master Wei reached out and took Xiao Yen's left hand in his, forcing her to look at it. A scratch with beaded blood went across the back of it. It didn't hurt. It took her a moment to realize where it had come from. When the crane had passed its head next to her cheeks. The remembered feeling of silk feathers.

Master Wei lifted Xiao Yen's hand, making her stand and walk to the altar. He dipped his fingers into the ashes and coated the cut. The stinging brought sudden tears to Xiao Yen's eyes.

Master Wei held her hand up and examined it. "I want you to cover that with cloth for ten days. You will develop a small scar on the back of your hand, a reminder of your first day as a paper mage."

Xiao Yen swallowed hard around the sudden lump

in her throat. Master Wei had only called them "students" before. He'd never referred to any of them as "mages." Amazement flooded through her, along with joy. She was sure her happiness was strong enough to carry her to the moon and beyond.

Xiao Yen had to knock at Master Wei's door a second time before he responded. She let herself in and looked around with curiosity. Though she'd been at the school for four years, she'd never been in Master Wei's private quarters before.

The room was attached to the back of the Hall of Receiving, as long as the hall but skinny. Shelves holding a menagerie of paper creatures filled one long wall: lions, bears, dragons, snakes, elephants, mice, horses, and creatures Xiao Yen couldn't name. Squeezed between the shelves were windows. In the far corner on the left sat Master Wei's bed. A small fireplace was set in the wall next to the head of the bed. Xiao Yen was envious—he must be warm in the winter, while her building caught every cold wind that came from the west. Closer to the door stood a large desk covered with piles of papers. Master Wei sat behind the desk, still reading.

When Master Wei looked up from his papers, his eyes bored into hers. Xiao Yen felt like dissolving under the intensity of his gaze. She knew he didn't like her to be timid though, so she folded her hands behind her back, stood up straight and said, "You asked me to come see you before I leave for Bao Fang, sir."

"What are you going to do when you graduate, Xiao Yen?" Master Wei asked, almost to himself. "Well?" he said after a moment's silence.

"Get hired as a paper mage?" Xiao Yen asked. That's what Wang Tie-Tie had told her she would do when she graduated. And anything Wang Tie-Tie wanted, she got.

"I wonder," Master Wei said. He stroked his thin

scholar's beard and leaned back in his chair. "Who will hire you?"

Xiao Yen replied, "I don't know, sir. But, my Wang Tie-Tie, she—"

Master Wei interrupted. "They say old ginger is the sharpest, but Wang Tie-Tie is sharper still. She's strong enough to browbeat anyone into doing her bidding. But will there be a second commission after the first? Or a third? Xiao Yen," he said, then hesitated. "We have to work on your fighting skills."

Xiao Yen blurted out, "Fu Be Be says girls shouldn't fight."

Master Wei replied, "Your mother doesn't think you should be here, does she?"

Xiao Yen pressed her lips together and didn't answer. Wang Tie-Tie always said to wear your broken arm inside your sleeve. Telling your problems to people outside your family never solved anything.

"Xiao Yen, what do you want to do?" Master Wei asked.

"To do my duty," she responded, as she'd been taught. She didn't see any other choice.

"Your duty to your family, Xiao Yen? Or your duty to yourself."

Master Wei didn't ask that as a question, so Xiao Yen didn't respond. Besides, weren't they the same thing?

"Listen," Master Wei instructed as he turned and looked out the window.

Xiao Yen listened. She couldn't hear anything. She knew Fat Fang, Long Yen, and some of the other students were playing ball in the other courtyard, but she couldn't hear them.

"The silence of this room is a great comfort," Master Wei said after a while. "Sometimes, it's a sorrow as well. Would you like to live in a room like this someday?" Master Wei turned back to Xiao Yen, leaning forward in his chair, his arms resting on his knees. "To be surrounded by your work, by your creations, with silence running like a clear stream through all your days? To shine like a light in a watchtower outside of town, outside of everything? Or do you want to be in the center, surrounded by your family and your descendants?"

Xiao Yen looked around Master Wei's room, at the hundreds of creations on his shelves, the small bed that would never be shared, the space that was his and his alone. The stillness in the room penetrated her bones and touched a responsive chord in her. The peacefulness attracted her more than it frightened her.

Xiao Yen solemnly faced Master Wei again. "Yes. I like the quiet."

Master Wei's eyes widened. He looked surprised. "I would think a girl would choose her family first, but then again, my sister would exchange places with me in an instant." He chuckled. "You don't remind me of her at all, though she's the reason why I decided to let any girls into the school at all. She's like black ice on a late winter morning. Everything slides off her, around her. Our mother wouldn't let her train with me. Though she was very good at the few things I showed her. . . ." Master Wei fell silent again and studied his student.

Xiao Yen's ears burned with embarrassment at the intimacies Master Wei shared, but she didn't squirm. Her time at the school had taught her how to be still.

"We need to work on your fighting skills," Master Wei repeated, turning from her and picking up a paper from his desk. "You're too trusting. Too nice. You felt bad about beating Fat Fang this afternoon, didn't you?"

Xiao Yen agreed, not meeting his eye.

"You shouldn't. You have more imagination than those two combined. You need to compete when you're in a contest. There has to be a winner, and it isn't wrong for you to win."

"But they're boys."

"So?"

Xiao Yen didn't know how to reply. Wasn't it obvious? As a girl, how could Xiao Yen hope to be better than her male classmates?

With a loud sigh, Master Wei leaned back, picked up a piece of paper from his desk, and handed it to Xiao Yen. The paper had been folded into a square, the center sealed with a bright red stamp. "Please give this to your aunt," he said.

Xiao Yen stood for a moment, unsure if he was finished. He no longer watched her, but stared at the ceiling. She bowed low and turned toward the door.

Master Wei called out after her. "Yes, they're boys. But you"—he paused—"are Xiao Yen."

Xiao Yen looked back over her shoulder. What did that mean?

Master Wei stood up and bowed to her, bending his gaunt frame almost in two, until he bowed to her like an equal. Xiao Yen bowed back, her spirits shooting toward the ceiling. When she straightened up, Master Wei gestured toward the door. Xiao Yen was dismissed.

She picked up her sack from outside the door and walked across the outer courtyard. What had her master meant? Of course, she was herself. She was also part of Wang Tie-Tie's family, a daughter and a sister. Even if she had a room like Master Wei's, she'd still have family.

Xiao Yen sighed and shook her head. It was too much to think about. Wang Tie-Tie would take care of her, see to her future, get her a good commission. She had no reason to worry.

Chapter II

On the Trail

The quality of the silence coming from the cave behind Xiao Yen made her shoulders tense. Every sound was muffled, indistinct, oppressed. The rat dragon slept somewhere in the tunnels of the hill she rested against. Udo had to be there, too, lost, maybe dead. Xiao Yen had to find him. But she couldn't get up. Not yet.

Xiao Yen took another deep breath, trying to breathe past the rising bubble of terror threatening to choke her. Her quiet place was impossible to reach, as if it had never existed. She even pushed down with her hands as she exhaled, seeking to push away her fear. Though her hands stayed steady, her fear remained. She had to go into the cave now, or she never would.

She made herself stand up. The shadow of the hill had grown since she'd sat down, stretching across the flat plain. Xiao Yen could see everything for many *li* in front of her. Nothing moved. Khan Hua lay on the horizon like an empty black bag a giant had dropped. Smells of rotting fruit, moldy cloth, wet fur, and urine rose from the garbage heap to her right. It looked as though a lazy maid had swept all the refuse from the tunnels out one of the holes, letting it collect at the foot of the hill. Young Lu had been right. It had been very easy to find this place. Xiao Yen was sure Udo had found it too.

Xiao Yen opened her pack. It bulged with a light-weight knotted fishing net. She pushed the net to one side and pulled out a paper lantern and a candle. The lantern had thin strips of bamboo along the sides and top to give it structure. The top pieces snapped in and out of place, allowing Xiao Yen to fold the lantern flat. She uncreased the paper where it had been folded, then she lit her candle and impaled it on a thorn placed at the bottom of the lantern. She had four candles in her pack; enough, she hoped, to get her through the cave.

Many sharp rocks covered the floor of the entrance to the cave. They bit into Xiao Yen's boots. She walked carefully and told herself it was like the time Master Wei had made his students walk on river rocks to release the energy in their feet. Her high-pitched giggle held so much hysteria she stopped again and checked her hands, holding them out in front of her. She couldn't see any trembling. She didn't want to look too long. She forced herself to move forward.

The wide cave entrance narrowed into a downward-sloping tunnel. Xiao Yen had to bend over, as if bowing to an equal, to avoid brushing her head against the roof. The light from Xiao Yen's lantern didn't extend beyond her feet. She placed her free hand against the tunnel's sloping sides. There were too many protruding rocks for her fingers to glide across the wall as she walked. Instead, with every step, she deliberately put her hand out, like an old man placing his cane as he walked.

She walked as quietly as she could. Young Lu had told her there was a rumor that the rat dragon slept in the afternoon, but she didn't know for certain. Xiao Yen's heart jumped every time she dislodged a rock or made any sort of noise. She strained, listening for Udo, scared she'd hear scampering clawed feet. Only oppressive silence greeted her ears.

Soon the tunnel forked. Her aunt had said that

though there were many tunnels, finding the rat
dragon would be easy—Xiao Yen just had to follow
her nose. Getting out was another matter. She
wouldn't be able to smell fresh air until she was close
to the end of a tunnel, and even then, it might lead
to a sheer cliff. Xiao Yen knew she'd never keep right
and left straight in her head. Xiao Yen did know how
to memorize a series of paper-folding instructions.
When she turned and went down a tunnel to her right,
she made a mountain-fold in the imaginary creature
she built in her head. When she turned left, she made
a valley-fold. If she had more choices than that, she
did an inside-reverse fold, crimping the fold to adjust
for the tunnel order.

Finally the down-sloping tunnels opened up into a
larger tunnel. Xiao Yen stood up straight and eased
her back. She held her paper lantern above her head.
To her left, she sensed a wide open space, maybe a
cavern. She gratefully gulped down the fresh wind
blowing from that direction. To her right, the humid
animal smell was stronger than ever.

Xiao Yen took one slow step after another, her
heart thudding in her chest. She held her eyes open
wide, trying to see in the darkness. Her mouth dried
up. Though the arm holding the lantern was steady,
she trembled inside. The tunnel dead-ended in a round
room, with a large boulder to the left of the entrance.

The boulder moved.

Xiao Yen froze.

The boulder stayed in one place, but the top of it
moved up and down slightly.

It was breathing.

Xiao Yen forced herself to back up and stop. The
light continued to move. Xiao Yen didn't understand
what was happening until she looked at her lantern.

Her hand was shaking.

Xiao Yen placed the lantern on the ground and
drew the net out of her bag. It wouldn't hold a heavy
fish, but Xiao Yen hoped that, with the knot magic,
it would hold the rat dragon.

Xiao Yen needed to surround the rat dragon on all sides with the net. Luckily, the tunnel entrance the rat dragon slept behind wasn't that tall. She stood on her toes and threw one end of the net up, snagging it near the ceiling. She carefully hooked one edge of the net, then the other, on protruding rocks about waist height on either side of the opening. The bottom of the net dragged on the ground.

Xiao Yen closed her eyes and concentrated on shrinking the knots, turning the net gossamer and thin. Wind blew on her back from the large cavern, sending chicken flesh across her shoulders.

When she opened her eyes, two red orbs glared at her.

Xiao Yen heard herself say, "Oh!" She put her hand to her mouth and took a step back and to the side, away from her net. She made herself move slowly, controlling her urge to run.

The red orbs followed her. As the rat dragon pushed forward with its long snout, the net fell and draped itself across the rat dragon's back, reaching all the way to the floor behind the beast. The dragon took two more steps, bringing the front of the net underneath it. Xiao Yen released the illusion of thinness and worked its opposite. In her mind's eye, she saw the strings as ropes, thicker than her forearm, each knot as big as a melon, pressing down on the armor plates protecting the rat dragon's back. Irregular black, white, and brown bristles covered the armor, as lichen grew on rocks. Leatherlike wings pushed up against net, trying to lift it. The rat dragon twisted its long snout from one side to the other, biting at the ropes that appeared out of nowhere. The snapping jaws were within an arm's reach of Xiao Yen.

Xiao Yen raised her shaking lantern to find the edges of the net, where it flowed off the dragon's back and touched itself. She blended the adjacent ropes into one, forming a solid bag out of the long net. Then she pulled the knots tighter, shrank the spaces between them. The rat dragon twisted its head from side to side, but it couldn't get free. Its long golden whiskers pressed up against the sides of its snout. It lifted one horribly naked pink scaly foot, pushing at the net with yellowed claws. The net strained, but held. The rat dragon hissed at Xiao Yen. She found herself panting as if she'd just run many *li*.

Udo's voice suddenly called out from behind her. Xiao Yen felt a momentary relief. At least he was nearby, and not completely lost in the tunnels. The rat dragon's ears perked up, dried flaps of skin poking between the holes in the net. Its tail stuck out beyond the net, scaled and pink, like its feet.

Xiao Yen took a step back. She couldn't turn around and walk normally, exposing her back to this monster.

The rat dragon started gnawing the ropes.

The sound sent shivers up Xiao Yen's spine. It grated on her nerves, sawing across her calm. Long fangs ground together, biting at the illusion. Xiao Yen shuddered. The ropes wouldn't hold forever—sooner or later those teeth would sink into her skin. She had to find that hairpin. Fast.

Udo called again, calling for the rat dragon to come to him, challenging it. Xiao Yen couldn't let herself worry about his arrogance now. She backed up some more. She didn't turn around until the bulk of the rat dragon had disappeared into shadow and she could only see the two pinpoints of red light glaring at her. She had little time to find the hairpin, then to find Udo, and get away.

She walked toward the main cavern, stopping at each passage and peering into its dark entrance, even venturing a few steps down, trying to find the treasure room. Young Lu had heard stories about gold at the end of one of the tunnels. Xiao Yen assumed the hairpin would be there.

The sound of gnawing harassed her. Udo's calls irritated her. He was always shouting. Now he was going to get himself killed and it would be her fault for not protecting him, though he was the one being stupid, who'd left before they could make a solid plan.

Xiao Yen walked into the large cavern at the end of the tunnel. At the far end, two streaming pillars of sunlight came through holes in the ceiling. She looked away from them and waited for her night vision to return. The gnawing continued. It seemed closer now.

To her right was another passage. It held its own source of light. She almost didn't go down it, but she had to check every nook.

At the end of the passage, sitting in its own spot of sunlight, lay a treasure heap. Xiao Yen, blinded by the light, started walking straight to it.

The toes of her right foot touched air.

Xiao Yen threw herself backward, landing hard on her bottom and elbows, the breath temporarily knocked out of her. She crawled forward. A large chasm gaped between the edge of the tunnel and the treasure. Xiao Yen couldn't see the bottom of it. She dropped a pebble down the side, and heard it land before she'd counted to two. It wasn't that deep. She could possibly climb down. But how was she supposed to climb back up the other side? Even if she had ropes, she didn't know how to climb. Neither Wang Tie-Tie or Master Wei had made her learn that.

Xiao Yen stood again, held her lantern high, and examined the treasure pile. It was difficult to look at. The bright sunlight reflecting off the gold, silver, and jewels made her eyes water. On the left side of the pile she saw a protruding stick. If she squinted her eyes, she thought she saw a blue shadow.

Xiao Yen sat and thought for a moment. The gnawing tore at her concentration. The teeth were getting closer. She imagined the sound of the rat dragon's naked claws scrabbling against the hard rocks, coming to get her. That large rat, with its foul breath, desecrating her body, tearing it to pieces, so she would never have rest, but be tied to this plane forever.

That rat—Xiao Yen stopped. She took a deep

breath and pulled out a piece of paper from her bag. Then she started folding. The familiar actions helped her relax, letting her shoulders loosen and her breathing deepen and slow. She finished the piece reluctantly, pulling the long tail out from the body of the piece.

She kept the piece in her hands and looked deep into creases that represented its eyes. She pushed as much intelligence and cunning into her creature as she could, stolen from those few moments of staring into the red orbs of the rat dragon. She imagined its long golden whiskers shortened, stiffened, whitened; the long nose twitching, sniffing out the magic hairpin; the claws scraping on the rock, first going into the crevice, then up the other side; and finally, bringing the hairpin back to Xiao Yen.

When she opened her eyes, a brown rat stood there, resting on its rear paws, like a little man ready to do her bidding. She placed it on the ground gently. Without hesitation, it ran for the chasm and scrambled down the cliff. Though Xiao Yen listened hard, she couldn't hear it above the monotonous gnawing. Udo's cries were fainter as well. Xiao Yen hoped he was giving up and turning around, though she was afraid that if he got lost, she'd never be able to find him.

After what seemed like forever, her little rat climbed out of the chasm and ran to the treasure pile. It scrambled up the side where the hairpin stuck out of the pile like a column on the side of a mountain. The little animal pushed against the hairpin until it broke free from the surrounding jewels and skittered down the pile. The rat ran after it and picked up the hairpin in its mouth. The long pins attached to the gold leaf top dragged on the ground, even though the rat lifted its head high. It couldn't see as it walked, so it would take a few steps, put the hairpin down, then take a few more steps.

Xiao Yen silently urged it to go faster.

Finally, it reached the edge of the crevice. It put down the hairpin and walked to the lip of the ravine.

It looked down, then looked at the hairpin. It paused for a moment, then turned back to the hairpin and shoved it with its nose.

Xiao Yen called out, "Don't!" It was too late. The rat shoved the hairpin over the edge, letting it tumble to the bottom of the ravine. Then it scrambled over the edge.

How was she going to get the hairpin from the bottom of the crevice? Her little rat couldn't carry it. Gnawing teeth continued at her back.

Her rat scrambled up her side of the crevice, without the hairpin, as she knew it would. It shook its head at her, ran to the edge, then back to her. She knew the hairpin was at the bottom.

"I don't know how to get the pin," she said. The sound of her voice echoed in the tunnel, startling her. The rat sat still. Its whiskers bounced with its rapid breathing, and its tail swished against the rock.

Its broad, ropelike tail.

Xiao Yen indicated with her hand that the rat should go back down the cliff. She took out her practice string and looked at it. She concentrated, trying to see her rat's tail between her fingers. Gradually the image formed. It had short hairs on it, and dark rings at the thick end, stiff, barely bendable. Xiao Yen carefully placed a single knot in it, toward the end.

Xiao Yen listened as her creation came back up the cliff. The rat popped over the edge, dragging the hairpin after it, attached to its tail with a knot. Xiao Yen felt a glad smile tugging at her mouth, probably the first smile she'd had all day. When Xiao Yen touched the rat's tail, the knot undid itself. Without another sound, her rat scrambled down the cliff again.

The head of the hairpin was a gold phoenix, with a graceful neck and trailing wings. Its legs started thin and curved, but straightened out to form the two prongs that went into a woman's hair. Xiao Yen put the hairpin into her bag, then got out another candle. Her first had burned down to a stub. She replaced it, then used the stub to burn the remains of the paper rat. She closed her eyes, breathing in the silence, speeding the rat on its way to much more treasure.

Her eyes popped open.

Silence.

When had the gnawing sound stopped?

Xiao Yen stood up. She didn't want to be trapped in this tunnel, with no way out but down the crevice. She hurried back toward the big cavern, surrounded by darkness.

Two red points detached themselves from the darkness and came toward her.

Xiao Yen backed up, but she had nowhere to go. Remnants of the net clung to the beast's back. She had no cranes or tigers pre-folded to defend herself. She didn't even know if paper magic would work. Xiao Yen backed up until she was pushed against the rock. She closed her eyes and held herself still, dreading that first cold touch of its claws.

A whistling sound filled the air, followed by a sharp crack. Startled, Xiao Yen opened her eyes.

Udo had attacked the rat dragon.

The beast turned its back to her and faced the new threat.

Udo roared at the dragon. He held a curved saber in his right hand, and had a round shield buckled onto his left arm. They looked foreign. Maybe he'd taken them off one of the defeated men down here. Xiao Yen moved to one side, trying to get away from the fight. Udo roared again and pushed the rat dragon back. The armored plates around the neck and head of the rat dragon protected it from Udo's blows. Udo changed styles and, instead of swinging the saber, stabbed with it, trying to dig at the rat dragon's eyes, but he wasn't fast enough. The rat dragon moved its snout so quickly that Xiao Yen could barely follow it, snapping at Udo's sword with its long teeth.

Now the rat dragon pushed forward, trying to get under Udo's guard, to nip at his feet. Udo backed up, one slow step at a time. Then he pushed forward again. It was like a dance. Back and forth Udo and the rat dragon went, Udo yelling and hacking, the rat dragon growling deep in its throat.

A new sound came. Udo's panting. Xiao Yen watched carefully. Udo no longer swung the saber as high as he had. When he connected with the rat dragon, the sound was duller, the blows not as strong.

Udo yelled at the beast. Xiao Yen didn't understand the words, but she heard the frustration in his voice. He attacked again, pushing the rat dragon against some boulders. The rat dragon curled its tail around a column when Udo pushed it back.

Xiao Yen had an idea. If Udo could hold it there for just a moment . . .

She pulled her practice string out of her sleeve and untied the knot already in it. She closed her eyes and ran her fingers along the rope, feeling the smoothness of it, the hardness at the core of it, linking the string to the rat dragon's tail in her mind. Then she tied a slip knot in the string, so that if one end were pulled, the knot would tighten.

When she opened her eyes, she saw the magic had worked. The rat dragon's tail was tied around the column.

"Back up!" she called to Udo.

He didn't seem to hear her, but after a moment, he took a step backward. Then another step. The rat dragon tried to follow, but couldn't. It turned its back on Udo to see what held it.

Xiao Yen called to Udo, "Run!"

Udo hesitated, his saber held high. He smashed it down across the spine of the rat dragon, then he ran. The rat dragon let out a terrible howl, angry and high pitched. The sound raked across Xiao Yen's back teeth.

"Quick," she said as Udo joined her. She ran toward the tunnel from which she had come.

"The treasure?" he called.

Xiao Yen stopped and turned around. "Impossible," she said.

Udo swayed on his feet. The gnawing had started

again, but this time it was a deeper, more threatening sound, the sound of rocks being crushed between long rat teeth. Xiao Yen wanted to run, but she couldn't leave Udo behind. She tried to show him the situation with her hands. "Gold," she said, miming a large mound. "Deep hole," she indicated, next to it. "No bridge."

Udo nodded. He looked down at his saber and ground his teeth together. His jaw stuck out, as if a magician had cast a spell and turned it to granite. The muscles in his neck strained.

Xiao Yen walked back toward him, took his arm and said, "Run. Now."

Udo dropped his head, defeated. He allowed Xiao Yen to lead him back to the tunnel. The horrible gnawing from the rat dragon was soon muffled. Xiao Yen had to drop Udo's arm. The tunnel wasn't wide enough for them to walk side by side. She hurried as much as she could, pausing a few times as she reconstructed the folding instructions she'd memorized as she'd come in. She listened for the scrabbling of naked claws from behind, but all she heard was Udo stumbling over rocks as he followed. She held her lantern low so he could watch where she placed her feet. This time her hand never trembled.

Xiao Yen smelled the fresh air before she felt it blowing on her face. She heard a pattering sound as they stepped out of the tunnel into the cave entrance. She paused, then held up a hand to stop Udo.

"What is it?" he asked.

"Shh," she replied. The sound drew nearer. Xiao Yen pushed Udo against the wall, then flattened herself against the cold hard rock. "No move," she said. "No talk." Udo stayed silent. He must have seen the fear in her eyes.

A rush of wind came from deep in the mountain, pushed out by the fast-moving rat dragon. It appeared as a brown blur as it passed Xiao Yen and Udo. It didn't pause when it reached the top of the tunnel,

it raised its

reaching fo

again as it

And dow

The rat dr

the rock its

the beast fo

too late for

Its snout

the rat drag

shook, as if a

Yen heard s

her feet: the

tumbled back

tied there cr

its snout in t

sault down th

to the pile o

Udo shout

Xiao Yen

to kill the d

credit for it.

but hurled itself out the cave entrance, into the air.
Its batlike wings creaked as they spread out.

Xiao Yen's heart leapt as the dragon disappeared.
Had the dragon missed them? She walked to the entrance of the cave and looked out. "Oh, no!" she exclaimed. Her heart sank to her toes. They had been so close.

Udo asked, "What's the matter?"

"The plain," Xiao Yen responded. "It"—she moved her hands in frustration, one over the other, trying to show the shape of the plain, not remembering the foreign words—"Dragon can see us. No place to hide."

Udo stepped up to the mouth of the cave and looked out. He grunted and nodded. The flat plain offered no shelter from an airborne dragon.

"Look," he said. "What's wrong with the dragon?"

The rat dragon flew in an erratic path across the sky. It flapped its wings hard to gain height, then rocked back and forth, as if heavy winds buffeted it.

Xiao Yen pointed and said, "The tail!"

The rat dragon still had a large chunk of rock knotted into its tail.

Like a ship with a broken rudder, it couldn't steer.

The rat dragon acted as if it heard Xiao Yen, and aimed straight for the cave entrance where they stood. It issued a high-pitched scream that ran sharp nails down Xiao Yen's back. She stepped away from the edge, tugging at Udo's sleeve.

Udo didn't budge. He raised his saber and issued his own battle cry, harsh and guttural.

The rat dragon swung from side to side as it dived, but the swinging seemed to be controlled now. The rock-laden tail hung below it like a pendulum. The beast folded its wings closer to its body to give speed to its dive. The red glowing eyes fastened on Udo.

Xiao Yen put a hand up toward Udo, then dropped it again. She couldn't stop him or save him. She took a deep breath and waited to see Udo's fate.

Just before the rat dragon got to the cave entrance,

it raised its head and extended its wings, braking, reaching for Udo with its hind claws. It screamed again as it glided forward.

And down.

The rat dragon wasn't used to the extra weight from the rock its tail still held. While momentum carried the beast forward, the rock dragged it down. It was too late for the beast to compensate with its wings.

Its snout smashed next to Udo's feet. The rest of the rat dragon's body hit the hill hard. The ground shook, as if a small earthquake had just occurred. Xiao Yen heard several loud snaps as she tried to stay on her feet: the rat dragon's ribs breaking. Then the beast tumbled backward. Its tail came up, and the rock still tied there crashed into the rat dragon's face, snapping its snout in two. The rat dragon continued to somersault down the hill, and landed with a loud crash next to the pile of garbage. It didn't move again.

Udo shouted with joy, raising his saber in victory.

Xiao Yen wanted to laugh. He hadn't done anything to kill the dragon, but he was going to take all the credit for it. He was such a foreigner.

Chapter 12

∞

Bao Fang

"And Liang Ko Fu's family? They have a large house in Bao Fang, of course, but an even larger one in the capital. Its gardens are said to rival the Emperor's!" Gan Ou bragged.

"The harvest here wasn't too large, but down south, it was tremendous. I've doubled our contract for millet, and our profits too," said Wang Tie-Tie.

"Do you have enough blankets at night?" asked Fu Be Be.

Xiao Yen almost laughed. Though the dinner Wang Tie-Tie had ordered was supposedly in her honor, no one had let her say a word until now.

"I have plenty of blankets. I'm learning many things at school too. Master Wei is a good teacher."

A pained look crossed Fu Be Be's face. "Have some more *huo qiezi,*" she said, passing a plate of fried eggplant with fire sauce.

Xiao Yen sighed, depressed. Her family expected her to do well, to pass all her exams and excel at being a paper mage. Conversely, they acted ashamed of her attending school, and would never let her talk about it.

"What happened to your hand?" Fu Be Be asked.

Xiao Yen followed her mother's stare to her left hand, holding the plate. She knew she should minimize the importance of what the cloth covered, but she couldn't.

"Today, at the contest, my crane . . . well . . . we . . . uhm, interacted, and he pecked me." Xiao Yen didn't know how to explain the importance of the event.

Fu Be Be pulled back in horror. "Your creature attacked you?"

"No, Mother. It didn't attack me. It scarred me, marked me as a paper mage. Master Wei even called me a paper mage."

"No child of mine is going to have scars on her hands," Fu Be Be said, unwrapping the cloth bound around Xiao Yen's left hand. She gasped when she saw the ash covering the wound. She got up, pulling Xiao Yen with her.

"Mama, Master Wei said I should keep it covered for a week," Xiao Yen said.

Fu Be Be responded, "Proper ladies don't have scars on the backs of their hands. That's the sort of thing a superstitious peasant woman would do. You're going to have nice, beautiful hands."

Xiao Yen didn't argue. She didn't want to start one of their usual screaming fights. She wanted the time she spent with her family to be happy. She didn't see them very often. She let her mother clean her hand, put healing herbs on it, then bandage it again.

Xiao Yen also vowed to herself that she would reopen the cut and put more ash in it later that night. Her mother wouldn't know, and Xiao Yen could still have the scar marking her as a true paper mage.

"Did I show you the writing set my fiancé sent me?" Gan Ou asked Xiao Yen. Before Xiao Yen could reply, Gan Ou leapt off their shared bed and started rummaging under it. The three candles sitting on the window ledge behind her threw her shadow across the bed and up the wall.

Xiao Yen stretched, then lay down, across the bed, her head near the edge where Gan Ou sat. She grinned at her sister, though Gan Ou couldn't see it.

It was fun to see her sister so excited about something. Ladies never indulged in simple enthusiasm, so Gan Ou always pretended to not care as well.

Gan Ou dragged a large, off-white bundle of cloth from under the bed. The knotted cloth covered an eight-sided box, lacquered in an elegant, emerald-and-cherry colored design. The sides interwove at the corners, showing excellent craftsmanship. Gan Ou stood up and placed the box on the bed, next to Xiao Yen. Then she fetched one of the candles from the window.

Gan Ou handed Xiao Yen the candle so the older sister could lift the lid off the box with both hands. Nestled in luxurious crimson silk lay three brushes, lacquered like the box, with fine straight bristles. Next to the brushes lay a slab of ink so black it was like a solid piece of night. The ink stone, used for grinding and holding the ink, was just as black. A slim knife with a pearl handle, used for trimming the brushes, glittered in the light.

"Surely that ink stick is so fine that twelve tiny dragons will want to live in it, like in Wen Zhang's, the god of literature!" Xiao Yen proclaimed.

Gan Ou said, "I hope so." She sighed, and gazed for a moment at the contents of her writing set. Then she sighed again, put the snug-fitting cover on the box, and placed it back in the center of the cloth.

"Why do you keep such a fine gift under the bed? Why isn't it displayed on your table, or in the Hall of Receiving?" Xiao Yen asked.

"It's part of Wang Tie-Tie's strategy," Gan Ou said as she tied the final knot. "She won't let me display it until Ko Fu sends a more expensive bridal gift."

Xiao Yen had never heard such a tone in Gan Ou's voice; at least, not when talking about family. Normally, she reserved that disparaging tone for merchants. Xiao Yen peered at Gan Ou after she replaced the box, but the flickering candlelight made it difficult to see any details in her sister's face.

"Fu Be Be says Wang Tie-Tie is a miserly harpy, like old man Ti, that elder who wouldn't give any of his gold to help the goddess Nü-gua."

Xiao Yen was shocked. Fu Be Be and Wang Tie-Tie argued, often, but always in private. Neither Xiao Yen or Gan Ou were ever included. Puzzling over the content of their battles had been a source of more than one late-night conversation between the sisters.

"Did Wang Tie-Tie actually tell you that you should receive a more expensive bridal gift?" Xiao Yen asked.

"No. She just said this gift was inappropriate. He should have sent jewels or something, a gift just for me. She said the writing set was a selfish present. That he gave it to me to keep it in his family, not so that I might enjoy it. But I *would* enjoy it! I'm not some illiterate peasant who doesn't know how to write her own name. I compose poetry that even Fu Be Be says is good."

Xiao Yen weighed both sides of the argument. It was an expensive gift, well made and beautiful. She believed Wang Tie-Tie was right though. It wasn't appropriate for a young bride. Gan Ou should have something that was hers alone, not something an unscrupulous husband could "borrow" and never return.

"Wang Tie-Tie's just looking after your interests," Xiao Yen said, trying to smooth things out.

"No, she isn't. She only wants to protect *her* interests, to further *her* plans."

"That's not true," Xiao Yen replied. "She's looking out for the family."

Gan Ou snorted. "She isn't part of our family. She's our uncle's wife, not our mother's sister."

"She took us in when our father died," Xiao Yen pointed out.

Gan Ou looked away, then glanced back with a sly smile. "So, if she's looking out for us, tell me about the husband she's found for you. Tell me when you'll be meeting with the matchmaker."

Xiao Yen looked down. Her hands lay still in her lap. Master Wei had punished her often enough for fidgeting that she no longer did it. The silence grew tangible, dripping off the walls like wax dripping off the candles.

Gan Ou plucked at the bedspread. She started to say something, but stopped when Xiao Yen stared at her. Gan Ou bit her lip and wrung her hands, uncomfortable in the growing silence, while Xiao Yen took a deep breath and relaxed, her soul expanding in the familiar quiet. Gan Ou grew more agitated. Xiao Yen hid her smile. Finally, here was something she could do to tease Gan Ou.

Xiao Yen let the silence expand another few moments before she took pity on her sister and replied. "I don't know who Wang Tie-Tie has picked out for me to marry. Maybe no matchmaker has approached her, or will approach her, until after you're married. Or maybe she has someone in mind, but she hasn't told me yet. I've only been home for one evening. But I *know* Wang Tie-Tie has my best interests at heart."

Xiao Yen heard the lie even as she said it. Wang Tie-Tie *was* selfish. She wanted Xiao Yen in the paper mage school for her own reasons, not because it was best for Xiao Yen. "I must do my duty," she added, almost whispering.

Gan Ou emitted a harsh bark of laughter. "Your duty? Your duty is to your family, to your mother and me."

"Wang Tie-Tie is the head of our family," Xiao Yen said. "Every year she goes through the dedication ceremony and swears to follow the tenets listed in our family poem." Xiao Yen's most treasured possession at school was a scroll with two of the stanzas from the family poem written on it. Wang Tie-Tie had copied them for her. Xiao Yen marveled at the calligraphy every time she studied it. Though Xiao Yen could fold for hours without lowering her arms, her hand would never be as graceful as her aunt's.

Gan Ou shot a skeptical look at Xiao Yen and said, "You've always been naïve, little sister."

Xiao Yen was tempted to let the silence grow to

make Gan Ou uncomfortable again. Instead, she said, "I still wish you ten thousand happinesses for your upcoming wedding."

Gan Ou's smile made the room seem brighter. "Fu Be Be said Ko Fu is handsome, and his neighbors say he's kind. And he's smart too! He passed his civil exam on the first try."

"The first try! Really! You must be very proud of him," Xiao Yen said. "I passed my school exam on the first try," she added.

Gan Ou acted as if she hadn't heard Xiao Yen. "Ko Fu comes from a small family, but he says he wants many children, to make up for it."

Xiao Yen giggled with Gan Ou. They both knew what it took to achieve "many children."

"Fu Be Be said she knows a woman who had a cousin who married a woman who owned a magic pearl that—"

"That's impossible," Xiao Yen interrupted.

Gan Ou looked startled. A younger sister wasn't supposed to contradict her older sister like that.

Xiao Yen made herself continue. "Only artifacts can be made magic, not elements. Maybe this woman had a magic pearl ring or necklace. She couldn't have had just a magic pearl. That would take too much strength, too much energy from the mage when he'd made it."

"How would you know?" Gan Ou asked in her most annoyed older sister voice.

"I study magic," Xiao Yen said. "What do you think I do at school? We don't just sit around folding pretty flowers all day."

"Why can't, what, an element, be made magic?" Gan Ou asked, still challenging.

"Elements are more . . . permanent," Xiao Yen said, trying to use terms that Gan Ou would under-stand, and not talk in the manner Master Wei always did. "Artifacts are made, and can be unmade. Paper is an easy element to enchant, because it doesn't last. Cloth too. A ring, anything metal, is harder to make magic, because it lasts so long. It has a life all its own, so it takes a lot of a mage's strength, and energy, to make something like that magic. A mage might have to die to make something like a pearl magic." Xiao Yen paused. "Maybe that's what happened. Maybe a mage gave his life to enchant the pearl. Maybe that's why the pearl is magic," Xiao Yen ended, trying to mollify Gan Ou.

Silence crept back into the room. Xiao Yen tried again. "What was this magic pearl supposed to do?"

"It was supposed to help the woman have many sons," Gan Ou finally said, looking away.

"I will pray day and night that you have many sons," Xiao Yen said in the most pompous voice she could. "May you never have the bad fortune of having a daughter."

Gan Ou giggled, then continued in a more serious tone. "I have wished for at least one daughter too. 'Sons to protect you, daughters to warm your heart.' "

Xiao Yen reached out and held her sister's hand. Their mother had often quoted those words to them when their male cousins had teased them too much.

They smiled at each other for another moment, finally at peace.

Xiao Yen handed the candle to her sister, then climbed under the light cotton blanket and curled up on her side of the bed, closest to the wall. It was the coldest spot in the bed, so she, as the younger sister, always had to sleep there. Gan Ou placed the candle back on the window ledge, blew all three out, then climbed under the covers as well.

"Sweetest dreams of nothingness," Xiao Yen said.

"The same for you, dear heart," Gan Ou replied, part of their usual ritual.

Xiao Yen lay awake, listening to her sister's breathing grow slower, more even. She listened beyond the room as well, catching the unfolding silence, holding it to her like a second blanket. Funny how she needed the quiet now. She remembered when she'd first started at the paper mage school, more than four years before, and how she'd hated the stillness.

Xiao Yen drifted in the quiet, resolved to not think about her conflicting duties: to Wang Tie-Tie; to her mother; or even, as Master Wei pointed out, to herself.

As sleep came, Xiao Yen dreamed she danced with her crane again. She lifted one arm over her head, then the other, in a graceful imitation of flying. The crane jumped into the air, straight-legged, long toes pointed down. Xiao Yen jumped too, the happy jumps of a child, playing.

At one point the crane reached its long beak across the space dividing them. Xiao Yen thought it was going to peck her feet, but it picked up a figure that had been dancing, unnoticed, next to Xiao Yen. It flung the doll shape over its shoulder, much the same way her crane had flung Fat Fang's birds out the door that afternoon.

Xiao Yen tried to see whom the crane had flung. Had it been Wang Tie-Tie? Her mother? Some mysterious stranger she was supposed to marry?

It didn't matter. The dance went on.

Chapter 13

∽

On the Trail

Xiao Yen and Udo pushed through the crowd in the street gathered outside Young Lu's complex. The gate was open, but they couldn't see beyond the spirit wall. A broad peasant woman, with froglike eyes set almost on the sides of her face, stood with her mouth open, gaping. Xiao Yen asked her what had happened.

"The horse soldiers came. Looking for thieves," she said.

"Oh no," said Xiao Yen. She made her way to the gate.

"Wait!" Udo called from behind her.

Xiao Yen ignored him and hurried through.

No one stood in the outer, formal courtyard. The brass bells hanging under the eaves of the Hall of Ancestors rang with quiet sweet notes across the empty space. It seemed peaceful, but something wasn't right. Xiao Yen took a deep breath and it came to her. She couldn't smell incense. Young Lu always burned incense to honor her ancestors. She'd never let it go out unless something was terribly wrong.

Xiao Yen ran to the gate that separated the formal courtyard from the family compound. Udo stopped her before she could go through and asked, "Are you sure it's safe?"

Xiao Yen couldn't take the time to answer, to try

to explain. Maybe it wasn't safe. But Young Lu was family. Maybe Xiao Yen could help Vakhtang's soldiers find the thieves. She had to try.

The family courtyard was in chaos. Beds, wardrobes, dishes, clothes were scattered everywhere. No one seemed to be in charge. Soldiers—men wearing Vakhtang's badge, the stylized horse—stood clumped together. One group shared a jug of wine. Three soldiers came out of one of the buildings, carrying a heavy wardrobe between them. They heaved it out the door. When it hit the ground, it split and spilled its contents. A few soldiers cheered, and the group went back into the building.

Xiao Yen put her hands over her mouth, too shocked to say anything. What were the soldiers doing? Why were they destroying Young Lu's things? Where were the thieves? She backed up a step. These weren't good men. Udo had been right. It wasn't safe. Someone in the household had betrayed them.

A strong hand gripped her upper right arm. She heard Udo cursing and struggling. Xiao Yen looked back. A man with greasy hair leered at her. A scar streaked from his right eye to his lip. Two teeth were missing from the upper right side of his mouth, under the scar. He lifted the bag from her back and handed it to another soldier.

Xiao Yen forced herself to look away. Maybe if they didn't realize how important her bag was they wouldn't destroy everything inside of it. How would she recover the hairpin?

The man holding Udo struck him hard enough to make Udo drop to his knees. Udo's head lolled to one side before he straightened up. He didn't say anything more, but just glared at his captors. Then the soldier holding Xiao Yen yanked her arm, making her look forward.

Another of Vakhtang's soldiers, wearing a leather chest plate, walked across the courtyard toward her. He picked his teeth with a short knife as he walked. A group of men followed him, like an honor guard.

The soldier with the knife stopped in front of Xiao Yen, then looked her all over, pausing at her face, hands, and boots. Xiao Yen didn't struggle. She stood tall, and willed her gaze to be ice.

The soldier took his knife out of his mouth and called one of the honor guards to him. He said something in the man's ear. Xiao Yen listened hard, but he spoke too quietly for her to understand. The guard made a half-bow and rapidly walked away from the group. The man with the knife went back to picking his teeth and looking at Xiao Yen. Udo shouted, asking who he was, what they wanted. Xiao Yen stiffened when she heard the blow. Udo stopped asking questions.

The man with the knife continued to watch her with interest. Xiao Yen stared at the man's face, willing him to challenge her gaze. He wouldn't meet her eye. Was he afraid of her? Xiao Yen wasn't certain.

She stared so hard at the man with the knife she didn't see the guard return. She only looked up at Udo's gasp. Gi Tang, Bei Xi's guard, the one they'd left with Ehran, stood there. Xiao Yen glanced at him, then went back to staring at the man with the knife. Ten thousand questions fluttered inside her. How had Gi Tang escaped from Ehran? Where was Ehran? Was he hurt? Was he captured? And Young Lu? Had she been taken into custody because she was Xiao Yen's aunt? What about the rest of Young Lu's family?

"That's her," Gi Tang said. Xiao Yen continued to ignore him. She didn't want to show any fear.

The soldier that held her arm pulled it back, and grabbed her other arm as well. Rough rope slid across her wrists. Gi Tang stopped the soldier, saying something that Xiao Yen didn't catch in the horsemen's dialect, the language of the kingdom of Turic. Gi Tang looked around, then grabbed a peacock blue silk jacket from one of the broken wardrobes. He tore a strip off it and gestured for the man behind Xiao Yen to turn her around. They made her clasp her fingers together while they tied her wrists. They took a long while, tying many knots.

At any other time, Xiao Yen would have laughed. They took such care, as if she were some great mage, not a student, barely graduated, on her first commission.

They weren't as careful with Udo. His face had already bruised from where he'd been hit. The soldiers bent Udo's arms up behind his back when they tied them. It looked painful.

The soldiers circled Xiao Yen as they marched across the formal courtyard, around the spirit wall, and out the gate. The crowd shouted insults. What if Vakhtang killed her, and hung her body on the city walls like a common thief? Wang Tie-Tie would be so disappointed if word ever got to her of how Xiao Yen had died.

The crowd grew louder, and more bold, when they saw Udo. He was taller than everyone around him. Nothing could mask his foreign looks or hair. Xiao Yen shook her head. He didn't belong here, in the Middle Kingdom. At least the crowd wouldn't throw stones or rotten vegetables at him. He was too closely surrounded by soldiers. No one would risk accidentally hitting one of them.

Xiao Yen wished she could close her eyes and wake up in her quiet room at school. This wasn't a visit from Xi Mong, the bringer of nightmares. What was happening was real. She was going to have to face it.

The soldiers were taller than Xiao Yen was, so she couldn't look over their shoulders and see where they were going, but there was only one possible destination. She and Udo had never planned how they were going to get into the governor's compound to see Vakhtang. She had wanted to work that out with Young Lu once she and Udo had returned from the rat dragon's cave. They didn't have to worry about that now.

Xiao Yen tried to take deep breaths and stay in her center, but she was scared. More scared than she'd been in the rat dragon's cave. That beast would have just killed her. Men knew about torture. Plus, Vakhtang could suck the soul from her body, use her essence to make the bubble surrounding his heart stronger. There'd be no hope for rebirth for her until he was killed. Even the knowledge that she wouldn't have to kill him brought no respite.

The soldiers turned and led them off the street. The gate was wide enough for wagons to pass through. The spirit wall wasn't just painted; the dragon bulged out of it, as if breaking free, ready to attack. The gray courtyard stones fit so well against each other, it was like they were a single piece of rock. Nothing could escape between the cracks. The buildings, what little she could see of them, were all stone, not wood, with colorful murals covering the walls. Some even seemed to be two-stories tall.

They passed through two more courtyards and were about to go into a third when someone called out a command. The group stopped abruptly. The soldiers surrounding Xiao Yen stood up straight. Xiao Yen smelled their fear.

A soldier grabbed Xiao Yen's arms. Before she knew what was happening, he'd cut the cloth binding her. She brought her arms down to her sides, flexed her fingers and her toes. It surprised her how solid the ground felt beneath her feet with her hands freed.

A man approached them, followed by another group of soldiers. He asked a question. His voice rumbled like water falling down a mountain. Xiao Yen felt the power of the man coming from the inner gate, though she couldn't see him clearly. The soldier with the knife lost all his casualness. He called Gi Tang forward.

Even Gi Tang spoke with much respect. Xiao Yen blessed Bei Xi for teaching her something of the kingdom of Turic's language. She caught a few words. He said "Bao Fang," "trail," and "thief," pointing at Xiao Yen.

"I'm not a thief," she said loudly in her own language, drowning out the other man's words.

The soldiers around her froze like a cage of icicles.

The man with power laughed. The menace held in that gentle sound caved in Xiao Yen's stomach. The sweat in her mouth tasted stale. The soldiers in front of her parted.

A single man faced her. His dark brown eyes were like a greedy whirlpool, sucking in everything they saw. They stared at her above a thin, spiked nose. Deep lines ran from next to his nose around the ends of his mouth. A few long hairs—known as a scholar's beard—grew out of the bottom of his chin. His broad forehead had three furrows running the length of it, with matching lines running from the corners of his eyes; lines the sun had beaten into his face, lines that power ran along.

Xiao Yen had never met another mage before, besides Master Wei. She wished she didn't have to confront this one.

The man looked at her for a long moment.

Xiao Yen wondered if he'd understood her. She didn't meet his eye, but kept her gaze demurely unfocused.

"If you aren't a thief, what are you?" he said, the words rolling from him, wrapping around her like a wet tongue. He spoke the language of the Middle Kingdom with a thick accent, using formal terms.

Xiao Yen drew herself up straighter and replied, "I am Bei Xi's maid. This"—she paused and flicked a scorn-filled gaze at Gi Tang—"man?" She deliberately made it a question. "He made inappropriate suggestions. I refused. That is the only reason he's accusing me."

The man with power looked over his shoulder at Gi Tang.

"I do see the lust in his eyes," he said. "But," he added, turning back to Xiao Yen, "I still think you stole something from me."

Xiao Yen waited. He obviously wanted her to ask what she'd stolen. Gan Ou had played that game. Xiao Yen had learned how to not respond. She took a deep

breath, willing herself to be calm, and even smile at
the man challenging her. She drew strength from the
ensuing silence.

The man didn't seem disconcerted by the silence
either. After a while, he bowed his head to her, as if
in defeat, gave her a crooked smile, and said, "You've
stolen Bei Xi. You turned her into a snake."

Xiao Yen laughed as if she had no fear and replied,
"How could I turn someone into a snake? That would
take a great magician. I am small and powerless.
You're talking nonsense. Take me to Lord Vakhtang."

The man in front of her said something over his
shoulder, in the soldiers' language. The men behind
her laughed. Then he turned back to her and said, "I
am Lord Vakhtang."

"Excuse me, my lord. I didn't recog—"

Vakhtang held up one hand to stop her. He pulled
on his long beard hairs, considering. Then he raised
his head and sniffed the air between them. "You have
a delicious strength," he said. "I was told that Bei Xi
traveled with a woman who practiced magic."

Xiao Yen tried to turn her fear into anger. She spat on
the ground near Vakhtang's feet and took a step forward.
"Do I look like a grave-robbing Taoist?" she asked. She
held up one hand, sleeve drooping. With the other hand,
she pulled back the material, revealing her polished fin-
gernails. "Do these nails look like they muck around with
dyes and potions all day, searching for immortality?"

"No," Vakhtang replied. "But they might be the
hands of someone who works with paper and string."
He grabbed her wrists and caught them together with
just one hand. Then he held her arms up and delved
into her left sleeve.

Xiao Yen twisted and cried, "Let me go! How dare
you touch me!"

From inside the deep corner of her left sleeve he
pulled out a knotted piece of cord. He held it up before her eyes, dangling it like a hangman's noose.

Xiao Yen said desperately, "That isn't mine! Gi
Tang placed that in my sleeve!"

Vakhtang looked at the string, rubbing the amulet-sized knot between his fingers. He wrapped his hands around it, then closed his eyes. When he opened his hands, the illusion melted from the knot.

Xiao Yen swallowed with dread. It took strong magic to return something to its natural state. Master Wei could do it, of course, but she couldn't.

"Strip her," Vakhtang said in her language, stepping back and folding his arms over his chest. The men didn't need the words translated.

Xiao Yen lifted her head and tried to catch Vakhtang's eye, but she couldn't see over the shoulders of the guards surrounding her. She wanted to stare at him, have an anchor outside of herself, a physical thing on which to focus her anger.

The man with the knife came forward. He held the blade against her cheek, like a lover's hand. Xiao Yen closed her eyes. Her stomach dropped. She felt nauseous. The cold metal knife rested on the side of her neck, branding her with fear. The hard back of the knife pressed against her collarbone, then abruptly disappeared. The first frog of her outer garment snapped off. The men laughed, making a game of catching the flying buttons as they fell.

Xiao Yen shivered once, violently, as her robe was torn from her, exposing her breasts and thin waist. The men around her laughed, making jokes about her anatomy. Xiao Yen was glad she couldn't understand their language very well. No one had seen her this undressed, not even her mother, since she had been a little girl. Hands touched her, stroked her back, her sides, tweaked her nipples, making her jump, which made the men laugh more. She flinched with each touch.

Though Xiao Yen took short breaths, and her sides trembled, her arms were still. She sent whatever peace she could find, whatever part of her mind that wasn't screaming with fear, embarrassment, and rage into her fingers, her clever fingers, which would save her, get her revenge, later, if they could.

The cold knife rested against her belly, then slid

down, beneath the waist of her pants. She sucked in
her breath so the tip of the knife wouldn't cut her.
Xiao Yen was jerked forward as the man with the
knife tried to cut through the ties around her waist.
She heard someone cursing, harsh and guttural. Xiao
Yen shivered at the menace in his voice. He would
just as soon cut her as cut the pants. While he sawed
at the strong cord, someone said something in her
language: "Be careful. When she's presented to me,
she must be in one piece, still complete."

Xiao Yen's eyes snapped open. She would get another chance at Vakhtang? He stood behind the
guards, his face visible between their shoulders. Xiao
Yen stared at him, her hatred fanning to life, her fear
and her revulsion of taking another's life forgotten. If
she could change herself into a tiger, she'd leap over
the other men and claw his throat out in an instant.

"You will get your wish, little mage, and be presented before me, though not in the fashion you had
imagined. I like virgins. And I desire your strength.
But first, we have to temper your will, encourage you
to obey."

The fear returned, dropping like a weight against
Xiao Yen. Even if she had wings, she was so heavy
now she couldn't fly away. Vakhtang barked some or-
ders to the guards, then turned. Xiao Yen closed her
eyes again. She was naked, embarrassed, cold. She
didn't know where her aunt was, if she was in some
prison; what had happened to Ehran; or what they
were doing with Udo.

She shivered, striving to ignore the hands touching
her, desecrating her.

The worst was yet to come.

Xiao Yen had never seen a man's bone flute before,
let alone had one shoved into her face, her mouth.
She gagged, wanting to vomit, to force the men away.
She bit down without thinking. The man withdrew and
struck Xiao Yen across her cheek. Her vision darkened and blurred. She tasted blood in her mouth. No
one had ever hit her like that before.

She couldn't help herself. She started crying. Her tears shamed her as much as her nakedness.

A man shoved her arm up behind her back. Another forced her mouth open.

Xiao Yen tried to hang on, to exist without feeling. Then someone probed her back passage. Xiao Yen fled deep inside herself. She found her silence running through her like a sluggish river, clawed her way into it, and endured what she had to, kneeling on the cold dirt between the two courtyards. She stayed in her silence, a deeply buried seed, unconscious in a moving tide of filth. She no longer heard the men's jeers. She clung to herself, her core, and kept it apart from the atrocities being performed on her body. It was little consolation that her maidenhood wasn't being violated.

After a time she would never be able to measure, she heard, but did not hear, high-pitched scoldings coming from behind the wall of soldiers. She saw, but did not see, a young woman with bright red lips, dressed in a flimsy, emerald-colored robe that was improperly tied, who hit the soldiers with her folded fan. She felt, but did not feel, a woman with white braids, wearing a long silver robe, touch her arm and tug her to her feet. She heard, but didn't hear, the giggles and squeals of other women as she was led into one of the buildings at the back of the courtyard.

Many candles burned in the room, but Xiao Yen shied away from the light. Four women, dressed in bright indoor robes in all the colors of the rainbow, led her farther inside. A large copper tub, filled with warm water, waited on a cold tile floor.

First, the women bathed her standing up, outside of the tub, washing the dirt away from her knees, her palms, and back, soaping her and pouring warm water over her. They brought her a bucket that she vomited into. Then they led her to the tub, made her sit down, and scrubbed her all over, as if they knew how she felt.

Xiao Yen didn't try to understand what the women said to her. She let their words run together, like in a song. Maybe they were singing to her. She couldn't tell. The women ran their hands over her body while they washed her, as if trying to erase the pressure of those other hands. They brought her a musty-smelling tea, and held her head while she vomited again and again.

When Xiao Yen's fingertips were as wrinkled as an old farmer's face, the women dried her in a soft chamois cloth, wrapped her in a blanket, and led her to a bed. They directed Xiao Yen to lie down. Then a woman lay down on either side of her. They held her between them. At first, Xiao Yen squirmed and pushed them away. She didn't want anyone touching her. The women wouldn't go, or leave her alone.

Xiao Yen fled deeper into herself, building up her silence like thick walls. She didn't realize she was crying until she felt a tear fall off her nose and splash onto the pillow. She stayed detached, letting her eyes cry the tears she couldn't allow herself to feel. The women on either side of her didn't say anything, just held her and rocked her. Finally, she slept.

The women tried to interest Xiao Yen in the robes they chose for her, the food they brought to her, the music they played for her. Xiao Yen stayed locked in a small kernel, deeply buried in the pit of her belly. Her walls of silence were many *li* thick. She didn't count the days she stayed there, how many times the women bathed her, fed her, or dressed her. It could have been as few as three, or as many as all the days of her life.

She dreamed once of being a small girl in the Garden of Sweet Scents. She smelled the flowers and the incense, felt the warm sun on her skin, heard her cousins playing in the family courtyard. Then Wang Tie-Tie came and demanded that Xiao Yen tell a story. Xiao Yen tried, but every story she told disappointed

Wang Tie-Tie. No matter what Xiao Yen said, Wang Tie-Tie said it wasn't good enough, *she* wasn't good enough.

One afternoon, the women seemed agitated, like a flock of cranes about to migrate. They vibrated in their brilliant colors. The women explained to Xiao Yen that she was to be presented to Vakhtang. At this news, Xiao Yen felt a heavy weight press down upon her walls. She didn't let herself be bothered by it though. It was just one more thing to ignore.

Then the older woman with the white hair, braided like a crown, touched Xiao Yen's cheek, and said that she hoped Xiao Yen would come back from her evening, and stay with them.

Xiao Yen managed to chip a tiny crack through her silence and said, "I would like that too." Her voice was hoarse from disuse. She would like to be friends with this woman. Xiao Yen was certain this woman had been kind to her through the countless days. Thinking about being friends with her was easier than not thinking about what would happen that evening.

The woman with the white hair turned to two of the other women and argued with them for a moment. Xiao Yen didn't understand, didn't want to understand. She thought maybe she heard "Jhr Bei," but decided she was wrong.

The older woman won the argument and made Xiao Yen follow her. She led Xiao Yen to a small closet, holding buckets and brooms. The old woman had Xiao Yen stand in front of her. Both of them could barely fit. The woman rested her hands on Xiao Yen's head, then looked skyward for a while, lips mumbling. It slowly occurred to Xiao Yen that the woman was praying for her.

When the woman finished, she took Xiao Yen's right hand in her own, and made her reach out and touch the wall. A vague outline of a woman resting on a snake tail was sketched there. Xiao Yen opened her mouth to ask, but the older woman shook her head. Xiao Yen let the silence close back down around her.

The woman with the braids led Xiao Yen to a side room. Only two items filled the room: a low bench heaped with pillows, and an elegant wooden dressing table. Xiao Yen sat and looked straight ahead as different women applied makeup, eyeliner, rouge, and color for her lips. She traced the pattern of leaping fish edging the top of the table, losing herself in the design. The women continued to be gentle with her, flitting around the room like butterflies.

One woman came up from behind, took Xiao Yen's hair down, and began brushing it. Xiao Yen closed her eyes and let herself enjoy the sensual strokes. She *would* like to be friends with these women, if she survived her night with Vakhtang. Maybe, they could help her recover. She took a deep breath, her first in uncountable days. She let the air fill her belly, then expand upward, loosing her ribs. It felt good. She concentrated on her next breath, when the woman who had been brushing her hair, twisted it, pulling it sharply. Xiao Yen didn't open her eyes, but tried to breathe again. Then the woman behind her jabbed a hairpin into her hair, hard enough that it scraped Xiao Yen's scalp.

Xiao Yen opened her eyes and looked in the mirror.

Bei Xi stood behind her, holding a second, very familiar, hairpin in her hand.

Hope flared through Xiao Yen, like fire blossoming across dry prairie grass. Her legs twitched. Her fingers tingled as they came alive, all the knowledge of her years of study flooding back into them. The water she hid her full consciousness under drained away. She half turned to Bei Xi, to ask her how she'd gotten there, how she'd gotten the hairpin, what they needed to do now.

Bei Xi lifted a single finger to her lips, asking for Xiao Yen's silence.

Xiao Yen made herself turn back around, keeping

her movements languid. Bei Xi didn't want to be recognized, not yet. Xiao Yen still had to deal with Vakhtang by herself. A rush of vengeance swept through her.

She didn't feel the second hairpin going into her hair, but she felt the weight on her head. She looked in the mirror again. Bei Xi was gone. Xiao Yen nodded to herself, opened her eyes wide, and looked around the room. She yawned and stretched, as if she'd just come awake after a long sleep.

Then she began to plan.

Chapter 14

Bao Fang

Xiao Yen walked through the southern gate of Bao Fang as the early morning bells rang in the hour of the Dragon. The air still held a little of the evening cool, but the sun would soon bake it away. A man selling sweet steamed buns—Xiao Yen's favorite—called to her, but she hurried past. She didn't want to be late.

No one greeted her at the gate to her family's compound. They hadn't been expecting her. It was only by luck that she'd been able to come. In the competition for the privilege of going home, Fat Fang had won just the day before, and would be home for three days. However, during the night, most of the students had come down with a stomach sickness. Master Wei had canceled all classes.

Xiao Yen did, but didn't, want to go home that day. On the one hand, it was Wang Tie-Tie's birthday. The entire family, as well as many guests, would be there. Xiao Yen should be there too. On the other hand, Xiao Yen needed more time to study. There was always too much to do at school. Besides her own studies into the essence of nature and its creatures, she now had younger students to whom she taught basic folding. Plus, Xiao Yen feared the inevitable fight that she'd have with her mother.

The off-white tiles in the Yard of Greeting glittered. Old Gardener had sprinkled water mixed with oil around the courtyard. The quiet seeped into Xiao Yen's skin. She stood for a moment, admiring the solid nature of the Hall of Politeness. The dark wood, the shape of the building, made it seem like a hill, placed there by the King of Heaven, immovable, immutable. Xiao Yen wanted to stay and listen to the brass bells under the eaves tell their secrets, but she had other duties.

She stepped through the round moon gateway separating the formal courtyard from the family courtyard. Chaos reigned there. Servants hurried from one end to the other, carrying food and platters from the kitchen storage areas to the Garden of Sweet Scents. They also carried pillows, small tables, and trays loaded with wrapped packages from the storage rooms. Xiao Yen heard her mother yelling at one of the servants, then saw the woman scurrying out with an outfit, obviously the wrong one.

Xiao Yen slipped out of the courtyard into her old room. A pristine cover lay across her bed, three new candles sat in the holder on the windowsill. No one stayed in the room now. Gan Ou lived with her new husband. She'd already birthed one feisty son and was expecting her second child. Xiao Yen's cousin, Wang Tie-Tie's youngest son, had recently had a baby girl, who might inherit the room when the girl grew older. For now, it was saved for Xiao Yen on her infrequent visits.

Xiao Yen opened the dresser and pulled out a jacket her mother had given her on New Year's Day. It was made out of silk dyed the same orange as a setting sun in autumn, with golden bamboo circles sewn on it. Bamboo represented youth because toys were often made from it. It simultaneously represented old age, as the tree was an evergreen. It was the perfect symbol for a gift from a mother to her youngest child. Xiao Yen also liked it because paper was often made from bamboo, though she was certain

her mother hadn't thought of that when she'd had the
jacket made.

Xiao Yen slipped out of her school clothes, a simple
dark blue jacket with no embroidery, into the other
jacket. It fit tightly across her chest when she buttoned
it, and when she held her arms straight out in front
of her, the jacket pulled across her back and the
sleeves slid up to the middle of her forearms.

Xiao Yen sighed, hoping she could hide from Fu
Be Be how small the jacket had grown in half a year's
time. Her mother thought her daughter's muscles un-
seemly, and had commented more than once that Xiao
Yen resembled one of the boys who carried buckets
of water from the city well to the shops and temples.
Xiao Yen rolled her shoulders. She had to be strong
to do her magic, to hold her hands out in front of
her and fold for hours, her arms weaving, graceful,
supporting nimble fingers. She liked the way her muscles felt when she rubbed her hands over them. She
resolved to keep her arms close to her chest, folded,
and to try to not reach for anything.

Xiao Yen took a deep breath, catching at the silence
Master Wei had shown her, the one that lived deep
inside her. She glimpsed her quiet place—the river,
the bright sunlight, the verdant pines. She had an impulse to wrap it around her like armor. She laughed
at herself. What was she protecting herself from? She
was with her family. She should feel happy and safe.

She listened for a moment. The chaos in the courtyard continued. Xiao Yen couldn't hide any longer.
She hoped the guests might soften her mother's
tongue when she saw her youngest daughter. Xiao
Yen pulled a folded item out of her bag, tucked it
into her too-short sleeve, then opened the door just a
crack, and looked from side to side. She could still
hear her mother, but she didn't see her. Xiao Yen
sneaked around the courtyard, staying next to the
shadowed wall. She bowed her head as she passed the
hurrying servants.

Wang Tie-Tie's room stood on the sunny side of the

courtyard. One of her aunt's maids opened the door at Xiao Yen's knock and bowed to let Xiao Yen enter.

Wang Tie-Tie sat before her dressing table. The powder she applied to her face made her skin glow in the candlelight like a pink peony, but it couldn't hide the wrinkles lining her eyes and mouth.

Xiao Yen went to Wang Tie-Tie, knelt next to her feet, and placed her forehead on the cool floor. "Happy birthday, Wang Tie-Tie," she said. "May you have ten thousand more years to brighten all our lives." She reached into her sleeve. "Please accept this inadequate gift from your unworthy niece," she said, handing her aunt a beautifully folded peach made out of paper dyed an orange-yellow with red tinges.

"My dear Xiao Yen," Wang Tie-Tie said, accepting the gift. "I shall treasure this more than any other gift I receive today."

Xiao Yen had employed special folding techniques to make the peach seem round. The paper was so fine that when Wang Tie-Tie held the peach up to a candle, light streamed through it, making it glow like a little sun. Master Wei had ordered the paper for her from the Emperor's papermaker in Xian, the capital. A second piece, dyed green and folded into a serrated leaf, accented the peach-colored paper.

Wang Tie-Tie called over a maid and handed the gift to her. "Place this on the table of gifts, so all the guests may see it."

The maid bowed low and carried the peach in both hands, careful to not crush it.

Wang Tie-Tie took Xiao Yen's hand and looked at her. The skin on the back of Wang Tie-Tie's hand felt softer than the ermine fur Master Wei had brought in for the students to study. The bones underneath it were like winter twigs. Even in the dim light, Xiao Yen felt the intensity of Wang Tie-Tie's gaze. She stayed very still, as though she'd been transformed into a small creature under Master Wei's examining glass.

Finally Wang Tie-Tie turned to the remaining maid

and said, "Go fetch a pillow, you lazy thing. Xiao Yen shouldn't have to rest on the cold floor like a peasant." The maid winked at Xiao Yen as she hurried to the next room.

Wang Tie-Tie turned back to Xiao Yen, let go of her hand, and asked, "Are you doing well at school?"

"Master Wei's an excellent teacher. It's a privilege to study under him. Every day I learn more about nature and the creatures within it," Xiao Yen replied. Not even her aunt really wanted to hear what she did at school. Or how overwhelmed she felt.

Wang Tie-Tie continued peering at Xiao Yen as she said, "You'll need to study more. You need to learn about things beyond your paper folding. I'll send you some books. I expect you to do well in *all* your studies."

"I will, Aunt," Xiao Yen replied. She didn't let her despair show in her face. She was already drowning in work. What did it matter if her aunt poured a bucket of water on her head? She reminded herself that she was lucky to be at school, lucky to have such an aunt. Maybe she could sleep less. . . .

Wang Tie-Tie sucked in her breath, then asked, "How are the mock battles going? Are you doing better?"

Xiao Yen replied defensively, "I fold well. I'm the best at the school. Not just my creatures, but the way I do it. Master Wei says I follow nature in both my folding and in what I fold. I assist him in the beginning folding class."

Wang Tie-Tie smiled a very possessive smile. "You spent much time observing nature when you were a girl. I made sure of that. You've always been good at imagining. You could work harder, I'm sure. But your fighting. Master Wei said you had some problems."

"Maybe it isn't in my nature to fight," Xiao Yen said.

"You're *my* niece. You can fight, and win. And you will. Or do you want to shame your family?"

Xiao Yen looked down at her hands, sitting so still

on her knees. A knot formed in her throat, holding the tears Xiao Yen never dared to shed.

"My precious jade flower, my little sparrow," Wang Tie-Tie said, her voice now soft and gentle.

Xiao Yen looked up. Wang Tie-Tie rarely used this voice with her anymore.

"Do you think I don't know it's hard? So far from your family, every day with strangers, learning a difficult, demanding craft? But if jade isn't polished, it can't become a thing of use. And you want to become a priceless jewel, the star of your family, don't you?"

Xiao Yen felt her jacket strain as she took a deep breath. She looked beyond Wang Tie-Tie to the small altar dedicated to Zhang Gua Lao against the wall. In the twinkling candlelight, the immortal's eyes remained hard, as unimpressed as small black pebbles.

Wang Tie-Tie's voice grew harsher. "Don't you want to do your duty, your *xiao,* to your family?" Wang Tie-Tie asked this question of her almost every time they met.

Xiao Yen replied, "Yes, I do."

"And that is?" Wang Tie-Tie asked, the next phrase in their litany.

"To study hard, do well at school, and do great deeds," Xiao Yen replied by rote.

Wang Tie-Tie reached out, and with her soft, wrinkled fingertips, caressed Xiao Yen's cheek. "Old Zhang will notice you. You'll perform some great deed, and he'll offer to reward you."

Xiao Yen didn't know what to say. She never did.

She'd asked Master Wei about great deeds. He'd said they were most often performed in battle. Though there were rumors of raids by the horsemen who lived up north, against the villages that bordered their lands, there were no wars. The Middle Kingdom had been at peace for all of Xiao Yen's life. The Great Merchant route to the west was open. Foreigners and foreign goods poured into the capital every day. Where would Xiao Yen perform her great deed? Would she have to go to some frontier? The only fighting she ever heard about happened with bandits. Could she perform a great deed by fighting a bandit and his minions?

Wang Tie-Tie sat up, her backbone becoming like iron. She looked away, but kept her voice soft as she asked, as always, "And you'll remember your ancient Wang Tie-Tie, and everything she's done for you, won't you?"

Xiao Yen's words tumbled out of her mouth, "Of course, I'll remember you, Wang Tie-Tie. You've done so much for me. You've made everything possible for me. Of course, I will remember you if I meet Zhang Gua Lao."

Wang Tie-Tie sighed. She patted Xiao Yen's head and paused before she continued her line of the litany. "I'm so tired of this endless circle. I've been on this earth too many cycles. I want to leave this valley of tears, and watch over my descendants, and their descendants, and theirs as well."

Xiao Yen thought she saw the glitter of a tear in the candlelight. She looked down, and when she looked up again, the tear was gone. Maybe she'd just imagined it.

It took a moment for Xiao Yen's eyes to adjust to the sunlight when she stepped from Wang Tie-Tie's candlelit rooms. She knew she must go greet her mother. Before she could make herself do so, she heard Gan Ou call her name.

Xiao Yen hugged her sister, hard, then pulled back a little to examine her. Though Gan Ou's face had always been round, now it was rounder, like a melon about to burst. Her breasts had filled out, too, giving her a woman's curves. She felt more solid, more like Fu Be Be, and she smelled like sweet rice, roses, and musk.

"I'm pregnant again with another son," Gan Ou confided to her sister.

"A son? How wonderful!" Xiao Yen said. "How do you know?" she asked, curious.

Gan Ou replied, "I've prayed so many times at Jing Long's altar, it must be a son. Besides, another son would make Ko Fu so happy. I want many sons."

"No daughters?" Xiao Yen asked, puzzled. "No girls to warm your heart?"

Gan Ou pulled away from Xiao Yen, her mouth open in shock. "Why would I ever wish for a daughter? All she would do is cost money. After I had raised her to take care of our household, I'd have to give her away. Daughters aren't a good investment."

"I see," Xiao Yen said, but she didn't. What had made Gan Ou change? Her sister stood as a stranger before her.

Gan Ou wrapped one arm around Xiao Yen's shoulders and turned her toward the moon gate. "Come," she said in a conspiratorial tone. "Fu Be Be is still dressing. She doesn't need us. Let's go greet guests as they arrive at the Hall of Politeness."

Xiao Yen smiled. Maybe her sister hadn't changed that much. "Greeting guests" was an easy job, and the sisters had always vied for it. It was a good method for getting away from the turmoil of the family courtyard.

The sisters walked arm in arm to the Hall of Politeness and made themselves comfortable sitting on cushions on the front steps.

"Did Wang Tie-Tie tell you about the husband she's chosen for you?" Gan Ou asked.

"No, she didn't," Xiao Yen replied, guarded. "Do you know who he is?" she asked. She didn't think Wang Tie-Tie would choose a husband for her. Not yet. Not until after she'd done her duty.

Gan Ou shook her head in disgust. "There isn't a husband for you. It's so improper. Wang Tie-Tie says you have to finish school, and"—she dropped her voice—"work."

Xiao Yen shrugged. Though Wang Tie-Tie had never told her directly, she knew that it was expected of her.

"For foreigners," Gan Ou added.

Foreigners? Xiao Yen stopped herself before she

asked Gan Ou anything more. Maybe that was why Wang Tie-Tie wanted her to study additional things. Though looking for work with foreigners made sense. Very few from the Middle Kingdom would hire a girl for protection. Girls weren't supposed to fight.

Xiao Yen looked at Gan Ou. Her sister peered back at her. Gan Ou wore one of her sharp smiles, both predatory and confident in the kill.

"Of course, I will do my duty, go where the head of our household sends me, and make our family proud," Xiao Yen replied, trying to give her sister no excuse to pounce.

"Getting married and having many sons would make your *family* proud," Xiao Yen heard from behind her.

Both Gan Ou and Xiao Yen stood to greet their mother. Xiao Yen stayed bowed for a moment longer than her sister, searching unsuccessfully for a thread of stillness inside herself to hold on to, but it was like grasping at leaves frozen under ice.

The powder and the sunlight on Fu Be Be's face made it glow as white as the full moon. Lipstick the color of ripe cherries brightened her mouth, and her eyebrows were mere wisps, like the feelers of a butterfly, accenting her broad, intelligent forehead.

"Fu Be Be, you look so beautiful!" Xiao Yen exclaimed.

Her mother sniffed. "And you have more muscles than ever, I see. I can't keep buying you new jackets. Wang Tie-Tie says you don't need any fancy clothes while you're at school. *I* think you should dress better. And I *am* your mother."

Xiao Yen stayed silent.

"You have a duty to me as well," her mother said.

Xiao Yen knew better than to reply. She and Fu Be Be had had this fight as often as Wang Tie-Tie had told her to do something of merit, worthy of an immortal peach.

Fu Be Be turned away from the girls and walked toward the front gate. The first guests had arrived.

Xiao Yen glanced at Gan Ou, but she wouldn't meet
Xiao Yen's eye. Shoulder to shoulder, they stood,
greeting guests, but each was ten thousand *li* away.

Xiao Yen dropped to her knees the instant the servant announced Governor Fang had arrived. No one
had told her that the governor was coming to the
party. She stayed with her forehead on the cool
ground an extra moment, composing her face, wrapping it in stillness. She didn't want to be accused of
excess pride, though the governor had never visited
her family before.

When Xiao Yen had first started school, her family
hadn't been important enough to mix with the ruling
family in Bao Fang. Wang Tie-Tie had made their
family rich and improved their social standing since
then. Xiao Yen hadn't seen Bing Yu for years. She
hadn't been allowed to socialize with her friend because of her family's status. Maybe now, though, she
could.

Xiao Yen stayed kneeling while her mother was
presented to Governor Fang and his latest wife. He'd
brought five sons with him, including Fat Fang, and
three daughters, including Bing Yu, all dressed in fine
colorful silks.

The governor's servant introduced the children. His
voice didn't rise or lower as he spoke, as if he were
reading a list. Then the servant said in bored tones
that the Lady Fu could introduce her offspring to the
governor's wife. Xiao Yen stood and walked with Gan
Ou to be presented. She tugged at the sleeves of her
jacket, hoping they wouldn't appear too short.

The governor's wife stood a little taller than Fu Be
Be. Her face was just as beautifully painted, but nothing could hide the length of her jaw. The tiny thin
eyebrows painted in the middle of her forehead only
accentuated that her face wasn't round like a delicate
fruit, but long, like a horse's. Her eyes were large and
round, with irises like liquid night. They could have
been her best feature. Xiao Yen saw a spark of cruelty

deep within them, making them more terrible than all of Gan Ou's smiles.

Xiao Yen bowed low as she was presented. Bing Yu stood behind her mother, her face somber, though a smile kept flitting across her lips at seeing her friend. Fu Be Be explained that Gan Ou's husband was attending Wang Tie-Tie, and would be presented later. The governor's wife inclined her head indulgently. She turned away, then turned back, and called Fat Fang to her side.

He wore a sky-blue jacket that draped across his shoulders well, showing off their breadth, while at the same time hiding his belly. Embroidered carp and waves flowed across his chest and around his cuffs. His brown trousers were tied tightly around his calves, showing the muscles there as well. Fat Fang looked as handsome as a lord in the Emperor's court, though Xiao Yen would never tell him so.

Fu Be Be bowed low and said, "It's an honor to be presented to such a distinguished young man."

The governor's wife said, "*My* son will be responsible for guarding Bao Fang when he graduates from the paper folding school. The training *he* gets won't be wasted." With another nod, she walked past Fu Be Be toward the moon gate.

Xiao Yen glanced out of the corner of her eye at Fu Be Be. Her mother's face was calm, of course. She wouldn't overtly react to such an insidious insult. Xiao Yen knew better than to reassure her mother that Wang Tie-Tie would find work for her when she graduated, that her training wouldn't go to waste.

Wang Tie-Tie joined the party after everyone had arrived. She walked slowly to her place at the head of the garden, leaning on the arm of Old Gardener. The dark candlelit room where she'd first greeted Xiao Yen had hidden her age more effectively than the piles of makeup she now wore. The sunlight made her skin seem transparent, like thick paper. From the way she relied on Old Gardener, it was apparent she couldn't walk unaided. Her arm trembled when she raised her teacup, as if the slight exertion were too much effort.

The guests filed by one at a time to greet her, like dignitaries at court, their brightly colored silk robes and jackets moving like a living rainbow. Wang Tie-Tie exchanged extravagant compliments with the women on their children, and witty sallies and quips with the men. Everyone left smiling after their few moments with Wang Tie-Tie. She still had a brilliant mind, and was the star of the party.

After greeting Wang Tie-Tie, the guests spread out among the flowers in the Garden of Sweet Scents like flowers themselves. Xiao Yen waited until the latest group of guests had moved away from Wang Tie-Tie before she approached.

"Can I get you anything, Aunt?" she asked.

Wang Tie-Tie just shook her head, then said under her breath, "Maybe a little friendly company."

Xiao Yen looked hard at Wang Tie-Tie. Had she really just said what Xiao Yen thought she'd said?

Wang Tie-Tie reached out one soft hand and patted Xiao Yen's strong hand with it. "Don't mind me," she said. "At my age, sometimes people think you can't hear or see as well as you can. My legs may be going, but my mind isn't." She sighed, then continued. "Don't worry, little one. You'll grow used to their stares and whispers and ill-formed rumors. Because you have something you want more than their approval."

Wang Tie-Tie paused again. "I've been stared at, whispered about, ever since my husband went to the Heavenly Palace. I've been told to allow a man to take over our family's trading business. But I've persevered. As will you. We're different from them. We're not willing to float like a leaf on a stream, letting the current take us where it wills. We make our own way. Let them stare."

Xiao Yen didn't know what to say. To be stared at all her life? She drew in a sharp breath as the realization stung her. She would be. She was always going to be odd, outside her family, her society. She'd always thought she'd be able to combine her family with her magic, somehow. Now she realized she'd never have both. It was going to have to be one extreme or the other. Either Wang Tie-Tie or Fu Be Be. They couldn't both win.

And neither could Xiao Yen.

She was never going to be in the center of anything. She would always be an outsider, always on the edges, looking in. The inevitable lonely years crashed upon her like a cold ocean wave. Her luck couldn't save her from the life she saw. Nothing could.

Maybe Fu Be Be was right. Maybe Wang Tie-Tie wasn't doing the proper thing.

Xiao Yen pushed down on the thought, trying to drown it, but it bobbed to the surface again. Maybe Wang Tie-Tie was just being selfish. Maybe Xiao Yen should quit school, get married, and have the children her mother wanted.

It was the first time Xiao Yen had ever allowed herself to feel the doubts she'd had. Though she hated them, it was a relief to face them. She closed her eyes for a moment. There was no calm inside her, just a whirling mass of conflicting priorities.

"Xiao Yen!" Xiao Yen realized her mother had called her name, and it didn't sound like it was for the first time.

"Do some magic for us, Xiao Yen," she said.

Gan Ou repeated, "Some magic!" A few of the children also joined in.

Xiao Yen looked in horror at her mother. Do some magic for them? Like a sleight-of-hand trickster at the market who made scarves and coins disappear so children would laugh? Her magic was serious, for defense, not for entertainment. Did her mother take Xiao Yen's work as lightly as that?

Fu Be Be glared back at Xiao Yen. Prove your worth, was what she seemed to say.

Before Xiao Yen could respond, Wang Tie-Tie

raised her hand. "My niece is not going to perform for you. She had just come to me to excuse herself from the party. She needs to continue her studies."

Xiao Yen felt the strength flowing from Wang Tie-Tie, a warm protective curtain that her aunt tried to cover her niece with. Wang Tie-Tie's strength wasn't as certain as it had been, though. Fu Be Be had her own defenses. Wang Tie-Tie was aging, and sooner or later, Fu Be Be was going to wear Wang Tie-Tie down.

Maybe that wasn't as horrible as Xiao Yen had once thought it was.

Xiao Yen hurried through the crowd, leaving the garden, going to her own quiet room. She wrapped the silence around her like a soft shawl that let evening breezes through. Xiao Yen clutched her amulet, and wondered if she was that lucky after all.

Chapter 15

On the Trail

Xiao Yen walked back to the main room from the makeup room. She noticed for the first time that paintings of flowers covered all the walls, giving the impression of being in a garden, though there were no windows. Holders for candles stood everywhere, emanating soft light and heat. No wonder the women didn't wear jackets under their robes. Pillows and low tables filled the floor. Fans, scarves, flutes, mandolins, and more flowers and candles lay scattered across the tables. At least a dozen women sat around the room, talking, gossiping, or playing music.

Two more-properly dressed women stood to one side, listening to the woman with the braids, the one who had taken Xiao Yen to the picture of Jhr Bei. Three other women stood before them, silent. They wore clothes Xiao Yen saw as immodest, as well as more makeup and jewelry than the first group. It was obvious the first group talked about the second, debating something.

Xiao Yen went up to the woman with the braids. The women fell silent as she approached.

"Excuse me," Xiao Yen said. She cleared her throat. Her voice was still harsh from not being used. "May I speak with you a moment?" she asked the woman.

The woman bowed to the other women and walked a short way from them with Xiao Yen. Xiao Yen wanted to go back to the makeup room. Their conversation would be heard by everyone else here. No matter. Xiao Yen took a deep breath. She wasn't sure how to begin.

"I am called Kai Ju," said the woman, introducing herself with her informal name. "I'm glad to see you've found your tongue."

Xiao Yen smiled, and said, "I'm called Xiao Yen."

"Yes, we know. What would you like to say to me?"

"I, ah, I need your help."

"You need our help?" asked Kai Ju. "Our help with what?" Her smile held sadness and pity.

"I know how to free . . . Our Lady." Xiao Yen remembered Young Lu's reluctance to say Jhr Bei's name aloud. Young Lu had known that Vakhtang had subsumed the goddess. Xiao Yen hoped these women knew as well.

Kai Ju dismissed Xiao Yen with a wave of her hand. "Many of us know how to free Our Lady. But we must have something of hers to use against that coward, Vakhtang. Nothing survived his rampage after he . . . took her. Nothing," she said, her voice plain and stripped of hope.

"I have something of Our Lady's," Xiao Yen said, pulling the hairpin free. Some of her hair fell from where it had been balanced on her head. She ignored her hair and held the hairpin up for Kai Ju to see.

Kai Ju looked from the hairpin to Xiao Yen's face. She laughed and shook her head. "Little one, you carried nothing with you when you arrived here."

"It's Our Lady's hairpin. I can't tell you how I got it. But it's hers."

Kai Ju laughed again. A mean tone flavored the edges of it. "All the women who pass through here are desperate. We're sorry, little one. But this is your fate. We helped you when we could. It is not worth our lives to help you more."

"Please," Xiao Yen said. She didn't know how to

continue. There must be some way to prove the hairpin was what she said it was. She held it above her hand. The flickering candlelight didn't cast strong shadows, so she couldn't show them the blueness of the hairpin's shadow. She glanced around the room. One of the three women—the women being judged, Xiao Yen was certain of it now—had a blue ribbon loosely tied around her long hair.

Xiao Yen walked over to the woman with the ribbon. "May I borrow this?" she asked.

The woman handed the ribbon to Xiao Yen, then followed her back over to where Kai Ju waited. The women Kai Ju had been talking with earlier also came over and circled the pair.

Xiao Yen didn't know if she could work any magic. She'd been trapped in her silence for so long, not practicing. But she had to try.

She tied a bowline in the ribbon, the same kind of knot she'd tied the first time she'd tried knot magic. When she tightened it, pulling on the hanging bit of ribbon while holding the rest with her other hand, she was left with a large loop, closed tightly with her knot.

Xiao Yen closed her eyes, ignoring the women around her, forgetting her past, her future, concentrating on the knot, and it alone. She followed the loops and twists in her mind, shrinking and tightening the knot, willing it to be what she saw.

The silence that lay inside Xiao Yen clawed at her awareness, calling her, wanting her to come back, to escape. That path looked so easy. To just give in.

Xiao Yen was not going to give in. She threw her anger now into the knot, the sickening feeling she got in her stomach when she thought about the rest of the days of her life. She didn't hear anything from the women who surrounded her. The mood of the room changed though. Xiao Yen opened her eyes.

In the center of her palm, connecting the two parts of blue ribbon, lay a hard black bead. The color disturbed Xiao Yen. Was she really that angry? She couldn't worry about it now.

Kai Ju picked up the ribbon and tugged at the bead. "Very nice," she said. "You've proven you have some magic. That doesn't prove anything else." Kai Ju stared at Xiao Yen, as if willing her to back down.

One of the women who had been in the group with Kai Ju took the bead from Kai Ju. She studied it, then said, "Kai Ju, you should . . ." She fell silent when Kai Ju held up her hand.

"The next step," Xiao Yen said, as if this was what she'd planned all along, "is to break it."

"That's not possible," said the woman holding the knot.

Xiao Yen smiled and motioned for the woman to continue. It was much better if the women learned about magic from one of their own.

"You can only change the form of something, not the essential essence," said the woman. "Not unless you drain your soul."

"Or you use something that has stronger magic," Xiao Yen countered.

The woman nodded. She looked again at Kai Ju, who stood with her arms crossed over her chest, standing in judgment over Xiao Yen.

"Please," said Xiao Yen, handing the woman the hairpin.

The woman examined the hairpin for a moment, then closed her fist around the head of it. She raised her arm above her head and struck the bead in her palm with force. A loud crack filled the air, like a clay pot breaking. The momentum of the blow carried the ribbon from the woman's hand. When it reached the floor, instead of being a single piece of ribbon, there lay three pieces, with jagged ends where it used to be connected.

"Now will you test it?" the woman asked Kai Ju, handing her the hairpin.

Test? There had to be another test? Xiao Yen trembled. What more would she be asked to do? She couldn't do any more magic. She felt as exhausted as after her first days of class. She wasn't certain that she could escape her silence another time.

"I didn't want to hope . . ." started Kai Ju. "Come with me," she told Xiao Yen, turning abruptly.

Xiao Yen followed Kai Ju to the closet containing the small picture of Jhr Bei. The other women crowded behind them.

Kai Ju stood in front of the picture for some moments, head down in prayer. Without turning around, she said, "If you have tricked us little one . . ." She let the threat hang in the air.

Xiao Yen shivered. The women themselves, of course, wouldn't do anything to her. But they might encourage the soldiers to take her again, and . . .

Xiao Yen was so involved in her own revulsion that it took the sound of the other women crying out to bring her back. Kai Ju had touched the picture of Jhr Bei with the hairpin. Light brighter than sunlight filled the small space, spilling out and blessing the women behind her. Xiao Yen was close enough to see that the picture had changed, growing as white as a snowy crane, and fully fleshed. The picture retreated to its normal colors and proportions as Kai Ju removed the hairpin.

Kai Ju turned around, tears streaming down her face. "We have hoped, for so long. . . ." She sank to her knees, her head bowed, and handed the hairpin to Xiao Yen with trembling arms.

Embarrassment filled Xiao Yen. This older woman shouldn't be paying respect to Xiao Yen like this. Xiao Yen took the hairpin, then took one of Kai Ju's arms and pulled on it, making Kai Ju stand.

The look of adoration from Kai Ju made Xiao Yen anxious. She laughed a little and offered the hairpin back to Kai Ju. A puzzled look filled the woman's face. Xiao Yen turned around and said, "I can't put the hairpin back properly by myself."

Xiao Yen felt her hair lifted off the back of her neck, gently twisted, balanced, then captured by the hairpin. "Thank you," Xiao Yen said, turning back to the older woman.

Kai Ju stared at Xiao Yen. "I was a priestess at the temple of Our Lady." Her voice was low, husky. "Vakhtang has kept me alive, a plaything, to watch the other women suffer, for more years than you could know. It's just so hard to have hope." She shook her head. "You said you needed our help. What can we do?" Her voice now sounded normal.

"I'd like information about my family, my aunt. And also about a golden-haired foreigner who was brought in at the same time I was. And if any other foreigners have been brought in as well."

Kai Ju walked back to the main room, the other women following her. She called two of the women sitting in the corner to her and talked to them quietly for a moment. The two hurried from the room. "What else?" she asked Xiao Yen.

"I must scratch Vakhtang with the hairpin, just break his skin." At least that's what Bei Xi had told her. "This may kill him," Xiao Yen said. She took a deep breath. When she'd been at school, thinking about her future, she'd imagined she'd battle her opponents in the same way she fought her classmates—creature against creature, not mage against mage.

Xiao Yen forced herself to continue. "It may not. It may only stop him, or put him to sleep, or something." It would only be a little scratch. And though Xiao Yen wanted vengeance for what Vakhtang had let his men do to her, she was hesitant to kill him. It wasn't right. "After—afterwards—if I'm still alive, is there some way to signal you?" Xiao Yen felt she had to concentrate on getting out of the room alive. It was her hope, the only thing that gave her the strength to go forward. She didn't want to count on Bei Xi rescuing her. The other women had to help.

"The third bell cord on the back wall will ring a bell in the kitchens," Kai Ju said. "Vakhtang uses it when he wants tea served in his room. We'll come and serve the tea. The soldiers won't count how many women go into the room. Or how many come out."

Xiao Yen said, "Good." If she managed to survive Vakhtang, if he didn't suck the soul out of her body, she had a way out. She needed to think about that, and not the coming battle.

"How do you plan to scratch Vakhtang?" Kai Ju asked.

This was the part of the plan that Xiao Yen felt most uncomfortable with. "I need to, or rather, he needs to . . . be . . . distracted." That was all she could say. She didn't want to think about what it was going to take to distract Vakhtang. She didn't want to give up her maidenhood to him. No one would marry her then—not that anyone would marry her now.

One of the improperly dressed women came up and put her arm over Xiao Yen's shoulder. Xiao Yen started. She didn't like to be touched, not since the soldiers had touched her.

"Men love swords," the woman said. "The longer the better." Some of the other women laughed.

Xiao Yen squirmed, uncomfortable. Why was this woman stating the obvious?

"You could ask him to teach you about men's swords, about fighting. It's worked for me before."

Xiao Yen didn't want to hear this. She didn't want to hear techniques for seducing men. She made herself listen though, because it might save her life.

"You could challenge him to a duel. You have two hairpins. You use one, and he gets the other. Just remember to laugh and smile, and not let the fight get too serious."

Xiao Yen caught her breath. She pulled away from the other woman and bowed deeply. "Thank you," she said. It might work. Xiao Yen knew nothing about flirting, while this woman obviously knew a lot.

The woman nodded her head in acknowledgment and walked away. Xiao Yen wondered if the woman had helped because she'd gained status that way. Or maybe it was to make up for something. She had been one of the three that Kai Ju and the others had been judging. Not all the women here were former temple attendants for Jhr Bei. Some were prostitutes.

Kai Ju turned to Xiao Yen. "I have one piece of advice for you, too, little one. As cruel as Vakhtang is, as powerful as he may seem, he is still scared. Now come. We must dress you for this evening."

Xiao Yen turned to see two women carrying a mock wedding dress. Xiao Yen bit down on her lips to prevent any tears. She was sure it was the closest thing to bridal clothes she'd ever wear. The red had a tinge of orange to it, like the color of maple leaves in the fall, not the happy red of a summer poppy. It didn't have a collar. Xiao Yen hadn't realized how long or white her neck was until she saw herself in a mirror. Though the dress hung over her hands and dropped over her feet, properly covering her, it was cleverly made and came undone with just three ties and two little hooks.

Another woman approached her with a veil. Before it covered Xiao Yen, the two women that Kai Ju had sent out came rushing back. They told her that Young Lu had escaped to her son-in-law's house, and he'd paid enough in bribes to keep her safe. Udo was held in another part of the compound, with other prisoners. They didn't know how badly the guards had tortured him. No other foreigners had been brought in, so Xiao Yen didn't know Ehran's fate.

Just as she didn't know her own. The women draped the veil over her head, her eyes. The details of the world disappeared. All Xiao Yen saw were vague shapes. She swallowed hard. Not being able to see clearly meant she had to rely on those around her. This wasn't a problem here, with the women, but what would happen when she was alone with Vakhtang? Xiao Yen took a deep breath and tried to calm her pounding heart, certain that everyone could hear it.

Xiao Yen's entourage gathered around her. Seven women—more than one hand's worth—hopefully enough to confuse the guards. Xiao Yen tried to keep her hands still under her long sleeves, but she found herself clenching and unclenching her fists. She willed herself to be calm, her fingers to be still. Inside, she still trembled.

Xiao Yen heard guards call out a challenge, and the party came to a halt. She ignored the dark laughter that came from the men, laughter that raised chicken flesh across her shoulders and down her spine. One of the guards reached out and started lifting her veil. Xiao Yen closed her eyes. She would not see them, would not admit them into her consciousness. Her river of silence stood ready to accept her, to drown her.

The women in the party shrieked in false fright and batted at the guard. A deep rumbling voice called out, echoing in the close corridor. Abruptly, silence filled the hall. Xiao Yen opened her eyes, but all she saw were outlines of figures.

The women led Xiao Yen to the center of a room. Out of the bottom of her veil she could see a low table and pillows heaped on the ground. The room seemed small, and had an odd, peaked ceiling. Vakhtang was just a blur of silver. He greeted the women and talked with them for a while. He laughed, a warm-hearted sound, and the women responded in kind. When he thanked them, he used formal terms, then bade them good night.

Xiao Yen stayed where she was, looking forward, while Vakhtang walked the women toward the door. She couldn't hear him return. The floor was padded, and he wore soft shoes, and he walked lightly. He circled Xiao Yen, like a cat circling its prey.

"Remove your veil," he ordered.

Xiao Yen lifted the veil above her head with two steady hands. Vakhtang took it from her, raising the elaborate headpiece straight up. He wore a long silver jacket over forest green pants, in a style looser than what Master Wei wore, more like a lord's holiday clothes. Xiao Yen was relieved that he wasn't wearing false wedding clothes like she was.

She took a closer look at his jacket. It had rivers of complicated knots flowing over it, sewn with white thread. Xiao Yen wanted to touch the knots, to study them, to see how they were made, and trace their rolling patterns. She tried to follow them with her eyes, but they kept shifting—magic, she realized. Each knot was linked to the next with tiny chains, covering the silk with protection. It was her own knot magic, being used against her.

"I'm glad you like my outfit," Vakhtang said in amusement.

Xiao Yen gasped and blushed. She sank to her knees, lowered her forehead to the ground, and said, "This unworthy person begs your forgiveness for not greeting you properly." Her cheeks burned with embarrassment and her hope landed in the pit of her stomach. How could she fight against someone protected by such magic?

"I forgive you," Vakhtang replied in a silky voice.

Xiao Yen felt her hope sink even lower. Power emanated from this man, more power than from Master Wei when he did his exercises.

Hard fingers grabbed Xiao Yen's chin and forced her to look up. Dark brown eyes sucked at her soul, greedy to possess her. Vakhtang's face was as tan as a farmer's, but he didn't have the laugh lines a farmer would.

Xiao Yen made herself smile and let the pressure from his hand raise her to her feet. He towered over her. She only reached his mid-chest. His arms were like round barrels underneath his jacket, straining the silk. She looked down and away from him.

Blankets, fur rugs, and pillows covered the entire floor, like in those forbidden stories Gan Ou had read to her. Long strips of cloth, muted reds and browns, hung from a hook in the ceiling and along the walls, hiding the straight lines of the room. They made the room seem smaller, like there was no place to hide.

Vakhtang followed Xiao Yen's wandering gaze. He

said, "I like to remember the tents I was born in when I'm in town."

He indicated with his hand that she should take a seat on the pillows next to the table. His tone of voice indicated that she shouldn't ask more about his birthplace.

Xiao Yen sat down, taking care to appear graceful, arranging her long skirts over her legs so the fabric draped nicely, as Bei Xi had taught her at a campsite many lifetimes ago.

Vakhtang took a seat on the other side of the table. He sat so his back wasn't facing the door. Though he had the bubble around his heart and was supposed to be invulnerable, he was still scared, just as Kai Ju had said. Maybe Xiao Yen could hope.

Xiao Yen smiled, and to hide it, looked down at the table. The dark top was carved and inlaid with two lighter-colored woods, making a pattern of fish jumping through waves. It was an older piece, the kind traditionally inherited from one generation to the next in a family. Xiao Yen wondered from whom Vakhtang had stolen it. A tea service sat on the table. The pot was made of plain red, baked mud, in the shape of a rooster, appropriate for a bachelor. The cups were made out of similar material, the handles in the shape of leaves and vines.

"Were you born near this town?" Xiao Yen asked as she poured two cups of tea.

"Yes, north and east of here," Vakhtang replied, his tone low and guarded.

"Have you been back to see your family?" Xiao Yen asked as she handed him a cup. She kept her head averted so he wouldn't notice her secrets.

The teacup grew heavy in her hand. The silence in the room coalesced. Xiao Yen turned her head so she could look at Vakhtang out of the corner of her eye. When her gaze touched him, he broke into laughter.

"You imp!" he said, pounding the cushions next to him with one hand while taking the proffered cup with

the other. "You knew I didn't want to talk about
seeing my village, but also that I needed to talk about
it. Are all paper mages trained as well as you?"

Xiao Yen picked up her own teacup and took a
calm sip, proud to see that her hands weren't shaking.
She didn't meet his eye, but did turn to face him. She
smiled demurely, hoping that was answer enough.

"Why do you ask about my family?" Vakhtang said,
swirling the tea in his cup and peering at her.

"I"—Xiao Yen paused, unsure if she should tell the
truth, but she forced herself to plunge on—"need to
please you."

She didn't add what she was truly thinking, "Or I
am quickly dead."

Instead, Xiao Yen said, "To do that, I must learn
about you. Wang Tie-Tie always said a man without
a past was like a tree without its roots, easily blown
over in any storm. You"—Xiao Yen paused again—
"aren't about to be blown down. So I asked about
where you were born, your family."

Vakhtang looked at her thoughtfully. "Is that really
why? Or haven't we tempered your will enough?
Maybe I should call the guards and let you play together again."

Xiao Yen hastily placed her cup on the table and
prostrated herself on the ground. She forced her hands
to show the trembling of her heart. "My only thought
was to please you, my lord. That is all."

Vakhtang snorted. The silence in the room grew.

Xiao Yen continued to make her hands shake. She
knew Vakhtang's threat was an idle one. He wouldn't
call the guards again. Kai Ju had been right, though
she didn't know the full extent of it. Vakhtang wasn't
just scared; his fears drove him. Because he was fear-
ful, he needed to be feared.

It was the key to his character.

Finally, Vakhtang said, "Rise, little mage. If you
need more tempering, I can do it myself."

Xiao Yen sat up slowly. She tried to mix the emotions on her face, to remain calm and yet show some

fear. She took care to not show any of the hope she felt. Vakhtang seemed satisfied.

Xiao Yen didn't know what to say now, whether to ask again about his family or to talk about something else. She took a sip of tea, letting her hands fall back into their natural, calm state. The silence continued. Finally it occurred to her what he wanted.

"What would you like to talk about, my lord?" she asked, giving him all the control he sought.

"My family." Vakhtang paused, then looked straight at Xiao Yen, his gaze drilling into her. "My family gave me this future. My father was chieftain of our tribe. My uncles taught me the art of war. My eldest aunt taught me of magic, of knots and fire and how to look through the skin of a man to see the strength of his soul."

Vakhtang paused again. "You have a delicious strength," he said. "There is so much more to you than meets the eye."

Xiao Yen laughed, the sound like a frightened bird breaking into the room. "I am a weak willow in your overpowering wind," she said. She needed to deflect the point of this conversation. "Tell me of your uncles."

Vakhtang smiled as he sipped his tea. "I wanted more than the tiny patch of ground we called ours. My uncles counseled tolerance. The hypocrites. So I took the village closest to us, killed the men and boys, made slaves of the women, and burned everything to the ground." He considered his teacup for a moment.

"My uncles opposed me. Said what I'd done was evil. But it wasn't, don't you agree? I'd done what they'd taught me. What's more, I'd done what they'd wanted to do, in their secret hearts, the ones they showed no one. I found that out when I took their souls." He sighed and shook his head, his eyes faraway.

Xiao Yen said the first thing that came to her mind. "Was it hard to take your uncles?"

Vakhtang laughed, a short bark that was almost a

cry. "Yes. It was. I had become"—he paused—"invulnerable, in my person. I needed their strength to help me stay that way. They were weak, too weak. It took too much of my energy to suck them dry. They had nothing left to give me at the end. They taught me to only use people with enough fire." He looked again at Xiao Yen, considering her.

Xiao Yen couldn't help her curiosity. "What is it like? To be invulnerable?"

Vakhtang smiled at her, like a master proud of his student. "Nothing can kill me, but I'm still not safe."

Xiao Yen nodded to herself. She'd been right. Fear drove Vakhtang, fear of death, fear of life, fear of everything unknown.

Vakhtang continued. "What would happen if someone captured me, made me a prisoner? I'd be trapped forever in some dungeon. Or worse, if I fell under a torturer's care?" Vakhtang's tone was bantering as he said these things.

Xiao Yen heard the undercurrent of terror running through his words.

"So I will secure my kingdom, controlling everything from one horizon to the other. I *will* be safe."

Xiao Yen breathed deeply to hide her shiver. He sounded so determined. How could you control everything? It went against nature.

"Tell me about your most important battle," she said. She had to keep his thoughts moving around, away from eating her soul, taking her strength too. There weren't enough souls in all the world to keep him safe, but he couldn't see that.

"That was the sword fight with Er Tso, the great general, who opposed my uniting the tribes. It lasted three days and two nights. People still tell tales of the night of the thundering ride, when I threw him from Mount Tang."

Xiao Yen had heard this tale too, but in Young Lu's version, the good general had refused to fight Vakhtang, accusing him of being evil and an unworthy opponent. So Vakhtang had had the general poisoned, then trampled to death by his own horses.

"Did you ever learn Wu Xu sword form?" she asked, naming the only form she'd ever heard of.

"Yes, with both one and two swords," Vakhtang said proudly.

Xiao Yen sighed. "I never learned how to use any weapons. I only ever learned the folding poses Master Wei taught us." She looked at Vakhtang, forcing hope into her voice. "Would you teach me how to use a sword?"

Vakhtang laughed. "I don't think I want to teach you how to fight."

Xiao Yen saw her opening. She lowered her eyes and looked back up at Vakhtang through her lashes, imitating how Bei Xi had looked at Ehran sometimes. "I don't know anything about men's swords," she said.

Vakhtang laughed again, throatier. He'd understood her meaning. "I'll show you," he said. "Come over to this side of the table."

Xiao Yen laughed, trying to keep her tone clear and light, like a young girl at a picnic. "No, silly. That wouldn't be fair. I'll stay on this side. Wang Tie-Tie always said the best way to learn is by doing." She pulled the two pins from her hair, letting it tumble down her back, and tossed one to Vakhtang, while she kept the other, the gold phoenix.

"Guard well!" Xiao Yen said as she flourished her hairpin. Then she reminded herself to smile. The phoenix was almost as big as her palm, and its beak poked into her flesh when she closed her hand around it. It felt awkwardly balanced.

A high-pitched, metal-against-metal sound occurred when the two hairpins came together. Vakhtang grinned. Xiao Yen laughed and said, "Well done! Well done." She brought her hand down, then bent her wrist back, like the Snake Striking Wall pose that Master Wei had taught her. Vakhtang was too quick for her, and parried her blow.

She tried another light blow from the same side, and again Vakhtang stopped her. Then he reversed his angle, and pricked her wrist with his hairpin.

"Good blow!" Xiao Yen said, forcing a laugh.

Vakhtang grunted, as if that was expected. He attacked again, first from one side, then the other, but slowly enough so that Xiao Yen could defend herself. He pushed his arm forward, forcing Xiao Yen to pull back, until she was defending herself almost in front of her chest.

Xiao Yen took a deep breath, breathing strength into her arms. She pushed her arm forward, now forcing Vakhtang to retreat. She tried to laugh. A squeak escaped. This was supposed to distract Vakhtang from subsuming her. He was far too serious. Now his defenses were up. He would think of her as a threat. The sound of metal on metal filled the air, a continual tinging, like from a copper shop.

The war spirit seemed to have possessed Vakhtang. His face was wiped clean of emotion. His eyes grew darker, large pools of black water, absorbing everything. His hand moved quickly, though in restricted motions. The white knots on his jacket expanded, growing closer together, in order to protect him from any blow.

Xiao Yen had to stop this. She was just going to have to distract Vakhtang that other way. She let Vakhtang push her back and hit her hand. The blow stung, and she dropped her hairpin.

"Oh, sir! You've beaten me," she said, lowering her eyes. "Will you come collect what you've won?" she continued, raising her head flirtatiously.

The stone held Vakhtang's face for another moment, then it broke apart. He grinned and said, "Come here, little mage."

Xiao Yen rose and walked around to his side of the table. Butterflies filled her stomach.

Vakhtang didn't rise. He reached up with one arm and grabbed hers, then pulled her down into his lap. "Oh, my sweet," he said, breathing into her neck.

Xiao Yen wrapped her right arm around his back. Vakhtang kissed her neck, nipping and lapping at it, like a cat with a fresh bone. She hated his touching her; she hated anyone touching her, but she would endure it. She turned her head away from him, hoping he couldn't feel the trembling at her core. He sucked at her neck now, pulling the skin into his mouth.

She felt herself rise out of her body, as if she watched from a great distance. Time slowed down. She watched how her left arm stretched out across the table, the long sleeve brushing first against her thigh, coming up to the edge of the table, over the top of the table. Then her small white hand peeked out from under the red silk, the scar on the top of her hand flashing in the candlelight while she retrieved the hairpin.

Like a log freed from where it was stuck in a river, slowly her arm turned and came back toward her body, back toward Vakhtang, the end of the hairpin leading the way. She used the hairpin on his neck as if she was carving the first stroke of her name in a tree. Just one small stroke. The skin barely tore. Xiao Yen watched the blood in fascination as it welled.

Then time speeded up. Vakhtang stopped kissing her and made a choked sound. Xiao Yen stood up, her heart beating in her bruised throat. She dropped the hairpin on the table. The metal ends hissed and dissolved, as if dipped in acid.

Vakhtang stayed seated and stared straight ahead, his hands flat on his chest, pushing against it. His dark eyes filled with fear. At first, the side of his neck pulsed, as though a great heart beat under the wound. Then the skin swelled and ripped, as if something crawled under it, pushing against the hole, trying to escape. Vakhtang tried to speak, but his throat had been pulled too tight. He made one last hoarse intake of breath. Blue crept into his face as he choked. Then he didn't make any noise at all. The sizzling hairpin was the only sound in the room.

A vivid blue liquid crowded out the blood of his

scratch, dripped down his neck, and stained his jacket. Vakhtang froze, then crashed down on the table, shattering a teacup. A soft sigh escaped and a scent like gardenias filled the room. It was similar to Bei Xi's scent, but sweeter, lighter.

Xiao Yen wanted to smile. Jhr Bei had escaped. She could now go to await rebirth.

While Xiao Yen stood in a tented room with a dead man.

Dogs barked outside. Xiao Yen heard the guards talking in the hall. She knew they wouldn't disturb their master for the sake of some broken pottery. They expected to hear sounds of violence.

She walked to the back wall and pulled the third cord.

Xiao Yen longed to run from the room. Instead, she forced herself to kneel at the end of the table, next to Vakhtang. Her knees felt as old as Wang Tie-Tie's. She arranged her gown over her legs, draping it in the most attractive way. Everything grew quiet. Xiao Yen folded her hands in her lap and listened to the silence death left in its wake. It had a different quality than a living silence: more was expected from it. Xiao Yen half expected Vakhtang to sit up, his face frozen in a grotesque grin.

He didn't move.

Xiao Yen sought her inner silence. She plunged deep into it, searching for a place where she didn't have to think, didn't have to feel. The river running through her calm place welcomed her, sucked her into itself, and held her.

She'd killed a man.

It didn't matter that Vakhtang had been evil, or that he'd ordered his soldiers to do unspeakable things to her. She'd killed him. She was no better than a foreigner or a barbarian. She didn't allow herself to think of Fu Be Be, or what she might say.

Dead silence in a cold river was all that was left to her.

Chapter 16

∾

Bao Fang

"When will you come home again?" Gan Ou said.

Xiao Yen felt both gratitude and despair at Gan Ou's question. Gratitude that she'd asked the question while they were alone, and not in front of Fu Be Be or Wang Tie-Tie. Despair, because she could only answer the form of the question, not the essence.

"I'll be home again when I win enough contests," Xiao Yen said.

"You mean you can't just come home when you want?" Gan Ou asked, incredulous.

"No. I have responsibilities at the school. I teach younger students to fold. And I have my own studies. All of us older students have much more work than time. So Master Wei makes us hold combats. After you win a number of them, you get to go home for a while. The person with the most losses takes your responsibilities while you're gone."

"You battle?" Gan Ou said, shock raising her tone until it was almost a shriek. "The men?"

Xiao Yen shrugged helplessly. It was a major part of her school training now. Someday, if Wang Tie-Tie could convince someone to hire Xiao Yen, it would be her job to defend property or people. Gan Ou and her mother would never understand, or accept a woman fighting.

Maybe they were right to be ashamed.

Xiao Yen pushed the thought aside.

Gan Ou stared at Xiao Yen for a moment, then deliberately turned her back on her younger sister and walked out of their old room. Xiao Yen closed her eyes, hoping that maybe by blocking the sight she could escape the pain.

No wonder she consistently lost contests for the first half moon or so after she visited her family.

"Guard well!" Xiao Yen called, using the traditional phrase Master Wei had taught them.

Fat Fang didn't reply. He stared into the small, egg-shaped arena that lay between them. The walls were wooden, about the length of Xiao Yen's arm. Each end of the oval pointed at a student. On Fat Fang's side lay a cherry-colored ribbon—the prize of their contest.

A short dog stood at Xiao Yen's end of the arena, golden brown along the flanks, mud brown around its head. It loomed over the scorpion waiting at the other end. The dog's left lip curled in a snarl. The short dark hair along the back of its neck stood straight up. The scorpion waved its tail at the dog, like a daring boy with a pendant. The dog lunged and snapped up the scorpion in its mouth.

Before the dog could bite down with its sharp canines, the scorpion flexed its tail and stung the dog on the side of its snout. The dog opened its mouth, letting the scorpion fall and scuttle back to the end it was protecting. The dog stood shaking its head, opening and closing its mouth.

A high-pitched twitter came from behind Xiao Yen. She jumped, then forced her shoulders down, taking a deep breath to squelch the flame of anger that surged through her. She had to admit the dog looked humorous standing there, working its jaw like that. That didn't give Bing Yu, Fat Fang's sister and her former friend, any right to laugh.

Xiao Yen took another deep breath and focused on

her dog again. It had to get beyond Fat Fang's scorpion to the ribbon, the prize the scorpion guarded. If her dog could just grab that ribbon, Xiao Yen would win a contest. She'd lost almost every contest the students had held for the last three moons, much longer than usual after coming back from visiting her family.

The dog stared at the scorpion, showing its teeth. It bunched up its hind legs, almost like a cat, then leapt at the scorpion. This time it got stung on its tender nose.

Again and again the dog attacked the scorpion, trying to get past Fat Fang's creation to the goal. Every time it was stung, beaten back.

The soft ding from the water clock indicating that the hour had passed brought Xiao Yen back to the room. She'd lost. Again.

She looked to where Master Wei stood at the end of the table, in front of the altar. He wore a long, dark blue robe, embroidered with circles of lucky white bats. His face was expressionless. Maybe, because she'd tried so hard, maybe, this time she would . . .

Master Wei turned his head and indicated that the contest had gone to Fat Fang. Xiao Yen watched with envy as Fat Fang took his paper creation up to the brazier on the altar and placed it on the fire, releasing whatever spirit he had captured with his folding and animating. Fat Fang smirked at her as he took his seat and picked up the prize ribbon. Then Xiao Yen burned the remains of her dog.

Xiao Yen heard a rustle of silk behind her, footsteps that approached, then stopped. She forced herself to turn around. Bing Yu stood there, looking as if she wanted to say something. She wore an iridescent robe of lavender silk, covered with a pattern of intertwining gold grapevines, representing wealth and fruitfulness. Between her petite nose and the paleness of her makeup, Bing Yu looked more like a perfect statue than a living person.

Xiao Yen bowed and said, "Thank you for watching

this unworthy person battle your successful and talented brother. Though we do not deserve the grace of your presence, I beg you to come again, and soon."

"Though this unmeritous person wouldn't presume to give you advice . . ." Bing Yu paused, turned her head to look at Fat Fang, then looked back at Xiao Yen out of the corner of her eye.

Xiao Yen said what was expected of her. "I would greatly appreciate any advice you may deign to give me. But you do not have to give advice to this undeserving person. Do not trouble yourself." Xiao Yen's voice went down on the last phrase, the ritual words turned personal. She couldn't win a contest. She wasn't a worthy mage.

"Come," Bing Yu said, slipping her hand into the crook of Xiao Yen's arm, like her sister Gan Ou did. "Let's go for a walk in the courtyard, and talk." She turned the pair of them and bowed to Master Wei, saying, "That is, if your esteemed master will allow us."

Master Wei said, "Please. I grant Xiao Yen permission to walk with you instead of watching the contest between Fat Fang and Long Yen."

Xiao Yen bowed low to hide her bristling, then turned with Bing Yu and walked out into the courtyard. Master Wei had found reasons for Xiao Yen to not watch the other students compete more than once. How would she learn if she couldn't observe them? Master Wei had told her to observe herself more. What did that mean?

Bing Yu asked after Xiao Yen's family as they walked across the sunny courtyard. Xiao Yen told her of Gan Ou's wedding, and that her sister was expecting again. Xiao Yen was careful to not mention that Gan Ou had taken to her bed. She'd lost the second child late in her pregnancy, and so was being extra careful this time.

Bing Yu, on hearing the name of Gan Ou's husband, exclaimed, "Oh! We're cousins now!" She looked meaningfully at Xiao Yen.

Xiao Yen replied politely, "Really?"

Bing Yu explained, at great length, how their families were related through a second cousin on her father's side. "This means that we'll never be *more* than cousins," Bing Yu finished with a pointed look at Xiao Yen.

Xiao Yen didn't understand what she was supposed to see.

Bing Yu sighed dramatically, like a heroine portrayed by a street performer, then tugged on Xiao Yen's arm, leading her to the far corner of the courtyard. She looked around, as if making sure they were alone. Finally she turned back to Xiao Yen. "Do you think Gan Ou, and the baby, will live?" Bing Yu asked, enunciating clearly, making each word a separate, hard spike.

Xiao Yen took a sharp breath, too shocked to speak. Of course, Wang Tie-Tie and Fu Be Be were worried. No one ever spoke of such things aloud. To say evil was to attract it to you.

Before she could recover, Bing Yu asked, "How about my brother, Fat Fang, eh? Do you ever want to 'hide the pearl' with him?"

Xiao Yen put her hand over her mouth. What could Bing Yu mean? She'd never . . .

Bing Yu inclined her head toward Xiao Yen. "Now you know how I felt when I saw you competing. Your attacks are as clumsy as my words. You're unbalanced. You have too much *yang,* not enough *yin.* You attack with aggression, head-on, like a man. You need to think more like a woman. You need to attack sideways, like a crab."

Xiao Yen pondered what Bing Yu had said. Was that what Master Wei had meant by learning from observing herself? Was that why she no longer won contests? The boys were coming more into themselves, becoming men. Xiao Yen had no one to guide her, no other women living at the school to help her, no one at home to talk with.

Xiao Yen stood still, feeling the solid tiles beneath

her feet, letting their cold seep through her soles, letting herself become stone. She created the best creatures of all the students in the school because she followed nature. She needed to tap into that same spring for her animations. Not to create better creatures, but to lend them part of her own spirit as well.

Bing Yu fluttered next to her, like a butterfly in a breeze. She didn't know quiet. She felt connections though, and thought sideways. Like meandering water, she always got to her goal, though sometimes through a seemingly backward course.

Xiao Yen bowed deeply to Bing Yu.

Bing Yu started to talk again, telling her things she'd heard in Bao Fang: of the rumor that the head priest at the White Temple had a new mistress; of the sighting of a gold dragon that would mean good crops that year; and of the rain that would or wouldn't come.

Xiao Yen listened, but didn't comment, trying to see where Bing Yu was leading, trying to think outside of the straight lines of boys and devils.

This time, a fat crab, twice the size of Xiao Yen's palm, faced Fat Fang's scorpion. It scuttled sideways toward the scorpion, then at the last minute, pivoted and slashed at the other creature. The scorpion stung the crab's hard shell to no avail. The crab pushed with its claw, trying to move the scorpion out of the way, seeking the ribbon. The scorpion gave some ground, then rushed forward again, its mandibles under the crab, lifting the crab up so only one set of its legs touched the ground. The scorpion pushed like an old man with a shovelful of dirt until the creatures were halfway across the arena.

When the crab got all of its legs on the ground again, it scuttled away from the prize, then with amazing speed changed direction and went straight for it. The scorpion barely got in front of it in time.

Back and forth they went, the crab approaching the scorpion and the prize from oblique angles, but always being repulsed at the last moment. It touched the ribbon once, but was pushed aside by the scorpion before it could grasp it.

Finally the scorpion got enough leverage and flipped the crab over onto its back. The crab struggled to right itself, but there was nothing for it to grab, nothing it could gain purchase on. The contest was over. The crab had been subverted.

Xiao Yen sighed as she watched the victorious Fat Fang fondle his latest prize. He had quite a collection in his room. As did Long Yen. Xiao Yen had a pitiful few. Why couldn't she animate a creature that could win?

She'd tried the boys' tactics, ramming straight ahead. That hadn't worked. She'd tried a woman's tactics, things that Wang Tie-Tie or Bing Yu or even Fu Be Be would have approved of. That hadn't helped either. What kind of tactics did she need for herself? What would work for her?

She reached up and rubbed her lucky amulet. If only she could call on her luck. But her luck only came when she wasn't expecting it, not when she counted on it.

Rubbing her amulet harder, it occurred to her to try to trick her luck. Pretend that she didn't need it. Xiao Yen took a deep breath and rolled her shoulders. She closed her eyes and thought about that first big contest, when she'd danced with her crane. How good it had felt to move to that unheard rhythm that had filled her head. The wonder of her crane's glorious flight as it leapt toward the sky. How proud she'd felt when Master Wei had first called her a paper mage.

Xiao Yen imagined her mind as a clear jade bowl. It filled with the essence of whatever creature she folded. Then she poured it out, poured all her thoughts and feelings and knowledge into her creation, leaving nothing behind. It was like a meadow, flooded with moonlight at night, with no traces of that silver light left in the morning.

Xiao Yen didn't notice what she'd folded until she'd

finished. She was a bit dismayed to find she'd folded a mouse. What good would a mouse do against the snake Fat Fang had folded?

Again, Xiao Yen turned her thoughts away from defeat, and toward happy times.

The contest was short. The mouse stayed shaking at Xiao Yen's end of the arena while the snake leisurely made its way across. Then, just before the snake struck, the mouse darted away, sprinting toward the other end. The snake couldn't glide back fast enough. Xiao Yen's mouse had the prize in its mouth before the snake returned.

Fat Fang huffed out loud at Xiao Yen's victory. He obviously hadn't expected her to win.

Master Wei congratulated Xiao Yen, saying, "You see? You just needed to find yourself."

Xiao Yen disagreed, but she didn't say anything. Though she'd been more relaxed, more herself, the real reason she'd won was because of her luck. She'd pretended she hadn't needed it, so it had come.

What would happen if she ever lost it?

Chapter 17

❧

On the Trail

Xiao Yen stayed swaddled in her silence. She didn't look up when the giggling women came into the room. Two stayed in the corridor with the soldiers. Once the door closed, the women's casual attitude disappeared. One pulled an under jacket; another, a pair of pants; and a third, an outer jacket from under their own clothes. Two others urged Xiao Yen up and stripped her "wedding" gown off before she'd realized what was happening. They concentrated on dressing her, not wasting a look at Vakhtang.

Xiao Yen rubbed the back of her left hand, hoping that some luck remained there.

Then they were out in the corridor, walking away. The guards were so involved with the women entertaining them that Xiao Yen wondered if they'd even seen the group leave the room.

The smell that greeted them in the women's quarters made Xiao Yen wrinkle her nose. She still swam deep inside herself. The silence she'd sought after Vakhtang's death wouldn't let any words slide out.

Kai Ju, her braids undone and her hair hanging loose down her back, bowed low to Xiao Yen as she entered the room.

Xiao Yen returned the bow. She'd done what she said she would do. How to live with it though? She turned to Kai Ju, curious about the smell, still unable to ask about it.

"Hope and miracles, little one. That's the smell of hope and miracles." Kai Ju laughed, a younger laugh than Xiao Yen had thought the older woman possessed. "Come," Kai Ju said. She led Xiao Yen to the baths.

There, Udo soaked in a tub. The sun had been taken from his hair. His skin was pale and sickly. The lines around his mouth held pain. Dark circles lay underneath his closed eyes and the lids were smudged, as if a child had drawn them on with charcoal.

Xiao Yen wanted to ask Kai Ju about Udo, but she couldn't force the words out of her deep waters. Kai Ju answered her as if she'd asked anyway.

"He appeared in our midst, cloaked from prying eyes by Our Lady. He's had some rough treatment. He was hung from his arms for a while. Then from his feet. But neither his shoulders or his hips were dislocated. He was made to roll in his own refuse, but he wouldn't eat it, so he was filthy, and starving, when he appeared. Our Lady instructed us to care for him." Kai Ju beamed at Udo, as if he were her own son. "If he can be rescued, a foreigner, then surely our own men can be too?"

Had Jhr Bei come back from the dead? Why would she rescue a foreigner first? The answer came before Kai Ju could continue. Bei Xi entered the bath chamber, her sweet perfume banishing the foul odor of the prison. Even Udo opened his eyes.

Xiao Yen turned, hoping for absolution from Bei Xi's lovely face. She wanted assurance that she'd done the right thing. She'd killed a man. Would he haunt her now? Must she burn incense night and day to appease his angry ghost?

Bei Xi's entrance prompted the women bathing Udo to get him out of the tub, dried, and clothed in a matter of moments. While they worked, Bei Xi instructed them in a low voice, building alibis for them. They hurried from the room. Finally she turned to Xiao Yen.

"Little Sister," she said, taking Xiao Yen's hands. "Can you ever forgive me? I would never have sent you had I known what was going to happen. I know that jade must be polished to become a thing of beauty, but even jade can crack. Please, please forgive me."

Silent tears rolled out of Xiao Yen's eyes. Of course, she forgave Bei Xi. It wasn't Bei Xi's fault that the guards made her . . . touched her . . . Xiao Yen pushed the thoughts away, sinking them deeper inside herself than where she'd been hiding.

Xiao Yen struggled to speak, to tell Bei Xi she was all right, but she stayed locked in her silence. She couldn't swim out of her river of calm. All her life, all her time at school, her silence had comforted her.

Now it threatened to drown her.

Bei Xi wrapped her hands around Xiao Yen's head and pulled it to her chest. Heat from the goddess burned through Xiao Yen, melting her glass walls. She popped up above the water and took a gasping breath.

"It is still my privilege to call you 'Little Sister.' " Bei Xi's words floated down, through Xiao Yen's hair, into her ears.

Xiao Yen hadn't realized she'd longed to hear those words until she did. She drank them down like steaming hot tea on a cold day, feeling their warmth seep into the quicksilver core of her soul. Bei Xi accepted Xiao Yen for who and what she was, no matter what had happened to her, what she had done. A tiny seed of pain lay at the bottom of her soul, where she'd buried it. Her silence no longer trapped her.

"Thank you," Xiao Yen said as she pulled away.

Bei Xi motioned for Udo to join them. He walked slowly and swayed a little when he stood. His exhaustion emanated from him, like Bei Xi's perfume flowed from her.

"You must go, and ride through the night, toward the east," Bei Xi said slowly and carefully in Udo's language so that Xiao Yen could understand. "Ehran travels with another merchant. You'll find him there. Vakhtang's body won't be discovered until morning. The soldiers won't come after you for a long time. If ever. Vakhtang's second in command is ambitious. He'd thank you for taking Vakhtang out of his way before he killed you." Bei Xi laughed softly, with little actual mirth in her voice.

Then she turned to Xiao Yen and added seriously, "He'll attack Bao Fang soon."

Xiao Yen drew in a quick breath. Attack her home? She told Bei Xi, "Then I must go to Bao Fang. Wang Tie-Tie's sick. And if the city's going to be attacked . . ." Though Fat Fang had always teased Xiao Yen about doing a man's work, he'd listen to her and mount a defense for the city. He had to.

"No," Bei Xi said. Now she spoke rapidly in the language of the Middle Kingdom. "You have to ride with Udo to the coast first. The king of Turic will break the treaty they signed with Emperor Dezong soon. The horsemen's raids against the border towns are just a start. War is coming, war I can't prevent. And Udo and his brother must be gone before it starts. They *must* go home. They'll be trapped—and killed—if they stay."

"But Bao Fang . . ." Xiao Yen started.

Bei Xi held up her hand to stop Xiao Yen from continuing. Bei Xi put her head to one side, listening to her other voices, before she said, "Bao Fang is safe until next spring. I make that promise to you, Little Sister. You have time to go to the coast, see the brothers on their way, then make your way back to your home, and prepare your defenses."

Xiao Yen bit her lip. She wanted to fly back to her home, see Wang Tie-Tie, warn Fat Fang. If Bei Xi said Xiao Yen must do other things first, Xiao Yen would acquiesce. Bei Xi was a goddess, after all.

Udo and Xiao Yen rode through the night, silently, determined to put as much distance between them and

Khan Hua as possible. They took a short break at dawn. Udo's exhaustion overtook him as soon as he lay down. Xiao Yen didn't want to set up any defense; they were stopping for less than an hour. She'd planned on staying awake and keeping watch, but her own tiredness betrayed her.

Xiao Yen didn't sleep long. A silent Vakhtang, still in his silver jacket and green pants, awaited her in her dreams. He wouldn't approach her, or say anything. He just stared at her. Xiao Yen couldn't determine the expression on his face. Resignation? Remorse?

Xiao Yen forced herself away from Vakhtang, out of her sleep and back to the empty plain. She woke Udo, and soon they rode again.

"Please tell me about your travels. Why are you here?" Xiao Yen asked Udo. Udo had gathered strength as they'd gained distance from Khan Hua, and the short break had helped, but he was still exhausted. Xiao Yen decided to keep him talking so he'd stay awake.

Brilliant morning sunshine made the dew in the short grass sparkle, and warmed Xiao Yen's face. They rode straight east, and hoped to catch up with Ehran on the main trade route before nightfall.

"Ehran and I are banished from our land," Udo said.

Though Bei Xi had already told Xiao Yen this, she couldn't stop herself from blurting out, "You unlucky. Like me."

Udo paused before he replied. "No, not unlucky. We've seen cities with domes out of beaten gold, statues carved out of mountains, black people, yellow people, red people. We haven't been unlucky. A man makes his own luck, and ours has been good."

Xiao Yen didn't know what to say. How could you make luck? She could never force her luck. Then she remembered Wang Tie-Tie saying, "If you grasp opportunity as it passes, you don't need lucky dreams." Was that what Udo meant?

A high-pitched whoop sounded ahead and to the

left of them. A sienna-colored pika stood on its hind legs, watching them approach. It whooped again, then scuttled back into its hole. Xiao Yen heard other creatures rustling in the grass, and saw two brown streaks run in front of the horses. She pulled up her reins, giving the pikas time to get to their homes. Udo stopped too.

"Careful here, many holes," she said.

"Yes, we don't want to hurt these beauties, do we? Let's go around," Udo replied, leading his horse to the right.

At first, Xiao Yen had thought Udo was concerned about the horses because they represented money. Finally she realized he treated them like how she'd treat Gan Ou's children.

Udo sat with his hands loosely holding his reins, relaxed. He swayed a bit in his saddle. They'd have to stop again soon. Xiao Yen looked over her shoulder again, checking to see if they were followed, but no one was behind them.

The silence grew between Udo and Xiao Yen. Normally, Xiao Yen enjoyed time for her own thoughts, but twice now, she'd been forced to retreat into her silence to protect her sanity. Once with Vakhtang, watching his dead body grow cold, surrounded with thoughts of killing and death, and before, with the guards. . . .

"Why you banished?" she asked. The embarrassment of asking inappropriate questions was less painful than her memories. Plus, it was possible Bei Xi hadn't told her everything.

"It's a long story," Udo stated, his voice trailing away at the end, not finishing his sentence.

"And?" Xiao Yen asked, prompting him.

Udo laughed. "Curious, eh? I like that."

Xiao Yen's cheeks grew hot, followed by a warm glow that went all the way through her center.

"My story, well, it's hard to know where to start." Udo paused again.

Xiao Yen looked at him expectantly.

Udo smiled at her, and began. "I was promised to marry Frauke," Udo said.

"Frauke?" Xiao Yen asked, rolling her tongue over the new name. This was something Bei Xi hadn't mentioned. She wondered if the goddess knew Udo's story. Bei Xi had only showered her attention on Ehran.

"Frauke. We were friends from childhood. She's always been the only woman for me," Udo commented, almost to himself. He took a deep breath, then seemed to force himself to continue.

"I was the eldest son, the only son, supposed to inherit my father's farm," he said, watching his hands holding the reins. They were no longer loose.

Xiao Yen was puzzled. "But Ehran? He your brother?" she asked.

"Yes, but he's a bastard," Udo said with a sigh.

"Excuse me, what is 'bastard'?" Xiao Yen asked, guiding her horse around another pika hole.

"A son born to an unwed woman."

"So not concubine or second wife? But unwed girl?" Xiao Yen asked, surprised. Wang Tie-Tie would never have let the brothers hire her if she'd known Ehran's true status.

Udo smiled. "Yes. Does that happen here?"

Xiao Yen bit her lip before she replied. "It happens here. It is a shame on family, a shame on girl. Often she kills herself."

They rode in silence a short while before Xiao Yen asked, "So what happened with Fra . . . Fro . . . The woman you marry?"

"Frauke. When my mother died, my father brought Ehran's mother to our farm, and Ehran. My father had been, uh, friendly with her for years, ever since my mother had taken ill. I didn't know Ehran then, but I could see right away that he was a gambler and a spendthrift. Yet my father treated him like his second son. It made me so mad I left the farm. I traveled to the capital of Charlemagne's empire, Aachen, with one of the local cloth merchants, supposedly to make enough money to marry Frauke, but mainly to get away."

Xiao Yen didn't follow everything Udo said, but she caught the gist of it. They rode for a while in silence. Shrubs now dotted the plain. The edge of the forest was no longer a splotch on the horizon. Xiao Yen smelled pine mixed with cooler air, air that came from the shade, up ahead.

"What happen, you come back?" she asked, hoping that was the right question.

"When I returned, everything had changed. Ehran had helped my father run the farm, been responsible, probably for the first time in his life. He'd changed, for the better.

"But my father expected me to come back and take my old place, the place Ehran had been filling. I was so happy to be home, I didn't think about Ehran. So he went back to gambling." Udo paused.

"And the woman you marry?" Xiao Yen asked.

"Frauke was being intimidated by Habel, a bully who had terrorized me, and everyone, as a child. He was blackmailing her, saying if she didn't marry him, he'd force her family off their land.

"I went to see him one night, to talk sense into him. Ehran had gone to see him that night as well. Habel had tricked him into gambling away our father's farm. It wasn't legal, but Habel, well, he was a powerful man. He could have made it legal. Do you understand?"

Xiao Yen replied, "I understand." Bei Xi had told her this part of the brothers' story. Corrupt officials lived everywhere.

"Habel wouldn't change his mind. Ehran got angry. There was a fight. I don't think Ehran meant to kill him, but he did." Udo fell silent.

Xiao Yen shivered as they passed under the shade of a tree. Ehran was such a barbarian. A sudden thought made her catch her breath. What right did she have to judge Ehran? She'd killed a man too. Her guilt darkened the morning.

"I got there too late to stop him," Udo continued

after a moment. "In addition, someone saw us leave. Both of us were charged with the murder. Though Habel was powerful, he wasn't well liked. We were just banished, not executed."

When Bei Xi had first told Xiao Yen the brothers' story, she'd been shocked that the whole family hadn't been punished. Now, she almost understood why foreigners only punished the perpetrator of a crime. On the one hand, Wang Tie-Tie and her family were responsible for everything Xiao Yen did, because they'd laid the seeds for her soul. Now, Xiao Yen herself was responsible for how those seeds had grown. It was a strange thought for her.

"And Frauke?" she asked, putting the thought to one side, for a while.

"I told her to marry someone else. I guess I expected her to vow undying love for me, like in the poems. She agreed it was best to stay. I heard later that she married someone else within the month." Udo laughed his biting, barking laugh.

"Can you ever go back to your village?" Xiao Yen asked.

"If we had enough silver, and put it in the right hands, I think we could. That's why I wanted the treasure from the rat dragon's cave."

"Not make money close to home? Why come here?"

Udo laughed again, gentler this time. "I've thought about that a lot. I think I kept pushing us to travel because I needed to run away. To forget about Frauke." He turned and looked at Xiao Yen.

Xiao Yen tried to look down, but the intensity of his stare caught her.

"And maybe, I have," he said.

"How?" Xiao Yen didn't want to speak. The word was forced out of her, drawn by Udo's eyes, the color of thunderclouds.

"You've protected me this whole journey. You killed Vakhtang. You defeated the rat dragon. You've never betrayed me. Frauke can't compare to you."

Finally, Udo looked away and Xiao Yen was able to look down at her hands. They'd twisted her reins tightly through her fingers without her realizing it. Whatever warmth she might have felt from Udo's unexpected praise was overwhelmed by his unspoken question.

When would she betray him as well?

Finding Ehran along the main road was easy. Many merchants camped next to the side of the road; all Xiao Yen had to do was point to Udo and ask "where?" Everyone knew where the other foreigner camped.

Dusk had gathered at the tops of the trees by the time they arrived. The sour and meaty smell of the camp's evening mash mingled with scents of pines, sweaty men, and dusty horses. A few crickets had begun their nightly chorus. The air chilled as the sun dipped below the trees, making Xiao Yen wish she could get at her head scarf, but it was buried at the bottom of her saddlebag.

Ehran challenged them as they rode up. Udo responded. Xiao Yen recognized that they were swearing at each other, and was glad she didn't know exactly what they were saying. Udo hopped off his horse, gave his brother a big hug, and pounded his back. Ehran responded in kind.

Xiao Yen slipped off her horse and stood nearby, watching. The resemblance of the brothers struck her again: though Ehran was fat, and Udo was skinny, one was dark, the other blond, they had the same chin, the same ears, the same frightening, tooth-filled smile.

When they stopped swearing at each other, Udo asked about all the horses, naming each in turn. It sounded to Xiao Yen like an old uncle asking after his brother's children. A strange thought occurred to her: maybe they were Udo's children, since he'd never had any of his own.

When the brothers finished talking, Udo turned to her and beamed. Xiao Yen wasn't watching him though.

Ehran's face had turned pale, drawn, and his shoulders had stiffened. Udo turned back to Erhan.

"What's wrong?" Udo asked.

"I didn't think you'd bring her here too. I thought you'd leave her behind at Wolfgang's."

"Vakhtang's. Why should I do that? She saved my life, more than once." Udo's eyebrows drew together in a single frowning line.

"She's a woman! I thought you didn't like her," Ehran sputtered.

Udo looked at him sternly. Xiao Yen held herself still. So it hadn't been her imagination. Udo hadn't liked her.

"I've changed my mind," he said. "She's proven herself, more than once, that she's worthy. Why is it a problem that she's here?"

Ehran had the grace to look embarrassed, even as he defended himself. "After that guard escaped, I didn't know how to find you, or if you'd be coming back. I waited, but when this caravan came, needing horses, I agreed to go with them, and wait for you on the coast." Ehran lowered his voice. "This caravan already has a mage to protect it."

Xiao Yen looked at Ehran. Had she understood him correctly? There was another mage here? A sinking feeling weighed her down. Master Wei had warned his students again and again that any mages they met outside their school would be unfriendly. Vakhtang certainly had been. Was she going to have to fight someone else?

Udo asked, "How much are we paying her? And for what services? Can we renegotiate the contract? And just pay her for whatever magic she does?"

Ehran laughed, long and mean.

Xiao Yen wanted to shake him. Why was he laughing? What did he know that he wasn't telling his brother? That he wasn't telling her?

"She's turned you around, hasn't she? The new mage is a man. We're part of the general caravan. We don't pay anything, and they get the use of two of the horses to pull their wagon. We're on our way to the mage's home, Kuangho, which is also a port city, with ships going back west."

Udo stroked his chin, nodding. "So Xiao Yen could also be part of the caravan if she agrees to help defend it, right?"

"Sanchen? Yes, she could. That is, if Tuo Nu allows it. He's the mage guarding the wagon."

Udo and Ehran narrowed their eyes and stared at each other in the growing twilight, trying to see what lay inside the other's head. Their expressions were identical. If the situation hadn't been so serious, Xiao Yen might have laughed.

A small thin man, with dark hair, creamy golden skin, and eyes that marked him as someone from the Middle Kingdom, walked up. He had a long scholar's beard growing out of his chin, similar to Vakhtang's. His forehead was broad and wide. Xiao Yen wondered if he shaved the front of his hair to make his forehead seem larger, and himself more intelligent. His nose had a crook in it, as though it'd been broken and not set properly. His eyes also reminded her of Vakhtang's, greedy and sucking in everything they saw.

He kept his hands inside the sleeves of his dark red jacket. Xiao Yen wondered what weapon he was hiding, then chided herself. If she had to fight this mage, it would be magically, not physically. Besides, the evening was chilly. This mage probably had nothing up his sleeve except his hands. Gold braid ran around the cuffs and down the front of his jacket, like some kind of official's. A thicker brown braid was tied around his waist. He wore his hair pulled back, bound in a short ponytail worn high on the crown of his head, looped over and pinned back down, every hair in place, neater than even Fu Be Be's.

He bowed over his folded hands to Ehran, then to Udo. When he looked beyond the men to Xiao Yen, he hesitated. Xiao Yen bowed deeply to him. Power emanated from this man. With her mind's eye, Xiao

Yen saw him filling the clearing with a warm glow. The trees seemed to bow with him, as well as the grasses at his feet. He'd cast a strong blue shadow when she saw him in the daylight. She hoped he would be friendly.

He bowed just as deeply back to her, saying in the language of the Middle Kingdom, "I thought the moon had risen early. Now I see it's just your mage light."

Xiao Yen wasn't certain what he meant. She'd never heard of anything called "mage light." She'd only ever seen blue shadows, and images in her mind's eye. She glanced around. There wasn't enough sunlight left to see clear shadows. Maybe this mage was much stronger than she could tell, able to see magic in shadows, while she needed the light.

"Oh, no," Xiao Yen replied. "I am still young, and learning. I have small magic, compared to you."

Tuo Nu shook his head again, opened his mouth to say something to Xiao Yen, then changed his mind. He turned his head and addressed Ehran.

"Since your brother has arrived, should I set up the defenses for tonight's camp?" he said smoothly in their language.

Xiao Yen caught her breath. He spoke Udo and Ehran's language so well she could barely follow him. He spoke the language of the Middle Kingdom. His home was far enough from the capital that he probably spoke a third language, his own people's dialect, as well. How was she ever going to compete with him, or other mages like him?

Ehran said, "Sure," while at the same time, Udo said, "No." The brothers stared at each other for a moment before Udo continued. "Let Xiao Yen set up the defenses for this evening."

Tuo Nu turned and bowed to her. "Of course. It would be a great honor for me."

Xiao Yen replied, "I can't. I need to practice. Not tonight." Xiao Yen hadn't folded anything since the rat dragon's cave. She normally practiced every day. To fold a creature that wasn't perfect, and then to animate it, would be a disaster.

"Don't be modest," Tuo Nu said. "I've heard so much about your magic. I would enjoy seeing it." He smiled at her, but in a foreigner way, showing his teeth like a predator.

"I can't," Xiao Yen said. She looked at Udo, to plead with him.

He stared back at her, measuring her refusal, measuring her against the other woman in his life. "Please," he said. "Please, you can do it."

Xiao Yen couldn't refuse.

Xiao Yen sat without a cushion, letting the cold earth seep into her legs. It was a distraction and a comfort at the same time. She sought her silence, the stillness that formed her life, that was an integral part of her magic. It came roaring in her ears like floodwaters. She tried to clear her inner ear, to only see with her mind's eye. The silence beat at her, like a giant heart pounding beneath ocean waves. There were too many things outside her silence, forcing their way in.

She lowered herself to the ground and touched her forehead three times. She sat and prayed to Zhang Gua Lao for a moment, but she couldn't clear her mind. She was hungry, the ground was cold, her legs hurt from riding a horse. She took another deep breath and brought her hands out in front of her. At least they were still steady.

Udo had wanted her to do something flashy, like the tiger again, to show off in front of Tuo Nu. Xiao Yen had disagreed. She didn't have the calm necessary for such a great beast tonight. She wasn't sure she could control even a rabbit, let alone fold anything.

Xiao Yen wished she had more time. Maybe doing some of the forms, folding her body like she folded paper, would have helped. Sunset was imminent, and she needed to get the defenses for the camp set up before it was fully dark.

She'd agreed on a hunting dog to circle the camp. She based the dog on one of the deer patterns she knew, heavy and strong through the body, but with light, thin paws. She realized her mistake after the first half-dozen folds, when she brought the legs out from the center mass of paper. The dog's paws would be too scrawny to support its body. She tried to refold the ends, but she didn't have enough paper to work with.

So she started again. Her arms, though still steady, felt leaden. She was no longer in good shape to fold. She rolled the initial marking folds, trying to give more substance to the legs, and to give herself more room to work, but this time, the legs were unevenly thick. One front paw was like a club foot, while one of the back paws was just a twig.

Xiao Yen took a deep breath. Should she start again? She could correct the club foot, some, but not the skinny one. Her deafening silence had leaked out a little. On the edges, she felt her calm returning. Folding was familiar to her, and though she was under pressure to perform, it still soothed her.

She got out a third sheet of paper from her bag. Her arms trembled when she raised them. Her fingers felt drained of blood. Her calm circled her slowly, eating at the darkness of her panic. Instead of radiating out from her, it approached from the outside and worked its way inward. She lowered her arms and let the night speak to her, the distant crickets, a soft breeze rustling the pine needles, the whisperings of the occasional bat overhead. She breathed deeply, and felt places in her shoulders that she hadn't realized were tight, loosen. A wind sprang up and blew in her face, not strong, but noticeable. She ignored it and went back to her folding.

Suddenly, she heard a crashing behind her. Xiao Yen scrambled to her feet.

An elephant towered above her.

Xiao Yen put her hand over her mouth to stop herself from screaming. The elephant trumpeted at her, lifting its long nose high over its head to proclaim its anger. Xiao Yen picked up her bag and held it in front of her while she took a step back. Why hadn't she finished the first piece? If she had, at least she'd have some protection.

The elephant didn't lower its tusks and charge her. It raised its left ear and turned its head, as if it were listening for instructions from behind it. Then it pulled up a clump of grass and put it in its mouth. Xiao Yen watched in fascination as it masticated and flapped its ears at her.

Tuo Nu appeared behind the elephant, slapping it hard on the rump, saying something in a language Xiao Yen didn't understand; the mage's native dialect, she presumed. The elephant nodded and moved away. Xiao Yen was surprised at Tuo Nu's appearance. His face was pale, even in the dark, and his hands shook.

"I saw you were having difficulties," he explained as he came up. "I know it was presumptuous, but I thought I would do the protection for tonight. It will give you time to practice, so you can do the defense for tomorrow night."

"That elephant is magic?" Xiao Yen asked. It affected the mundane world, seeming a natural part of it, actually. Tuo Nu must be a powerful mage indeed, though he sounded out of breath, as if he'd just run a long race. Was his magic so different? Did he work more closely with the elements?

"Yes, I conjured it," he said, taking deep breaths, struggling to keep his breath even. "It took a little effort."

Xiao Yen shook her head. What had she been thinking, to ever believe she could make a living as a mage? When there were such powerful mages already in the world? She walked silently next to Tuo Nu into the camp. Udo's eyes followed her, but he didn't say a word. Xiao Yen didn't know what to say to him.

She sighed and went to her tent, wishing she was ten thousand *li* away. Her magic didn't affect the mundane world like Tuo Nu's. She didn't know if Fat Fang or Long Yen's creations were now as powerful as Tuo

Nu's, if it was something to do with age, or with her being a girl, or if Tuo Nu's magic was that much different from hers.

She lay down on her comforter and didn't cry, though she felt deep holes torn through her heart. She missed her luck, Wang Tie-Tie, Fu Be Be, and Gan Ou. She resolved that she'd see her family soon. She'd warn them of the coming war, make them safe.

Then she'd never leave home again.

Chapter 18

Bao Fang

"We're so attracted to each other," Bing Yu confided, leaning closer to Xiao Yen. "The moon god must have tied our ankles together with a red ribbon when we were born."

Xiao Yen couldn't keep the shock out of her voice. "You've met your fiancé? Did your family arrange it?" She knew mores and customs were different at various levels of society, but she didn't think Governor Fang's family would be that dissimilar to her own.

Bing Yu shook her head and laughed. "No, silly." She looked behind her and on either side, scanning the crowds of people in the street for someone who might know her, before she continued, "We met in private. My father doesn't know."

"Oh," Xiao Yen replied. She didn't know what else to say. How could Bing Yu do such a reckless thing? Her reputation would be ruined if anyone found out. Her father might renounce her and kick her out of their home.

Bing Yu laughed again and said, "Xiao Yen! Your eyes are as round as your mouth saying 'Oh.' You shouldn't be so shocked. Everyone meets before the wedding, these days."

"Without their family's knowledge?" Xiao Yen asked.

"Shh," Bing Yu said. "Keep your voice down. Everybody does it. No one talks about it."

Xiao Yen didn't ask any more questions as they walked through the market. It was nice to have a day off from school. She'd won the last large contest, and had gained the privilege of going to the city for three days. Though she was enjoying Bing Yu's company, Xiao Yen still felt guilty. She should be at home, with her family, since she saw them so infrequently. Her mother hadn't wanted her to go when Bing Yu had asked, but Wang Tie-Tie had overruled Fu Be Be, saying it was good for the family to have high connections. As Wang Tie-Tie spoke infrequently now, when she did say something, it carried a lot of weight.

There seemed to be more people in the streets than Xiao Yen remembered from when she was a child. There were just as many shops crammed together, selling everything from fancy keys to bundles of candles to copper bowls and braziers. Xiao Yen's favorite shop was the big paper shop on the east side of the market square, which had everything from imported fragrant dragon paper, which was thick and had incense imbedded in it, to flimsy gold paper in the shape of coins that people burned to show respect for their ancestors.

In addition to the shops, people sold goods on the side of the road. A few of them were merchants. Most of them looked as though they were selling their belongings, whatever they had with them.

When Xiao Yen had asked Fu Be Be about them, her mother had sniffed and said, "Refugees. From the north. Don't go near them. They bring bad luck."

Master Wei had explained about the treaties the Emperor had signed with the kingdom of Tibet, to the west, and the kingdom of Turic, to the north. Some of the Turic horsemen, also known as the Uighiers, now ignored the treaty, and raided border towns, driving the people who lived there south.

"Let's go to the silk shop," Bing Yu said, taking her friend's arm.

The shop was several streets away, down a skinny

alley that twisted like a tangled ribbon. Two wide
doors draped with undecorated but gaily colored cloth
stood open to all. The shop seemed dark after the
bright spring sunshine. Bolts of cloth lay everywhere.
The center of the shop held a low table, covered with
off-white muslin.

Bing Yu paused in the doorway to take off her
shoes, then waited for Xiao Yen to stop gawking and
do the same. One clerk brought them slippers to be
worn in the store, while a second clerk rushed through
a door at the back of the shop.

The proprietor came running out in a moment. He
was a skinny man dressed in purple silk so rich Xiao
Yen wanted to rub her cheek against it.

"Ah, Fang Bing Yu!" he said, bowing deeply over
his folded hands. "What an honor it is for you to visit
our poor establishment again." He turned to Xiao Yen
and squinted at her, backlit by the light coming in
from the street. "And may I have the honor of being
introduced?" he asked.

"This is my friend Fu Xi Wén," Bing Yu announced. "She also needs a new jacket."

Xiao Yen and the proprietor exchanged deep bows.

"Welcome to my humble shop," he said, then he
peered behind Xiao Yen. "And your gracious
mother?" he asked hopefully.

"She's not with us this time."

"Oh," said the proprietor, crestfallen.

Xiao Yen hid her smile behind her hand. The shop-
keeper knew Bing Yu had no money, and couldn't
buy anything, even on credit, without her mother.
They were just browsing that day, not buying.

He made the best of it, replacing his brightest smile
with his second best while saying, "Please, come into
my shop." He indicated that they should sit at the low
table. He instructed his assistant to show them any
cloth they wanted, then excused himself, returning to
the back of the shop.

Bing Yu ordered the assistant around, having him
display first one bolt of cloth, then another. She fin-

gered each, and asked Xiao Yen's opinion on the quality of the silk, the weave of the cloth, the color, and the pattern. Xiao Yen liked tighter woven cloth. Wang Tie-Tie had told her it would last longer because it had more threads. Bing Yu liked the looser woven cloth, because it draped better, and would be cooler in the summer.

They also disagreed on colors and patterns. Bing Yu's favorite was a shocking pink, brighter than the petunias in the Garden of Sweet Scents, embroidered with golden cranes. Xiao Yen liked the darker colors and more subtle patterns. Her favorite was a rich blue, the color of the river Quang on a cloudy day, covered with rings of lucky bats done in a lighter blue.

After the temple bells tolled once to mark the hour of the Sheep, Bing Yu and Xiao Yen left the store. Xiao Yen felt sorry for the poor clerks who would have to put away all the bolts of cloth scattered across the table. She knew better than to say anything to Bing Yu.

"Where do you want to go now?" Bing Yu asked Xiao Yen as they put on their own shoes.

"I should return home," Xiao Yen replied. She felt guilty for being gone so long. Yet it had been nice to be with a friend for the afternoon.

"I'll walk you halfway there," Bing Yu said, linking arms again.

Xiao Yen pretended to know the people Bing Yu gossiped about as they walked, adding an appropriate, "No," "Really?" and "She didn't!"

When they reached the main road going south, Xiao Yen, instead of turning toward her family's compound, turned north and said, "I'll walk with you a little farther."

Bing Yu asked, "Why? I thought you needed to get home, and be a proper daughter again."

Xiao Yen didn't pay attention to the teasing tone in her friend's voice. "I do need to go home. But I want to stop at the well and make an offering to Jing Long first."

Bing Yu laughed so loudly that another pair of girls stared at them as they passed by.

"What's so funny?" Xiao Yen asked. More passersby stared. Xiao Yen blushed. What had she said?

"Now I understand why you seem unbalanced!" Bing Yu explained. "Don't be angry," she added quickly. "It's all part of a pattern, see? When I told you about meeting my fiancé, you were shocked, like an old woman. When we went shopping, you liked somber colors. Now, you want to go make an offering to Jing Long. Only old people believe in those stories or make offerings to the city dragon anymore." Bing Yu paused dramatically.

Xiao Yen didn't understand the point Bing Yu was trying to make.

With an exaggerated sigh, Bing Yu continued. "Don't you see? You're a perfect replica of Wang Tie-Tie!"

Xiao Yen jerked her head back as if Bing Yu had slapped her. How could Bing Yu say that? It sounded like something Fu Be Be or Gan Ou might say.

"I am not just like Wang Tie-Tie," Xiao Yen said. Wang Tie-Tie was beautiful and elegant. Fu Be Be had told Xiao Yen often that her broad shoulders made her ugly. Wang Tie-Tie was old and wise. Xiao Yen felt like an infant next to her.

Bing Yu said, "It might be your fate. Or it might not be. Maybe you could try to be someone else. Like your sister. Or even"—she paused—"like me."

Xiao Yen held herself still. Who did she want to be like? Most children were like either their mother or their father. Did she want to be similar to Wang Tie-Tie? At the edge of her mind's eye she saw another figure approach, someone else that she could be like.

Bing Yu interrupted Xiao Yen's thoughts before Xiao Yen could get a good look. "Do you believe in the stories of Jing Long? That it will rise up out of the well and defend Bao Fang if it's attacked?"

"Of course," Xiao Yen replied. Why shouldn't she

believe that? Everyone knew dragons lived in water. The two city dragons, Jing Long and the river dragon, had battles every spring, fighting for dominance. That was why they had thunderstorms. Hadn't Bing Yu heard them?

"Fat Fang says there's no magic at the old well. He said he's never seen any."

Now it was Xiao Yen's turn to smile. "Master Wei has never taught us to 'see' magic. He says it's possible, but unreliable. I'm not surprised Fat Fang has never seen magic at the well."

"So you don't know for certain if the dragon is there or not?" Bing Yu asked.

Xiao Yen paused. "I get a feeling something is there. . . ."

Now it was Bing Yu's turn to be surprised. "Really?" She breathed out the word as if she didn't want anyone else to hear. "Let's go look." Bing Yu grabbed Xiao Yen's arm and hurried with her through the crowded street.

Xiao Yen regretted saying anything. This was worse than Wang Tie-Tie's birthday party, with her mother asking her to perform.

The well sat in the center of Bao Fang. The streets from the four main gates ran to it. A waist-high wall of red, rounded bricks surrounded the well. On the south side of the well the water boys plied their trade. There were always a couple around, ready to help someone carry water to their compound for a fee. Some of the boys had regular routes, and came at certain times to fill up their buckets.

On the north side of the well sat a small wooden altar on a spindly table. Every spring the monks repainted the altar red, and touched up the picture of golden Jing Long rising toward heaven in the center. The altar looked as solid as the bricks, with three flat planks rising out of a base. Below each plank, in the base, three cups had been carved.

Two of the younger water boys watched Xiao Yen

and Bing Yu as they approached. One sniggered when they went around toward the altar. An older man cuffed him.

Xiao Yen bowed as she approached the altar. From a distance, the altar looked impressive. Up close, she saw it hadn't been taken care of. The flowers placed on it had dried long ago. The bowls were empty, even the center one that should have had pure water in it for Jing Long's use, should the dragon choose to manifest. Though the altar was painted every spring, now it was fall, and the paint was faded and chipped.

After Xiao Yen bowed to the altar, she walked back around to where the water boys stood. Without a word, she handed the old man a coin. He bowed in return, glaring at the younger boys who sat giggling. He gave Xiao Yen a small silver cup, filled to the brim with water. Xiao Yen's hands grew cold instantly when she wrapped them around the cup.

She went back to the altar, poured the pure water into the center bowl, and sought the peace she generally felt at a temple. But she couldn't find her calm. She was too distracted by the noise of the boys getting more water out of the well, the people passing behind her, the calls of a fish merchant. She said a brief prayer for her family, then started walking back home.

"Wait!" Bing Yu called.

Xiao Yen stopped. She'd forgotten her friend.

"Did you see any magic?"

Xiao Yen had to admit she hadn't seen or felt anything.

"That's because there's nothing there," Bing Yu said triumphantly. "And you looked like a silly old woman, pouring water on that altar. The boys will steal the water back and sell it again."

Xiao Yen shrugged off her friend's comments. It was right to show respect, even if Jing Long didn't live at the bottom of the well. She was certain the dragon existed. Pretty sure.

Bing Yu peered at her friend for a moment, then walked next to the well. She cleared her throat. For a horrifying moment Xiao Yen thought Bing Yu was going to spit in the well, but instead, she spat next to it.

When Bing Yu turned to face Xiao Yen again, she broke into loud laughter. She came up to Xiao Yen and put her arm around Xiao Yen's shoulders. "You looked so much like Wang Tie-Tie just then, so proper and shocked." She leaned forward, kissed her friend on the cheek, and said good-bye.

Before Xiao Yen could go, Bing Yu caught her hands and asked seriously, "If you're so old now, when will you be young? When will you be young enough to get married and have children?"

Xiao Yen didn't know the answer. She rubbed her lucky amulet as she walked back to her family compound, hoping it would show her a sign, but it didn't reply.

Chapter 19

❧

On the Trail

Stark streams of sunlight poured through the trees, striking Xiao Yen's arms, then sliding off as she moved. Mossy ground gave way under her feet. She pulled breath deep into her belly, letting the dark pine forest smells warm her nostrils. Birdsong came alive over her head.

Xiao Yen stepped out widely, then had to shift her foot. She'd landed in the wrong pose. Again. She rested in her stance—Spreading Phoenix Feathers—and forced herself to concentrate. Her mind kept going back to Tuo Nu's powerful elephant, to Udo's sudden warmth, to her overpowering silence in the days after those men in the courtyard . . . to Vakhtang, growing cold beside her . . . to her dream of him, the second night in a row, staring and silent. She'd tried to approach him, to speak with him, to say that she was sorry, but her words had no sound.

Xiao Yen exhaled sharply, coming back to the streaming light and dark forest. She did the next step in the form, and the next, concentrating on pushing off the ground, the flow of *qi,* and her breath. As she warmed up, her movements began to flow. She went from one pose to the next, folding her body as she would fold paper, bringing up one leg, then discovering it and pulling it out, like how she found the legs of a deer from the center of a folded piece and brought them out.

Though Xiao Yen kept her eyes open, she ignored her surroundings. Instead, she tried to see her quiet place, the glassy river, clear, quiet, calm. The familiar movements helped. She did, but didn't, want to find it. She missed her calm, almost more than her luck or her family. Without deep waters, she felt diminished, and magic was almost impossible. On the other hand, the river frightened her. It had overpowered her, locking her in thick walls of silence.

Her place came into focus, piece by piece. Unfiltered sunlight beat down on the brilliant green banks. The water shone silver and gray, reflecting the light like a mirror. Xiao Yen stood some distance away from the flowing river. She didn't want to get any closer.

She knew she must.

She concentrated on her feet, not on the flowing water, and took a step forward. Then another.

"Xiao Yen!"

The pine forest surrounded her again. She no longer saw her center. She flowed from the pose she stood in—her left arm across her chest, hand extended, the other curved behind her—to the next, reversing her arms, hoping to recapture where she'd been.

Someone shouted her name a second time.

Xiao Yen let her arms drop and bowed her head, as if in prayer. Next time she'd get closer to her calm. She ignored the sinking feeling in her chest. She *would* get closer.

Someone called her name a third time.

Before she could reply to the caller, someone else, close behind her, replied for her.

"She's here."

Xiao Yen turned around. Tuo Nu stood under the trees behind her.

"What were you doing?" he asked. "Were you practicing your magic? I saw traces of your mage light, over your head."

Xiao Yen put away her grief and studied the man in front of her. His scholar's beard moved in a slight breeze Xiao Yen didn't feel. His eyes engulfed her, devoured her, trying to puzzle out everything about her. He hadn't been hostile to her, even though she was a rival mage. He was unfailingly polite at all times. She still didn't trust him. She didn't want to answer his questions either. Instead, she asked, "What do you mean by 'mage light'?" Bei Xi had taught her to see magic in shadows, not light.

"Don't you see magic by light?" Tuo Nu asked.

Xiao Yen refused to give in to his questioning. He wasn't as bad as Gan Ou, but only slightly better. She started walking toward camp and returned his question with a question. "Is that how you see magic? Through light?"

"Sometimes," Tuo Nu replied as he hurried to catch up with her. "But it isn't reliable. Were you just practicing magic?"

"I was trying to find my center," Xiao Yen said. She regretted the words as they slipped out. When was she going to learn to not say the first thing that came into her head? She no longer had her luck to protect her when she said the wrong thing.

"Your center? That's interesting. When I seek my center, I stay completely still, in a dark place. I can't move in bright sunlight and find it," Tuo Nu replied.

Xiao Yen slowed down. Maybe she should talk with Tuo Nu. She'd never talked with another mage about magic.

"I can find my center without moving, too, at night, when I'm lying on my bed," Xiao Yen replied as she walked into the clearing.

"You're so powerful," Tuo Nu said.

Xiao Yen snorted.

"You are!" Tuo Nu protested. "I can only find my center using one method, not two."

Xiao Yen stopped and looked at him. "Maybe our magic is just different," she said.

"Maybe," Tuo Nu replied in a noncommittal way.

Udo called, "Xiao Yen!" He hurried over to them. "Are you well?" he asked, staring at Tuo Nu.

"Of course," she said. What was Udo worried about?

The horses and the wagon stood just beyond the trees. One of the horses' halters jingled as it shook its head.

"What were you doing, out in the woods, alone? Haven't I told you not to go off like that?" Udo kept staring at Tuo Nu.

"She was practicing magic," Tuo Nu said.

"Were you?" Udo turned to look at Xiao Yen. His gaze softened.

Xiao Yen whispered, "I was."

"You're sure you're not hurt?" Udo asked. He reached out a hand to touch her elbow. Xiao Yen shied away. She didn't want anyone touching her, didn't like to be touched, not since Vakhtang's. "Xiao Yen?" Udo asked.

Finally, Xiao Yen understood. Her cheeks grew warm. She remembered the last time Udo had found her alone in the woods, with Ehran. He was trying to protect her from Tuo Nu.

"I'm fine, Udo. Tuo Nu was like lord in other lord's garden." She wanted to tell him that Tuo Nu wasn't Ehran, or like those guards, those men who forced her to . . .

She squashed the memory and said, "Let's go."

"You be careful, *ja?*" Udo said. He shot one more glare at Tuo Nu, then walked away, toward Ehran.

The brothers were happy to be reunited, though Ehran had avoided Xiao Yen last night. She suspected he was still embarrassed that she'd "saved" him from Bei Xi.

Xiao Yen shrugged at Tuo Nu, indicating her puzzlement, then went to her horse. Udo obviously didn't trust Tuo Nu, and wanted her to stay away from him. Xiao Yen wanted to follow Udo's wishes, but that would be difficult. Tuo Nu was a mage who spoke her language, and who asked many questions.

*   *   *

The torrent from Tuo Nu continued while they rode. "Do you have special times of the month when you practice? Or are all times good for you? Is that just you, or for all paper mages?

"Who do you pray to? Do all paper mages pray to Zhang Gua Lao? Or is it just you?

"How do you choose your paper? Do you all do it that way?"

Xiao Yen tried to respond with her own barrage of questions, but Tuo Nu always asked two questions to any one she asked. After a while, she saw a pattern, and said, "Why do you keep asking me if all mages do it the way I do?"

Tuo Nu was silent for a moment before he replied, "I've never met, or even heard of, a female mage."

Xiao Yen didn't reply. Of course. Girls were supposed to stay at home, get married, give birth to sons. Not practice magic, go traveling with foreigners, or fight.

Or kill.

She pushed away her guilt and pulled on her reins to slow her horse so she no longer rode beside Tuo Nu. She knew she shouldn't blame the other mage. If she continued to practice magic, she would always be treated like this, always stared at, always questioned. No wonder very few people ever saw or met mages. No wonder only their works were visible. She sighed. It seemed like such a hard life, always being alone, even with other mages. Maybe she should get married when she returned. Gan Ou or Fu Be Be could find her a husband. Giving up her magic didn't seem so difficult now. She'd already lost so much peace. She felt ten thousand years old.

Xiao Yen watched the trees, trying to draw comfort from their silence, since her own remained elusive. They were shorter than the trees behind Master Wei's school. Many pines mingled with the hardwoods. Yellow lichen grew on the west sides of some of the trees, and large mushrooms blossomed like ears. The wind usually blew from the east, and sometimes Xiao Yen thought she caught the scent of salt from the ocean. The ground was mossy, moist.

Tuo Nu came back to ride next to Xiao Yen after a while. "I've been selfish, haven't I? I ask you many questions, and never reply to yours. What do you want to know?"

"What are we protecting?" Xiao Yen asked. She'd asked this question more than once, but neither Ehran or Tuo Nu had responded.

"The wagon," he said, gesturing toward it.

It was a two-wheeled wagon, rimmed with iron. It held tents, cooking gear, and three round, wooden barrels.

"Spices?" Xiao Yen asked. She knew some spices, like black pepper, were worth a lord's ransom.

"Better. Magic herbs. We call it 'the Breath of God,' or 'the Wind of God.'" Tuo Nu chuckled. "When I was with my master, the other apprentices and I called it 'God's Glue.'"

"Oh," Xiao Yen said, still not enlightened.

"Don't you use magic herbs sometimes to help you in your magic?" he asked, incredulous.

Xiao Yen replied, "No, my master thought it was unnecessary. He said discipline, practicing every day, should be enough. If you relied on powders, you were less of a mage. He also said he'd heard many claims about many different powders, but he'd never known any that had worked."

"Your master sounds very wise," Tuo Nu said. "Was he very old?"

"He was," Xiao Yen said proudly. "He had much experience as a mage."

"Oh," said Tuo Nu, disapproving.

Xiao Yen bit her lip and didn't comment. She pressed her knees against her horse's ribs, urging it forward. She didn't want to hear Tuo Nu disparage Master Wei. Plus, why wouldn't he venerate someone who was as old as her master? Though Tuo Nu looked like someone from the Middle Kingdom, he was as foreign to her as Udo.

Tuo Nu kept talking, as if to himself. "I mean, who wants to practice, and practice, and practice every day? It's so much work. And for what? Just to be old before your time. Better to use the herbs," he ended.

Xiao Yen rode up in front of the wagon. Tuo Nu was right. Magic was a lot of work. Generally, she loved practicing, but then there were times, like now, when nothing seemed to go right, when practice just meant work with no reward.

What if she never found her peace again? Her luck was gone. She didn't want to practice, not like this, every day, for the rest of her life. Maybe she should quit, get married, and raise sons. That would please her mother, but disappoint Wang Tie-Tie. Who was ill, dying. Xiao Yen still needed to do something worthy of an immortal peach. Soon. Before Wang Tie-Tie passed beyond the Yellow River.

Maybe she already had. She'd faced down Vakhtang. He'd been evil, stealing people's souls so his own life could continue, preventing them from a chance of rebirth. She remembered her dream from the night before, his searching eyes. She'd killed him.

Xiao Yen's spirits sank far below her into the earth. There would be no reward for killing.

Xiao Yen got out her practice string and started tying knots. It didn't take any work to do her knot magic. She'd already found out how to do it without reaching for her quiet. And it took her mind off the cold future ahead.

Vakhtang came to Xiao Yen in her dreams again, still dressed the same as she'd seen him last, the white knots of the silver jacket expanded as if protecting him. His face held a light blue color this time, a pale reflection of the magic that had kept him alive.

Xiao Yen pushed her way across the darkness to

where Vakhtang stood. It took all her courage to speak. "Why are you here?" she asked.

Vakhtang stayed frozen for a moment more. Then his face rippled, like the surface of a pond. "As a reminder," was all he said.

A reminder? Of what?

Suddenly, she felt paper in her hands. As she started to grasp it, something on the other side of the paper, that she couldn't see, tried to pull it away. Xiao Yen played tug-of-war with an unseen assailant for what seemed like a long time. The paper was resilient, but she couldn't pull too hard on it, or it would tear. Vakhtang watched her the whole time, his face tinged with regret.

Xiao Yen noticed that as she pulled, Vakhtang grew less real, more like a painting. She sent a quick prayer to Zhang Gua Lao, then pulled the paper one last time. Vakhtang shrank as she pulled, then drained away. Xiao Yen looked down at the piece of paper she had won. It was a portrait of Vakhtang, done with a few strokes in black ink, just enough to capture the essence of the man, the cruelty of his deeds showing in his tight lips, the fear that drove him haunting his eyes.

Xiao Yen quickly folded the portrait into a box, with the picture on the inside, locking Vakhtang away forever.

As soon as she put the box down by her feet, she felt another piece of paper in her hands. For the rest of her dream, that was all Xiao Yen did. Take portraits of Vakhtang and fold them away. Her hands and arms were a blur. Sometimes she grew tired. Then she'd take a deep breath, and find the strength to continue.

Xiao Yen awoke smelling dawn in the night air. She didn't know if Vakhtang would come back and haunt her again. It didn't matter. He'd served his purpose, reminding her of one of the basic truths of her life.

If she continued to fold, to do paper magic, sooner or later, she'd have to kill again.

Xiao Yen couldn't bear the weight of another death on her soul.

She realized her face felt cold. When she reached up to touch it, she found her cheeks were wet, her eyes shedding tears. She rolled over onto her side and faced the dull center of her life. When the tears stopped, she slept.

Xiao Yen crawled from her tent the next morning, unrested. She didn't meet anyone's eye, but walked next to the fire and announced loudly, "I'm not practicing magic anymore."

Ehran nodded and said, "Good."

Udo cuffed his brother, then came up to Xiao Yen. "I don't understand," he said. "Why would you give up your magic? Why would you give up such a large part of yourself?"

Xiao Yen blinked back her tears. She couldn't believe the irony. Someone finally understood how important her magic was—after she'd renounced it.

Tuo Nu came up as well, and asked Xiao Yen in a low voice, in her language, "Are you sure you want to do this?"

Xiao Yen considered for a moment. Maybe she could explain to him why. Though Udo understood some things, his essential nature was too violent, too aggressive, to understand this. "The price is too high," she said. Killing went against all her Buddhist teachings, against her mother's and sister's wishes. It pressed too hard against her soul.

"Ah, the, ah, Wind of God lowers the price," Tuo Nu said.

Xiao Yen thought for a moment, then replied, "Thank you, no." Forgetting what she had done wouldn't make it better. She didn't want the Wind of God to blow away her pain. What would prevent her from becoming like Vakhtang if she couldn't feel remorse?

She helped herself to the still-warm porridge. She only gave herself one spoonful, and had problems finishing that. She packed up her tent and gear without saying a word to anyone. Udo saddled her horse for her and strapped her things to it.

As they left camp, Udo rode next to Xiao Yen. "I don't understand," he said.

"It's wrong to kill," Xiao Yen responded. She didn't know how else to explain it, didn't know how to tell him of her Buddhist teachings, of her mother, her culture, her soul.

"Vakhtang was evil," Udo said simply, as if that should absolve her.

Xiao Yen merely looked at him. After a while, Udo pulled forward, up to Tuo Nu. They talked urgently, but Xiao Yen couldn't make out their words.

Xiao Yen wished she could pull forward, make her horse run, all the way to the coast, then back home. Though Bei Xi had promised the attack against Bao Fang wouldn't come until the next year, Xiao Yen felt anxious. What if Bei Xi didn't make a distinction between an attack and a raid? What if bandits set up closer to Bao Fang, threatening the merchants and the markets? What would happen to her family?

Xiao Yen tried to distract herself by naming the trees as they passed. Elm, oak, blue pine, rock pine, scrub pine, bilberry bush, pine . . . Bored, she pulled her practice string from her sleeve and began tying knots, as she always did. First she grew the knot big in her mind, then small. The familiar movements brought her a little calm.

"What's that?" Tuo Nu asked.

Xiao Yen stared at her hands with a shock. She was practicing magic again. She threw her string to the ground in horror.

"Nothing," she said, nudging her horse around him. How could she have forgotten her vow so quickly? She flexed her fingers. At least her arms never trembled. She bit back her laugh, afraid she'd never stop if she started. The sun still warmed her back, the pines still smelled sweet. But she'd killed Vakhtang. And one day, she'd have to kill again. Now she knew why no one wanted to hire her. It was awful enough for a man to kill, but for a woman . . .

Maybe she should let Tuo Nu help her, try the Wind of God, lower the payment made by her soul.

Xiao Yen tried to eat the stew they cooked for lunch, but only managed a few bites. She still wouldn't talk with anyone. After lunch, she sat on the ground next to her horse, moving her hands restlessly. She wanted to go into the woods, just for a short while, go through her poses, maybe find her center. That smacked of practicing magic though, which she'd given up. She sighed, frustrated.

Tuo Nu approached her, carrying a steaming cup of tea. Udo stood behind him. Ehran stood farther back, his arms folded over his chest, looking on in disgust.

"Here," Tuo Nu said, handing her the cup. "Drink this. It will help."

Xiao Yen looked up at him, then at Udo. He nodded, then spoke slowly, using simple words, so Xiao Yen would understand him. "Tuo Nu said your essence hurts from killing. But without magic, I think your essence hurts more."

Xiao Yen took the cup, letting it warm her hands for a moment. The tea smelled like dirt and bitter herbs. She hadn't known what the Wind of God was supposed to smell like, but she knew that anything this powerful wouldn't smell sweet.

She drank the whole cup in one gulp. "Now what?" she asked.

Tuo Nu took the cup and helped her lie down on the ground. "We wait. It should only take a short while," he said.

Xiao Yen closed her eyes and tried to find her center.

There it was. The cool running river, flashing like quicksilver. If she bathed in the waters, maybe she would feel clean. She let her core expand. A dead tree, one she'd never seen before, had fallen on the far side of the river. It was being reabsorbed by the forest. Young plants grew out of it.

Xiao Yen's heart beat hard in her chest. Death was

just another part of life, the endless cycle. She could make offerings for Vakhtang, remember him in her prayers, and hope for the best for him in his next life. It wouldn't be enough, but it could be a start. Maybe her guilt would abate, and her soul could heal.

She walked toward the river, knelt, and put her hands in the cool water. Blood streamed from her fingers. She'd never be able to wash her hands clean. This death would follow her through this life and all her others. It might prevent her from being able to leave the cycle of death and rebirth.

She pulled her hands out of the river, carrying dripping water to her face. She stopped before she drank any of it. Something was wrong. The river in front of her bubbled, frothed, growing more chaotic, then exploded, like someone had set off a firecracker under the surface. Water flew everywhere, like a frightened flock of cranes. What had happened?

Xiao Yen heard wind. It blew through her, blew away her calm. She opened her eyes, shocked. The wind still roared in her ears.

"What is this?" she asked.

"It's the Wind of God," Tuo Nu replied.

"It doesn't make you forget?" Xiao Yen asked. Udo looked at her strangely. She realized she'd been shouting over the sound of the wind. No one heard it but her.

"No," Tuo Nu replied. "The wind blows strength to you, so you don't have to use your own. It blows you to your center."

Xiao Yen shook her head. "How can you think with all that noise?" she asked.

"The sound of the wind is a great comfort to me. Isn't it to you?"

Xiao Yen replied, "No." She struggled to hear the silence of her river. The wind ripped it away from her. "How long will this last?" she asked, struggling to sit up.

"Forever," Tuo Nu said.

Xiao Yen blinked. Forever. Her luck was gone. Her calm, her center, gone. Her magic. Gone. Forever.

Chapter 20

✺

Bao Fang

Xiao Yen waited, without fidgeting, to be presented to Master Djong, the official visiting from Huang Hwa, a large town east of Bao Fang. His town was investigating different defenses. They'd contacted Master Wei about hiring one of his students. The trouble up north continued to grow. Though the treaty held, there were constant raids. Rumors of a great warlord, and the horsemen uniting under him, circulated through the marketplace. Many merchants no longer took their wares to Tan Yuan, the next large city north of Bao Fang. Xiao Yen was certain this wouldn't be the last time Master Wei had his students "perform" for potential clients.

Xiao Yen couldn't decide what to make of the official. His cheeks were as fat and round as the Buddha's, but he didn't look serene or jolly when he smiled. He wore a brilliant pink silk robe, with golden chrysanthemums embroidered so finely around the cuffs and hem that the flowers seemed painted on. Yet Master Djong's beard held tiny white flakes, and maybe a drop of soup from lunch.

A breeze shook the bright orange canopy. Xiao Yen elongated her neck to catch more of the cool wind, wishing she could fan herself. The spring sunshine was unusually hot this afternoon. However, she and the other students had to sit absolutely still on the hard dirt of the outer courtyard and wait to be presented. After all her years of training with Master Wei, it wasn't hard to sit motionless, with a quiet heart, waiting as a river waits for the rain. As the youngest of the three senior students, she would be presented last. Earlier that day all ten students from the school had been presented in an assembly. Now, only the most senior students were allowed to approach the dais where Master Wei and Master Djong sat.

Fat Fang, being the eldest student and Governor Fang's son, went first. His body resembled the official's: round belly, small eyes under a protruding brow, fat Buddhalike lips. The differences between them were more subtle. Strong muscles molded Fat Fang's shoulders, his back was as straight as a sword while he knelt, and he projected calm like a boulder sitting next to a river. He still teased Xiao Yen, but it seemed more out of habit now than out of spite. He never listened to her folding ideas. When his sister, Bing Yu, came to visit, he bragged about how he was the best student in their class.

Long Yen sat next to Xiao Yen. He waited like a willow tree waits for the wind. His nose had grown sharper as he'd matured, protruding like a sheer cliff in the middle of his face. His eyes had grown sharper too. He always saw when Fat Fang took more dessert, or when Xiao Yen had spent the morning missing her family. He still had creamy skin and a sweet, wide smile. He was also the laziest of the three students. He folded well when he concentrated, but he preferred sleeping to studying.

Master Djong pulled a small bag from his sleeve and presented it to Fat Fang at the end of their interview. This was a not-so-subtle bribe, so that the students might consider employment in Huang Hwa if a position was offered to them. Fat Fang thanked the official many times. He fingered the bag as he walked back to his place to sit down, trying to count the number of coins in it.

While Long Yen was being presented, Xiao Yen thought about the upcoming mock battle for the pleasure of the official. She didn't know what the boys planned to fold. Long Yen had hinted at a large creature, since they were outside. Fat Fang had warned her that a mere crane wouldn't defeat him this time. She smiled, thinking of the stag she'd been practicing, with its delicate hooves and sharp antlers. In her mind, she practiced the folds again: the gentle creases to set the shape into the paper, the false fold to give the hind legs their power, the little tug to bring the face down and expose the antlers.

After Long Yen sat down, also carrying a small bag, Xiao Yen rose and walked forward. She stopped a respectful distance away, her head bowed. The official turned to speak with Master Wei, so she waited, not listening to their conversation, as that would be impolite. A sweet fragrance came from Master Djong, sweeter than incense, a foreign scented oil. Finally, there was a pause in the conversation. Master Wei inclined his head, indicating that Xiao Yen should come closer.

Xiao Yen walked up, knelt, and bowed, touching her forehead to the earth three times. She stayed kneeling and sat back on her heels.

"This is Fu Xi Wén," Master Wei said, introducing Xiao Yen with her formal name.

Xiao Yen bowed again.

The official turned to Master Wei and said, "A student? Not a servant? I thought you only had two students."

Master Wei didn't respond. Xiao Yen hoped that Master Djong felt as uncomfortable in the silence as Gan Ou did.

"We had heard rumors about the girl," Master Djong finally continued. "Of course, you are well known for your charity and gracious heart."

Xiao Yen felt her cheeks catch fire. She kept her face impassive, not letting her eyes burn with anger.

She was not here on charity. She had just as much skill as the boys.

"I shall have to send the *girl* something from the road," Master Djong said, his voice coated with oil.

The words hit Xiao Yen's chest like a series of swift kicks. How dare he? Xiao Yen had never heard such condescension in someone's tone. He obviously had money for her, and didn't plan on giving it to her because she was a girl. Xiao Yen's rage held her chest in a vise so strong she couldn't take a deep breath, even if she tried. She looked at Master Wei, but his face told her nothing.

The official cleared his throat. He had nothing to say to her, though he'd talked with each of the boys for a while.

Xiao Yen hid her face with another set of deep bows, then returned to her seat.

Neither Fat Fang or Long Yen looked at her, but she knew they'd seen her empty hands. Master Wei and Master Djong continued conversing. Xiao Yen wanted the tournament to begin immediately so she had a place to focus her anger, but she had to wait for the signal.

She reached for her calm while she waited. It wasn't there. She tried to think about her creature instead, to lose herself in its folds, but all she could think about was the stag ramming its antlers into the fat official, tossing him into the air, then trampling on him after he hit the ground. She shook herself mentally, shocked at herself. What would Fu Be Be say? Girls weren't supposed to think such things. The stag kept growing in her imagination, filling the courtyard, until he wore the bright orange canopy like a scarf woven through his antlers. With a single leap he cleared the wall around the school. Xiao Yen flew with her stag into silent woods filled with green jeweled trees, sipping water so cold it chilled her core like melted snow water.

Abruptly, Xiao Yen came back to the courtyard.

The men still talked. She looked at the space she had to work with. In her mind's eye, she placed her stag in it and tried to proportion her creature to the space. The stag kept growing. She'd never be able to contain it, to make it follow her bidding. She was too angry, and the stag would reflect that. She needed a still heart for such a creature.

What else could she fold though? That was what she'd prepared. She needed the perfect creature, particularly after Master Djong had suggested she was a charity case. She studied the official. Maybe if she made a creature that resembled him, he would be impressed. She watched the quick darting way he moved his hands, how he always moved his head and shoulders together, how his wet eyes were alive, searching the corners of the courtyard for hidden treasure. Then he moistened his lips with just the tip of his tongue, suggesting . . .

A tail.

Xiao Yen knew what she wanted to fold: a scorpion—sly, tricky, noxious—an appropriate representation of the official. It was also a difficult creature to fold. The tail was complicated. She considered for another moment. If her scorpion grew larger than normal size, that would be okay. All the better to even the odds with the other full-size creatures she was sure Fat Fang and Long Yen were folding. A scorpion could be mean, take all her anger and use it.

Finally Master Wei announced the start of the contest. Xiao Yen, Fat Fang, and Long Yen rose and went to their spots in the courtyard. When they were in place, they bowed to each other, then sat down together. Xiao Yen picked up the paper before her and prayed to Zhang Gua Lao, the immortal, the patron saint of paper folding. She closed her eyes and breathed the hot courtyard air. The dust and the clay smell baked her bones, her resolution. It was the ideal scent for a scorpion. She opened her eyes, touched her amulet with both hands, just the fingertips, to bring luck. Then she started folding.

This was the first time Master Wei had let the students do battle outdoors, with large creatures. Normally, they did mock battles or contests, with one seeking a prize while the other guarded, with small creatures like birds or dogs or snakes. This "battle" had been at the insistence of the official, who'd been unimpressed with the earlier presentations. He appreciated strategy, but he wanted to see blood. Fat Fang already had a position when he left the school. He'd see to the defenses of Bao Fang, protecting all his "children," as he called the townspeople. Both Long Yen and Xiao Yen could use a prominent post when they left the school, so Master Wei had agreed to this demonstration.

Master Wei always judged the students on how gracefully they folded, as well as the success of their creation once it was animated. Xiao Yen suspected that Master Djong wouldn't know graceful folding from ungraceful, so she didn't worry about the fine points like keeping her elbows always pointed in one of the three directions of Heaven, or finishing each long fold by drawing out her hand. Instead, she concentrated on the tricky figure itself.

More than once, Xiao Yen felt her shoulders folding themselves up around her ears and had to force herself to relax. Sweat trickled down her neck and her sides. Occasionally, she heard the faint tinkling of the bells under the eaves of the Hall of Reception. The wind stirred the surrounding trees as well, a quiet rustling, like pieces of paper being shuffled.

Xiao Yen finished pulling out the second set of four legs, pursing her lips in disappointment. They were longer than the first four. Her creature was lopsided. She should start over again, but she had no time.

Xiao Yen had just finished the front pinchers, trying to rectify the different sizes with extra folds, when she heard faint applause. She sneaked a quick glance. A large black bear growled at a towering stag. Xiao Yen smiled and looked back to her creation. Though her scorpion was small, and maybe a little lopsided, at least she hadn't folded the same thing as one of the other students. Xiao Yen blessed her luck, touching her amulet once more, then focused on her creation, blocking out everything else in the courtyard.

Xiao Yen rolled the tail up in one smooth motion. It didn't bend at the natural creases, so she spent time she didn't have pulling, pinching, and prodding the tail into shape. By the time she finished, it looked much better, but the boys had started their combat. The stag had claw marks down its sweating sides. It circled the bear, who had an antler prong—like the stub of a wooden knife—stuck in its chest.

Xiao Yen placed her scorpion in front of her, wiped the sweat from her brow, then closed her eyes. She focused her anger and concentrated on impressing her creation with one thing: winning.

When she opened her eyes, her scorpion had already run into the center of the courtyard. It had grown to the size of a small dog, and fearless. It pinched the bear's hind legs, then darted toward the deer as the bear reached out with a huge paw to swipe at the annoyance. Again and again, it stung or pinched the two larger animals. They attacked each other in frustration, unable to reach the fast-moving scorpion. The stag kept going up on its hind legs and using its sharp front hooves to batter the bear, which slashed and clawed with deadly force at the stag. The scorpion scooted in, pinching higher and higher, until it severed a tendon in the back of the stag's leg.

The stag crumpled. The scorpion came in and stung the stag's nose, while the bear stomped down with all its weight, breaking the stag's neck.

Xiao Yen felt the pit of her stomach fall. The stag had been so beautiful, its coat like soft down. It had been a terrible thing to kill it wantonly, even if it was only a created thing, infused with essence, without a soul. Tears threatened to spill from her eyes. She bit her tongue and looked at Master Wei. He sat with an impassive face. His right hand tightened sporadically into a fist. Xiao Yen gulped. She didn't want to face the wrath of her master.

Just then he looked at her. He didn't smile at her, but there was a broadening of his mouth, the slightest loosening between his eyes that only the most perceptive of observers would notice. He wasn't angry with her. He bowed his head slightly, then returned his attention to the battle.

Necessity drove them all, from the fighting beasts to the people who created this combat. The scorpion had severed tendons in two of the bear's legs, making it impossible for it to stay either upright or up on four paws. Then it aimed its front claws for the neck, stinging the bear's face, keeping its sharp teeth to the side. Soon, it was over, and the scorpion scrambled up onto the bear's chest, waving its stinger like a flag in a parade. Then it scrambled off. Xiao Yen's heart stopped for a moment, fearing that it would run up and sting Master Djong. Instead, it ran out the gate, seeking its way into the wild.

Xiao Yen and the other students picked up the delicate remains of the original paper creatures they'd folded and carried them to a waiting brazier set just outside the canopy. Long Yen went first, as his was the first creature to fall. Xiao Yen admired the beautiful lines of his stag's chest, its proud antlers. She wanted to tell Long Yen it had been a fine creature as he consigned it to the flames. As had been Fat Fang's bear, beautifully rendered, standing on its rear legs, its front paws ready to attack. Then she gave her little lopsided scorpion to the flames.

She didn't mark the center of her forehead with her creation's ashes. She felt no pride in this victory. Her creature had just been meaner than the other two, not more graceful or beautiful. She'd been angrier, and luckier. She sighed, then turned, walked back to the dais, and knelt in front of it. She bowed low, touching her forehead to the ground nine times. Master Wei spoke loud words of praise for her. Xiao Yen kept her attention on the official. He returned her gaze, rubbing his chin with one hand, not saying anything.

Xiao Yen thanked her master with the standard phrases, then went off with the boys to eat the feast that had been prepared for the official. For once, Fat Fang didn't tease her and Long Yen didn't make her walk behind them. They walked shoulder to shoulder with her. They weren't angry with her for winning. Maybe they understood how hollow the victory was.

Xiao Yen wanted to be happy. She'd won. She'd get to go home the next day as a reward. But her heart stayed beneath the soles of her feet.

The next morning, just before Xiao Yen left for Bao Fang, a messenger arrived at the school. He carried a large bag of gold, twice as big as the bags Fat Fang and Long Yen had received. Xiao Yen refused to touch it, instead directing the messenger to take it to Wang Tie-Tie.

Let her family enjoy it. She couldn't.

"Little Bear! You're so strong!" Xiao Yen exclaimed as she reached the end of the courtyard with her nephew gripping her fingers. He still wobbled when he moved, but he also pulled himself up on tables. Soon he'd be walking without help. He ignored the shrieks of the other children chasing a ball in the far corner and concentrated on going forward. He pulled his mouth up and led with his chin, like a scholar deep in thought.

"He's so serious," Xiao Yen commented to Gan Ou over her shoulder.

"He's going to be a fine man when he grows up," Gan Ou replied. "Responsible and full of *xiao,* always ready to do his duty, eh?"

Ling-Ling and Han Wanju, two of Xiao Yen's cousins, politely agreed that he'd honor his parents as a good son should.

"Give him to his nurse," Gan Ou said as Xiao Yen turned around with her nephew, who seemed determined to walk all the way back without pause. "Come here and have your tea with us."

Reluctantly, Xiao Yen handed the boy to his nurse standing on the side of the courtyard. A part of her wanted to stay and play with the other children, rather than join her sister and her cousins. As always. Xiao Yen hid her smile at the thought.

She walked back to the stairs where the other women sat. Bright pink, green, and yellow unembroidered silk pillows lay on the steps. Gan Ou sat in the middle, on the top step, her legs curved under her. Her face had slimmed since the end of her last pregnancy, making her nose and chin seem pointed. Her smile glittered with secrets. She wore a bright gold jacket with fine white bells embroidered around the cuffs and down the front placard.

Han Wanju sat on Gan Ou's right side, her scarlet jacket blazoned with large black peonies. She'd never lost her round, childlike cheeks, even though she was also a mother. Her eyes still coveted everything they saw greedily, like a pig.

Ling-Ling also sat on that side, down a step, leaning back on one hand. Her sharp teeth were always present in her conversation. She wore a purple jacket with circular patterns of yellow-orange peaches dotting her front and sides. Her hair was pulled back from her face and piled high on her head with an elaborate set of jeweled hairpins. She'd always been the one most concerned with appearances.

Xiao Yen glanced down at her own plain school jacket. It was well made, but dark blue, with tiny flowers in lighter blue sewn only around the cuffs. She always felt fancy at school in this jacket. The boys wore dull colors, and never took care of their clothes. Yet, compared with her sister and her cousins, she looked like a servant. Xiao Yen knew she shouldn't feel ashamed, but a small part of her did.

Xiao Yen sat down at her sister's left. Gan Ou handed her a well-balanced cup, coated in a cracked white glaze, full of slightly bitter *gen mai cha,* a green tea made with toasted rice. Xiao Yen wrapped her hands around it and drew the smoky scent of the tea deep into her chest, letting it relax her.

The women slyly bragged about their sons. The older boys ran with abandon across the courtyard, absorbed in their game. The girls were more circumspect, listening to stories or taking care of their own pretend children.

Ling-Ling called attention to her newest jade bracelet as she asked for more tea. Xiao Yen, of course, didn't have any bracelets. They got in the way of folding. Gan Ou wore a plain silver one. Xiao Yen looked at her sister. Though the silk of her jacket was fine, the seams weren't straight. Gaps showed between the stitches along the back of her left sleeve. Plus, the cup she held was chipped along the rim. Xiao Yen wondered if Gan Ou's husband ever let her use the beautiful writing set he'd given her as a wedding gift, or if he was too miserly.

Just then crying erupted on the far step. Gan Ou's youngest son batted at his nurse's hands and pulled out of her arms, reaching for his mother sitting so far away. Gan Ou smiled and called, "Bring him here."

The nurse shuffled to where the women sat and handed over the boy. With a practiced movement, Gan Ou undid two side buttons and pulled out her breast. The boy began suckling with a happy sigh. Ling-Ling and Han Wanju talked with each other. Xiao Yen drank her tea and watched her sister out of the corner of her eye. A contented smile, one that Xiao Yen had never seen before, played on Gan Ou's lips. Xiao Yen, in her mind's eye, could see the magic bond between mother and son. Xiao Yen had never seen her sister look so happy. Could being a mother have changed her?

The women sat quietly for a moment, each thinking her own thoughts after the nurse took the baby away.

"Xiao Yen, do you remember Chieh-yeh Be Be? My matchmaker?" Gan Ou asked, calling Xiao Yen from her fog.

"I think so," Xiao Yen replied. "Wasn't she at Wang Tie-Tie's birthday party?"

"She was," Gan Ou replied, taking another sip of tea, and pausing.

Xiao Yen remembered Chieh-yeh Be Be's nose. It was flat, like a peasant's, and good for smelling gossip. She meddled in other people's affairs with her meaty hands, leaving sticky fingerprints behind. She'd been Fu Be Be's choice for a matchmaker, not Wang Tie-Tie's.

Gan Ou looked around the courtyard, making sure none of the servants was near. Ling-Ling and Han Wanju both leaned forward so they wouldn't miss a word.

"Fu Be Be and I talked with Chieh-yeh Be Be, and she's agreed to look for a husband for you," Gan Ou announced, her smile triumphant, but possessive and sharp around the edges.

Xiao Yen opened her mouth. No words came out. A husband? So she might have her own son? Have a piece of happiness as big as Gan Ou's? She grinned at her sister, unable to say anything.

Gan Ou clapped her hands and said, "I knew you weren't Wang Tie-Tie's pawn! I've already checked with my husband. You don't have to go back to school. You can stay here until we get you married!"

Ling-Ling said, "Don't you worry. We'll hide you. No one will know where you are." Ling-Ling put a thin, clutching hand out toward Xiao Yen.

Han Wanju, ever the follower, said, "We'll protect you." Her small eyes looked over Xiao Yen as if she were eyeing a new delicacy.

Gan Ou said, "It'll be so good to have you here, with your family, where you belong."

Xiao Yen pulled herself back from the three women. Of course, if she got married, she'd have to stop practicing magic. She'd have to leave her quiet room, the whispering trees, how good it felt to bring a creature to life.

"What do you mean, no, you won't?" Gan Ou

asked, her voice holding the sharpness her smile always hid.

Xiao Yen wasn't aware that she'd spoken, but she must have. "I have to go back to school. I graduate later this spring. Then, we can talk about . . ." She let her voice trail off. Talk about her giving up her magic? Everything that she'd worked so hard to do? What about her promise to Wang Tie-Tie, to do a deed worthy of an immortal peach?

But to have a baby . . .

"I have to go," Xiao Yen said, standing. Though the air in the courtyard was still, Xiao Yen felt a great wind blowing, tearing her apart. To continue with her magic? And always do what Wang Tie-Tie wanted her to do? Possibly to go to live with foreigners? Or to have a child? And maybe get a miserly husband like Ko Fu? Her luck couldn't protect her from something like that.

Xiao Yen leaned over and kissed her sister's cheek. Gan Ou wouldn't meet Xiao Yen's eye, her smile hiding her hurt. Xiao Yen bowed to Ling-Ling and Han Wanju, then left without another word. She knew they'd gossip after she left, gnaw over her words and suck at the marrow of her life. She hurried back to her own family compound to gather her things. There'd be no peace for her there either. Maybe the quiet at her school could help her decide where she wanted to go, who she wanted to be.

Fat Fang and Long Yen stood talking in the entrance to the student courtyard when Xiao Yen returned to school that afternoon. Long Yen was more animated than she'd ever seen him. Even his sleepy eyes were wide open.

"So my father placed a vote before the members, and they agreed. I'm to defend the big caravan, for the whole Weavers' Guild, the one with all the goods. And all four horses! From here to the capital," Long Yen finished in a rush, using his hands to indicate going from one place to the otter.

"Congratulations," Xiao Yen told Long Yen, awed. The horses were worth as much, if not more, than the cloth they carried. "I wish you the greatest success," she added, bowing low.

Long Yen bowed back, still grinning.

Fat Fang added, "It isn't as important as defending a big city like Bao Fang, but it's a good start."

Xiao Yen rolled her eyes at Long Yen. He winked, then ducked his head to hide his laughter. Fat Fang had bragged about his position since he'd arrived at school.

"Just think of all the things you'll see!" Xiao Yen told Long Yen. "The fancy puppet shows, the imported paper shops. Even foreigners perform in the markets there, or so I've heard."

"And if the caravan is successful, who knows? Maybe we'll go back every year. Maybe the Emperor will see our cloth and *ask* us to come back!" Long Yen said, building bigger dreams with his hands.

"Anything could happen," Xiao Yen replied, sharing in and trying to add to his happiness.

"What position will you take after graduation?" Fat Fang asked, turning to Xiao Yen.

Xiao Yen felt the question like a cold rain beating on her head. She prevented herself from jerking back, but just barely. "My aunt has many contacts with many caravans," she said, hugging the book Wang Tie-Tie had given her to her chest. It was a dictionary of the language of the foreigners, the ones that lived on the other end of the Great Merchant trail. It had been expensive, but Wang Tie-Tie said it was worth it. Xiao Yen needed to learn a foreigner's tongue for her work. If she spoke some of a foreigner's language, maybe they'd overlook that she was a girl, and hire her.

Fat Fang said, "I see."

Long Yen turned to Fat Fang and said, "Why don't you go practice or something? You're going to need it, with such an important position."

Instead of replying to the sarcasm in Long Yen's

voice, Fat Fang bowed his head to them and said, "I think I will." He turned and walked away, toward the student rooms.

Neither Xiao Yen or Long Yen could stop from giggling. Fat Fang held himself like a puffed-up priest, hands to his sides, while rocking his hips like a prostitute. He waved his hand at them without turning around, well aware of the picture he presented.

Xiao Yen smiled again. Fat Fang was pompous, but he hadn't meant to hurt her with his question. The play-walking was all the apology she'd get.

"Do you want to work with a caravan?" Long Yen asked. "I didn't know girls could do that. I thought . . ." His voice trailed away.

"You thought I'd get married?" Xiao Yen asked.

Long Yen replied, "Breathe deeply and let nature guide your fingers." He bowed as he said it.

Xiao Yen laughed out loud. Long Yen was so sweet, trying to cheer her up with impressions of Master Wei.

"Well, I, have to go," Long Yen said.

Xiao Yen started walking toward her room at the back of the courtyard.

"You know, you *are* the best student here," Xiao Yen heard from behind her. She turned to look, but Long Yen was still walking toward Master Wei's study. Had Long Yen said that? How could he think such a thing? She was a girl, as Fat Fang had pointed out many times. A girl, who shouldn't be practicing magic, or fighting, but who should be looking after her husband, and having babies.

Chapter 21

∽

On the Trail

Udo pointed to Khuangho and asked Xiao Yen, "Isn't it pretty?"

Xiao Yen gave him a sad smile. The town did look pretty from where they sat, high on the merchant road above the town. It wasn't a walled city like Tan Yuan or Bao Fang—shops and compounds sprouted in random clumps in a sheltered cove. Most of the buildings were made of wood or yellowish rock. Bisecting the curve of the cove was a long dock, sticking like a child's finger into the water, with brown lumps on either side; ships, Xiao Yen assumed. The sea sparkled brilliantly blue beyond the town. Xiao Yen had never seen such a large stretch of water before. It went out as far as she could see, until it touched the edge of Heaven.

Now that she'd seen it, she could leave. She'd done her duty. She'd seen the brothers and their goods to the coast. She had to get back to Bao Fang.

Sea wind, tinged with salt, blew the strands of hair that had escaped her braids into her face. She cocked her head to one side. This wind had a lighter tone compared to the wind she constantly heard in her head.

"I'm sorry," Udo said, for the ten thousandth time

in the week that had passed since she'd drunk the
Wind of God tea.

Xiao Yen replied without thinking, "My bad luck."

Udo asked, "What do you mean?"

Xiao Yen said, "I . . . I . . . I lost my luck. Before
I travel." She didn't add that she wouldn't have had
to go on this journey if she'd still had her luck.

Udo asked, "How can you lose your luck? You
make your luck, good or bad."

Xiao Yen didn't know what to say. Udo had said
that before. How could she make her own luck?

Ehran piped up from behind. "Udo's right. Luck
isn't given to you. A man makes his luck, his
opportunities."

Xiao Yen turned around, surprised. It was the first
time Ehran had said anything directly to her since
she'd returned. He looked sheepishly at his brother
and said, "Udo told me how you killed that foreign
lord and the rat dragon. You don't have bad luck.
How could you have done all that with bad luck?"

Xiao Yen had to admit Ehran had a point. It was
just that the cost of her deeds had been so high. Her
guilt over Vakhtang's death had shrunk some, now
that she'd realized he was on the natural path of
death, rebirth, and life, but she'd never be able to
justify her killing. Then there was the memory of those
men, in the courtyard, who . . . She refused to think
about it. It was getting easier. The Wind of God
hadn't helped her forget, but time and distance had.

She was curious though. "Udo not tell you before?"
she asked.

Ehran chuckled. "He told me. I didn't listen." He
turned and faced Xiao Yen. In the bright sunlight she
noticed a slight bruise under his left eye. The brothers
had come to blows? She'd never understand
foreigners.

The coastal road narrowed to a dirt trail north of
Khuangho. Xiao Yen took her time as she walked
along it, enjoying the afternoon sunshine, the crashing

waves, the fresh sea scent, the pale grass clinging to the cliff on her left. Black-tailed gulls swooped from their nests and dipped into the sea. The wind grew stronger as Xiao Yen headed up the coast. The sound almost drowned out the constant blowing she heard inside her head.

Tuo Nu said he knew of no way to stop the Wind of God. He'd promised to search his books for a cure, when he had time. Xiao Yen didn't blame him for not wanting to have much to do with them. He was home; he lived in Khuangho in rented rooms, and his family lived another half-day's ride south, down the coast. He no longer had any responsibility toward his fellow travelers.

Xiao Yen tried to not think badly of Tuo Nu, giving her the Wind of God—their forms of magic were more different than even he could have known. Sometimes, though, she suspected he wasn't sorry she couldn't practice magic anymore. Stopping her had removed his competition. Master Wei had said that all other mages would be enemies. Maybe Tuo Nu's teacher had said the same thing, and he'd taken the lesson more to heart.

While Tuo Nu did research, and Udo and Ehran sought passage on a ship, Xiao Yen decided to go to the local dragon temple, north of town, to pray. Maybe a dragon or a god would hear her, and lead her back to her center. Every time she'd tried to find her center, there had been no center to find, just a whirling cacophony of images, scents, and memories.

The trail split at the crest of the next bluff. One path went down the bluff, along the water's edge, while the other curved to the left, around the back of the next hill, then up to the dragon temple. Xiao Yen caught a glimpse of its curving roof before the trail dipped.

Rocks seemed to have overgrown the path. She paused halfway up the hill to catch her breath. The path had curled around. She was no longer next to the sea and assaulted by the wind. Bushes clung to

the hill. A few stunted pines forced their roots into
the rock. The gray boulders were smoother here, almost round, scattered over the landscape like the toy
balls of the giant Liu-Hua. Anchored under the rocks
grew bunches of yellow star-shaped flowers.

Xiao Yen knelt down to smell them. They had a
light, springlike scent. She stayed as she was for a
moment, eyes closed, remembering the Garden of
Sweet Scents, the glorious array of flowers always
blooming there. She saw herself sitting on the platform
at the end of the garden, as she had when she'd been
a child, waiting for Wang Tie-Tie. The heads of the
flowers in the garden bobbed in time to the wind she
heard in her head, then slowed.

The wind in her head abated.

Xiao Yen froze and held her breath. She brought
the picture of her river to her mind's eye. It formed
piece by piece, the sun glistening off the water, the
cool green banks, when *bam!* A mini-tornado spun
through the glade, scattering water everywhere.

She still couldn't find her center.

With a sigh, Xiao Yen stood up and continued
walking.

Coming over the crest of the hill, she saw the
dragon temple again. The sun, now at her back, shone
brightly on the whitish grass. The painted temple
looked dull in comparison. Beyond the temple the sea
reflected the sunlight like a dark mirror. The temple's
shadow flowed midnight black behind it, as solid as
the structure itself. Xiao Yen tried to see with her
mind's eye the mage light Tuo Nu had been teaching
her to perceive. She got the impression of a foggy
cloud wrapped around the base of the temple, but the
image was quickly dispersed by the wind in her head.

The slate-gray roof of the temple curved up on all
four corners of the building. When Xiao Yen drew
nearer, she saw murals painted just under the roof,
telling the story of the village of Khuangho and the
sea dragon. Xiao Yen walked around the whole building, reading it.

At first, men fought the dragon. Their battles were fierce and terrible, and many people died. At the same time, every time the townspeople drove the dragon away from his home in the sea, they suffered. There was drought and a plague that made everyone's face turn green. Finally, they had a brilliant leader—shown as enlightened with the round flame of Buddha springing from his forehead—who understood that the ways of the dragon were the ways of nature. He negotiated a peace between the town and the dragon, and now the town was prosperous.

Xiao Yen paused at the threshold to remove her boots before she walked into the temple. A tree of candles stood to the left of the altar, all lit. On the back wall hung a huge scroll painting of a dragon, made up of three bolts of silk sewn together. A thick red quilt covered the altar table. In the center gleamed an ornate silver bowl full of pure water.

Xiao Yen knelt in front of the altar and prayed. She praised the dragon for its wisdom, long life, and intelligence, for its working in harmony with the people in the town. Then she prayed to Yen Lo, the ruler of the dead, to judge Vakhtang lightly, praying his reincarnation wouldn't take too many ages. She also asked for Udo and Ehran to return safely to their land, for peace between the horsemen and her people, for Wang Tie-Tie to live a long time, for Fu Be Be and Gan Ou to be happy, for some quiet, and for her luck. The cold stone of the temple floor numbed her knees. A trace of incense remained in the air. Xiao Yen tried to drift with it, to float above her troubles.

An angry voice interrupted her, and a hand shook her shoulder. Xiao Yen turned, startled.

A fat priest in ochre robes with wide sleeves, and a swath of white silk cloth tied around his paunch, stood behind her, his eyes full of menace. The top of his head held a few wisps of silver hair. Behind thick, gummy lips stood a bright row of perfectly polished teeth, like a carnivore's. He spoke in Tuo Nu's dialect, a language Xiao Yen didn't understand.

"Excuse me," she replied. "I was praying."

The priest grunted. "What were you praying for?" he asked. He spoke with such a heavy accent that it took Xiao Yen a moment to grasp that he'd spoken in her language.

The first thought that came into her head popped out of her mouth. "Luck," she said.

"Luck!" the priest exclaimed. "You're a long way from your home. Did you come crawling here on your luck?" he asked, sticking his hands inside his sleeves over his round belly.

"No, I didn't," Xiao Yen replied. "But my magic—" she started.

"I can see you have magic. But your magic doesn't have a solid home. Do you wish to keep it?" the priest asked.

Xiao Yen sighed. She didn't know.

"What do you want, child?" the priest asked, in tones that reminded her of Master Wei.

Again, her words blurted out without thought. "My quiet."

"Everything comes with a price," the priest intoned. Now he sounded like Fu Be Be.

Did she want to pay that price? To live like a foreigner in her own land? Did she have any choice? The wind in her ears blew louder, and she shivered. That cold stream running through her was part of her core. Its depths reflected her being. The green mossy banks gave a spring to her step, kept her young. Without access to her quiet place, she'd die, like a flower without rain.

"Then go find it," the priest said, smiling at her like Udo did, showing all his perfect teeth.

Another shiver ran down her back. She got to her feet and bowed deeply to the priest.

"And don't come cluttering my temple asking for frivolities again!" he called out as she crossed the threshold into the brilliant sunlit morning.

Halfway across the clearing, Xiao Yen looked back. The temple still seemed wrapped in its own blanket of shadow. Afraid that it'd disappear before her eyes, she scampered down the side of the hill.

On her way back to town, Xiao Yen stopped at the split in the road. The sea had a lighter sheen to it than earlier. The wind blew straight into her face, lifting the hair around her temples.

Had that really been a priest at the temple? Or maybe, it had been the sea dragon. His teeth had been perfect . . . Xiao Yen giggled out loud at the thought.

Xiao Yen closed her eyes. She tried to imagine what type of dragon the old priest would manifest as. His stoutness transformed into length. His ocher robes dulled and darkened, and became the back of the dragon, while his white silk cloth belt elongated and brightened into a pearl-white belly. Wings like flames attached to his front legs and a sharply pointed ridge of yellow spikes ran down his back. Swirling patterns of gray and black ran along his snout, curls of smoke rose around his ears, and row upon row of sharp white teeth filled his mouth. His eyes were the color of the autumn moon and glowed with their own light. Golden whiskers flowed from his chin, draping across his body and over his shoulders.

Xiao Yen reached out one hand to greet the dragon and welcome it, then folded her hand back toward herself while she reached out her other arm. From that, she flowed into the exercises Master Wei had taught her, folding and unfolding her body like paper.

Without thinking about it, she sought her center. Abruptly, she was there. The river ran faster than she'd ever seen it. The wind still blew through the trees, bending the grass down, sending ripples across the water. It didn't blow all the water away this time, or push her back.

Xiao Yen let the vision fill her sight. She understood now.

Everything had its price.

Had the priest said that? Or Master Wei? It didn't matter. She was willing to pay it.

The quiet splashed over her, like a fine rain. She

let it soak through her clothes, into her skin, down into her very bones, along with her acceptance.

Her peace came with a high price, which included her willingness to be both alone and lonely, as well as take responsibility for what she did. She had to step beyond duty, into choice.

In her mind's eye, Xiao Yen walked forward, thrust both hands into the cold stream, and drank.

Xiao Yen came back to herself, standing, head bowed, still at the crossroads. She gurgled inside, the sort of noises her nephew, Little Bear, made when he was happy. The sound of the wind in her head had faded a little. Maybe sometimes it would gust and scatter her thoughts, but she was connected to her calm again. It was her choice.

Xiao Yen turned, then stopped. The old priest wouldn't approve of her going back up the hill to the dragon temple. So she gave thanks where she was, starting in a small ball, then unfolding her limbs, one by one. She followed the steps Master Wei had taught her, enjoying the ritual precision. She let the wind and the stream inside her add touches by bending more in this pose, flowing more in the next.

Xiao Yen saw a dragon again, rising from the sea. It looked different this time. She didn't understand how she could conjure two such different-looking dragons in her mind's eye. This dragon's body was the color of the sea, but its belly, instead of being pearly white, had a gray sheen to it, like polished metal. The spikes along its back were a dull orange, like an iron bell that had been left in the rain. Its wings were larger, and ran along its body like miniature hands. The snout had red streaks running on its sides. Its whiskers hung almost to its shoulders, looking more like gold wires than flowing gold fur. Its eyes were the color of the ocean just before a storm. Yet Xiao Yen still believed it was just a creature of her imagination.

Xiao Yen greeted the dragon and danced for it, recalling the dances for Jing Long she'd been taught as a child. She welcomed the dragon, told it that she was glad that it was rising, that the rains would come. She heard shouts from above her, telling her to stop. She ignored them. She knew who she was. She'd made her choice. She was determined not to care if people whispered and pointed at her, or even if they shouted.

She danced as the dragon took to the air, a mini-rainstorm of water dripping off its body as it left the sea. She waved farewell to it, and continued to dance for herself.

An angry fisherman ran up to her and shook his pole in her face, yelling at her. He held himself so stiffly the cords in his neck stood out like sticks of bamboo. When he realized Xiao Yen didn't understand his language, he grabbed her arm and pulled her down the path back toward the town. She went with him reluctantly; he smelled of fish, and of being at sea for many days.

She didn't hear the screams until they crested the next bluff.

The second dragon hadn't been in her mind's eye. It *had* risen from the sea, and now attacked the town. Its gray body shimmered in the sunlight as it blew great gouts of fire. People ran screaming from its path. It made a large lazy loop over the water and came back toward the town, flying lower so it could smash a building with its tail.

Xiao Yen turned to the fisherman in horror. "But I didn't . . . It didn't come because of me. . . ."

The man twisted her arm up behind her back, then marched her into town.

Chapter 22

❧

Bao Fang

Xiao Yen looked in dismay at the piece she'd just folded. The center line curved, making the horse look like an old nag with a bent back and low hanging belly. At least she'd failed alone, in the quiet of her room. Xiao Yen wanted to destroy the piece. Instead, she forced herself to study it, to see which folds had gone wrong. Just refolding wouldn't help her. She needed to see her mistakes and learn from them, to see how one wrong fold could warp the whole.

The youngest class of students played a loud game with hoops and sticks in the courtyard. She watched them from her window, wishing she could join them. Even if she went outside to watch, they'd notice an older student, and their enthusiasm would dim. She was stuck by herself.

She tried to study her horse. She held it in front of her and looked at it from every angle. Her mind kept skipping away. She found herself thinking about the Weavers' Guild caravan Long Yen would be protecting. Or about Fat Fang, and how pompous he could be. Or about Wang Tie-Tie, and the contract she was negotiating. With foreigners.

A chill ran down Xiao Yen's back, like ghost fingers walking down her spine. She looked around her room.

She'd leave it in less than a week's time. There was very little that marked it as hers. A few scrolls in the corner. Two of her better pieces, a crane and a grasshopper, sat on the shelf near her bed. Her three jackets hung in the cupboard. Candles, held upright by their own wax, stood on every flat surface; the shelf, the table, the top of the cupboard. Master Wei called her lazy because sometimes she needed three calls in the morning before she'd get up. Xiao Yen knew the truth. She worked best at night, in candle-light, letting shadows suggest meat and muscle before her creatures grew to full size.

Xiao Yen turned back to her horse. With a sigh, she folded another. Again her mind wandered, and the result showed it. Instead of standing on four solid feet, it was lopsided, the right foreleg longer than the back. Xiao Yen looked at the beast, turned it around in her hands. What was the use? If Wang Tie-Tie couldn't get her a contract, Fu Be Be would force her to get married. She doubted her husband would let her practice. If her mother could find anyone who would want her, with her large shoulders, strong arms, and strange upbringing.

She pulled over the foreign language book Wang Tie-Tie had given her. Only a few of the folded pages had useful vocabulary. The rest were filled with color-ful stories about the strange things foreigners did, like sleeping with their animals, rubbing themselves with bear fat before a battle, speaking out of their stomachs instead of their mouths. Xiao Yen didn't want to travel to foreign lands, but she had to do her duty.

Xiao Yen pushed the book away and picked up an-other sheet of paper. This time, she'd do it right. She concentrated hard, talking herself through every fold, holding her arms up in front of her face. However, she tried too hard, and ended up tearing the left back leg as she refolded a crease.

With the sound of the rip still ringing in her ears, Xiao Yen looked at the horse in horror. Was it an

omen? Long Yen was going to protect horses as part
of his duties. Would she have responsibilities like that
someday, and fail?

Then her anger took over. Xiao Yen threw the
paper to her table in disgust. She was no good. Nothing was right. Maybe she should have just stayed at
Gan Ou's, and not come back. Give up.

Xiao Yen glanced into the courtyard. The younger
students had gone to their afternoon classes. No one
expected her until dinner. Xiao Yen stretched her
arms in front of her and rolled her wrists. Maybe a
walk to Bao Fang would be good for her. Master Wei
didn't approve of his older students going into the city
without his permission, but he was busy with a class.

Xiao Yen leaned over her table, then stood up
straight. Her lucky amulet slapped against her neck.
She fingered it ruefully. Maybe she wasn't as lucky as
she'd once thought. Then she left.

Xiao Yen marched into town, sounding off with
each step: unfair, unfair, unfair. Little winds whirled
around her feet, spinning the dust in the road up to
her knees.

She could never please everyone.

If she got married, like Fu Be Be and Gan Ou
wanted, she'd disappoint Wang Tie-Tie, and all her
training would go to waste. She'd lose her quiet, her
calm. If she got a position with a foreigner, she'd disappoint and anger her mother. There was no way for
her to please them both. When Wang Tie-Tie died,
her mother would win. Xiao Yen would have to get
married. Wasn't that what girls were supposed to do?
Maybe her mother *should* win.

Xiao Yen shuddered at the thought of having to
work for foreigners, with their impossible language,
their dirty habits. She'd be cast out from her own
people forever.

Xiao Yen snorted. She was an outcast now. It didn't
matter what she did. People in Bao Fang would always
talk about her upbringing, even when she was as old

as Wang Tie-Tie. Things could only be different if she went someplace else. Yet in a new place she'd be a stranger, and talked about anyway. Her family would be far away, both a blessing and a curse.

As Xiao Yen neared Bao Fang, she modified her walk to a casual stroll. She didn't want people to stare at her any more than they already did. She decided to walk to the northern market, stare at the foreigners, see the worst of her fate. She rubbed her amulet hard. She'd always been so lucky. Maybe her luck would win out, pull her through. Xiao Yen closed her eyes and stopped on the dusty road for a moment. She breathed a brief prayer to Jing Long. Help her see a clear way out of this.

Then she remembered visiting the well with Bing Yu. She'd always been sure there was some magic there, but that last visit, she hadn't felt anything. Maybe there never had been anything for her to feel; maybe it was just an old well. She started walking again, then paused and spat in disgust.

"There!" she said under her breath. "That's what I think of you, old dragon!"

"Xiao Yen!" someone called from behind her.

She jumped and looked over her shoulder. Bing Yu waved at her, dressed in a coat so bright and yellow it glowed. Patterns of green pine and red berries dotted the front and sleeves. Her pants shone pure silver. Though Xiao Yen's coat was new, it was a dark forest green, with no embroidery.

Bing Yu's nurse was dressed in a coat the same color as Xiao Yen's.

Xiao Yen refused to let her plain clothes bother her. She waved to her friend. A sudden gust of wind buffeted her back, pushing her toward Bing Yu.

"You bad girl!" Bing Yu said, hitting Xiao Yen on the arm.

Had Bing Yu heard what Xiao Yen had said as she'd spat?

"Why didn't you tell me you were coming into town?"

Xiao Yen grinned in relief. "Oh, I just decided to go," she said casually.

Bing Yu opened her eyes wide. "Really? You didn't ask permission?"

Xiao Yen replied, "No, I didn't." Her voice sounded grim even to her ears.

"What's wrong? Why did you rebel?" Bing Yu asked.

Xiao Yen smiled, the tightness easing in her chest. There was real concern in Bing Yu's voice. She wasn't just searching for gossip. Maybe it would help Xiao Yen if she could talk with someone about her dilemma.

"My sister, Gan Ou, talked with Chieh-yeh Be Be, the matchmaker, and she's agreed to find me a husband. Wang Tie-Tie wants me to get a position protecting a caravan, but no one except foreigners will hire me. And Wang Tie-Tie's so old. Even if I get a position, my mother might take it away. I'm tired of practicing all the time, always studying, always exercising, and for what? That official from Huang Hwa thought I was a charity case. No one believes a girl can be a paper mage." Xiao Yen rolled the bitter words around her tongue, and spat again, trying to take the foul taste out of her mouth.

"What are you going to do?" Bing Yu asked breathlessly. "Are you going to give up magic?"

"I don't know," Xiao Yen replied. "If I get married, I'll get a bad husband, because I went to Master Wei's school. If I get a position, it'll be a bad position, because I'm a girl. No matter what I do, it's going to be bad. I don't know what to choose." Should she deny her Wang Tie-Tie? Forget her promise to do something worthy? There were still those scars on Wang Tie-Tie's arm to consider. Or should she deny her mother, her sister, all convention, and accept a position? If one was ever offered to her?

"If you give up magic, your aunt can't force you to travel with foreigners," Bing Yu told her, tucking her arm into Xiao Yen's and walking through the gate into Bao Fang. Her nurse followed at a discreet distance behind them.

"It would break Wang Tie-Tie's heart if I just quit. She's waited her whole life for someone in our family . . . to show potential," Xiao Yen ended, not wanting to spill family secrets to Bing Yu.

Bing Yu walked in silence for a while. They passed the street leading toward Xiao Yen's family compound. Here there were no beggars, but many more scholars and businessmen. There were also water boys, monks in their saffron robes, and mothers shepherding their children. Though the sun shone down warmly, there was still an occasional gust of wind to send shivers down Xiao Yen's back.

It wasn't until they were close to the center of the city, near the well, that Bing Yu spoke. "I know!" she said. "You don't have to tell anyone you're giving up your magic. You can just do something to make it leave."

"What do you mean?" Xiao Yen asked. She'd never thought of her magic as a part of her, like her hand or her foot. Her "magic" was her knowledge, her skill. She couldn't just forget everything she'd learned.

"You can spit at the altar of Zhang Gua Lao, your patron saint. That will show him that you don't want to do magic anymore, and he'll take it away from you," Bing Yu said.

Xiao Yen gasped, horrified. How could she spit at Zhang Gua Lao? It would be like spitting on the grave of her father. "I couldn't do that," Xiao Yen said.

"Sure you could," Bing Yu said. "You just need to work up to it in small steps. I know! You can start by doing what I did, and spitting at the altar of Jing Long." Bing Yu grasped Xiao Yen's arm. "Come on, it's right here," she said, pulling Xiao Yen down the street toward the well.

Xiao Yen dragged her feet, not wanting to get any closer.

Bing Yu didn't notice, and continued building her plans. "Then, after you spit here, maybe tomorrow, you could go spit at Jing Long's altar in the White Temple."

Xiao Yen pulled her arm out of Bing Yu's grasp. Her friend stopped, turned, and faced Xiao Yen, arms akimbo. "Nothing happened to me when I spit at this altar. Nothing will happen to you. Not by doing this. Or are you afraid the dragon will crawl out of the well and come get you, like some demon your old nurse told you about? You're the one who said you didn't see any magic in that old well."

"Bing Yu, there are too many people around," Xiao Yen said, looking for an excuse to not go near the well. The following week was Jing Long's birthday. Everyone in the city would line up to place offerings around the well, to wish the dragon luck. Preparations had already started. Monks were building a false temple around the well. They had already repainted the altar.

"Nobody will notice, silly. Come on. I'll do it first. It's a good start for you, to show you don't want to practice your magic anymore." Bing Yu dragged Xiao Yen to the west side of the well.

A temporary, brightly painted wooden wall stood on the eastern side of the well. To the south stood walls and an elaborate portico, the gateway to the well. By the end of the week, walls would be added to the north and west sides, too, plus a roof, enclosing the well in its own temple. After the celebration, they'd be taken down again, until the following year.

Bing Yu pretended to admire the wall on the far side of the well.

Xiao Yen shrank inside herself, wishing she could disappear like a ghost at sunrise. She didn't think that spitting by the well would affect her magic. Then she sighed. It would be easier to follow the path Bing Yu set for her than to follow her own path, a path she couldn't see.

No one paid any attention to the two girls standing next to the well. The monks were stabilizing the latest column they'd raised on the near side of the portico by attaching it to the existing columns. Then they went to the other side to do the same thing.

"They're gone," Bing Yu whispered to Xiao Yen. "This is our chance." She looked over her shoulder toward the street. Then, in a smooth motion, she looked toward the well and spat in that direction. A small patch of wet appeared at the base of the well wall.

Xiao Yen's mouth went dry.

"See?" Bing Yu said, grinning at Xiao Yen. "No thunderclouds or lightning bolts. There's nothing here, nothing to be afraid of but old people's superstition. Come on. Don't be a wet goose. Or do you want to be an old maid? Alone, never married, no sons or daughters to look after you in your old age? With only foreigners to call you friend?"

Xiao Yen didn't want the life Bing Yu described. She saw it unfolding before her, then folding back up with her inside. The loneliness made her clench her teeth. Even her family would turn their backs on her, once Wang Tie-Tie died, if she continued in her course. The only bright spot was her quiet river, weaving its way through her future, like a shiny silver ribbon. Xiao Yen shivered. Was that all that she could look forward to? Shadows lurked at the corner of her vision, like bobbing plants or dancing birds, but Xiao Yen didn't turn to look. She'd seen enough.

In one swift motion, she turned her head and spat toward the well.

To her horror, instead of landing at the base of the well wall, a gust of wind picked her spittle up and carried over the edge.

Xiao Yen felt the pit of her stomach drop as she imagined that her spit had dropped down into the well, mingling with the water. She froze in fear. What had she just done? Yen Lo, the ruler of Hell, would judge her harshly for desecrating the home of a dragon. She clutched her amulet with her right hand, but no prayer came to mind. Her thoughts tumbled over each other. Dread sank into her bones.

Bing Yu laughed at her expression. "See?" she said. "Nothing's going to happen."

Xiao Yen turned to look at the well. In her mind's eye, she couldn't see a dragon or any magic. She couldn't shake the feeling that something lurked at the bottom of the well, just out of her sight.

"I have to go back to school now," Xiao Yen told Bing Yu. "Good-bye." Xiao Yen hurried back toward the southern gate. Nothing good was going to come of this. Not even her luck could save her now, she was certain.

Chapter 23

❧

On the Trail

The two soldiers guarding the gate of the courthouse compound wore solid, scuffed armor, made of iron and leather. They didn't stop the fisherman from propelling Xiao Yen through the gate. Xiao Yen was surprised at the size of the crowd that followed them. Though the dragon had stopped its attack—Xiao Yen had seen it fly south, down the coast—parts of the town still burned. She wondered why the townspeople weren't occupied with water-bucket lines to put out the fires. All she could think was that there was more water in this town than in Bao Fang because it was near the sea.

The court sergeant, who stood guard at the door of the main hall, did stop them. He interrogated the fisherman, all the while watching Xiao Yen. His armor was more polished; the metal rings bound across his chest held a dull shine. His face was as grim and gray as a drawn sword. The bridge of his nose jutted out from where it'd been broken and improperly set, and a long scar followed the contours of his jaw. His eyes peered out with fierce intelligence beneath mere wisps of eyebrows.

The fisherman had bound Xiao Yen's hands behind her back with thin twine as they'd walked. Now he turned Xiao Yen around to show them to the sergeant.

The crowd stared at her as though she was a freak on display at the market. People whispered behind their hands to their neighbors. No one smiled or lowered their eyes politely when Xiao Yen looked at them.

The sergeant tightened the knots on her bonds and grunted. When he turned her around, he spoke to her for a moment in Tuo Nu's dialect.

She replied in her own tongue, "I'm sorry, I don't understand."

Everyone in the crowd seemed to catch their breath at the same time. The sergeant drew himself up taller and looked more fierce. He barked an order at the fisherman, then disappeared inside the hall. The crowd muttered to itself. Xiao Yen looked at her feet. She couldn't reach her calm, but the constant wind she heard in her head was almost a comfort.

The sound of wooden boards being piled together came from the hall. Xiao Yen surmised that shutters were being removed from the tall windows. A bell rang out, calling the court to order. The sergeant reappeared, took hold of Xiao Yen, and pushed her into the building. The crowd followed.

The hall was rectangular, with tall windows rising almost to the ceiling on the long sides. A battered railing separated the crowd from the accused. It didn't make Xiao Yen feel any safer. An imposing wooden desk made out of dark-colored oak stood at the front of the room. Above it hung a black-and-red plaque with golden characters inscribed on it: "justice outweighs human life."

Xiao Yen stiffened when the judge entered and sat behind the desk. This man had no innate power, just that granted by the court. She couldn't tell if he was corrupt or not. He was fat. His eyes were set so far into his face that he gazed out of rolls of skin, like a sleepy baby peeping out of piles of blankets and pillows. The look he gave Xiao Yen was of deliberate intelligence. His nose proceeded sharply down his face, skinny and at angles to everything else. His lips, too, were thin, and set in a neutral line. He wore a fine silver robe, with a white dragon embroidered across his large belly. His black judge's cap had silver rope edging the flaps that came down over his ears. The sharp contrasts in the colors matched the contrasts in his face.

The sergeant forced Xiao Yen to kneel and bow before the judge. She kept her head lowered while the sergeant spoke to the judge in a voice that sounded like churned gravel.

The judge replied in her language, using cultured, educated tones. "What is your name?"

"Fu Xi Wén," Xiao Yen replied, giving her formal name.

"Fu Xi Wén, you have been accused of being an evil mage, of casting a spell on the dragon, making it rise out of season, then directing it to attack Khuang-ho. I want to hear the fisherman's testimony, then you will be given a chance to speak. I warn you. If you move in a suspicious way at any time during these proceedings, I will have you whipped. Do you understand?"

"I understand, honorable judge," Xiao Yen replied, holding herself very still.

The fisherman spoke for some time. The judge translated for Xiao Yen. A small hope nibbled at the edges of Xiao Yen's despair. The judge wanted her to understand, so maybe he really would listen to her side as well. The fisherman didn't embellish his story much, though he did claim that Xiao Yen's eyes had flashed bolts of light at the dragon.

Finally, the judge asked Xiao Yen to speak.

"I didn't call that dragon," she started. Her knees hurt from kneeling on the hard floor for so long, but she didn't dare move.

"Did you stop by the side of the road, and move your arms in a magical way?" the judge asked. His voice sounded stern.

"I stopped by the side of the road to meditate," Xiao Yen replied.

Some onlookers in the galley of the court who understood Xiao Yen's language translated her words for their neighbors, while others jeered. "Meditate? How do you move and meditate? Everyone knows priests meditate by staring at their navels."

"What about you, Han Jao? Don't you meditate by moving? Thrusting?" Crude laughter filled the room.

The judge banged on his desk, then yelled at the court in their native tongue. The laughter gave way to an uneasy silence. The judge then repeated his words in Xiao Yen's language.

"Though you are a foreigner, Fu Xi Wén, these people will treat you with the same respect as one native born. I will have order," he continued, almost muttering under his breath. There was another pause before the judge directed Xiao Yen to continue.

Xiao Yen didn't look up. She felt heartened. "I'd stopped to look for my center, for my peace." Xiao Yen paused. The stillness in her core was unreachable, but just for now. A slight wind sounded under all her words. Her calm was still there.

Shouting started at the back of the room. The sergeant ran from his place next to the judge to investigate. His gravelly voice rode over the others for a moment, then the other voices drowned his out.

"Silence!" the judge yelled.

Even Xiao Yen understood the foreign word.

"Sir, sir," called another voice. Xiao Yen recognized Tuo Nu. He spoke to the judge in their own language.

The onlookers gasped as a whole, then fell silent. Xiao Yen hid her smile when she heard the new voices. Not only Udo, but Ehran as well had come to her defense. There was a moment of consultation between the brothers and Tuo Nu, before Ehran began to speak. He spoke clearly and slowly in his language.

Xiao Yen wondered for a moment, then realized it was better that Ehran, not Udo, speak. He looked more like someone from the Middle Kingdom. His words would be more easily believed. Tuo Nu translated.

"Honorable sir, please excuse this disturbance. But when I heard you were wrongly accusing the great dragon slayer Xiao Yen, I had to come. She killed the rat dragon, the one living outside of Khan Hua, by making it fly into a cliff. When she saw your dragon rise out of the sea, she didn't run or hide, or try to protect herself. Instead, she went into a deep trance, to raise her powers, so she could make your dragon fly into a cliff as well. She would have succeeded, if someone hadn't disturbed her."

The judge paused until the whispered translations of what Ehran said were finished. Then he said, "You are foreigners here. You do not understand our ways. That rat dragon of which you speak was an abomination. I'm glad that it has been slain. But our sea dragon is no *An Ao*. Even though it breathes fire, it isn't evil. It's a part of the cycle of our lives. To kill it would be to kill our town, our way of life. If it doesn't rise in the fall, there are no winter rains. Long ago, we negotiated a peace with our dragon. You have broken that peace, woken the dragon out of time, in the wrong month, with no offerings, no direction for where it should go. It needs to be lulled back into the sea."

Udo spoke now. He told everyone how clever Xiao Yen was, and that she could send the dragon back to the sea.

"Why should we trust your mage to send our dragon back into the sea, and not send it against Khuangho again?" the judge asked.

"You can hold me as hostage," Udo said.

The judge paused and considered for a moment.

"Besides," Tuo Nu added in the language of the Middle Kingdom, "who else can you *afford* to send?"

Xiao Yen kept her surprise from spreading to her face. Tuo Nu would charge the town for his services? Why? Didn't he consider this his home?

The judge cleared his throat. "Fu Xi Wén, the court will address you. You may rise," the judge said.

Xiao Yen stood slowly, her knees stiff from having

knelt for so long. She had to bend her head back very far to see his face, almost as much as when she'd stood before Bei Xi in her natural form. Xiao Yen stood motionless, mindful of the judge's warning that he'd whip her.

"I charge you with attempted murder. The only way for you to dispel the charge against you is to do the court's bidding, which is to convince the sea dragon to return to its home, and not to rise again until autumn."

Xiao Yen bowed her head, accepting the charge.

"Why won't you deal with the dragon? You're a much stronger mage than I am," Xiao Yen said, hurrying to keep up with Tuo Nu as he walked along the winding main street of Khuangho.

Udo kept up easily on the other side, also harassing Tuo Nu, like two peasants beating up on a merchant, trying to get a better deal. Three court soldiers marched after them. The judge had decided to not lock them up, but to let them roam the town, as long as they took the soldiers with them. He knew that no one would help the foreigners escape.

Four or five people trailed after the soldiers, onlookers from the court, staring at Udo and Xiao Yen. Ehran had his own soldiers, as well as his own crowd. He'd purposefully drawn them after him by producing dice and starting a game of chance in the common area of their inn. Though Khuangho was a seaport, and saw foreigners occasionally, the people still stared. Xiao Yen figured that more of the crowd stayed with Ehran for three reasons: though Xiao Yen was a foreigner, she didn't look like one; she was an unknown mage, with possibly dangerous and unlucky powers; and she stayed close to Tuo Nu, a known mage, that the people in the town probably didn't want to anger.

"I must be paid for my work. And they can't pay me enough," Tuo Nu said.

All the fires had been put out. Merchants had opened their shops again. The wine seller they passed had attracted many boisterous men, and the noodle shop next door was also doing a brisk business. Only a few children played in the street though, and Xiao Yen didn't see any farmers or fishermen hawking their goods, or any scholars. It was like the first day of ghost month, when no one bought or sold anything for fear of making the just-awakened ghosts jealous.

"Why would you charge so much?" Xiao Yen asked.

"You wouldn't understand," Tuo Nu said.

He turned off the main street into a narrow alley. The walls along either side were high and well maintained, made out of solid stone. Some of the gates were painted bright red, but most of them weren't adorned. About halfway down the street, Tuo Nu stopped and unlocked the plain wooden gate to his compound. As soon as it was open, Udo pushed himself past Tuo Nu, going in uninvited.

Tuo Nu looked after him for a moment, his mouth open. Then he shrugged, shook his head, and turned to Xiao Yen. "Won't you please come in and have some tea?" Tuo Nu said, making a low bow, like a courtier.

Xiao Yen accepted with the barest incline of her head and floated across the threshold like a courtesan.

Tuo Nu rented rooms in a shared compound, with other tenants. White and yellow pebbles covered the courtyard. A few weeds sprang up between the rocks. Wang Tie-Tie wouldn't have approved at all.

A one-story wooden building lined the courtyard walls. It was divided into several apartments. Slate tiles led from the gate to the center apartment. A broad wooden stoop ran in front of the building, and the roof extended over it. Two young children with dirty faces played in the southern corner. They squealed and ran inside the closest door when they saw Udo.

Tuo Nu invited the soldiers into the courtyard, but locked the gate against the other people who still followed them. One of the soldiers stayed next to the courtyard door. Tuo Nu led Xiao Yen and Udo up the path to the corner rooms on the southwest side. He opened the door to a dark room, then walked across and untied the shutters, letting the sun spill in.

The walls and floor were made of a pale wood, with many knots. Xiao Yen smelled pine trees. Wind blew through the rooms, a constant roar, like the ocean. The apartment was small, only two rooms—a general sitting room with many pillows scattered around a low table under the southern window, and a sleeping room, separated by a white silk curtain painted with a large blue-and-white vase holding brilliant red peonies.

On the shelves next to the window stood dull-silver foreign mugs, a dark green clay frog, and a small painting of four of the eight precious things of a scholar: books, money, pink flowered herbs of immortality, and clouds of good luck. On the opposite side, a shelf held a painting covered with a piece of dazzling yellow silk, that Xiao Yen assumed was a portrait of a god that Tuo Nu prayed to. Small empty cups stood under this painting, along with the ashy remains of incense.

Though the room was full of sunlight and wind, it reminded Xiao Yen of Master Wei's room, a room for study and consideration. Like her little room at the school. She suddenly missed it, and swallowed hard to beat down the lump in her throat. Then she took a deep breath. She could have a place like this too. She'd chosen her peace.

The two remaining soldiers arranged themselves on either side of the door. Udo continued to hassle Tuo Nu, asking him why he couldn't subdue the dragon, why it had to be Xiao Yen.

Finally, Tuo Nu turned to Xiao Yen and said in her language, "I'll explain it to you. I doubt this foreigner will ever understand."

Udo opened his mouth to say something more. Xiao Yen looked at him and held up her hand. He shut it again.

"My magic . . ." Tuo Nu hesitated, then started again. "My magic is different from yours."

Xiao Yen already knew that, having tasted the Wind of God.

"It isn't just the wind or the movement or stillness. I only studied with my master for three years—not because I was a poor student, but because that's all that was needed. My magic isn't about ritual, or knowledge, or discipline. I don't have to study and practice every day like you do. My magic is powered by my life. Every spell I cast drains years from me."

Xiao Yen understood now why Tuo Nu's magic was so elemental. Why it seemed so powerful. He didn't work with artifacts, like she did. And he paid a heavy price for it.

"That's why I'm so exhausted after I cast a spell. I need to get a good, profitable job now, while I'm young, so that when I'm older, I won't have to cast spells." Tuo Nu paused for a moment, then added, "You're lucky. Your magic doesn't steal your life."

Xiao Yen turned away. Her magic "stole" her life, just as much as Tuo Nu's. Her magic took away her ability to have a normal existence, to have children and a husband, to stay close to her family. There could be substitutes, like protecting horses or a town, but it wasn't the same.

"To make the dragon go back to the sea would cost me a big spell. Maybe take ten years from my life. The town doesn't have enough money to pay me for that," he said.

"Then I do it, I chase dragon away," Xiao Yen said in Udo's language, so that both men understood her.

"How?" Udo asked. "I thought your magic was gone."

Xiao Yen ignored his question and asked Udo one of her own. "Why you tell the judge I defeat dragon?" she asked.

"So you could escape," he said. "You did the same thing for me. You put yourself into jeopardy, at risk,

for me. I will do the same for you. Particularly after
I helped you lose your magic, hurt your soul."

Xiao Yen looked down, her cheeks burning hot with
embarrassment over his offer. No one had ever sacri-
ficed themselves for her. No one had even tried to
understand her magic. The memory of what happened
in that cold courtyard, with those men, brought familiar feelings of fear and revulsion, but the feelings
weren't as strong as before. She'd lived through the
actual act. Now she could live with the memory.

Tuo Nu, too, was curious. "Do you still hear the
Wind of God?" he asked.

"I do," Xiao Yen replied, still using Udo's language.
"But more quiet. My quiet back too. Mixed."

Tuo Nu would have asked more questions, but Xiao
Yen held up her hand and spoke again in her own
language.

"I need to practice. Please, may I stay here for the
afternoon and work?" she asked.

Tuo Nu said, "Of course. I may have something for
you to work with."

He went into the second room, then returned a moment later with a large, flat, unpainted wooden box.
Ceremoniously he carried it over his head, so his
breath wouldn't spoil the contents. He laid it on one
of the pillows and opened it with a great flourish.

Inside lay brilliant white sheets of paper. Xiao Yen
picked one up in amazement. She'd never seen paper
so white or pure. Both sides were smooth. It was
thicker than the paper she was used to working with.
It would be more difficult to create fine or delicate
creatures with this paper. For easier animals, or for
designs she was familiar with, it was perfect.

"Why—" she started to ask Tuo Nu, but he
interrupted.

"Every guild has their secrets," he said.

Xiao Yen didn't ask any more. She wasn't surprised
he used paper in his rituals. Many people made paper
effigies to burn during worship.

Tuo Nu insisted that she take all of the paper, transferring the sheets from his box to her bag himself. Then he ushered Udo out the door, taking one of the soldiers with him, calling over his shoulder, "We'll meet you for dinner."

Xiao Yen forced herself to forget the guard standing at the door. She turned and positioned herself so she looked out the window. The wind in her head abated, though it still gusted through her silence now and again.

When Xiao Yen felt her peace settle into her bones, she lowered her forehead to the ground three times. Then she reached for the first piece of paper, and started folding.

Chapter 24

∽

Bao Fang

Xiao Yen stood in line and tugged on her amulet. She stifled a yawn. She hadn't slept soundly the night before. If she were truthful, Xiao Yen hadn't slept much since she'd spat in the well the week before. She couldn't remember her dreams, but she'd woken every night sweating, her teeth clenched, and her hands tightened into fists, as if she'd been fighting demons.

Though the sun shone down brightly on the freshly scrubbed square, and the day was warmer than usual for spring, she still felt cold every time the soft breeze played with her long black braids. She'd spat into Jing Long's well. Now, on his birthday, would he enact his retribution? She couldn't avoid going to pay her respects. Everyone in Bao Fang was expected to take part in the ritual.

Fu Be Be stood in line before her, dressed in her best silver jacket with golden pine boughs embroidered on it. She chatted with Gan Ou and played with Little Bear, the baby. Gan Ou's jacket was made of shiny verdant silk and covered with patterns of dark green pine boughs and red berries. Even Xiao Yen could tell the material wasn't good quality.

Xiao Yen couldn't see over the heads of those standing in line in front of her, so she moved to one side. A large, wooden, brightly painted façade covered the well. Though she couldn't see them, Xiao Yen heard the musicians standing next to the entrance, banging their drums and cymbals. She rubbed her amulet harder, wishing she didn't have to go. The pit of her stomach rumbled warnings. She shifted the flowers she carried from one hand to the other.

Bing Yu emerged from the doorway to the well. She looked as happy as ever. Maybe she'd escaped. Maybe Jing Long wouldn't do anything to either of them. A nauseating dread still stalked Xiao Yen.

When they arrived at the false portico, Fu Be Be indicated with her hands that Xiao Yen should accompany her. It was too loud to speak with the musicians so close.

Xiao Yen stepped back, signifying her wish to face the dragon alone. Master Wei had performed her graduation ceremony the previous night. She was no longer a student, no longer a child. She was an adult. Fu Be Be sniffed her disapproval, but didn't say anything as she turned and went through the low entrance.

"Life is choice," Master Wei had told the students. Choose your weapon, choose your fighting space, choose your life.

Xiao Yen wanted to believe his words, but she was filled with doubt. She wasn't a man, able to choose a destiny or fight against fate. Either Fu Be Be would find her a husband, or Wang Tie-Tie would find her a position. Or maybe the dragon would choose. She could only wait, and see whose will was strongest. She'd given up fighting.

She'd given up her right to choose.

When Fu Be Be came out, she didn't look at either of her daughters. Gan Ou went into the temple next, holding her son close to her breast. Xiao Yen couldn't stand still. She clutched her luck with one hand, then the other. She closed her eyes for a moment, searching for any magic that might be around. She felt nothing. Maybe Bing Yu was right.

After Gan Ou finished, Xiao Yen entered. Though

she was shorter than three-month-old bamboo, she still had to bow her head to step under the false doorway. Everyone was made to bow this way to render them more humble, possibly so they wouldn't ask Jing Long for impossible things on his birthday.

Behind the wall it was quieter. Xiao Yen put her flowers on the table heaped with offerings, then knelt on the red cushions in front of the well. She bowed three times, and asked blessings for Wang Tie-Tie, for Fu Be Be, for Gan Ou and her two sons. She also asked blessings for Master Wei, and her classmates, Fat Fang and Long Yen.

She sat back on her heels. Arrows of sunlight pierced the roof, brightening the false temple. Dust swirled in lazy circles, rising up the lines of light. Tiers and tiers of candles stood on the narrow shelves covering every wall. Still, Xiao Yen saw shadows curling around the foot of the well out of the corner of her eye. They disappeared when she looked at them directly.

Xiao Yen felt the same now as she had when she'd tested her luck, so long ago, on the riverbank. Maybe the dragon wouldn't choose for her. Maybe she'd have to wait for Wang Tie-Tie or Fu Be Be to make the important decisions, to choose her life for her.

Xiao Yen rose up on her knees to look over the lip of the well. The light from the candles wasn't strong enough to pierce the darkness there. She had to do something, say something, even if there was no dragon living at the bottom of the well. A musky, mossy scent overpowered the perfumed flowers as she took a deep breath. She held it for a moment, then let it out in a rush with her words: "Honorable dragon, protector of this town, please forgive me. I . . ."

Something gold flashed. Xiao Yen's words froze on her lips. A dark hole ripped through the warm, still air, swallowing her last chance for happiness. Xiao Yen couldn't hear the clink of the metal on stone as it tumbled down, nor the splash at the bottom, if there was any.

The dragon *had* chosen for her, but not in a way she'd imagined. He'd taken her amulet, the manifestation of her luck. Reaching up to her now naked neck, she finished her apology, her tears chasing the words down the well.

"I'm sorry I ever doubted you. Please forgive this worthless person."

Her words tumbled into the empty space. She knew the dragon hadn't accepted her apology, because her luck was gone.

Chapter 25

❦

On the Trail

Four court guards, the court sergeant, Udo, and a group of onlookers accompanied Xiao Yen up the coastal road to where it forked. The festive mood amused Xiao Yen. It felt as if she were leading them to a celebration at the dragon temple. The guards wore blue-and-red shirts under their leather and iron vests. The court sergeant wore a fine mail shirt, obviously foreign, because it was too big for him. The silver flaps hanging over his ears made his face seem even longer.

Though none of the guards spoke Xiao Yen's language, they managed to communicate. They pointed out the local landmarks as they walked up the trail: a large rock jutting out of the sea that looked like a chicken's head; a series of tall rocks, one on top of the other, that looked like a temple tower; and Crane Bay, a shallow calm inlet with its accompanying marsh that cranes and other birds migrated to in the winter.

Xiao Yen smiled and thanked them, not paying much attention. She focused instead on the sound of the ocean wind that whistled as it blew through her elegant coiffure. She also concentrated on the immutable heat from the sun pounding down on her. Her calm surrounded her. Each step immersed her more in her stillness. Tuo Nu had loaned her a good robe, made of brilliant yellow silk with red dragons lazing on clouds embroidered on it. It was too long and flowed almost to her ankles. It fit her just right through the shoulders.

At the fork in the road, the court sergeant divided the party. He and two of the guards would accompany Xiao Yen to the dragon temple. The other two took Udo into custody.

Xiao Yen watched Udo while the sergeant gave his commands to the guards and to the crowd. The wind played with his golden curls, which shone almost white in the sunlight. He had deep, worried lines around his eyes. He almost looked elegant in Tuo Nu's light blue robe. It had a pattern of stylized tiger faces in black and crimson embroidered on it. The sleeves hung short on his arms, and though it was Tuo Nu's longest robe, it still only came to mid-thigh on Udo. He stood a head above the crowd, looking more foreign than ever. He didn't fit. He didn't belong in the Middle Kingdom. Xiao Yen would do everything she could to see he got back home.

The sergeant indicated with his hand that they should continue up the hill. He would lead, and the two guards would walk behind Xiao Yen. She forced them to walk slowly. She didn't want to be out of breath when she reached the top of the hill. The dragon had settled next to the dragon temple, making occasional forays into the nearby fields to steal an ox or burn another building. The people from Khuangho had brought it sacrifices, but it had either ignored them, or set flame on the would-be penitents. Everyone had their own theory on why the dragon was so angry, what had caused it to attack the town.

As they walked, the mood changed. The two guards behind Xiao Yen stopped speaking. The sergeant looked more grim. She studied the rocks they passed, observing how solidly they held themselves against the constant wind. She paused on the leeward side at the same rock she'd stopped at on her first time trip up the hill, next to the yellow star-shaped flowers. The wind in her head gusted—a familiar sound now, not a distracting force. She focused on the flowers, on the warm sun, and the almost familiar-looking boulders scattered over the hillside. If she allowed herself to think about what she was going to do, her knees would turn to soft bean curd and she'd crumple into a ball and weep for ten thousand years. She forced herself to continue.

Just under the lip of the hill the sergeant made them all halt. He indicated for Xiao Yen and the two guards to crouch down. Then he turned and went up toward the top of the path, going from one boulder to the next, hiding. After a moment, he returned. Though Xiao Yen didn't speak his language, she understood his words. The dragon still lay curled on one side of the temple.

Xiao Yen bowed to him over her hands, then she turned and faced east. She took out a folded piece from her sleeve. It filled the palm of her hand. She walked a few steps away from the guards, placed it on the ground, then placed rocks around it, at the first four compass points.

The two guards whispered to each other until the sergeant grunted at them for silence.

Xiao Yen knelt on the ground, then lowered her forehead to the earth. It smelled of dried grass warmed by the constant sunshine. The wind rushed by, making the grass rustle. Xiao Yen stayed in her center, hearing the ocean waves above everything else.

She grew her creation to full size, imbibing it with the constancy of the mountain underneath her.

The guards gasped.

Xiao Yen smiled. She picked up the umbrella as she stood. Though it was still the same brilliant white color of the paper she'd folded it from, it was as solid as the boulders around them. The umbrella was about as large as the bamboo umbrella Wang Tie-Tie had in the Garden of Sweet Scents. Xiao Yen mimed instructions to the sergeant, that neither he nor his men were to go near the ashy paper umbrella still on the ground behind her. The sergeant ordered the two guards to flank the paper remains. Xiao Yen bowed and thanked him. Not only would he and his men not touch it, they would make certain no one else did.

Xiao Yen, now prepared, walked up to the top of the hill. The expanse from the edge to the temple looked as wide as the entire city of Bao Fang, but Xiao Yen would have to cross it too quickly. The sun shone down on her from straight overhead. Rivers of whitish grass covered the flat plain. The corners of the temple jutted out beyond the dark gray dragon curled up on the side. The ocean sparkled as it marched out to the horizon.

The wind blew into Xiao Yen's face, forcing tears from the corners of her eyes. The dragon raised its head and sniffed when she stepped onto the plain. Though the wind was blowing from the sea, it still seemed to smell Xiao Yen, and looked at her.

Spiny hairs stood upright around the dragon's face like a mane. Its eyes were a washed-out gray, like snow-bearing clouds. Golden whiskers hung down past its chest. The bright red streaks running down either side of its snout pulsed with living flame. Its segmented belly looked hard and armored in the bright sunlight.

Xiao Yen froze in place for a moment. The wind inside her head died down to the faintest whisper. Her heart thudded in her chest, as if it wanted to escape. The dragon had seen her. Even if she wanted to, she couldn't run away. She had to go through with her plan. She kept her mind on the rocks as she walked across the flat expanse, appearing as unconcerned as a young maid on a picnic.

The dragon, just as casually, twisted its neck farther in her direction, and belched fire at her.

The flames rolled off Xiao Yen's umbrella and dripped down its sides like heavy rain, then fell to the ground and burned the dry grass on either side of her. Xiao Yen stayed in her calm place. She didn't see the dragon, or feel the heat. Cool water poured around her, as if she were standing under a waterfall, the water surrounding, but not drowning, her.

After a second blast of fire, the dragon stopped. It nodded its head at her, as if saying, "Your turn."

Xiao Yen reached her right hand into her left sleeve and pulled out two paper cranes. She'd used Tuo Nu's red ink, the one for signing official documents, to color their vermilion crowns. She placed them on the ground next to her feet, so they would be protected by the umbrella. Then she closed her eyes and grew them. Their necks elongated and stretched toward Heaven. Their legs, thin but sleek, grew like delicate tree branches. Feathers filled in and fluffed up, covering the hard edges of the paper with softness. Their beaks grew sharp as knives below their red crowns, while their eyes shone like amber.

Xiao Yen filled them with the grace of willow trees bending in the wind, the fluidity of a cool mountain stream, the charm of a courtesan's smile. She placed in them all her hope and longing, making them as beautiful and as desirable as possible. She imagined them as a mated pair, bonded for life, two halves of a whole.

When Xiao Yen opened her eyes, her two cranes had already reached shoulder height. A moment later, they were taller than she was, and walked out from under the protection of her umbrella into the bright sunlight, like two ladies from court taking a stroll. Their white feathers reflected the light, while the black feathers along their curved necks, and bunched at their tails, gleamed.

One crane stopped for a moment to groom itself. It tucked its beak under its wing, smoothing the feathers there. Then it flicked its head toward the sky. The other crane waited for its partner, indulgent and proud.

The two cranes looked at each other for a long moment. Then they sprang into the air, wings outstretched, toes pointed. They bobbed their heads and wove them together, moving as gracefully as silk flags blowing in the wind. Even Bei Xi couldn't move with such beauty. The cranes circled each other, their wings moving in complicated, complementary patterns. They were involved with each other, but they still moved toward the dragon.

All the wings on the sides of the dragon had been standing at attention when Xiao Yen had first seen it, but now they lay against its body, relaxed. The red streaks along its snout dulled to a somber color. The spikes around its head lay against its back, making the head more snakelike. Its whiskers moved like winter wheat blown by the wind as it bobbed its head in time with the unheard music the cranes danced to. Its eyes had softened in color as well, to a misty gray.

Now the cranes stood farther apart with their heads stretched toward each other, weaving back and forth with their necks. They stayed focused at first, the heads jerking with great speed. Then the pattern spread out, and they moved their heads more to the sides as they walked closer to the dragon.

The dragon looked pleased, as if being courted by two ladies.

Then one of the cranes struck out, snapped at and bit the belly of the dragon.

The dragon pulled itself back, more surprised than hurt.

Xiao Yen examined the sides of its snout. Was it going to blow fire again? No. The red streaks remained a dull orange. The spikes around its head stayed flat. It just looked puzzled. It pushed itself back a little, so it was outside the circle of the dancing cranes. A moment later, it was mesmerized again.

The next time, both cranes snapped at the dragon, one biting a wing, the other a foreclaw.

The dragon looked uncomfortable. Xiao Yen's magic had lulled it. The dance of the cranes was so beautiful.

The cranes snapped again. They obviously didn't want the dragon there. They were driving it toward the sea.

The dragon looked over the two bobbing heads at Xiao Yen.

Xiao Yen met the dragon's eye. She drifted in the gray clouds there. She could get lost in that fog, traveling through ancient mysteries, seeing foreign lands, dancing to the moods of wings and the tide. What she saw surprised her. The dragon had risen at her welcoming dance because it was lonely. Did she want to be like Lui Ji and live under the ocean in the dragon palace? She would be immortal at the dragon court, providing him with dancing cranes and other entertainment, learning more powerful magic every day.

Xiao Yen closed her eyes. She wouldn't be alone at the dragon court. Other mages would seek her out. She'd be respected, and honored, all her days.

She'd be a foreigner though, like Udo and Ehran. It would never be the Middle Kingdom. It would never be home. She had to see Wang Tie-Tie, even without an immortal peach. Plus, she had to warn Fat Fang about the coming attack. She bowed low to the dragon, honored. When she raised her head, she didn't look in its eyes again.

"Honorable Dragon, you must go home. It is better to venerate you from afar, than to have you near, and be afraid. Go home, sir. Please."

At the end of her speech, the dragon turned its head and looked beyond the temple, toward the gray sea. One of the cranes nipped at it. The dragon moved back a little more without turning around.

Xiao Yen started to sing. It was an old song, written by a soldier, filled with all his longing for his home, the watery fields, the cool evenings, the cry of the cicadas. The dragon shook its head, once, twice, as she sang the last verse. Then it launched itself into the air, like a snake sliding into water. The two cranes followed it.

Xiao Yen felt her heart rise as well. Would the dragon go home? Or would it circle back and attack the town? She watched it gain altitude, then dive, a

gray streak, into the sea. The cranes flashed their
wings and dove with it. Relief splashed over Xiao Yen
like an ocean wave. The puppet strings that had held
her upright were cut. She wanted to slump to the
ground, and weep and sing at the same time, yet there
was something more she needed to do.

Xiao Yen inverted her umbrella, picked up the two
ashlike paper cranes at her feet, and placed them in
its bowl. She walked to the edge of the cliff and
looked down to the sea where the dragon and both
the cranes had disappeared. She waited until the wind
abated for a moment before she turned her umbrella
back over. The paper cranes fell out. The wind picked
up the ash and scattered it on the waves. She hoped
that the cranes would stay with the dragon and dance
at its court. The dragon might be lonely, but at least
it had a home. She let her umbrella fall as well. She
had no more use for it.

When she turned, she saw something glimmering
where the dragon had been sitting. Her heart skipped
a beat.

She walked to the glistening spot. A whisker had
fallen from the dragon's chin. It was as wide as her
little finger. Xiao Yen picked it up, folded it in half,
then twisted it upon itself. It shone like the purest
gold, and didn't untwist. She tied it around her neck
with a strong holding knot. The whisker warmed to
her skin instantly.

"Luck is what you make it," Xiao Yen thought as
she started walking back across the plain.

As was the rest of her life.

Epilogue

❧

On the Trail and Bao Fang

Xiao Yen pushed through crowds as she left the dock. It was market day in Khuangho. Udo had spoken with pride about the ship he and Ehran were taking. It wouldn't take them all the way to their home—just to a port Xiao Yen had never heard of—but from there it would be only a short journey overland. The whole journey might only take them two years.

Xiao Yen hadn't been impressed. The body of the boat was shorter than the sea dragon's, and under the decks it was cramped and smelled of mildew. She wouldn't have voluntarily sailed around the harbor in the boat, so she decided to go to the dragon temple to pray for Udo and Ehran.

She also wanted to pray for her family and to thank the dragon once again for the emblem of her luck. Tuo Nu had helped her find a good position for going back to Bao Fang, with an easygoing merchant who'd wanted some extra protection traveling to the capital. She was leaving the next day. She didn't know how Tuo Nu had talked the merchant into accepting a girl to provide his protection, but she was glad he had. She needed to get back to Bao Fang, to warn Fat Fang of the coming attacks. Even though she'd failed Wang Tie-Tie, she still looked forward to seeing her family.

Merchants and farmers sold their wares on the main road of Khuangho, lining each side. They called to her as she passed, offering to sell her wheat, millet, onions, carrots, tea (both packaged and prepared), to fix her shoes, or tell her a story. Every second stall burned incense, thankful their town still stood. The sweet scent mingled with the slightly salty air, blessing everyone. Xiao Yen paused once to buy a steamed bun, filled with a sweet, nutty paste. The man at the cart recognized her as "the lady who charmed the dragon," and wouldn't take any money from her.

The sky was blue from end to end, with only a few very high thin clouds. Tuo Nu had told Xiao Yen they were leftover trails from the dragon's flight. Though the sun was warm, the wind blew sharply from the ocean. Xiao Yen warmed her fingers on her bun as she nibbled at it. The sound of the wind from the outside was louder than the sound she heard inside her head. She enjoyed both.

As she neared the end of the main road, where it narrowed to just a trail, the number of people selling things thinned. Xiao Yen suddenly felt anxious about going back to the dragon temple again. Her heart pounded with each step. Should she go? What if the dragon returned? Or that angry priest? If it even had been a priest.

Then she heard a rattling sound, rhythmic and hollow, like metal against a dry reed. A singsong voice accompanied the beat. A crowd gathered around the last man on the road. Xiao Yen paused. Maybe it would be all right if she didn't go to the temple immediately. She walked to the side of the road to watch with the rest of the crowd.

An old fisherman stood on the side of the road. The woven basket next to him contained the fish that he sold. He shook a bamboo pole. Something inside the pole made the clacking noise that had first attracted Xiao Yen. His face held only a light map of wrinkles, yet Xiao Yen had the impression he was extremely old. His eyes held on to the dark brown color of a young boy. His jacket had faded to a muddy beige from too many washings. Muscular calves bulged beneath his rolled-up pants. Mysterious bags hung from his wide leather belt. His teeth flashed like brilliant pearls in the sunlight.

The fisherman told stories about every fish as he sold it. The person standing next to Xiao Yen translated the fisherman's words for her: this fish hadn't gone to school, that fish had never seen the sun before so it had the whitest flesh, the next fish was young like spring bamboo, and just as tender. The crowd melted away when the fisherman sold the last of his fish. Xiao Yen was walking away, too, when the fisherman called to her.

"Pretty girl in the dark blue jacket! Won't you help me for a moment?" The fisherman called to her in the language of the Middle Kingdom, using a rich, cultured accent.

Xiao Yen turned back. The fisherman grinned at her like a foreigner. His teeth were faultlessly placed—no gaps or irregularities—white with fine shading, like high-quality jade. The wrinkles around his eyes reflected many summers of looking into the sun. The eyes themselves held depths greater than the ocean. There was something more to this man than Xiao Yen could see, much more.

Xiao Yen picked up one of the woven baskets, while the old man took the other three. It was heavier than she'd expected—the inside was lined with leaves, then covered with wax to make it waterproof. It smelled of fish and saltwater. She followed the fisherman to a small shack. All the way there, the old man chanted in a language Xiao Yen didn't know, like a priest saying his morning prayers on his way to temple.

He placed his baskets under the eaves of the shack, next to dozens of other baskets, then indicated Xiao Yen should do the same. When she turned around, she found the old man was staring at her intently. She felt like a pika under the gaze of a plains hawk.

"Thank you Xiao Yen," he said, bowing low. "This

town is indebted to you. *I* am indebted to you, more than you know." He straightened up, leaned on his bamboo pole, and tilted his head to one side. "Would you do an old man a great honor and accompany me for a short while? We have things to discuss, you and I." He smiled at her again, like a father looking upon his first son.

Xiao Yen heard herself agree, though the words came out of her mouth without her volition.

The old man said, "Good." Then he turned and headed up the road again. Xiao Yen followed. A little way along, where the road narrowed into the coastal trail, he took a side path that Xiao Yen hadn't noticed before. It wound between boulders bigger than the fisherman's shack, a small brown ribbon through the bright grass. The wind blew constantly from the sea, ruffling Xiao Yen's hair, driving away the heat from the sun.

Xiao Yen and the old fisherman didn't talk. She followed him along the trail and tried to see who or what he was. She thought she saw blue in his shadow, but then the wind blew it away. She tried to see him with her mind's eye. The image of a solid, burning core—like a flaming sword—came to her. The flames burned stronger than the sun, like they would burn forever.

Xiao Yen paused, one foot in midair.

Wang Tie-Tie's stories of a fisherman with perfect teeth came back to her.

Her foot hit the ground, jarring her. Butterflies fluttered in the pit of her stomach. She took a deep breath to calm herself. She couldn't stop shaking inside.

When they crested the next hill, Xiao Yen caught her breath in surprise. They were approaching Crane Bay. The marshy grass waved in the wind, the green sparkling as though wet emeralds were strewn through it. Three herons stalked the edges of the marsh on their stiltlike legs. A few black-tailed seagulls bobbed on the waves. The far side of the bay was protected by a tall craggy cliff. Shelves jutted out from the vertical face, with the remains of nests sitting on them and long white streaks of droppings. The wind died down as they dropped below the head of the hill.

A brightly painted pagoda lay ahead of them. Its gray-tile roof curled up at the corners, supported by large red-lacquered poles. Green planks ran at waist level between the pillars, perfect for leaning against and watching the cranes. It housed a small altar dedicated to the White Crane boy, who'd excelled in good deeds when he'd been alive, and now sometimes brought answers to prayers from the gods.

The old fisherman led Xiao Yen to the pavilion, sat down on one of the benches, and invited her to join him. Xiao Yen approached hesitantly. She wanted to kneel and press her forehead on the ground before him, yet she didn't want to seem presumptuous.

She sat down on the edge of the bench and peered at the old man, wanting a sign from him to tell her how to act, how to treat him.

He smiled at her again, showing his perfect teeth, then laughed. "You know who I am, don't you?"

"Oh, honorable sir," Xiao Yen began, slipping off the bench and sinking to her knees. How could she dare to have her head at the same level as the patron saint of her chosen profession, the immortal Zhang Gua Lao? The same man who'd loved Wang Tie-Tie so many years before?

"My dear girl," he said, interrupting her. "Please, sit, and talk with an ancient man. You can call me Old Zhang," he said, patting the bench beside him.

Xiao Yen rose and sat next to him, her back stiff, her hands folded in her lap, her eyes on the floor. She wanted to stare at him, to touch him to make sure he was real, but she didn't want to be rude or treat him like a foreigner.

"I am in your debt, you know," he said.

Xiao Yen replied, "No, it is I who am in your debt, for allowing this unworthy person into your presence."

Old Zhang continued as if he hadn't heard Xiao Yen. "Vakhtang killed my family. All of them. I have no relations left to walk this earth, to watch over. I swore revenge, but my fellow immortals cautioned patience. Vakhtang kept living, kept doing evil deeds. You put an end to that. I am in *your* debt," he finished, bowing his head low.

Staying bent over, he twisted his head so he was looking at her almost upside down. He looked so comical Xiao Yen started to laugh. She put her hand up to cover her mouth so he wouldn't be offended. "A cautious one you are," he said, straightening up. "But bright. And steady as a mountain, now." He bowed his head toward her, approving.

Xiao Yen blushed and looked at her hands again. Old Zhang didn't say anything for a moment. She heard a rustling. She glanced up. He was taking things from the bags on his belt and placing them on the bench between them.

"I want you to choose your reward," he said in a tone that reminded her of Master Wei.

Two items sat on the bench. One was a gleaming, white-paper box. Loops twisted upon themselves covered the top. It glowed with its own internal light.

The other item was a peach. It also glowed, a warm miniature sun. Just looking at it calmed Xiao Yen. It was perfectly proportioned, with a slight red blush down one side.

"The box," Old Zhang explained, "contains the gold from the rat dragon. The peach is from the garden of Xi Mong Yu. It's sometimes called a peach of immortality. It will take you to Peng-lai, the Isle of the Blessed, where you can live forever in peace. I know that your short time on the wheel of life has been trying."

Xiao Yen's urge to kneel and place her head on the floor returned. She gulped back her wonder at his understanding and forced herself to consider his offer. She stared at the peach, then at the box, for many heartbeats before she responded. The wind in her head rustled, and her calm solidified.

"I see three choices, not two," she started.

Old Zhang smiled, pleased.

Xiao Yen continued. "The box is two gifts. First is the box itself. You would have to show me how to open it. With diligent study, my master, Master Wei, I'm sure, could learn how to recreate it. After many years of practice, if I proved not to be too stupid, maybe I could learn the form as well. That is a selfish reward, just for myself. I will not choose it.

"The gold inside would not be for me, but for my former client, Udo. He and his brother are banished, and need money to buy their way back into their land. Though I consider them my friends, they are still foreigners, not from the Middle Kingdom. So I do not choose this gift.

"My Wang Tie-Tie, Wang Kong-Jing, met you when she was a young girl. She's always dreamed of having such a peach, so that is what I would choose as my reward, that I might bring it to my aunt, that she might live forever in peace, off the wheel of death and rebirth."

Xiao Yen's quiet expanded up to her shoulders and sent a shiver through her arms, behind her ears, and up to the top of her skull. The cliff in front of her was as solid as her resolve.

Old Zhang looked surprised. "Wang Kong-Jing?" he asked.

"You met her in Bao Fang, before she was married. Her maiden name was Li."

Old Zhang stared at the floor in front of him, thinking hard. A slow smile crept across his face. "Mei-Mei," he said, caressing the name with his tongue. A golden light sprang up in the spot where he stared. It was full of dust motes, some shiny, some dark. They rearranged themselves into the outline of a beautiful woman in long robes, holding a fan. "Mei-Mei," Old Zhang said again. Then he blew at the light. It faded and the motes scattered to the corners of the pavilion. He looked sad now.

Xiao Yen didn't know what to say.

After another moment, the old man picked up the

peach, raised it to eye level, bowed his head, and handed it to Xiao Yen. Just as formally, Xiao Yen accepted the peach and placed it in her sleeve. She slipped off the bench, knelt, and bowed low to Old Zhang, then left the pavilion.

She hadn't taken more than a few steps up the dirt path before he called her back.

"Come, Ehran," Tuo Nu said, helping the portly foreigner to stand. "Time to go back to your inn." Both Udo and Ehran had drunk a lot of wine celebrating with Xiao Yen and Tuo Nu. The next week, if the weather was fine, they would begin their journey back to their land. Xiao Yen started back to Bao Fang the next day. They'd gathered at Tuo Nu's rooms for one last evening together.

Ehran turned and bowed toward Xiao Yen, then said something. It took a moment for Xiao Yen to realize that he'd tried to say something in her language.

"Good journey you too," she said, bowing from where she was seated. She smiled at him, and wondered again what Udo had said to him.

Udo started to rise as well when Xiao Yen stopped him.

"Stay," she said.

Udo sank back to the floor with a grunt. Though he'd had his share of the wine, he didn't seem as drunk as Ehran. He did seem tired, maybe from all the planning and fierce bargaining for their trip.

"Tuo Nu, could you walk Ehran home? Udo will follow soon," Xiao Yen said.

Tuo Nu let Ehran out the door, then turned back. "Are you sure you don't want a chaperon?" he asked, indicating Udo with his chin.

Udo gazed at Xiao Yen with a satisfied look, like a man just finished with dinner and staring at dessert.

Xiao Yen said, "No, I can handle him. He *will* be along in a short time."

Tuo Nu said, "All right. If you shout, the neighbors will hear."

Xiao Yen was outraged. What did he mean by that? Before she could respond, he stepped out the door.

"I have present for good-bye," Xiao Yen told Udo. She picked up the small wooden box she had sitting next to her. From inside the box, she took another box made out of white folded paper. She placed the paper box on the table before them.

"What's that?" he asked.

"Puzzle," she said. Eight rings decorated the top of the paper box, made of strips of paper that had been twisted once, then folded together. "You must learn puzzle to open box. Very important," she added, when he looked skeptical.

Xiao Yen counted through the rings, from the smallest to largest. Then she showed him how to untwist them, starting with the second and fourth rings. He seemed intrigued, and learned faster than Xiao Yen had hoped. Finally, they were at the last fold. Xiao Yen made Udo practice every twist up to the last fold twice, to make sure he had it memorized. Then she moved the box to the center of the small table, undid the last fold, and blew on the box.

It unfolded itself rapidly, fold upon fold, like a giant lotus blossom. A deep tone, like echoes from a bronze bell, filled the tiny room. Twice more the paper unfolded, then it lay on the table like a blanket, its secret revealed. In its center sat a large glittering pile of gold, silver, and jewels.

Udo's eyes were more round than Xiao Yen had ever seen them. His mouth opened and shut, but no sounds came out.

"This rat dragon treasure. For your banished," she added.

"Banishment," Udo corrected her, without taking his eyes from the pile. "Why?" he asked, unable to articulate more.

"You foreigner. This not your home. You go home now," Xiao Yen said, wishing again that she could speak his language better. She longed to tell him how alien he was, how much he belonged in his own land. Or how much his understanding had helped her.

"Thank you," he said, turning to look at her. Some of the age in his eyes had turned to wonder, taking years off his face.

"Last fold, not strong," she instructed. "Only open box, one, maybe two more times. Understand?" she told him, starting to fold up the box again. Udo nodded. She didn't think he could only open it a couple of more times, but she didn't want him to show it to Ehran, not yet, not until they were on their way home.

Xiao Yen showed Udo how to crease the four corners, then gather them together so the folds touched. The dazzling white paper folded so stiffly, but felt like smooth silk when she stroked it. She tugged on it three times, then let go as the paper folded itself back up. Soon it was in its compact form again. Xiao Yen picked up the box and handed it to Udo the same way Old Zhang had handed it to her, hands held high with head bowed.

Udo accepted the box. He grunted when he felt how light it was. He shook it. No sound came from within it.

Then Xiao Yen gave him the wooden box that she'd had a cooper make that afternoon. Udo put the paper box inside the wooden one and gazed at it for another moment. The paper reflected every bit of candlelight in the room, and shone against the red silk lining the box.

Udo closed the lid reluctantly. The top of the wooden box had a twisted gold chain painted on it. He touched the painting and asked, "What's this for?"

Xiao Yen touched the matching twisted gold dragon whisker around her neck and replied, "For luck."

Xiao Yen slipped into Wang Tie-Tie's room as quietly as a mouse slipping away from a cat. She'd arrived during the middle of the day, when the household napped, thereby avoiding seeing anyone else. She'd wanted to see Fat Fang before she saw her family, but he'd refused to see her without an appointment, which she now had, one hour hence.

Wang Tie-Tie didn't wake up until Xiao Yen reached out and touched her. Then her eyes snapped to attention. Only they held life. The rest of Wang Tie-Tie's body didn't change. It had betrayed her, grown weak while her mind stayed alert, alive.

"Did you?" was Wang Tie-Tie's question.

Xiao Yen suppressed her smile. Of course, Wang Tie-Tie wouldn't waste time asking Xiao Yen of her journeys or express surprise at seeing her. She would only ask of Xiao Yen's duty. Wang Tie-Tie had chosen her course, as surely as Xiao Yen had chosen her own.

Silently, Xiao Yen brought the peach out of her sleeve and presented it to her aunt, holding it above her head. When she heard Wang Tie-Tie's intake of breath, she lowered her hands and allowed herself to look at her aunt. The wonder suffusing Wang Tie-Tie's face filled Xiao Yen with joy. She wished she could somehow bottle the moment, like a magical elixir that she could later open and enjoy again and again.

Wang Tie-Tie looked past the peach into Xiao Yen's eyes. "Thank you," she said, her voice breaking.

"I was only doing my duty," Xiao Yen replied.

Wang Tie-Tie sighed. "You *have* done your duty," she said. "Nothing less would ever satisfy either you or me. You are my true heir."

Xiao Yen bowed her head, knowing she'd just received the highest praise Wang Tie-Tie could give. To her, only duty mattered. Nothing, not love, gratitude, or family, was as important.

With great ceremony, Xiao Yen gave the peach to Wang Tie-Tie.

The peach glowed like a candle in Wang Tie-Tie's pale fingers. It lit up her face as she brought it closer, illuminating the wrinkles around her eyes, the translucent quality of her skin.

With the first bite, the peach dissolved into a golden

blanket, like ten thousand dust motes spinning in evening sunlight. The light wrapped itself around Wang Tie-Tie's body, encasing her in a fine, translucent veil. Then it lifted up, taking Wang Tie-Tie's soul with it, through the ceiling, flying to the Isle of the Blessed.

Xiao Yen stayed kneeling on the hard floor for a long while. She'd just caused another's death, another black mark against her soul. It seemed to be her fate.

Xiao Yen reached up to hold Wang Tie-Tie's hand. It was already cool to the touch. The wrinkled skin felt softer than Gan Ou's new baby, as if all the living Wang Tie-Tie had done had polished her skin until it was smooth like silk. Her aunt had been such a strong influence in Xiao Yen's life. She was glad that Wang Tie-Tie would now watch over Xiao Yen forever, through every cycle of Xiao Yen's death and rebirth. This made her smile through her tears.

Xiao Yen kissed the back of Wang Tie-Tie's hand, then placed it on the bed. She stood up slowly, as if some of Wang Tie-Tie's age had found its way into her knees.

Wang Tie-Tie's eyes were already closed. The lines of her face had softened in death, and her cheeks seemed more filled out.

Xiao Yen thought of the golden outline of the girl Mei-Mei that Old Zhang had shown her, and could see the resemblance now in Wang Tie-Tie's face. What a beauty she'd been. Xiao Yen bowed again to Wang Tie-Tie, as deeply as she'd bowed to Old Zhang. She slipped out the door as quietly as she'd come.

It was time to see Fat Fang and warn him of the coming danger.

"I know it isn't adequate, for a great mage like you, but I pray that an honorable person like yourself can find it in your heart to accept such lodging from our humble village." The headman stumbled over his tongue many more times as he walked with Xiao Yen past the edge of the village, into the fields.

Xiao Yen fanned herself as she walked. She'd have

to get used to the hot, humid weather in this province. She'd never been so far south before.

A shack stood at the end of the first rice paddy, its door facing north, with windows on all sides. The village was giving it to her in exchange for her protective creatures and spells. It was made from a light wood, with a plain roof. Fields surrounded it on three sides. A limestone cliff stood to the west. Xiao Yen felt the quiet rising from the rock, through the chatter of the headman.

"It will be perfect," Xiao Yen said. She needed to be out in the fields to watch for animals that may come and trample the crops, and to give the village warning if bandits or soldiers approached.

The front room held a desk and chair, with a few pillows and some shelves. The back room, with a window facing the cliff, had a platform bed in it, piled with covers. Both rooms smelled musty. Though the air was still, Xiao Yen heard a wind blowing in her head, a comforting rushing sound. She would be just fine here. She'd always wanted a room of her own, like Master Wei's or Tuo Nu's. She'd be alone here, and possibly lonely, but with calm and magic running through the core of her life, through her choices.

She thanked the man again as she ushered him out the door. She breathed a quick prayer of thanks to Master Wei, for helping her with this appointment. She would make him proud.

After Wang Tie-Tie's death, Fu Be Be had at first assumed Xiao Yen would get married. Xiao Yen hadn't fought with her mother like she had while she'd still been at school. Xiao Yen had just insisted, quietly, continually, that she was going to continue her life as a mage. Eventually, her mother had given way, and even helped her get this appointment. Xiao Yen still wasn't sure why. Maybe it was because Fu Be Be had grown resigned to Xiao Yen's avowal of following her magic. Maybe it was because of the siege and attack on Bao Fang, and she thought that sending her daughter south might keep her out of harm's way. Or maybe it was because this village was close to her mother's home village. Xiao Yen had assured her mother many times that she'd look after all the people in the whole area.

Xiao Yen might never have a child of her own, but she could adopt all the people here as her children, as Fat Fang had the people in Bao Fang.

Xiao Yen looked around the room trying to decide where to hang the copy of her family poem, the one Wang Tie-Tie had given her when she'd been in school. She needed to burn incense for Wang Tie-Tie, for Vakhtang, for the others she'd known who now walked beyond the Yellow River.

Xiao Yen took a deep breath, taking in the quiet. Her soul expanded to fill the empty places in the room. A deep joy bubbled inside her, sounding like a sparkling stream full of spring rain. Her choices might not be easy, but they were hers. She had her own life, her own duty to follow. There was much work to do. Now she had the time and place to do it.

It felt good to be home.

Bibliography

This isn't a complete bibliography of all the research sources I used for this novel. It is a good starting point for readers interested in the Tang dynasty and in all things Chinese.

Non-Fiction

Beckwith, Christopher I. *The Tibetan Empire in Central Asia*. Princeton University Press, 1987.

Capon, Edmund and Werner Forman. *Tang China: Vision and Splendor of a Golden Age*. Macdonald & Orbis, 1989.

Cave, Roderick. *Chinese Paper Offerings*. Oxford University Press, 1998.

De Mente, Boye Lafayette. *NTC's Dictionary of China's Cultural Code Words*. NTC Publishing Group, 1996.

Eberhard, Wolfram. *A Dictionary of Chinese Symbols*. Routledge & Kegan Paul, 1983.

Engel, Peter. *Folding Universe*. Vintage Books, 1989. (This is actually a book on origami.)

James, Peter and Nick Thorpe. *Ancient Inventions*. Ballantine Books, 1994.

Lu, Henry C. *Chinese Herbal Cures*. Sterling Publishing Co., 1994.

Schafer, Edward H. *The Golden Peaches of Samarkand*. University of California Press, 1963.

Smith, Arthur H. *Village Life in China*. Little, Brown and Company, 1970.

Spring, Madeline. *Animal Allegories in T'ang China*. American Oriental Society, 1993.

The Red-Crowned Crane. China Pictorial Press.

Waldron, Arthur. *The Great Wall of China*. Cambridge University Press, 1990.

Williams, CAS. *Chinese Symbolism and Art Motifs*. Charles E. Tuttle Company, Inc., 1974.

Yang, Jwing-Ming. *Ancient Chinese Weapons*. Yama Martial Arts Association, 1999.

Myth

Bucher, J. Frank. *The South River Pagoda*. Fithian Press, 1988.

Carpenter, Frances. *Tales of a Chinese Grandmother*. Charles E. Tuttle Company, Inc., 1980.

Palmer, Martin and Zhao Xiaomin. *Essential Chinese Mythology*. Thorsons, 1997.

Walters, Derek. *An Encyclopedia of Myth and Legend*. Diamond Books, 1995.

The World of Chinese Myths. Beijing Language and Culture Center Press, 1995.

Fiction and Poetry

Hughart, Barry. *The Bridge of Birds*. St. Martin's Press, 1984:

Lao-tsu. *Tao Te Ching*. Translated by Gia-Fu Feng and Jane English. Vintage Books, 1989.

Lewis, Elizabeth Foreman. *Young Fu of the Upper Yangtze*. Holt, Rinehart and Winston, 1965.

Liu, Wu-Chi and Irving Lo. *Sunflower Splendor: Three Thousand Years of Chinese Poetry*. Indiana University Press, 1975.

Spence, Jonathan D. *The Question of Hu*. Vintage Books, 1989.

Tu Fu. *The Selected Poems of Tu Fu*. Translated by David Hinton. New Directions Books, 1989.

Van Gulik, Robert. *Celebrated Cases of Judge Dee*. Dover Publications, 1976.

Web Sources

Web sites come and go faster than spring flowers, but when last I checked (July 2002), all these sites were available.

Wonderful English-Chinese dictionary. Plus flash cards to help you learn Chinese, your name in Chinese, and many other fun topics:
   http://www.mandarintools.com/

Virtual tours of China:
   http://www.chinavista.com/discover.html

Deity worship through folk prints. Many articles on how Chinese use paper. Plus a shop:
   http://www.chinavista.com/experience/joss/joss.html

Mini-histories, plus news on what's happening currently:
   http://www.china-contact.com/e.html